The Warlock anc

By

Victoria Williams

ISBN: 978-1-918038-40-8

Prologue

A tale of two worlds colliding, mystic blends into the material, the dark battles with the light, faith and love conquer hatred and greed, a tale for Vincent.

Cad goddeu

Roedd galw ar y Creawdwr, ar Grist am achosion, hyd nes y dylai'r tragwyddol waredu y rhai a wnaeth. Atebodd yr Arglwydd nhw, Trwy iaith ac elfennau, Cymerwch y mathau o amser prif goed, Trefnu eich hunain mewn arfbais rhyfel, ac atal y cyhoedd, dibrofiad mewn brwydr law yn llaw, Pan fydd y coed yn swyno, Yn y disgwyliad o beidio â bod yn goed, Roedd y coed uttered eu lleisiau, O llinynnau o gytgord, Daeth yr anghydfod i ben, Gadewch inni dorri dyddiau trwm byr, A benyw atal y din, Daeth allan yn gyfan gwbl hyfryd, Pen y llinell, y pen yn fenyw.

The Creator was called on Christ for causes, until the eternal should dispose of those who did. The Lord answered them, By language and elements, Take the kinds of time chief trees, Arrange yourselves in the arms of war, and restrain the public, inexperienced in battle hand in hand, When the trees are charred, In the expectation of not being trees, The trees uttered their voices, O strings of harmony, The dispute ended, Let us cut short heavy days, And female stop the din, It came out altogether lovely, Pen the line, the head is a woman.

https://www.ancienttexts.org/library/celtic/ctexts/t08.html

FABLE ONE. THE SLUMBERING ...... THE SHATTERING...

The planet Mithos nestled verdant and brilliant in bosom of the earth mother, his siblings, the sun, moon, and star Alwyn, Alluan and Anwen, a graceful marriage of companions forever twirling and entwining in ancient timeless waltz, Like some infinite courtship, with an eternal reverence, a ceaseless sonata of the heavens.

constellations ornamented the clement scene with a peppered backdrop of sparkling stars which twinkled like diamonds charting out a divine map of utopia, in some never-ending intertwining nemesis, forever journeying forwards into creation like the eons old mother ever carrying her descendants.

Upon the planet's façade, darkness had shrouded the realm beneath its shadowy mantle; wisps of soupy night air swirled and writhed into dense pendulous clouds which loitered tenaciously above the Terras surface beneath Alluans immortal persona glittering hoary and magical against the cobalt sky, his bewitching glare painting the landscape beneath in swathes of eerie silver capturing every aspect with a glinting frost bitten concealment

Moon beams cast silhouettes across every aspect of the frosty scene, as if a giant spider had cast a silken thread across the realm to capture man and beast amongst its silvery snares.

Darkness began to shroud the realm beneath her shadowy mantle, wisps of soupy night air swirled and writhed into dense pendulous mists loitering like Specters tenaciously above the surface, the mood was as still and soundless as the tomb itself, as if somehow it seemed to timorously anticipate the approaching encroachment, fearing it would rip asunder and devour the poignant silence like a howling wind of torment.

The quiet breeze gently began to stir, whipping up a moaning wind that seemed to wail and groan through the trees splintered boughs.

The twirling opaque mist clawed across the ground spinning and weaving as the Spectral shapes transfigured themselves into more dense contorted apparitions as if summoned forth by some foul sorcery.

Far off in time in the distant realms the foul enchanted army advanced toward the gateway under the sorcerers command, his words like adders poison floated upon the wind, mercilessly sullying and fracturing the harmonious soundless demeanour of peace as they wove through the still air crackling into a thousand splintered and shattered shards as time and space were hewn asunder as the portal opened her gaping jaws, the charged atmosphere crackled and spat with violet sparks against the airs innocence, enchantment conjured into existence from the ravenous blizzard, as the deranged sorcerer spoke his poison upwards, birthing Menacing inky clouds which cracked asunder the icy environment, swirling and contorting as they collided head on, with the charged torrid air creating loud peals of echoing thunder that violently shook the land, flashes of lightning forked down from the raging storm clouds like the tongue of some great venomous snake striking down at the dominion beneath searching for prey.

Upon the horizon a murky silhouette loomed vast and imposing against the crystal backdrop of the moonlit sky, the ghostly conjuration of the dilapidated gaol tarnished the landscape with an unspoken air of decay, winds whistled around the turrets echoing the whisperings of sorcerers malevolent chant, cursing the air as it rang out lamenting and snaking around the ragged ramparts polluting the air spectrally weaving its portent of disease, snaking wisps spilled over the gaols edge like a bubbling cauldron the dark tendrils reaching out across the land like a decayed hand snatching and grasping to destroy anything in its wake, spiders and insects spewed forth from every crack and crevice of the long decayed walls creating a writhing carpet as they spilled into the shadows, , screeching corvids circled the turrets a murderous black army of feathered generals awaiting their masters command, the multitude of black wings blocked out the moons beams like a rancid angel of death conjured by sorcery.

Savage winds lashed fiercely at the cloaked figure defiantly domineering the pinnacle of the shadowy turrets, the sorcerer cast his arms upwards toward the silvery moon, throwing back his head as the raging winds snatched back the cowl concealing his visage, mercilessly revealing his countenances terrifying features in stark display under the moons rays.

Raul the Necromancers dead dark flesh glowed with a repugnant grey incandescence, deep scars and open lesions desecrated his form. staring up at the heavens through deadened milky eyes glowing with a surreal animation.

Malicious laughter broke from the fiends' lips as he curled them back into a leering snarl, his reptilian silver fangs protruded from his decaying mouth glinting maliciously in the silvern light, Wispy tendrils of ebony hair writhed and contorted in the storm like a pit of Adders as they licked at the Necromancers cadaver like visage, his ragged cape billowing behind him like the tattered wings of some repulsive fiend as he gave the invocation to release the assault in shadow speak, “Mors diligere” The words cut into the cracked heavens ripping open the ethereal portal, like a key into a lock discharging the foul legions of Dust Dervishes, Blusters and Zephyrs, the immortal army who would mercilessly carry out the diabolical assignment to which they were bound.

The creature endured the raging elements as he summoned the spirit of the tempest, chanting wildly, ravelling his dark sorcery, age old magic’s created before time summoned from the shadow realm, The potent magic spat through the charged atmospherics cut through the torrid atmosphere like violet lightning bolts as they split asunder the heavens, unleashing the necromancers’ foul legions free from the shadow realms through the portals gateway in time, cadaverous eyes surveyed the legions, infecting the air like some vast black vulture.

If you got past this point, Well done!!!

The overlord’s campaign was diabolic and simple; to devour and destroy the heavens star rendering all to dust and ashes.

Raul had served his master well weaving the freezing carousel of curses that had been commanded, The Overlord would have his revenge….

Inside the mirrored chamber the Overlord Saeb, oozed a malignant aura atop the icy throne of flames, his violet eyes shone with malicious glee as he callously beheld the fractured facet of the obsidian scrying glass in front of him, cackling cruelly as the shadowy mirages played out eerily across the shattered glass, his deformed hand gently stroking the soft snowy fur of the Siberian Snarl resting obediently at his side.

THE TIME RIP.

(The other side of the portal …The mirrors reflection….)

Centuries earlier in the age of the serpent….

Ossian and Alwar of the race of the Mentharl Relaxed back upon the damp dark grass, blissfully entwined within loves embrace they wistfully gazed upon the vista of the heaven's constellations.

"What is that star up there, it seems fiery and strange?" Alwar whispered to her love, but Ossian was far more preoccupied with thoughts of wilful caress, than that of the heavens and cosmos.

"I do not know my love" he commented before casting his eyes up-wards from loves sweet gaze towards the ecliptic horizon.

The inky skies were ablaze with fury as the sun's fiery trail engulfed the nocturnal scenery of the planet, as if the mighty serpent himself, had been unleashed from his ethereal shackles to spit fire and rage across the cosmos.

The sudden unnaturally stark brilliance of the celestial sky commanded Ossian's attentions. "How strange!" he stated to Alwar, with a timid undertone, she did not reply but instead called to her hound who lay slumbering beneath the majestic oak Myrddin.

Alwyn and Ossian observed the scene with fearful reverence as the wolf Apollo slumbered on blissfully unaware nestled safely beneath the protective branches of the mighty oak.

The Flaming night sky cast a surreal backdrop against the mighty Myrddin's silhouette, the lone ancient oak commandeered the summit of the tump like a forgotten general of the forest as the fervent comet blazed with all the intense ferocity of a blistering inferno, hurtling towards it's earthly charter, the phosphor trail ignited upon entering the stratosphere plummeting downwards into the atmosphere on its trail of pursuit towards the land, gaining heat and momentum as it accelerated on its course, blocking out the heavens and creating an ecliptic vista in its wake.

The race of Mentharl, beasts and men gazed upwards at the heavens in both wonderment and dread as they anxiously observed the intense radiance of saebs fury emanating forth from the burning sorcery.

The seas and streams boiled colliding into tumultuous barricades of scalding water as their currents were thrown out of synchronicity, Volcanoes erupted spewing blistering torrents of molten lava like gaping wounds gushing forth their very life's blood.

The immense pressure caused the terra to split and crack asunder as rocks and gaseous vapours were violently ejected out of the planets very core.

Colossal billows of hot ashes, dust and gasses were unified, creating an apocalyptic power of cosmic energy that writhed and morphed ever contorting in form with a ravenous and malicious zeal.

Apocalyptic energy unlocked the portal releasing the legions of Zephyrs and dust dervishes, entities that savagely cloaked all they encountered within scorching clouds of ashes rendering their innocent victims to petrified stone.

The cloud of Dervishes viciously accelerated across the surface hungrily devouring and baking every living thing that lay in their wake into statuesque formations, whirling Zephyrs followed like a cloud of disease to embrace the stone remnants of beasts and men and devour their essences, malformed shifting energy of torment transcended into the vision of a toothless haggard old crone as tall as the mountains themselves she loomed down ominously scouring the landscape for prey, her opaque vapours pouring stealthily across the nocturnal scene like a plague of pestilence.

The heavens observed as the dense cloud of undead advanced, children screamed as mortals and animals scattered heading for any evident cover as the spectral Zephyrs and Dervishes invaded.

Seers and sages across the realms looked up from their watchtowers in wonderment and dread, what could this extraterrestrial event be a wondrous revelation, a gift from the gods, or the ending of their existence, as the Mentharl became a silent memory.

NARCIS... THE MIRRORS REFLECTION...

Generations later in the constellation of Amadis the majestic Lion....

The county of Thygorshire nestled a quiet little village named Buck-spur, The vale as it was named locally was sat upon the seat of a great gorge, as if it had nestled down in a snug little crack between two cushions.

Buckspur had a ragged appearance, causing you to imagine that the land had been ripped apart by the immense hands of some great deity.

The valley displayed a fissured appearance, and its horizon was ornamented by immense megaliths which were positioned around the hilly valley known as the stone seers, this stony grove of rocks composed a magical and atmospheric perimeter to the little village and was known as the circle of slumbering sentinel's.

Legend stated that a weary companion of giants had settled down to rest before nightfall after a hard days mining they had slept so soundly that the cocks crow did not awaken them before dawn, Consequently as the sun's rays touched them they were transformed to stone and so there they rested for evermore ready to awaken at the great battle of time little was the true tale known.

Around the valleys rim perched a collection of twisted black and white timber framed cottages sporting odd crooked chimneys, seemingly observing the land below like a peculiar council of the watch as they leaned over the cliffs edge, any hefty gust of wind threatened to send them crashing down into the craggy fissure below to become firewood, gnarled Apple trees precariously teetered upon the hillsides, their lopsided roots reached outwards like grappling fingers trying to claw a hold in the loose tumbling soil, it seemed that any moment now they might stumble and slide into the ravine beneath.

Matted flocks of grimy sheep idly grazed upon the lush green slopes of the ravines basin, occasionally glancing up from their pasture to observe a lamb or the shepherd Bedwyr and his mischievous sheep dog Bracken, the shepherds collie had a mottled grey and white shaggy coat which shone with a clement vibrancy, she viewed you through piercing grey eyes which seemed to question your motives and reflect her intelligent persona, her favourite past time was skulking around the sheep on her haunches and keeping them in check with an occasional nip, much to Bedwyr's annoyance!

The valley's focal point was an unusual standing stone hewn from pallid crystal and shaped with smooth curves that were stained with hues of pure white, the quartz megalith appeared as chaste as the first snows of winter, clear graceful water arose up from the stones heart in a mild babbling cascade as it playfully trickled over the megaliths sides tracing down its cracks and facets with a serene descent.

Tumbling crystal aqua captured the light of the Anwens rays as it voyaged downwards on its inevitable path towards the megaliths base, the clear flow created an abundance of miniature rainbows upon the quartz boulders many mirrored surfaces, like the weaving of a watery enchantment until it ultimately pooled in a fissure imprinted by the course of the stream at its foundation which danced and flowed into a picturesque lake at the megaliths base, the waters gently rippled as the clement wind teased the surface sending out rippled messages like whispers upon the shimmering facet of secrets yet to be spoken.

lake Narcis watery environment was home to a variety of flora and fauna that stood out in striking contrast to the environment, large Mauve tinted flowers fashioned like horns adorned the lakes edge, each blooms Centre stealthily hid over laden fingers of pollen as crimson as the blood of warriors, delicate cornucopia perched upon lofty midnight stalks thin and spindly as a spider's silken thread, each flower ostensibly threatened to bend under its consignment as the flora frolicked about in the winds whispering breath.

A tender breeze elegantly caressed the blooms creating a beautiful melody from the trumpets as it gently kissed them, they responded with a sound like the tender rustling of leaves coupled with the first promise of spring upon the realm, exquisite birds descended upon the blooms in their quest for pollen, a vivid luminescent green in colour and their tiny scaled bodies were adorned with striking feathered wings as yellow as buttercups.

The flighted Nymphs descended gently upon the fluted purple leaves of the blooms and inserted their orange proboscis in to the abundant feast of pollen, signalling to each other with a melodic unearthly song as they buzzed furtively backwards and forwards from bloom to bloom, each one hoarding their prize upon their tails to the point of abundance, perilously curling and uncurled their tails out from their sea horse like bodies to take up a greater consignment, each new load was a threat to the carefully laden balance of treasure; once fully burdened to opulence they each descended towards the water's surface where they vanished with a splash and a ripple beneath the shimmering crystal depths below, as they proudly conveyed their ransom to the Nymph queen eagerly awaiting their return.

The mirrored lake Narcis spilled further downhill as the lucid waters tapered off into a crystalline torrent, watery energies cascading downstream into a dappled curtain of aqua, throwing up great sprays of foam on its descent through the valley creating bubbled froth from the dancing and leaping waters. Casting foamy mirages of salmon as it cut through the craggy ground creating a pebbled staircase into the valley below, vibrant liquids bore life to a sparkling stream as they wound downwards on their voyage, bending and snaking embracing the valleys terrain flowing ever onwards in the direction of a great forest.

The rivulet happily sang its watery tune enveloping the smooth pebbles and rocks within its watery cloak, gathering force and haste with a cascading descent, like a child laughing and tumbling downhill, before it disappeared into the tree line of Knight Shade Forest, it was spoken in lore that scrying the lake Narcis surface on a blood moon would reveal enchantments and sorcery shrouded in time.

KNIGHT SHADE FOREST

Knight Shade forest, encircled Buckspur like a shadowy defence, its ominous inhabitants cast out gnarled branches, and roots, clawing tendrils lying in wait to snare lost travellers.

Many rumours, folklores and myths surrounding its name, fable passed down for generations about the enchanted trees inhabiting the forest and the chilling statues dwelling within its shady heart.

Folklore and legends surrounded the forest like a shroud, villagers spoke in hushed dulcet tones handing down their tales to their children, many had strayed into the forest in search of adventure and exploration never to return, villagers and even poachers were too terrified to set foot anywhere near the place.

When the moon filled the sky, eerie howling could be heard emanating from the forests heart carrying eerily upon the strange singing winds, offspring were warned not to venture near the howling breeze lest the 'stone people' catch you and turn your blood to ice.

So fearful were the villagers that on every full lunar cycle they spent time together collecting lunar blooms and carving symbols of the Anwen upon their doors to protect themselves and charm the evil away from their thresholds.

Vast beacons blazed on the full cycle of the moon Alluan, around the village outskirts protecting inhabitants from what may venture from the tree line, each blaze infused with dried Lunar blooms every hour by the watchman Fyngar and his hunting hound Tarog.

Fyngar was a tatty looking individual who hid beneath a filthy green cloak, like a carpet of lichen, pacing nervously back and forth he rubbed hands together, muttering under his breath about taxes, as he drew heavily upon his clay pipe which flamed like an ember creating sweet woody aromas snaking into the air with an intoxicating wisp, as be he grumbled to his faithful hound Tarog for company as he was largely shunned by the towns folk.

Tarog was a scruffy mutt, his shaggy coat had the appearance of a dusty grey hearth rug, dolefully he glanced up at passersby from beneath his dirt encrusted beard, wagging his matted tail ferociously creating clouds of dog hair, he wasn't much of a watch dog, but more of a companion, more inclined to lick bandits then assail them to the ground, "What is it boy, do you smell them wolves" Fyngar stated, the hound replied with a solemn whimper skulking over to his master to lick the watchman's hand before cowardly skulking down. "Aye not much of a guard dog are ye?" commented Fyngar as he fed the blaze with a generous handful of Lunar blooms, releasing a pungent stench which hung about the air like a thick heavy blanket of smog, the scent heady, seductively overpowering and intoxicating undertones billowed upon the air, a sickly sweet smell perfume laced with an underlying stench of decay, the heady aroma invading the nostrils like a drunken necrotic bewitchment.

The legend of Knight shade forest only recounted by village elders was reserved for special gatherings, dark crisp Samhain nights, and frosty winters gathered around the blazing hearth, shadows dancing amongst flickering firelight, to an eager audience of small faces, the occasional spit and crackle of the fire making small silhouettes jump in fright, tales spoke that many centuries earlier two young children named love and virtue, had ventured into the shady forest one morning in search of their missing pet goose Wilbur,

THE TWO CHILDREN THE TALE OF LOVE AND VIRTUE

The twins Love and Virtue were inseparable from their pet goose, Wilbur was stout like an ale jug waddling around on his orange feet like a faithful hound, he adored the children and followed them everywhere like a shadow.

love and virtues father was a Knight named Gondril employed in the services of The Anwen Temple upon the mount at Theadran.

The twins were striking in appearance the male child Virtue had hair as silver as spun moonbeams with bright violet eyes which glistened like amethyst's it fell in ringlets about his face like dancing silvery snakes, his sister Love was the contrast with dark coppery gold hair which burned like fire, her hair straight against her features, she had eyes of steel grey wolverine in appearance, their dress was simple sackcloth tunics and woollen jackets, virtue was quiet and thoughtful, whereas Love was brave and outspoken.

The weary Knight arrived approached the ramshackle cottage after a hard nights watch, he thought it strange that no wisp of smoke trailed from the chimney upon approach, he reined in his horse and dismounted onto dusty earth, as he walked up to the rickety building the main door was ajar, cautiously he called out to the children and pushed the door asunder, venturing in he found it strange Wilbur was not here to greet him, kneeling by the hearth he raked through the ashes and cinders realizing that the fire had not been relit that morning, casting a glance over to the pot this was empty too, maybe the twins were still asleep?

Gondril cautiously climbed the ladder to the upper bed chambers, holding his hand over the hilt of his sword, he slowly stuck his head above the rafters, discovering that his two beloved children were missing from their beds, their straw beds lay unmade signifying they had up and left in a hurry, and mischievous Wilbur was gone too!

Only one explanation for this, Wilbur must of wandered off and the twins are out searching for him, Wilbur often waddled off to the mill and bake house in search of crumbs, The two children and the pertinent goose were a constant trio, Love and Virtue were all that Gondril had left, as his wife Ephhy had passed away the previous winter from the red plague which had be-fallen the realm like an enchanted cloud of pestilence, causing victims to appear blood red and perish from a fever that felt like fire, half the village had been claimed.

The knight strode into the courtyard and once more straddled the saddle of his mount setting off in haste for the mill, at a canter the already tired mare snorted heavily as her weary flanks rippled with the exertion, thundering hooves resounded through the coppiced meadows as they journeyed toward their destination.

Elgora was a snowy white mount with plaited golden tail and mane, beneath her saddle she wore the standard of the temple, a rampant lion emblazoned upon a gated turret, crimson and black, which stood out in stark contrast against her pale, proudly announcing their arrival to any onlookers, they slowed down to a trot as they approached the mill coming to a steady halt upon the cobbled courtyard, the Knight was met by the millers portly wife, dressed in sacking with a dusty apron and mop cap, she rubbed her floury hands down her apron and greeted the knight with a cheery smile, "what can i do you for today squire?" she asked, "Nothing today kind lady, it is the twins I'm seeking, have they passed by here?" Gondril replied.

"fraid not today master, nor that thieving goose that's always in my grain, I'll keep an eye out for sure, best you be on your way to find them, I wish you luck" phyillis replied; "thank you be sure to" he said touching his forrid and dipping his head in return he drove the mare off towards the village once more.

Gondrils heart sank at discovering that the children were nowhere to be found! he had half expected to be greeted by their shining faces, where could they be? pushing his heels into Elgora he thundered off in panic.

The pair searched frantically around the Vale for the children, calling out everywhere he went asking everyone he saw from the oak on the summit of the tump, down to the stream and watch house, before finally realizing with dread in his heart that the children had unwisely ventured in to the forest in search of their beloved pet goose Wilbur, Gondril returned home that day with a heavy heart, alas it was too late to continue the search as the shadows were drawing nigh, with Elgora too tired to continue he hoped that they had found safe refuge at the Wytchs cottage on the outskirts of the wood, they were capable children after the death of their mother and able to care for each other, he did not sleep well that night tossing and turning with dreams of trailing branches and shadows snatching at his cloak.

It was a cold misty dawn the next day when the knight set out on the back of his Mount, he would stop firstly at the Wytch Maeves cottage, as he rode into knightshade forest his nightmare crept back into his mind, the thorny gnarled branches snatching at his face and arms, he drew his sword to hack through the brambles hanging from the boughs like a thorny portcullis, and cursed as pricks of blood appeared on the mares flanks.

The footing was precarious as roots protruded from the earth like woody snares trying to catch the horses footing, calling out for the twins his shouts were muffled by the dense vegetation and eerie fog, bugs slithered across the forest floor like a writhing carpet, corvids rustled in the trees observing with beady eyes.

Gondril felt sleepy as the fog invaded his nostrils, his head swimming with the acrid stench of the rotting vegetation, it seemed as if he had going round in circles for hours, as he searched for the cottage, as he blinked into the gloomy shadows he began to make out a silhouette of a ramshackle building,.

The crooked little cottage sat huddled inside a grove of trees, tenaciously it teetered on the brink of collapse as smoke oozed from the chimney stack, toads hopped across the herb patch croaking in alert at the intruder, watched by the witch's ebony cat pendle.

Wearily Gondril dismounted from his saddle, he was feeling intoxicated from the mist and disorientated from the forest's enchantment, he had heard many rumours about the wytch and was aware to be respectful of her and her domain.

"They be not here" he heard from behind him, spinning round in alarm he was greeted by maeve the wytch shrouded beneath a mossy green cloak covering her features , she leant on a gnarled stick for support, "it is the children I seek" he replied nervously, she stood and observed him silently a while, "the forests heart you must find" she added, and returned to gathering herbs.

The black cat pendle crept over to the knight, with a whispering of the breeze he turned into a dark haired woman, black fur covered her body from head to toe, her emerald green eyes observing tentatively, raven black hair flowed down to her waist, and a black tail flicked behind her tauntingly, pendle clicked her fingers and was adorned in a purple cloak out of thin air, she would accompany him to the forests heart.

Pendle the cat creature lead the way from the cottage into the dense dark trees, looming like spectral woody monoliths over the search party, relentlessly the knight called out to his absent children as they wound ever deeper onwards into the gloom, the knight following his strange companion on less travelled paths as brambles and thorns clawed cruelly at the pair slowing them down as if in mockery, a few times he thought he lost sight of her amidst the shadows.

Gondril cried out in vain until his throat was hoarse, "Love, Virtue where are you?" his voice barely audible in the thick impenetrable fog loitering upon the forest floor like a billowing shield of concealment, Suddenly a familiar muffled Quacking rang out in the mist, his heart skipped a beat, dare he hope?

"Wilbur," he exclaimed in elation as the shadowy silhouette waddled out of the mist, the goose appeared somewhat forlorn as he slowly raised his beak towards the knight with a puzzled expression. "Why greetings my little fellow," laughed Gondril with an air of relief, the children cannot be far away now he thought! Pendle led on deeper into the gloom, "Have you found the twins Wilbur?" he asked the goose hopefully, Wilbur answered with a dismayed "Quack" bowing down his beak to preen his damp misty wing in shame, "Don't worry my friend we'll find them yet, follow me faithful Wilbur" declared Gondril in lighter tones feeling somewhat relieved to have a familiar presence in the menacing forest.

Gondril, Elgora and Wilbur wound ever deeper into the dense vegetation following the cat creature, like a trio of intrepid explorers.

"Love, Virtue, are you there?, I've found Wilbur he's here with me?" the knight called out in hope, "QUAACK, Quack" added Wilbur, pendle flicked her tail voraciously as she spotted a huge crow up overhead, whilst Elgora snorted and whinnied loudly shaking her head from side to side, they all listened hard till they could hear every leaf fall, but alas nothing but fog muffled silence met their ears.

Drawing deeper into the forests heart, Swirling vapours of mist snaked around the valiant travellers, ethereal and creeping, it deluded their direction as it cloaked the forests appearance in a taunting manner, even pendles fur began to bristle, even for a witches cat.

The surrounding terrain and trees looked strangely familiar to Gondril as they rounded the bend, his heart sank as he realized with dread that they wasted the morning traveling around in circles! “I think we may be lost faithful Wilbur” announced the Knight in dismay to the waddling goose, the gander gazed unhappily back at Gondril displaying a dejected expression and let out a Long Subdued, “Quack”

“Let us not lose heart dear Wilbur, for we have ventured this far” replied Gondril, trying to keep their spirits up, “We shall leave a trail to guide our way” he added pulling a muslin cloth from the depths of his saddle bag.

Wilbur nibbled nervously at his feathers; he was not sure that was such a wise idea? Still his master knew best, the dishevelled goose waddled off faithfully behind Gondril and Elgora as they followed pendle, Gondril wondered if this was a trick by the witches familiar to lead them deep into the forest travelling in circles, but he dare not discharge her guide, he would keep his own trail. Every so often along the journey the knight would toss some bread crumbs onto the ground behind them, but alas poor Wilbur had been right, Gondril had not accounted for the wood Flyghts!

For as soon as Gondril had ventured onwards the menacing Flyghts hungrily advanced toward the crumbs erasing the companions trail.

Wood Flyghts stood no higher than a Black Bird, their bellies were rotund and bulbous giving off a disproportionate appearance against their skinny limbs, the nesting of Flyghts observed the bounty of crumbs upon the forest floor with huge blinking hazelnut coloured eyes which twinkled with a ravenous delight, flygths hides were varying leafy colours ranging from muddy brown; through to russet red depending on the variety of tree that they dwelt in, and Silvery yellow lichens grew upon their damp mouldy skins like jerkins of Armour, they had moss like hair which poked out from beneath the Flyghts acorn cup hats, but their crowning glory were their elaborate peacock butterfly patterned wings in all the hues of the rainbow which they used for treetop flight.

Wilbur on the other hand had not missed the spectacle of the mischievous Wood Flyghts, he watched on in annoyance as a pesky scoundrel fluttered down from the branch of a horse chestnut tree and greedily advanced upon a morsel of crumb.

"HIISSSS, QUACK" hollered Wilbur as he charged at the Flyght with outstretched wings.

But the Flyght was already wise to this and had been eyeing up Wilbur all along, it flitted about annoyingly around Wilburs head, then let out a taunting giggle as it took flight with the loot, Wilbur snapped at the air, but the Flyght just chuckled and released a Conker from its pouch with a "PLONK" onto Wilbur's head before vanishing into the tree tops.

Meanwhile Gondril had missed the escapade that had been going on behind him, he was much more absorbed in the swirling mists that were dancing around them, Gondril was sure that he had witnessed the vision of his children in the hypnotic billows, the twins had beckoned for him to follow them, but now they were nowhere to be seen, and where was Pendle? He stared hard as a billow of mist writhed and contorted taking on the deceptive form of his children, "Children is that you?" he called out with a quavering undertone to his voice.

The Myst wraiths smiled a malicious grin as they nodded beckoning him to follow them deeper in to the forests heart, "Come let us hurry Wilbur at last we have found them!" the knight proclaimed joyfully, scooping the portly goose up onto his saddle, unknowingly the comrades followed the Myst wraiths to the very inner most point of the forest.

Suddenly they emerged into a clearing , all was quiet and still in the forests heart not even a bird's song could be heard, dead leaves crunched noisily underfoot as Elgora and her riders advanced into the clearing, Overhead a nesting murder of crows protested, crawing loudly to announce the arrival of the weary band of travellers.

The knight looked up at the squawking birds and shuddered, in doing so, he failed to notice the swirling mists mysteriously retreating as the Mystwraiths spectral vapours skulked widdershins across the ground in an unearthly fashion like a cloud of smoke being sucked back up a chimney!

Slowly in their place a whirlwind of dust and dirt began to emerge spinning towards the trio with a relentless crescendo, the sprinkling sound of the soil drumming against the earth commanded Gondrils attentions, snapping him out of intoxicated bewitchment, as he stared at the forest in horror at the approaching tornado, he tightly grabbed the struggling Wilbur with one arm amidst the frantic flapping as he tried to take flight from the woods, Gondril raised up his other arm in attempts to shield his face from the barrage of swirling earth as the zephyr ejected dust into the knight's eyes and mouth, and spattered Wilbur who let out a frightened "Honk!"

The knight tightly closed his eyes and mouth against the dust storm, hanging on for dear life to the saddle with his legs, After what seemed like an Aeon the pelting of dirt began to subside as the swirling dirt and howling wind subsided to all but a mere whisper and the eerie forest again fell silent

What strange portents we have witnessed, this place is surely cursed proclaimed Gondril to himself spitting the dust free from his mouth, as he slowly drew his shaking hand across his blurry eyes clearing away the dirt.

The knight blinked hard in a vain attempt to regain his sight, Gondrils eyes slowly began to refocus, distortedly revealing the abomination which loomed before him!

He stared on aghast, the windstorm had created a foul manifestation a ravenous beast stood towering above them!

What was this abomination? A vast creature loomed above the trio, it observed them over its long tapered reptilian snout staring out from behind moss green eyes that glinted richly with malice, Two sharp barbarous fangs protruded down from its crocodilian mouth, hot pungent sulphurous breath rasped down upon the intrepid comrades as the beast tasted the air with its drooling venomous tongue hunting for scent.

The brute had the regal form of a golden lion and was covered in ancient long healed battle scars, upon its powerful hide grew a thick coating of foliage shaped scales resplendent of all the red fires of autumn, Tauntingly it flicked its two pronged tail through the air like a whip, a formidable and menacing sight to behold.

Four gigantic paws flicked their scythe like talons savagely as the soil serpent observed Gondril, Elgora and Wilbur with a sadistic sense of amusement like a cat stalking its prey.

"QUACK, HONK" let out Wilbur in protest as he struggled to free himself, Gondril swallowed hard and tightened his grip upon the goose his attentions were drawn elsewhere towards the ground beneath the serpent.

The knights heart filled with dread, as either side of the Beast were his children, stood frozen and motionless in time by some evil sorcery, They had been cast into statues of cold stone, Gondril vainly spun Elgora about in an attempt to flee for his very life, but alas it was too late, he felt the hot pungent breath rasp on to his face.

The monster lashed its tail with a menacing crack like a clap of thunder and curled up its cruel lips in delight, Its emerald eyes portrayed an evil glint as it spat fire and earth on to the Knight and his companions rendering them to solid stone beside the children love and virtue, The Soil Serpent cackled with delight as it took flight from the woods back towards the wytchs cottage.

Knight shade forest stood shadowy and sinister as the stone family watched the forest through their blank unseeing eyes.

Three centuries passed…..

BUCKSPUR

At the forests edge a pack of Centaurs rested amongst the lush green clover after a hard nights hunt, they had ridden hard not willing to give up the chase, paying off well as they had trapped and slain two stags and a brace of rabbits, the catch should last the herd a few days.

"Cadog, what is that small boy up to straying into the forest?" questioned Adair the sentry and second in command

The leader of the centaurs Cadog was striking in appearance, thoughtfully he observed the outskirts of Knight Shade forest as a small grubby boy sunk beneath the tree line. "I do not know brother what he is up to, but it is not our place to interfere in the lives of men; should he survive he'll not return again" he replied.

Centaurs were powerful beasts, it was rumoured that the gods themselves had moulded them from clay to defend the forests, their form had been crafted into that of a man, thickset and strongly built, deeply bronzed skin stretched taught across their vast muscles, which they skilfully used to release their arrows at unwitting prey, Their torsos sublimely blended down into the form of a stallion's rippling flanks which gave them advantageous speed for the chase, the coats varied greatly from chestnut through to palomino depending on the herd they originated from.

The most visually striking of the herd was the stallion Cadog, his lower half was coloured in grey and white dapples, like the silken coat of a winter hare caught in the morning's frost, from his rump grew a thick elegant tail of pure spun silver, Cadogs eyes were a piercing sapphire blue, setting a stark contrast against his pale hide seeming to bore right through you, searching the inner-most depths of your soul to seek out your intentions.

His features were crowned by a flowing mane resembling silvern moonlight in all its resplendent hues, it burned and crackled like silver fire as if it was a separate entity in its own right flickering with tones of azure blue as the flames licked up and down the beasts neck in a never ending blaze a bewitching sight to behold.

"Come let us journey back brothers" announced Cadog arising gracefully from the meadow.

"We had best to cook and smoke the catch before it spoils," the herd snorted their approval as they were now well rested, centaurs began to rise from their patches of indented grass stamping their hooves and flicking their tails impatiently waiting for Cadog and his deputy Adair to harness the kill upon their backs.

"Let us journey forth into the wooded realm" commanded Adair majestically, suddenly there was a great drumming of hooves upon the ground as the herd of Centaur galloped off at speed, vanishing into Knight Shade forest.

Meanwhile the small grubby boy seen earlier continued along the winding stream that coursed throughout the forest, mindlessly chewing at a piece of straw and humming along as he explored.

The child's face wore an expression of eagerness and mischief only seen in the young, he sported a crop of ebony coloured hair curled in tight ringlets about his head which hung down in coils around his face seeming to dance with a life of their own as he went on his way, framing sparkling mischievous eyes a dazzling liquid gold like the Anwen, an unusual colouring for his tribe.

Celts were generally red headed as foxes or as blonde as hay and had piercing steel grey blue eyes set within a fair skin as pale the spring's snow, whereas the boy displayed a small stature for his age with a rich tanned skin the colour of caramel, dressed in a grimy linen shirt ripped covered in mud from a morning's youthful explorations and adventures, covering a pair of itchy woollen britches which he hated.

"Mother will cuss me; I am in a frightful state again, no supper for me" announced the young boy looking down at his clothes and bare feet which were as black as coal.

In the vale of Buckspur Smoke wound up in to the air wafting the aroma of succulent roasted boar upon the breeze, an enticement which seemed to reach out and pull you inwards, capturing every hungry man and beast.

Smoky trails from the pit billowed in a dance of ever changing forms as they reached upwards toward the heavens, loud raucous Laughter and music could be heard floating upon the air, and people stood idly gossiping around the village.

"Hey merthyl, did you hear about the rumour in the ox last eve?" asked the neighbour Emergaid, "Nay Emergaid, what be that then?" she replied ,"I'll tell ye but don't mention it to anyone will ye?" added Emergaid, "Nay I shan't, just tell us will ye?" said merthyl impatiently.

"Well," began Emergaid, "Thou must Ave eard bout the new king Kalthor?" she questioned.

"Aye I have" replied Merthyl with interest; "Well, my Will says the inn keeper Theoeard the traveller; said Kalthor's descended from them evil Valanthians!" retorted Emergaid, "Never, Emergaid!" stated Merthyl in alarm.

The realm had recently crowned a new monarch King Kalthor all but a moons cycle ago following the untimely demise of the previous king Bryce, perished at the hand of an unknown plague, amid fierce rumours and speculation that he had been bewitched..

King Kalthors subjects were already revolting due to the unfair hike in taxes since Lord Saul had been appointed Regulator and Treasurer, Pockets of bandits had erupted all over the kingdom like an infection, the watch would have to spread themselves thin to keep order in the realm of Buckspur.

The sheriff of the watch Argan stood guard at the village gates ready to challenge any traveller's or strange folk passing through Buckspur, a middle aged local man, who presented a stern formidable persona.

Argans stood on sentry duty, his bulky silhouette outlined, illuminated by the blazing torches, flickering shadows were cast down from the watch fires, they danced across his handsome face obscuring his features and wagering no clues to his identity, Just the sheriffs muddy boots could be seen protruding out from the hem of his concealment.

Warm breath misted upon the chill night air as Argan sternly observed the black horizon from beneath his sodden cowl, his hand rested un-easily upon the hilt of his broadsword ready to wage battle in an instant; Dangerous times lay ahead, rumours Spake that the dark ones were marauding once more.

A peaceful settlement resided within the city walls, it was home to many families and their livestock, Chortling pigs truffled around in the sludge, geese honked and protested at passers-by and chickens pecked at the ground, chased by Laughing grubby groups of children racing around the mediocre wood and straw dwellings that they called home.

Basic and functional they were constructed from branches, mud and horse hair, rotund in shape with animal pelts hanging over the entrances and windows, each dwelling kept a fire burning in its centre to provide heat and cooking for the family within, the aromatic smoke wound upwards escaping through a vent in the roof, which often gave rise to a thick blanket of smog and seasoned wood smoke descending upon the village like a scented culinary fog.

The focal point of the settlement was Hross Hall, the elaborate structure had been crafted with ornately carved timber frames of inter-woven braids, panelled with thatched fencing which had been plastered together with mud and horsehair, the focal point was the Threshold beautifully adorned with an elaborate painting of three interlocked Celtic horses painted in red, orange and green, representing truth, loyalty and honour, each animal was portrayed as biting the others tail as they eternally circled the golden Anwen, representing the regal status of the inhabitants that dwelled within there.

Hross hall was the abode of the chieftain Bynar, an aged stocky man built like an ox, he had a mane of tousled auburn hair which was worn in braids to match his beard, intricately braided and entwined with small ornate bronze beads.

His stature was hearty with thick trunk like arms, decorated by tattooed patterns of interlocked horses and his wrists were adorned with detailed copper and gold bangles.

Bynars knowing expression greeted you with a welcoming friendliness, pale grey eyes set a piercing contrast against his tanned visage.

Bynar wore a wrapped a pleated woollen kilt around his broad girth, in red, orange and green all the colours of his tribe which he coupled with a rich elaborate tunic fashioned from crimson cloth with a gold brocade, he adorned the tunic with a delicate coverlet of pure bronze chain mail that had been crafted by Elven smyths.

Bynar held a truly regal persona as he stood observing his village, The chiefs overall attire reflected his status and set him apart from the other settlers simple clothing.

The chieftain's favourite item was a breastplate of gold, inlaid with orange and red jewels, creating the emblem of the blazing Anwen in its centre, resplendent battle attire to dazzle and impress the enemy with its status, his broad sword which he wore strapped to his right side at all times as a mark of status, The sword named Bradwriaeth passed down lineage had been smelted from an unusual red metal which burned like the harvest sunset, the blade itself had been decorated with a band of runic inscriptions running down its edge, and Tigers eye stones studded the weapons hilt, the blades centre piece was a large amber stone which stared out like a vast orange eye, appearing to blink when the light of Anwen caught it.

The blade glinted majestically as the sun's rays reflected off the burning hues of metallic ochre as the in scripted runes smouldered magically in Flames word, the meaning had been lost down the ages.

On his left side he wore a dagger, a gift from the new monarch King Kalthor of which he was immensely proud, a serpents head grasping a green stone, cut as a flame blade resembling the serpents outstretched coils, it bore markings up its blade in runic depiction of Kalthors kingdom, which were ENVY, GREED and MALICE, kalthor had stated it was to banish these from Bynars kingdom when he had bequeathed him the sword.

The chieftains rank of heraldry, a hefty golden shield rested at Bynars sandaled feet, it truly breathtaking, the defence had been painted with a scarlet backdrop split into a gyronny of amethyst inserts, Emblazoned across the centre were a pair of battling beasts, the dominant creature was an ochre lion in a rampant stance, who prevailed over a violet phoenix, they raged in a never ending war against the backdrop of the brilliant yellow Anwen.

Bynar thoughtfully watched a group of villagers returning from the fields, his ochre cloak whipped about In the wind like a portent of the looming storm on the distant horizon.

“Anwens Afty all” bellowed Bynar against the elements, “Anwens Afty Bynar” rang back the many replies.

The everyday inhabitants of the encampment toiled hard, reaping their living from the land, women were clothed in simple felt dresses with pelts tied around their feet, and the men of the village wore a simple sack cloth shirt coupled with a felt kilt tied about the waist with cord, worn over thick woollen britches, hair was worn long in braids tied with leather thong, Every member of the clan even the children wore an amulet of the Anwen fashioned out of bronze, which hung down from their neck on a leather thong, as if it were a uniform charm of protection given by the chieftain to each new born as a mark of clanmanship.

The village folk worked long hours labouring from dawn until dusk most days, whatever season of the cycle it was, the mammoth task of ploughing was the job of the villager's livestock of Oxen.

Land Oxen or Yamak, stood tall as a hay cart upon limbs as stout as barrels, they were coloured russet and buttermilk with long shaggy coats, which trailed through the field's mud and sludge until they were spattered a mucky earthen colour, Crowned upon the oxen's head were a pair of long curved horns like mighty ploughs of their own

After a long days work the settlers loved to unwind in the local alehouse, "The Oxen and Plough", The Oxen and plough was a tithed barn thatched with fusty yellow straw which harboured many a birds nest and rodent, Over the door swung a worn out wooden plough with some unfortunate Yamak's skull bound to it, Loud music, drunken song and raucous cheers could be heard emanating from the alehouse, as far away as the outskirts of the settlement by the sheriff Argan and his men.

Inside the ale house many ruddy-faced folk were clanking and supping tankards which spilled over with a rich dark ale that trickled down the outside of the pewter mugs like a frothing cascade of intoxication, Slops of ale descended into small puddles soaking the carpet of straw underfoot creating a muddy quagmire of the earthen floor beneath, the scented aroma of fermented hops, wheat and berries, sweetly fragranced the air, the heady bouquet was a byproduct of the publicans intoxicating hobby of Ale and wine brewing, his Damson sherry was legendary, and rumoured to floor a fellow in just one sup, but Buckspur folk were well accustomed to it.

A red faced inn keeper stood behind the pen constructed from straw bales and wooden timbers, the cramped space behind him was stacked up to shoulder height with wooden kegs and leather flasks of all shapes and sizes, it had been a good year for brewing Theo thought to himself as he poured another tankard of Gryphons fire, as he watched the inns inhabitants having a drunken arm wrestling contest with great delight, between the chieftains son Fynlach and his brother Sulien, Fynlach was thick set and built heftily, whereas Sulien was small and agile, it could go on a while yet Theo chuckled heartily to himself wiping his hands down his leather apron.

Rhys, the local Tanner approached the bar, Rhys was a skilled crafts-man who fashioned custom battle jerkins from any pelt, his garments were undeniably the best in the realm and It was even rumoured that they were charmed with protective enchantments.

"Anwen's Afty Theo, a flagon of your finest Dragons Rage Ale if you please?" commanded Rhys banging his Tankard down on the bar with a clang. "Certainly my good friend, how goes it today?" questioned Theo.

"Trade has been kind today Theo the Anwen is with us, that regulator Saul has been in and requisitioned that I fashion him a hefty order of leather armouries, nearly three score and ten suits!", "The Anwen has blessed you indeed" commented Theo, "Funny thing is though, he's only wanting them three-quarter size, a the only race as I knows they'll fit is damn trolls!" added Rhys in a whisper.

Theo wore a puzzled look as he released the stopper from the keg of Dragons rage, he looked deep in thought as he allowed the amber liquid to flow over the tankards brim before noticing and replacing the cork back in the barrel, "Ay that seems sinister all right, what with the prophecy an all." Theo replied wiping his hands on his leather apron sounding troubled.

Suddenly the conversation was brought to a halt with a loud clattering as Fynlach and Sulien's arm wrestling became more raucous, flagons, ale and men fell rolling on the floor as they laughed boisterously jesting to one another, " I bet you a tankard of centaurs cider Fynlach that you'll not beat me!" taunted Sulien, "I'll better that my man, I'll bet you two tankards of Minotaurs mead, and a dance with my sister I do!" bellowed Fynlach.

"We shall see, but it'll not be this day!" retorted Sulien to loud out-pourings of cheers and laughter, as he jested with his gathered onlookers.

Dusky light cast through the hessian drapes of The Oxen and Plough faded as outside the sun gradually descended beneath the horizon at Cuchulainn's farm.

The day's work had drawn to an end and the nights revelries were now well underway.

Cuchulainn's farm was a rural one without livestock save for the Oxen, its main purpose was to feed the settlement.

This year the offerings to the goddess had been plentiful they were counting on a good harvest this cycle the goddess be willing, they needed surplus crop to trade for goods in the town of Thygor at the next market.

Perhaps Bynar would grant a day of rest with merriment and feasting in celebration of the goddess?

Freyja and Solomon

THE WYNDING BOGART

Meanwhile in Knight Shade forest the young Uther was resting beside the winding stream that wove throughout the forests tree line, Kneeling down the small boy diligently sifted through the streams shining bed of pebbles as he hunted for an unusual stone to add to his collection, "Aha this one is beautiful and shiny" he announced washing the silt from a chunk of obsidian. Holding up the pretty stone , he admired the intricate white pattern adorning the black stone like a speckled bird's egg, Uther was far too preoccupied with his new found treasure to notice the green slimy hand stealthily arising from beneath the placid waters of the stream.

Suddenly.. the marsh bogart snatched Uthers wrist! catching him unawares, the boy startled tried to snatch his wrist back, back the slimy tendrils held him fast, he began to panic as the icy water began to envelop his body, snatching his breath from him with the stark coldness as it dragged him beneath the icy waters which burned like a thousand frozen pins.

Bubbles arose on the streams surface as uther tried to scream out for help but alas it was too late he began to descend like a stone beneath the water, as the wynding boggart sank with its prize!

Uthers lungs started to choke from lack of air, his mouth threatening to fill with the murky waters as he gasped for breath, clamping his mouth tight shut he blinked frantically trying to focus his vision beneath the murky depths, but he was cruelly blinded as the cloudy water sullied his eyes like an inky invasion, fighting back he kicked and struggling battling to break free of his slimy captor, but alas the more he struggled the more the slimy hands tightened their vice like grip, cutting into his wrists and ankles like weedy shackles!

Uther plummeted ever downwards towards the secret caverns that lay hidden beneath the streams bed, the small boy felt his head swim as his consciousness threatened to leave him, fighting hard he battled to stay awake, as he wrenched his limbs defiantly in a vain attempt to swim up-wards against his unseen attacker kicking his feet hard in an assault against the weedy Specter, but alas it was to no avail as each attack caused him to become ever more entangled in the marsh bogarts strangling weeds!

The bogart smiled a spectral grimace as her prey flailed around under-water like a floundering fish, Caught like a rabbit in a snare, blind panic began to set in the small boys heart with the realization that he was trapped!

Uther felt utter despair creep into his heart as the cold dark waters closed in around him, like a blanket of frigid isolation it enclosed and challenged his every move.

Desolate thoughts such as "Would this foul place become his watery shroud and what would become of his family?" darted through his head filling him with dread hopelessness.

The fear pressed ever tighter like an iron vice squeezing out the last rays of hope, the child felt hopeless and was about to give up his desperate battle when a strange cerulean light appeared before his eyes, was this his life flashing before him? He thought, or was he already dead and it was a divine angel come to comfort him?

Transfixed by the peaceful light it seemed to draw him in, washing waves of calm over his body mind and soul he no longer felt the previous terror of his predicament only peace and restfulness, The light before him seemed to dance and flicker like a gentle flame pulsing as it gradually transpired into the vision of a beautiful translucent maiden, behind her floated a cloud of iridescent coloured hair like the delicate tentacles of jelly fish.

The torrent smiled at Uther as she swam circling around him, she drew him spinning into her whirlpool as the force of her vortex ripped him free of the Marsh Bogarts strangling hold

Uther span triumphantly out of the pond weed as the Ghoul loosened its slimy manacled grip, he looked down upon the loathsome beast as it sank in defeat to the murky depths.

The foul Specter that had ensnared him was truly a loathsome sight to behold, the bogart was almost skeletal in appearance, strips of putrid rotting flesh hung from its spectral frame, fetid pond weed embraced it's putrefying remains clinging to the torn remnants of its watery shroud, The marsh boggart's deathly features observed the Torrent through hollow orbits, its skeletal visage shrieking out in anger as the child was swept away to freedom.

Uther could contain his hunger for air no longer, his mouth gaped wide open as the sullied water gushed in like an invasion, Precious air rushed into the boys lungs making his head swoon explosively, He watched in amazement as a rush of joyous bubbles escaped his mouth effervescing before his eyes like a watery kiss; HE COULD BREATHE! Hungrily the boy gulped in mouthfuls of rancid pond water in his hunger for life giving air.

Consciousness began its stark painful return drawing Uthers senses back with a jolt into the cold dark environment surrounding him, snapping him cruelly out of his dream like state, and causing his body to ache in pain as a reminder of his ordeal, Uther gazed before himself in disbelief and gratitude upon the torrents pearly features as she smiled broadly back at him.

Large cerise eyes observed Uther with kind pity a truly a bewitching combination against her opaque skin, the torrent had a scaled body, with a large spiny fin running down her back which branched into rainbow coloured fins, her hair flowed out behind her like an iridescent halo of mauve and blue, however strange her appearance, she seemed like a blessed angel of the sea to Uther.

The watery Elemental gazed upon the small boy and spoke in a damp gurgling voice, "It is Not your time to die child of two halves from the whole, you have great deeds yet to perform, I am Aquaria and I have been sent to guide your way," spoke the Torrent.

And with this statement she arose to the pinnacle of the whirlpool like a water boatman before spinning rapidly upwards, creating an eddy in her wake which ejected Uther out onto the silty mantle of some the underwater cavern with a grounding THUMP! And then without so much as a ripple she had vanished as quickly as she had appeared!

Uther felt somewhat dazed as he lay upon the shingled floor wearily rubbing his eyes, everything seemed so sudden and unreal, where was he? He wondered woozily taking in his surroundings, was he dreaming?

Stalagmites and stalactites' protruded down from the dripping cavernous roof like the teeth of some great watery dragon of the under realms, Uthers surroundings were dank and gloomy, the ground was wet and a stench of Sulphur hung about the air, a cold drip of water trickled down his forrid as he gazed above.

The cavern luminesced with an eerie incandescence, as a gentle breeze whispered across the boys cold damp face chilling his skin and causing him to shiver violently.

Uther looked down at his sodden form, "I need to get back to the surface where am i? I shall catch my death in these wet clothes." He shuddered to himself.

The child pondered what was causing the strange glow in the distance before him, and the origin of the breeze, was it the faint last rays of Anwen for the day shining in through an air hole large enough to war-rant his escape?

The small boy felt worried, how on earth had he become trapped in this dismal dungeon, And what had that Marsh boggart and Torrent wanted with him? He felt afraid and mystified by these questions, was he special or cursed?

Uther nervously began to edge forwards crawling carefully along the caverns floor upon on his hands and knees clambering tenaciously over numerous sharp pebbles which littered the caverns floor, slinked along like an anxious beast cowering from its hunter, he felt almost sick with hunger and fear but still he pressed on, his head still swooning from the ordeal.

Uther sneaked along for what felt like an eternity, looking for a way to the surface, the once distant light of the cavern gradually began to grow brighter as he progressed deeper into the hidden heart of the antechamber.

The child recoiled in pain as something sharp sliced down into his knee, OW! He exclaimed tearfully feeling that he had had enough bad luck for the day, Uther glanced his wounded knee, blood streamed in small rivulets down his leg and dripped onto the floor below, what in Anwens name had he cut himself on?

Tenaciously he felt around on the floor until his fingers detected the sharp object that had caused his wound, Uther crouched down to inspect the jagged fragment carefully wiping away the grimy earth which encased it, holding the scale shaped shard aloft he stared intently upon its countenance aghast, what manner of object was this?

Sitting down exhausted upon the damp earth to question the origins of this peculiar object in his mind, its pocked surface had a strange meteor like appearance, shaped like a jagged crescent moon, “It fits nicely in the palm of my hand” thought Uther to himself as he turned the object over .

Uther suddenly recalled tales of a legend told to him by his father stating that the third sun, Alumayen ‘dragon of the skies’ had crashed deep down into this vale centuries ago, crafting the valley from the sheer force of that cataclysm, and from that point forward it had been called Ashard Vale by the temple knights upon the mount at Theadran, He had never dared believe the legend dismissing it as sheer fable, surely it couldn’t be true!

It was then that he terror and fear had begun to set in, parching Uthers throat and bringing tears of fright into his eyes for as he looked aloft, there sat before him a colossal fragment the size of a cart! Now he was afraid, it could not be! But yet the proof was here! Why me thought Uther?

The object lit up the whole cavern, and appeared to be ornamented with strange scales around its surface! Uther edged closer a hand at a time, shielding his eyes as he gazed at this commanding sight.

Whatever could this mean? He puzzled in bewilderment, these were similar to the drawings that he had seen on his father’s scrolls; symbols from the temple of the Anwen Knights of Crescents mound and the temple knights at Theadran!

The Large shining meteor blinked out like a closing eyelid snorting cloud of Sulphur which was exhaled into the dank air, It was at this point that Uther blacked out with fear, too many questions and bizarre images filled his head until he could take no more and unconsciousness embraced him in her velveteen blanket of stars in the realm of dreams.

DAY BREAK

Uther awoke the next morning safely embraced within the safe confines of his bed, for a brief moment he enjoyed the blissful ignorance of wakefulness until the memory of the previous day's events came flooding back to him like a slap to the senses.

Images of the ghastly Marsh Boggart filled his mind like a disease he shivered in frigid recollection until comforting memories washed over his consciousness of his radiant saviour the Torrent, lying in bed he considered these two visions a while trying to reason with himself what had led up to the bizarre events which later unfolded in the cave leading to the discovery of colossal meteor and the strange scale shaped shard!

What was going on, and how had he gotten back to his bed, had it all been some terrifying dream or bizarre vision?

Uthers rumbling stomach bought him back with a snap to the present reality around him, "I'm famished" he thought hungrily to himself, as the familiar smell of oats and honey hung upon the air, he was more than ready for his mother's hearty porridge this morning.

Uther stretched his legs out in readiment to swing down from his lofty bed, but was alarmed as a sharp stinging sensation greeted him, wincing he pulled back the eiderdown and gazed in horror at his badly wounded knee, his heart began to race and his throat parched dry, how would he explain this one to his mother? He couldn't even explain it to himself!

Little was the young boy aware that his uncle Wynnad had discovered him in the chamber of draco last night whilst on his checks to feed the beast, a bigger secret lay hidden from the child that was yet to be unravelled, wynnad and the boy's father his brother wynnauld and had decided moons ago that they would wait until the enlightenment began around the boy, when he had read the scrolls four festivals ago, now it looked as though the time was nigh, they had best to keep a closer eye on the child the enemy was aware..

Uther thought back to when he had secretly read his father's scrolls one night whilst his parents Wynnalud and Arianwen were sleeping, the small boy had stealthily sneaked out of his bed, dreading every footfall that he had nervously placed down upon the chilled quarry tiles as he headed towards his father's secret hiding place, like a nocturnal creature skulking about in the shadows.

Upon reaching the hearth Uther struggled laboriously to remove the loose brick above the mantle, carefully manoeuvring it out of place inch by painful inch wincing with each movement it made as the mortar ground loudly against itself loosening free clouds of dust which descended to carpet the tiled floor like a blanket of evidence.

Uther tried hard not to sneeze as particles of displaced dust frolicked upon the air.

He had composed himself stilling his shaking hands before timorously reaching inside the revealed vault as if he were descending his arm into a venomous vipers pit.

The small boy strained his ears until he thought they would burst as he listened hard for any stirrings in the bed chamber down the passage-way, but luckily his ears were met by the familiar snoring of Luna the wolf mutt who was curled up at the foot of his parents bed.

Sighing with relief he fearfully continued his search of the hidden compartment in hope of discovering the age-old musty scrolls.

Uther grappled along the bricks with his fingertips until he felt parchment, he held his breath as the concealed treasure gradually reached his grasp fearing to touch it in case the scrolls should disintegrate to ashes before his eyes, he carefully unrolled the scrolls toward himself as if his life depended upon it.

Slowly the fusty yellowed parchment came in to shadowy display be-neath the flickering embers of firelight, it held a strong acrid smell of moth balls and coal.

The young boy gazed upon the coveted treasure in awe, each of the three scrolls were bound with a faded violet ribbon adorned by a stamped wax seal displaying the symbol of a rampant gryphon, The excited child nervously surveyed his living quarters once more staring hard into the inky shadows for any sign of movement, his racing heart beat deafeningly loud in his ears against the muffled silence, After what seemed like an eternity had passed the boy decided that the coast was clear and triumphantly retrieved the first largest scroll, he turned it over in his palm noting every miniscule detail, strangely it felt warm to the touch?

Uther very carefully unravelled the scroll by the light of the dying embers, he strained his eyes as he struggled to decipher the faded runes inscribed upon the parchment by the waning firelight, deftly kneeling beside the glowing embers to gain better a light with which to read, as he did so something magical occurred.

Uther drew his breath in awe, surely it must be an illusion for as he drew close to the slumbering blaze the faintly etched runes upon the parchment flickered into life appearing to burn as flames upon the scroll in the age old Magic of Flamesword!

The small boy nestled down beside the cinders and read the fables of Galthoria, each scroll was related to legends that he had heard from his Father about the Temple of Anwen and the Menacing Gryphon riders!

The first scroll depicted the tale of the phoenix riders, Runic high Priests of Anwen who wore magical gold armour and rode upon fire Phoenixes, which were summoned from fire after battle from the blood of conflict a fearsome sight flaming and skeletal in appearance, the second smaller scroll told of their nemesis's the Gryphon riders and how they were clothed in the enchanted silver armour of Alluan, Gryphon riders were warlocks or enchanters and rode upon Grimm Gryphons, conjured from ashes and soil of ancient forests, feathered in leaves with talons like branches and thorns.

Both ranked equally in majestic sorcery conflicted against the other dark versus light, as they were dominated by different poles, two halves of one whole constantly striving against the other for supremacy, and so long ago began a battle until death between the one protecting the forests and land, the other harbouring battle and supremacy two fearsome enemies..

Legend had stated that both sets of riders were ‘born of the gods’ the phoenix riders all had one characteristic, piercing indigo eyes, set within wolverine features displayed beneath silver hair, they were hushed under a sworn veil of silence and never spoke to any man or beast, and bringing forth fear and awe in to the hearts of men.

In contrast gryphon riders were decorated with scarlet hair and bore eyes the radiant colour of gold upon lionesque features, their gait was pure majesty, they commanded respect and admiration from the hearts of men, they were not silent and had a loud and commanding tone.

Both services initiation was begun from birth, each were taught how to be victorious in battle, and strived constantly for valour and pride, battles between the two raged on for days like the onslaught of a tempest, protecting the forests from saeb the overlords attacks.

The scrolls told how on the full Alluans cycle the phoenix riders are abroad in their true form, Lycanthropes, And how they dare not ride abroad in the stark midday rays of the Anwen, for this is the hour of the gryphon riders, their true form is that of a man and a lion, for they are Felinethropes! The smaller of the two scrolls went on to explain that both factions were needed by the eternal balance, as everything must have its opposite.

The tale burned alive on the parchment as it told of how when the first two riders had clashed swords millennia ago, it had cast the cosmic balance out of synchronicity causing the third sun of peace Alumayen to come crashing down from the heavens to the land below.

The apocalyptic cataclysm caused such a monumental lesion that the portal of time herself ripped asunder leaving behind a gaping wound in her wake from whence could be unleashed the foul legions of the shadow realms, the gateway beneath the mirrored lake narcissus.

And thus so had allowed the evil overlord Saeb and his son Maleusius to summon draco from his utopian constellation, the gryphon and phoenix riders had ceased to exist when draco had flown his celestial shackles discontinuing the eternal reverence, yet two remained one man and one woman from each battalion and how they had rumoured to wed to create a son to unite the cataclysm fixing the rip in time keeping Saeb and Maleusius trapped behind the portal, balance must be restored once more and the riders pulled from the time vortex to regovern their temples, Uther struggled to take it in, surely this could not be true?

Lycanthropes and felinethropes abroad, the heavens crashing down and the monsters in the closet he had imagined were all real! with a shaking hand and quivering breast Uther hurriedly replaced the scrolls to their secret vault struggling to see clearly through the evident tears that now ran like salty rivulets down his boyish cheeks, he tenaciously slid the loose mantle brick back into place as fast as he dared without causing disturbance, quickly surveying the shadowy living quarters to check that his exit route was clear before speeding off toward his bed.

Wynnauld meanwhile observed his son from deep within the shadowy confines of his bedchamber, Arianwen was blissfully asleep her long red flame coloured locks adorning the pillow, meanwhile Luna snored and barked quietly in her sleep before rolling over onto his best russet cloak.

His heart went out to the small boy, but what could he do, the boy must know sooner or later he made up his mind that he would consort with his brother Wynnad later that day,

Brushing his long silver locks out of his eyes he best set off to sweep up the blanket of mantle dust before Arian found it in the morrow, meanwhile Uther dove down upon the fur pelts beside the bedchambers grate and pulled the largest pelt over his shivering head, it was some time before he fell in to a fitful nightmarish sleep full of lycanthropes and tum-bling skies….

TIME PASSED….THE DISCOVERY

It was in his fourteenth year when Uthers father Wynnauld instructed him leave for his apprenticeship, It's to be with the Smyth in Thygor Rhys, your to leave in the Morning he said, and thus was the end of Uthers childhood.

Morning came and the expectant Uther headed off towards the stables to choose his mount on his father's instruction a birthday gift, he had his mind set upon a fine Chestnut Gelding, The boy trudged through the muddy road that led up to the stable doors, mindlessly chewing at a piece of straw as he went along, Uther wondered with dread about which old cart horse would await his arrival as the familiar smell of fusty hay, horse dung and musk greeted his nostrils.

Uther drew level with the stable door taking a deep breath, he struggled to pull back the top bolt having to use two hands, the fitment grated in protest as he forcefully drew it back, Pulling a face at the grating sound, at last it wriggled free, Uther apprehensively grabbed hold of the large iron ring hanging from the door and swung it outwards releasing a thick cloud of dust and hay upon the air, he watched it swarm and dance about upon the bright morning air for a moment until it dispersed.

Uthers attentions were drawn back as he, peered into the stables interior illuminated by the stark Anwens rays, the boy drew in his breath sighing heavily in in trepidation for the sorry nag that he was about to meet and stepped forwards into the stable..

The sight before his eyes was not what he had expected, a beautiful flame Flyer stood regarding him bewilderingly, the beast held an aura of majesty which oozed from every pore of it's being washing over Uther like a flickering enchantment, the Flyers fur shone a rich golden brown smouldering with resplendent hues of autumn fire to captivate all who gazed upon him, the creatures eyes fizzed and crackled with hues of hazel observing the boy with a sense of questioning curiosity as if somehow the horse was trying to fathom out his intentions, his head bore a flash of white fur like an emblazoned white star which shone out like the heavens themselves, was this a magical beast Uther pondered to himself?

The stallion towered above his stall at almost fifteen hands high cutting an imposing scene against the shabby backdrop of the stable, uther wondered if it was a trick of the light as his steed seemed to blaze and flicker magically, The beast snorted shaking his mane, then stared Uther straight in the eye.

“Good morrow young master my name is ‘Minstrel,” he whinnied in a human like voice.

Uther stood there startled he wondered if the mead that he had taken with his breakfast had affected him, he glanced at the creature quizzically, surely that horse cannot be speaking to me he wondered?

“Yes, little master don’t look so alarmed, it was I that spoke to thee, I take it that you have not met a Flame Flyer before?” Uther gaped at Minstrel wearing an expression of complete alarm as his mouth dropped open, Man and beast stood regarding each other for a tense moment whilst Uther considered the possibility that he had gone stark raving mad.

Minstrel pawed nervously at the straw and said, “All beasts speak master Uther you have only to listen and you shall hear”, Uther composed himself closing his gawping mouth shut with a snap, and feeling slightly embarrassed he shifted nervously upon his feet drawing circles in the dust as he looked down at the floor.

After a painfully quiet moment considering his reply the boy faced Minstrel, held his breath and spoke. “Please forgive me for i have not before encountered a magical beast such as yourself and i am more accustomed to dealing with cart horses and nags, you must think me rude; i am pleased to meet your acquaintance Flame Flyer Minstrel”

“And I am pleased to meet yours master Uther” replied Minstrel, Uther continued, “My father has sent to choose a mount from this stable to embark on my apprenticeship with, it is a long and arduous journey” explained the boy before continuing, “I was shocked to discover you here, and invite you to accompany me on this quest would you be willing Minstrel?” he asked the Flyer in a hopeful tone.

Minstrel replied "Little master i have been sent here to surprise you by your father, to join you on your quest would delight me greatly, for I long for adventure i shall escort you to the ends of the realm and the kingdoms that lie beyond", And so it was set the two companions were bound to one another by a pledge in the spirit of adventure.

It was a bright morning in the spring of Uthers years when he rode off to the smiths forge in Thygor with Minstrel…

THE FLYGHT

Uther and Minstrel spent most of that sunny morning loading up their provisions for the long journey ahead whilst making each other's acquaintance, Minstrel revelled in telling legendary tales of his herd and their origins in Valanthia' whilst Uther on the other hand explained all he knew about the scrolls and his previous strange encounter with the Torrent and Wynding boggart, forming an allegiance together as they discussed their hopes and fears about the journey that lay ahead.

Finally once Uther had fully packed and loaded the saddlebags for both himself and minstrel, he swung into the saddle and they bade a cheerful farewell to his childhood home and family, once the companions had ventured beyond the farmyard gate and were well out of sight Minstrel halted and said to Uther,

"Now master we travel light, prey do not speak of this shortcut to your father" and with that the Flame Flyer ignited into a whirlwind of orange and crimson flames which licked and danced around Uther like a shimmering aura of heat, the boy recoiled back in shock lest he should be burned, Minstrel alarmed by the sudden movement reassured his rider by saying, “Fear not young master the flames shall not harm thee they are quite cool, reach out your hand and see.” Thinking the horse was mad, he wasn’t sure about this, minstrel expects me to put my bare hand into a sweltering flame? . “I dare not” replied Uther fearfully”, “I shall not harm thee, trust me friend” replied the Flayme Flyer.

Uther was afraid he had burnt himself on cinders at the cottage as a child and still bore the scars, sweat broke out across his brow with his heart hammering hard within his breast, I must show that I am not afraid he thought, tentatively he reached out his shaking hand towards Minstrels licking mane letting his instincts guide him as his eyes were clamped shut!, Slowly his hand became enveloped within the scorching licks of hair that ran down Minstrels nape, but gladly nothing but coarse horse hair met Uthers finger tips, no flame could be felt! Slowly Uther opened his scrunched up eyelids and laughed out loud, patting and stroking minstrels flickering mane in relief, “I am sorry friend it was just a shock” he said, “Not many horses burst into flames” he added jokingly.

The Flame Flyer laughed in return seeing the funny side, before adding, “I wished to impress you I’m sorry Uther, but now that you have seen my enchanted form we must travel, speak aloud our destination to the wind.” The boy held his head up high towards the billowing clouds and excitedly proclaimed, “To the Smyths Forge Thygor!” and with that came a huge gust of wind that blew through both boy and Flyer like a gale whipping Uthers hair across his face as it ignited the Flayme Flyer with an intense ferocity, the landscape around them vanished in a heady mirage of heat vapours, and a roaring sound like fire bellows met the boys ears as Minstrel took off to a gallop through the tempestuous thunder clouds with his magnificent Flames burning like a volcanic inferno.

Uther wished he could see the land below he knew they were up high he could feel it as the wind whistled through his hair and the rage of the flames met his ears, he had often wondered what it was to soar above the clouds like a buzzard?

The boy could almost taste the rain upon his tongue as the damp air around him fizzed and crackled releasing steam as the eye of the storm met the Flyers Flames, Thunder claps rang out in the air around them, as Thor smote his hammer in the forge of the gods, reminding Uther of his impending apprenticeship.

The Flame Flyer released Zeals of sheet lightning to the ground as his fiery hooves thundered across the atmosphere illuminating the realm below with flashes of stark brilliance, Uther was blinded by the visage of heat that enveloped him and Minstrel in their sweltering cocoon, After a while Minstrels pace began to slow until it became all but a trot, the raging wind died down to all but a whispering breeze and it felt as though they were descending back down towards the kingdom beneath them once more.

Minstrels surging flames began to flicker down to a mere smouldering as they drew level with the tree tops, a couple of corvids alarmed by the unusual sight took flight from a nearby Horse Chestnut tree, from the copse on the outskirts of Thygor, Uther could begin to sight the fast approaching landscape now that the flames were diminishing, a black and white wooded spire came into view marking out the local temple.

Thygor was now slowly coming into range, it appeared like specks on the distant horizon, wispy tendrils of smoke wound upwards snaking into the air as the villagers baked their wares,

The Anwen shone brightly ahead through the blustering clouds, cutting through the murk like an armoury of blazing swords, blades of stark light cut across the stormy scene temporarily illuminating the bowels of the pendulous sky, It must be late afternoon considered Uther raising his hand against the Anwens glare as they began their slow descent from the horizon

The heat haze surrounding Uther and The Flame Flyer vanished as minstrels hooves made contact with the dusty earth, the magical horse hit the ground at a steady trot before slowing down altogether and finally stopping by a weathered stone water trough in the village square, Minstrel hung his head low into the nectar and drew in large draughts of the cool crystal ambrosia, uther could of swore he saw steam arise from the horses nostrils as he swung down from the saddle stiffly stretching out his sore legs and rubbing his behind as he hobbled to the ground, it had been a magical but lengthy flight.

Minstrel had now finished drinking and stood retiring upon his aching flanks beneath the shade of the market hall which was now deserted by the many stalls of spices and trade from around the corners of the realm.

Thygor had a rich market trade offering anything from a multitude of vegetables and fruits through to aromatic spices, opulent dyed silks and woven enchanted carpets, The local tanner rhys also held a stall of armournents and battle wear which was rumoured to be visited by the kings regulator himself.

The market house was a peculiar building which teetered precariously upon four uneven stilts and was fashioned from timber and lathe finished with wattle and daub, Its treasury room was now guarded full time by fetch fairies due to the constant raidings on the coffers, Fetch fairies duty was to protect the money at any cost, they had nasty sharp teeth and flitted about on tattered looking feathered wings.

Each faery was assigned a bag of gold each, today had been taxes day resulting in a huge flock of them hovering about like a cloud of harpies, Fetch roosted ominously beneath the timbers of the building occasionally ruffling their dishevelled feathers and opening an eye here and there to observe the wayward travellers beneath the eaves.

Uther scanned the horizon as he took a swig from his flask, reaching down into his saddle bag he extracted some barley loaf that his mother had given him only that morning, now it seemed a life time ago.

He crudely broke off two sizable chunks and held one out to minstrel who gratefully nuzzled up the morsel, Chewing down upon the malty bread the boy considered their next move, should they find an inn and lodge down for the evening and find the Forge on the morrow, or should they press on and find the smyth tonight and risk running into a Lycanthrope as it was the full cycle of Alluan tonight?

Just at that moment a chill breeze sung around the buildings eaves before remorselessly biting in to Uthers flesh, this made up his mind for him, "Come friend let us bed down for the day, tonight you deserve a well-earned rest, we will press on in the morrow" stated the boy to the Flame Flyer with a shiver, Minstrel was pleased with this idea as he had laboured hard on the Flyght to Thygor, he didn't feel capable of any further explorations this day whinnying his approval so not to speak in public.

Uther collected up his saddle bag and canteen, then loosened off Minstrels constraining buckles and straps before burdening himself up with a hefty load as well, the two traveling companions then set off in the direction of thygors streets silhouetted timelessly against the diminishing light.

Uther shuddered as they began the approach up to the village gaols leading his companion through the winding narrow cobbled streets, the air was cold now and the wind had begun to pick up as it whistled around the gloomy timbers of the platform, rotten cabbages and egg shells lay strewn across the town square, Uther tried to avoid stepping on them wherever possible, but his boot squelched as he trod upon yet another rancid vegetable which released a pungent stench to greet his nostrils, in protest he pulled his snood tightly around his face to block out the festering aroma, the coarse woollen fabric irritated his skin but he dare not pull it down as they were now level with the gaols, the previous unlucky victim of the hang man's noose had been left to serve as a stark warning to all who defied King Kalthor and his evil regime.

Uther turned his face away as the rope creaked sickeningly in the wind, its consignment turned to face the boy with cadaver eyes, a large menacing crow glared down at uther from his macabre perch upon the gallows, making the boy shudder in repulsion at the scavengers next meal.

It was all uther could do not to wretch at this foul sight he was not accustomed to such barberry living in the quiet little farm all his youthful days, The Flame Flyer flicked his tail at the multitude of insects that had descended upon the fetid air the pair quickened their pace till they had passed the gruesome venue, traveling under foot had become somewhat easier now they were free of the town square and its carpet of rotten cabbages well-trodden cobbles now greeted their boots and hooves this pleased Uther greatly he reached up to his face and removed the itchy snood taking in a generous breath of fresh night air, the aroma of taverns and wood smoke hung upon the breeze like a welcome friend.

Uther and Minstrel now approached the row of taverns on Sunken Alley how were they to discern their choice of lodgings thought uther to himself observing the collection of bustling inns, The first One in the row had the grand title of "The Knights Rest" engraved upon a battered shield which swung from the buildings threshold, candles gently flickered at the windows like an ode to the weary traveller.

"Come let us try this one" remarked Uther to the Flame Flyer he lashed his steed to the wooden stall outside, and stepped hastily through the doorway following the enticing scent of boar upon his nostrils.

Uther entered the tavern somewhat nervously as this was the farthest he had ever ventured from home and he was not used to strange folk, the boy immediately felt out of place in the richly decorated room with its lustrous cushioned pews and elegantly carved tables, why even the floor was carpeted, you certainly wouldn't get that in the oxen and plough he thought to himself! looking around he observed the inns inhabitants curiously, a portly middle-aged noble man sat warming his cockles by the fireside, his stout frame filled his tapestry britches to bursting point which appeared comical against his over starched linen blouson, ornate well-polished buckled boots covered his mustard coloured socks whilst his ermine cloak lay strewn over the back of his chair like a discarded rug,

The portly man regarded the cabbage sullied Uther with a somewhat distasteful expression tugging at the corners of his Mustache before nonchalantly returning to his jug of ale and hearty platter of cheese, meats and bread.

In the corner sat a more sinister character Uther recognized as one of King Kalthors regulators, distinguishable by the cloak pin that he proudly displayed, a silver crescent moon set with one amethyst jewel at its centre, the foreboding figure was completely concealed beneath his vast ebony traveling cloak only the glow of his pipe could be seen as he slowly drew upon it, Uther suddenly changed his mind about their lodgings for the evening upon sight of this menacing individual and headed back out into the cold alley where Minstrel awaited him.

At that very moment the moon broke through the soupy clouds to illuminate the cobbled passage way in swathes of eerie silvern light, a blood curdling howl resounded upon the still night air, making the boys blood run icy cold through his veins, Minstrel pawed nervously at the ground they were out far too late night, had sneaked up around them without them noticing it.

Uther grabbed a hold of Minstrels reins with a shaking hand and the pair quickly disappeared like scotch mist into the courtyard of the Highwayman, This notorious inn was the favoured haunt of smugglers and bandits from all over the realm, they passed through the tavern to flog their plundering, trade for passage on galleons to far away shores and recruit new blood for their underhand plots , The Highwayman was a treacherous place at the best of times you always had one hand concealed upon the hilt of your dagger, but the way Uther saw it a lot more favourable than staying outside.

Uther lead minstrel through the grimy courtyard past discarded empty kegs that reeked of stale ale to the shabby stabling outback, The top half of the stable door swung askew in the silvern moon light, as the wind blew it to and fro like the pendulum of a great clock, banging it against the stable in an antagonizing manner like a precipitous ticking counting down to the witching hour.

Minstrel and Uther gladly entered the fusty warmth of the stables away from the cold windy night outside full of terrors and strange folk, the boy secured the door to their pen from the inside with a Wooden bar he hoped it would keep unwelcome visitors at bay should they come calling, he would pay the innkeeper in the morning, Once this had been completed they both collapsed exhausted upon the warm cushioned hay.

The boy yawned greedily as he deservedly stretched out his aching arms behind his head feeling a sudden stiffness stealthily invade his limbs like a creeping malady, sleepily surveying the dusty interior of their stall for hazardous objects or stealthily hidden ornaments, but discovered only a pail of water and a half a bundle of straw, his chest heaved with relief as he drew in the fusty air.

The familiar smell of hay, timber and horses met his senses with a somewhat comforting embrace, Uther lay there baffled and unable to move as his mind raced with the days onerous events, how could just one day make such an astounding difference to his future, testing the root of his beliefs, and shattering all his perceptions as it caved in the very foundations of his world and all he had thought was true, this time last week he had been a mere hand upon the family farm, now he was destined to become a smith and alchemist handling potent magical volva hewn from within the depths of the boiling Valanthian lakes that coursed through the treacherous crimson mountains of glass, strange beasts were rumoured to dwell within these volatile confines Uther was still to discover whether they were fact or Fable, resting his head down upon the belly of the slumbering Flame

Flyer beside him, the steady rise and fall of the beasts breathing lulled him into a prophetic sleep full of strange visuals and hidden codes that he could not decipher, like a screen of smoke that conceals the truth allowing only glimpses of what may lie beneath.

As the wind howled outside the stables a cowled stranger lurked within in confines of the shadows, drawing out his hand from beneath the folds of his damp traveling cloak he pointed a bony finger towards the stable door, Crimson and orange flames leapt from his fingertips, coursing like lightning bolts as they cut through the gloom, sputtering and crackling against the damp night air they wove their enchantment manifesting into a strange flaming tongue burning runes hung upon the air, fiery sigils and blazing words singed into the stables threshold creating a monumental Gateway of fire that no Lycanthrope nor beast could pass....

Beads of sweat trickled down Uthers furrowed brow as he thrashed around wildly in the hay, dreams of great flighted reptiles invaded his psyche, the boys ominous vision foretold a vast luminous dragon descending down from the heavens to reign down fire and pestilence upon the realm as it spewed forth white hot molten volva upon the kingdoms terra like a plague of asphalt decay, in his dream, Uther stood defiantly atop a mighty tor wielding all but a mere oaken stave, the boys brow furrowed as he slept, surely he would be destroyed as the dragon swooped in, heading toward the tump on its trail of rampage, the dream warrior Uther brandished his measly weapon in valiant defiance as the serpents leathery wings whistled through the air with an eerie cry, red hot flames and torrents of molten lava issued forth from its looming serpentine jaws as the tempestuous beast drew ever closer, an acrid scent of Sulphur loitered repugnantly upon the wind, Uther gagged choking on invisible fumes in his sleep.

The hot wind gained momentum as it whirled beneath the dragons wings assaulting Uthers senses raging toward him like a blistering inferno, Uther raised aloft his stave in a desperate attempt to shield his face from a scorching billow of air, as he did something magical occurred.

A brilliant flare of golden light ignited at the staves tip like a celestial fusion before radiating down the shaft of the stave like a magical tapering fuse, the beam of light totally engulfed the oaken rod in shimmering resplendent hues of the Anwen, the light spread out to form an impenetrable shield of light which shimmered like a dazzling rainbow, Uther observed the development in sheer wonderment holding his breath in awe, he could no longer feel the scorching air singe his face, or burning his skin, A serene sense of calm washed over him cleansing away all the fear and dread in his heart as he stood atop the Tor brandishing this mighty weapon of the gods.

The dread beat of leathery wings drew ever closer, resounding out like the beat of battle drums, Uther braced himself, the beast was nearly on top of him now! a few more heart beats and he would arrive at the Tor!

The boy stared skywards through his shield as the serpent came into view, the Anwens light became obscured as the mound became bathed in sullen drapes of shadow cast by the solemn beat of the dragons mighty wings, Uther shuddered in the chill shade they created, his heart skipping a beat as a Jurassic roar sang over the rhythmic flapping..

THE SHERIFF OF THE WATCH

The Night Wind howled around the ramshackle stable as the young boy tossed and turned in fretful throes of sleep meanwhile the Flayme Flyer Minstrel dozed on blissfully unaware of the outside world as he dreamt of riding against the tempestuous clouds earlier that day, and proudly reminisced how his mane and tail had charted a blazing a trail of fire against the inky utopian sky…

The howl of the wind was splintered as a chill cry rang out upon the air to chill the hearts of men, the beasts in the field took shelter beneath the hedges and trees, and any unfortunate folk who were abroad took shelter in the nearest inn or lodgings they could find….

The Sheriff of the Watch Fyngar stoked the blazing pyre, chucking on fresh faggots of seasoned wood and a generous helping of dried Lunar blooms, he stood back from the heat watching the wafting scent dance enchantingly as the pungent infusion snaked into the chill damp air like a smoky charm, rain lashed down unrelentlessly and peals of thunder could be heard In the distance, billows of smoke whipped up into contorted shapes as the wind whistled around the watchtower,.

An unearthly cry rang out a second time causing the hairs on the back of Fyngars neck to prickled, an icy cold shudder ran down his spine as if someone had stepped on his crypt, the sheriff nervously stamped his feet rubbing his mittened hands together against the cold, his useless forlorn hunting hound tarrog had long since slinked off to cower beneath the hay cart on the first howl, not much of a watch hound the sheriff muttered to himself as he nervously surveyed the villages perimeter for Lycans, it would be a long arduous night he thought to himself as he drew upon his pipe, his back turned to the forest Fyngar did not notice the cowled figure snaking through the tree line until it was too late, a fiery flash flew up to the towers turrets, unleashed from the strangers finger tips, hissing violet runes shot across the air, as a clap of thunder rang out to conceal the crackle of enchantment.

The spell hit the watchman Fyngar like a bolt of lightning, throwing him across the floor with force, rendering him unconscious on the ground, Tarrog growled beneath the hay cart hackles raised, as the Lycanthrope passed into the clearing from within the dark confines of knightshade forest, beckoned on by the enchanter Raul, the pair disappeared into the dark night, past the unconscious watchman like a pair of slithering adders as they ascended up the turrets , seen only by the cowering hound, the stormy night drew on, Alluan glared his hoary view upon the realm, a cosmodian sentinel on watch until daybreak where the anwen arose in her glory.

THE SMYTHS APPRENTICE

Dawn broke upon the threshold of Uthers apprenticeship, the Anwen sailed across the night sky flying her radiant sails of light as once more she welcomingly bathed the planet Nimrod beneath her conceptual embrace, Thygors horizon blazed with crimson hues as the sun ascended to her celestial throne at the horizons pinnacle, and the kingdoms landscape twinkled beneath the mornings frosty kiss, nocturnal hunters returned to their burrows and nests as the dawn chorus erupted like a graceful concert….

Uther awoke languorously that morning feeling as though he had waged a battle in his sleep. "I wish i could remember that dream!" he thought to himself with a sense of disappointment, the boy stretched and yawned, struggling to rouse his aching limbs as he arose from the beckoning bed of straw, defiantly vanquishing the urge to close his eyelids once more, laboriously he rubbed the gritty sleep from his eyes, sleepily surveying the interior of the stable he searched for The Flayme Flyer Minstrels whereabouts, miniscule particles of straw danced upon the bright beams of light breaking through the stables rotten timbers, illuminating the dusty interior of stall, but it was empty save for a few bushels of straw, a pail of water and the companions discarded travelling gear, Minstrel must of gone outside thought the boy to himself as he pulled himself upon his feet.

Uther steadied himself against the stable wall as he reluctantly pulled on his riding boots, his legs still ached from yesterday's ride, he drew in a deep breath, yawning and outstretching his limbs preparing for the long day ahead, after splashing his face in the pail and taking a swig of water from his drinking skin, Uther decided it was time to venture out into the courtyard of Highwayman..

Uther nervously pressed his face against the worm ridden wood peeking through a generous crack in the door, to spy any strangers that may be loitering around outside with unjust intent, Uther kept watch a while but encountered only a few crows hoping about, and a sleeping drunk before, he decided the coast was clear to emerge, steadily he pushed the creaking timbers that were holding the entrance closed and heftily pushed the aged door with a shove, suddenly a thought occurred to him, strange how could the Flyer Minstrel have passed through the threshold without disturbing the barricade? ."still it is a magical beast i suppose" he commented to himself with a bewildered expression.

The warm sun caressed the boy's face as he stepped out into the courtyard, the bright light illuminated his flame coloured locks casting the illusionary reflection of spun gold, the bright Anwen met Uthers eyes causing him to squint momentarily to adjust, the Highwayman sounded surprisingly peaceful in contrast to the previous night's merriments, raucous laughter, singing and jostling had sung out upon the air until the second unearthly howling had begun, an icy cold shiver ran down Uthers spine as he recollected the chilling sound that had surrounded them just before dawn, somehow it all seemed less scary in the cold light of day, the boy chastised himself for being so superstitious it was probably a vixen or wolf out on the hunt to feed its cubs!

Uther headed towards the highwayman in order to settle his board and lodgings and hopefully obtain some breakfast he would ask the inn keeper directions to the forge, still no sign of Minstrel, where was that horse he troubled to himself in annoyance.

The light in the Tavern was somewhat dingy, stale smoky air lingered about like a smog mingled with the odours of sour hops, wood smoke and tobacco, A pile of embers smouldered in the grate, remnants of the previous night's roaring hearth, the fizzing embers heralded a noxious black smoke as they spat and smouldered due to the unswept chimney.

Contorted melted stubs of candles lay littered about in dried puddles upon trestle tables covering every available surface, waxen seals of the local clienteles nightly debauchery, Up turned kegs were abandoned around the room now that their liquid nectar had been well drained.

A large and varying collection of pewter tankards clanked around Uthers ankles as he waded calf deep through the litter left behind from the brawl which had broken out between a shanty of scoundrels amidst the evenings revelries.

Uther scoured his gaze around the room looking for any sign of the inn keeper, but only dingy shadows met his gaze, sighing with relief he delved into his kid skin purse and extracted a silver Wyst which he quietly placed upon the bar in exchange for the nights' lodgings, and turned to leave, No sooner had Uther turned his back upon the room, he thought he heard a peculiar noise come from the hearth, it had sounded like a crackling voice had bade him thanks!

The boy span around in alarm to observe the origin of this strange voice, he had not seen anyone, fearfully but steadily he cast his eyes upon the grate hardly daring to look as he closed his lids to all but a mere slit, the smouldering embers seemed to ignite with a sudden intense ferocity spewing forth ash and cinders into the room as they blazed into life.

Uther shot back in alarm ducking for cover behind an upturned trestle as a large cinder singed into the rug where he had been stood not a moment before, timorously the boy raised his head above the level of the defence and stared bewilderingly at the heart, Out from the flames stepped a formidable character….

Soot cascaded onto the singed hearth rug like a ebony sprinkling of bewitchment as the stranger announced his presence in ashen foot falls, Uther beheld the spectacle with disbelief he was nought but a mere man! ..how could this be so?

The scent of singed hair and sorcery filled the smoky atmosphere with a choking reverence as the man stepped forward into the light, his hair was long and untamed and had a metallic coppery tone from years of smything, his once handsome face etched with deep furrowed lines, crafted from a life longs laughter, sorrow and toil, falling in intricate patterns around his features as if somehow detailing a sonnet of the soul within..

His knowing eyes commanded Uthers attention as he locked the boy within his smouldering gaze, the stranger had a sinister yet welcoming appearance, The smyth ran his hand across his heavily sooted brows, releasing yet more dustings of coke onto the floor before he summoned the breath to speak.

"I am the Smyth, and you Uther are charged with the task of learning the Anwen Fyre Magicks which i shall apprentice to you." The Smyth portrayed a commanding potency against the backdrop of the hearth, as if somehow he was drawing upon the flames raw energy, entwining himself majestically within their bewitching vigour as they ferociously devoured the cinders beneath, Blazing tongues of flame licked at the hearth like a ravenous beast, spitting out magickal sparks to rain down upon the air like a shower of singes.

The smyths words echoed with a booming resonance dominating the atmosphere of the hearth transforming the homely blaze into the manifestation of a fiery chasm.

Uther suddenly felt very afraid, how well did his father know the Smythe, and how had he emerged from within the flames, And why on earth was he here instead of being at home working on the farm where he was needed, it was a busy time of year approaching the harvest thought Uther to himself swallowing hard as he struggled to regain his composure for the sake of his father's embarrassment and his own, fearing that he would appear cowardly and not daring to ask the smyth himself!

Uther remained silently fixated upon the foreboding characters oozing aura of fear and knowledge, he tried to desperately to reason against his growing fears which knawed relentlessly at him like a rodent in the pit of his belly, Perhaps his father wished him to become skilled at Smything to forge tools for the farm, and shod the livestock, he could not fail him and disgrace the family and himself, his father knew best.

Uther put his hands in his pockets to still their trembling and focused his gaze back toward the smyth as he stepped forward, he drew out an ancient looking book from deep within the recesses of his robe and thrust it forcefully at Uther, he anxiously considered his next move, should he accept the volume or flee from this sinister character? before he could decide upon an answer he found himself reaching out his quavering hand to receive the mysterious volume, as if somehow he were strangely drawn to it, fearing the consignment would scorch his hand, but was unable to stop himself coveting this fiery trinket as if he were bound to it by some unknown sorcery.

The boys fingertips apprehensively claimed the shadowy volume into his sweaty palms as if it were treasure indeed, "how peculiar!" thought Uther to himself as he drew the prize closer within his grasp, it felt strangely warm to the touch like a pulsing heartbeat, It reeked with age and held a sinister looking quality about it, the bindings were shabby and frayed held together by archaic layers of dust and soot, Uther respectfully handled the ancient object as he tried to discern its origins by the firelight and solitary dusty ray of Anwen which sliced through the windows grime like a knife cutting through cheese.

The hide in which it was covered held an unusual wooden appearance about it like the dry aged bark of a tree trunk, and yet somehow the surface felt as smooth as silk, he turned the volume over to read the front cover, it had an incredibly odd appearance displaying a wrought gold binding depicting flames around the books edge, which appeared to burn and flicker into the cover as the morning light shone upon the coppery metal creating a captivating illusion.

Central to the cover rested a strange wrought copper symbol of an oak tree immersed in flames its roots were clearly visible and entwined in an elaborate pattern at the trees base spelling out one word, 'Flamesword', What could this mean? thought young Uther feeling perplexed.

Uther nervously thumbed at the books first leaf in eager readiment to discover its mysterious contents feeing like an intrepid explorer journeying into hidden realms, he closed his eyes tight shut and held his breath close in his breast not daring to breathe even as he expectantly lifted the page, The parchment made a thick satisfying crunch as Uther turned over the stiff parchment, the contents released a seasoned woody aroma like hearth logs at yule as the air caressed its surface with a gentle swishing embrace, hungrily he cast his eyes down upon the yellowed parchment, but alas only a surge of disappointment beat within his quavering heart as all but a blank page stared hollowly back at him, he blinked hard in disbelief. What manner of trickery was this?

He scrunched his eyes tightly together and willed there to be any manner of alphabet scribed on the page as he cast his eyes back upon the ancient page, but once more nothing but perplexing obscurity met his gaze, "why the blazes had the smyth given him an empty book?" he thought in anger to himself.

The Smyth observed the boy with a knowing smile from within the deep cushioned depths of his fireside chair, Uther frowned as he ran his hand over the woody parchment searching for any sign of hidden markings, but only emptiness greeted his fingertips.

The young boy spoke aloud to himself as he explored the labyrinth of his mind for guidance, "The lessons within are neither apparent nor visible" he stated questionably before looking toward the Smyth for guidance.

The smyth on the other hand was grinning broadly at this spectacle and clearly found it a wondrous source of amusement, he let out a quiet chuckle as he drew down upon his clay pipe issuing forth swathing smoky forms of dragons and fire rings into the taverns atmosphere, pondering a moment as he bit down onto the mouth piece of his pipe suspending it in animation between his teeth as he considered his reply. "Try soot boy" was the answer to Uthers question.

SOOT!, thought Uther to himself as he hurriedly scooped up a handful of jet coloured ashes from the hot grate, the soot felt warm and chalky in his grip as the boy rubbed the ebony pigment upon the yellowed parchment creating a charcoal palette thick with unseen forms that he had yet to master, Uther closed the book with a disappointed sigh, he had expected it to be too easy, he should have known there would be things to learn before he could decipher the smouldering text, he clasped the volume between his palms and looked toward his master, for guidance, the smyth sat regally beside the hearth like a lord of the fiery dance observing the young Uther with a pitying expression, he leaned forward in his throne grasping the velveteen arms of the chair with his shovel like hands as he rose to meet the naive boys gaze, observing his apprentice for a moment as he considered if the boy was ready for his initiation, but time was short, the battle must be won, he almost felt sorry for Uther as he steadily drew in his breath in readiment to command the Fyre incantating "IGNITE!!" The smyth bellowed forth the summoning, now it was done, the dye had been cast, the path had been chosen, the apprentice was shackled to the Flamesword.

The child like apprentice recoiled in shock as the searing hot metal emblem on the cover, branded down harshly into the naked flesh of his palm, white hot pain coursed up his arm like a boiling torrent of agony as the fyre Magick burned a searing path through his veins, the apprentice felt as though his blood might boil, snaking flaming chains weave up his arms, creating a flaming shackle between his arm and the almanac each chained to the other, the flames burned white hot momentarily before the chain extinguished and vanished, leaving the archaic Fyre Almanac to tumble crudely to the floor creating a cloud of dust and soot in its wake as it thudded with a muffled crash onto the hearth rug.

Meanwhile the screaming Uther was a picture of sheer torment, the fire pulsed through his veins, he clutched agonizingly at his dripping wet hair threatening to tear it out in hewn chunks, as the magic burned into his mind, Uthers once youthful face wore a visage of pure horror, contorting his features to display a portrait of suffering and wisdom far beyond his years, thick orange veins stood out like gnarled roots all over his visible flesh, thudding against his temples as they pulsed with the ochre radiance of raw Fyre Magick as it burrowed down into his every cell like an enchanted plague, Beads of steaming sweat ran from his every pore evaporating with a gentle hiss as they escaped into the cool atmosphere of the tavern.

Uther collapsed onto the floor, feeling as though his head would explode, images of vast red winged serpents flashed across his consciousness, they spat forth incinerating plumes of Magick Fyre sigils which raced through the tunnels of Uthers mind branding their burning glyphs upon his chaste memory with a scorching resonance, all the while the apparition of lava dragons beat their wings in a relentless steady rhythm mirroring the apprentices pounding heart until, the final ultimate sigil was brandished deep within the recesses of the labyrinth of his mind.

The wings fell silent as pure Nectarine light swept through Uthers mind reflecting out as it did so from behind his eyes like a voyeuristic beacon of sorcery bathing and healing his intellect as it closed down the rite, the incantation had been branded, The Smyth, bellowed the closing command of “SNUFF”, observing his apprentice through pitiful eyes as Uther collapsed into a crumpled semi-conscious heap upon the hard flagged tiles, The smyth sighed heavily to himself as he thought about whether it would finish the lad off or be his initiation, now his work had really begun….

Triad of Anwen

ONE MOON CYCLE LATER

Uther awoke late that evening in the autumn of his apprenticeship feeling as though he had slept for a thousand centuries, The apprentice drearily opened his eyelids gazing around at his whereabouts, his head swam woozily as he wearily tried to focus upon his swirling surroundings, Uthers vision appeared blurred and distorted like a water colour which had bled around the edges.

As he scanned his bleary eyes around the room distorted images slowly began to reappear, somewhat timorously the boy checked that everything about him was still in place by wiggling his toes and heaving his horizontal form to a slumped position in bed, Where am i thought the apprentice drawing up his hands in order to rub his sleep filled eyes, as he did so a strange marking caught his attention, apprehensively Uther turned his hand palm up for a closer look.....he drew a sharp intake of breath... what could this mean?

A large symbol sat brandished on his right palm in the exact same shape of the copper symbol cast upon the Almanacs cover! A mighty oak he nervously ran his finger over the ochre scar expecting a jolt of pain, but thankfully none greeted him only skin as soft as down met his fingertips, strange indeed pondered the boy it did not seem like a scar at all.

Uther lay back upon the soft billowy pillows taking a moment to reflect upon his situation, what had happened for him to be here, where were his family, and what was that strange marking on his hand?

The ancient fyre Magick in scoring its enchantments deep into the labyrinth of his mind had pushed him deep into the shadow realms to battle against death and oblivion at the jaws of a winged Cerberus, Uther upon emerging victorious had paid the Ferryman Charon's Toll by leaving behind all memories of his previous existence save for the Fyre Magick in the lake of Acheron...

The chamber surrounding Uther seemed sparse and shadowy amidst the smoky glare of the tallow all save for a wash stand and basin, the bed in which he lay, and a beaten up old trunk at the foot of the bed, A coppery glint caught Uthers eye as the tallow sputtered and flickered upon the washstand, casting a swaying smogy illumination as it did so like a flame fighting against the breeze.

The apprentice precariously leant over the side of the straw bed to discover the origins of the unusual glint, expecting to find naught but a coppery penny or shiny button at most.

Upon the floor lain on a dusty crack in the timbers sat the Fyre Magick Almanac! The excited boy reached downwards teetering upon the bed frame as he did so in order to retrieve the volume, he grasped at the woody cover, annoyingly this only pushed it further from his reach beneath the bed, Sighing in disbelief Uther threw back the covers and swung his trembling legs down from the cozy bed on to the floor, the warped boards greeted him with a coarse and slightly chilly feel which grounded him abruptly from his dream like state.

Uthers head began to sway around in circles like a spinning top as blood descended to his feet and legs, he momentarily teetered upon the threshold of balance before grasping anchor upon the bedstead, lowering himself gently down to the floor and carefully stretching out his burning legs he retrieved the almanac from its dusty hiding place beneath the straw stuffed bed.

Uther leant wearily against the bed frame cradling the book upon his lap like a long begotten treasure, he felt both elated to have found it and doubly afraid that it would burn his being once more, but the almanac was now imprinted into Uthers very essence. He could not resist unearthing the knowledge within he and the book burned together as one flame.

With a quavering hand the apprentice ran his fumbling finger tips across the smooth coppery emblem embossed upon the jacket, examining every aspect of its facet the copper seemingly smouldered resplendently, one word sprang to mind as he traced the metallic branches, "Emblazon" he found himself silently whispering the word as it flared across his thoughts, memories of the mornings events rushed back as he recalled vividly how the emblem had branded down into his palm sending a course of raw fyre magic scorching through his being like a torrent of lava, and now it looked so innocent and ordinary.

Uther carefully opened the book and looked down on to the once blank pages, where now a living manuscript now danced before his eyes, It was an alphabet made up of symbols which flickered like fire upon the parchment!

Uther instantly recognized the pictograms as being identical to those upon the colossal shard from his childhood that had sliced his knee in Draco's cave! But somehow now he could decipher their transcript, each glyph he read became script read aloud in his head by some unseen narrator, the apprentices eyes surveyed the page as the previous symbols disappeared leaving the page blank, as if he had absorbed the knowledge contained within, as if he was somehow taking on the tale of the book, Uther read on through the pages an incredible legend began to unfold as it dustily emerged from the dawns of time awoken from an eternal reverent sleep.

"When the third Sun Alumayen plummeted in to the deepest realms of Nimrod, cast down by the sorcerer Raul, it bore like a sword driven through the planets mighty heart, The shattered shards were split into five pieces and driven deep like fiery thorns into the very centre of the sphere issuing forth an intense heat and cataclysmic energy, boiling the planets clay, strata and ores, fusing them into life forms, the first were known as fire elementals, who evolved into "Embers" and their symbol was a sun.

The acceleration of this new life form was so vast that the pressures this birth created caused fissures which cracked like open like lesions across the entire globe as molten rivers of lava spewed forth unto the surface of the realm like birth waters leaving destruction in their trail, This enchanted lava or 'Volava' reached the mighty oak of life and knowledge named 'Myrddin' it was rendered into dust and ashes as the ravenous flames ravaged and consumed its very form and life force in a blazing gust of intense firestorm, But as with all death life is reborn from destruction,.

The almanac FLAMESWORD itself had been crafted from the druidic white leaved oak, which had stood for millennia , in a hidden little hamlet beneath the hills of the shire, but the oak having been smote to fire by the evil Raul in times dawn when he had sent fire and dust dervishes to the oak Myrddin to try to encapsulate its potent Magick.

A Druid warlock named Brandubh had resurrected the almanac from the ashes of the tree, using fabled rites of ogham alchemy, the almanac told how the legendary warlock had forged the first sacred armaments of FLAMESWORD in Volava, crafting the FYRE almanac from the red hot lava of the meteor sent by Raul , to engrave the ashes of the Oak Myrddin with Flamesword, Ancient Fyre Magicks were inset throughout the glowing volume, like a pulsing root of the once living oak Myrddin, the embers elementals bound to its pages could be conjured from the pages and incantations.

The first sacred Armament of sorcery had been crafted using the almanac named 'Flame Sword' the runes had been spoken into the sword Bradweith as it was forged, the legend stated that it held a vast blinking dragons eye within its lionesque hilt, and that an ember elemental resided within the stone, the tale both captivated and absorbed Uthers imagination detailed inner portraits depicting enchanted volcanoes, sword wielding warlocks and vast scaly serpents, his imaginative young mind continued to creatively narrate the tale as he eagerly read the following….

One moon cycle later foliage and life forms had resurrected from out of the carnage as ashes turned back into earth and energy took on form, and a magickal Almanac emerged from where the mighty Myrddin had once stood.

And so with the rebirth of the soil the second elementals were created out of the ashes these wizened creatures were known as a Morrows or earth elementals and had evolved out of the soil, clay and strata, their symbol was that of a four pointed star representing the points of the compass, this effect continued to spread over the terra as the supreme elemental energy left behind in the wake of the blistering Volava gave birth to boiling springs , steaming pits of sulphurous lakes and crystalline pools, and birth of the lake narcissus, with the ever changing tides of these waters governed by the moon Alluan, the lake narcissus bore into existence the water elementals known as Torrents and their symbol was that of the crescent moon.

Cataclysmic celestial winds reshaped and metamorphosed the acrid planes as huge blusters of stormy wind created patterns swirling throughout the ash and dust, spinning patterns and sigils across the soil, life forces transferred into the air creating creatures known as Zephyrs and their symbol was that of the lightning bolt.

With the Four elementals birth, a great enchantment was happening below the surface of the charred terra, the element of Ether that bore the elementals into existence came into form, crackling violet wisps wove around the five thorny shards of the fallen Alumayen that pierced Nimrods broken heart, Five spectral Wynder's engraved the five elemental symbols upon the shards facets to seal the summoning, the symbols were, a sun, a lightning bolt, a moon, a four pointed star and lastly a pentagram to represent the Wynder's".

At the tempests end sulphurous dust and ashes lay like a thick blanket cast untidily upon the ground, a light serene breeze blew across the landscape parting the ashes from the earth like a great carpenter blowing the shavings from his newly carved creation.

In the wake of the devastation and the end of the summoning, the earth cracked asunder to a deafening rumbling as two colossal crystal formations ejected from beneath the underworld, each on opposed ends of the realm like the conflicting ends of an immense magical force field ruled by the darkness and the light.

The ruler of light marked out the northern hemisphere, its formation being composed purely from chaste quartz crystal clear as glass, it created an optical illusion upon the senses, endless mirrored aspects courted the rays of the Anwen causing the quartz glacier to sparkle like a mirage, clearly apparent to the eye one minute and vanished the next rendering it virtually invisible to the naked eye.

A virginal stream of pure frigid water, flowed effortlessly from the base of the quartz megalith releasing its purity into the devastated landscape to fertilize the soil once more, a crystalline torrent cascaded with a vast force across the barren landscape cutting through jagged rocks and fissures as it snaked along its winding course, carefully smoothing the spiteful obtuse contours within its damp embrace as it sought out the cliffs edge, tumbling waters transcended into a roaring curtain of energy which fearlessly descended over the sheer drop into the swirling whirlpool beneath before ultimately collecting in a serene lagoon at the waterfalls end known as the Crystal Mirror of Anwen.

Its counterpart stood looming upon the southern hemisphere of the horizon loomed the immense amethyst Glacier known as the mirrored chamber of Alluan, the megalith resided within shadows as dark as an Alluanless night absorbing the sun's rays within its inky sword like surfaces, Each fractured facet seemed to pierce the horizon transforming it into chaos as the swords sliced upwards towards the heavens, with the uppermost peaks of the glacier threatening to penetrate the very stars themselves, zephyrs danced around its countenance, a low vibrating resonance sounded from the megalith as it spread its vitality out across the land like an unseen pitch of defence creating a shield of protection to be tapped into at will, lunar blooms grew all around the sentinel, delicate opaque mauve flora omitting a sweet heady scent intoxicating and entrancing.

Uther recognized the megalith Alluan as being situated by the fortress of the evil king kalthor , little had he known of its properties, the evil king and his regulators were trying to harness its energies warping and bending them to his own satisfaction for his master Raul the sorcerous cadaver.

The fortress Ravens peak, was an ominous plague upon the landscape, Thick pendulous storm clouds swarmed like a pestilence around the menacing keep, formations writhed around the turrets like spectral venomous serpents crafting a foreboding aura filling the poisonous atmosphere with noxious gasses, creating a sense of dread and loathing as swirling malformed shrouds writhed and morphed into corrupted contortions reflecting the tormented spirits of its unfortunate victims still trapped within its plagued embrace.

Eerie menacing sounds screeched defiantly against the tempestuous atmosphere as these unfortunate wraiths protested at their confinement, shrieking and wailing like a chorus of harpies, an unearthly sound of torment sliced down through the torrid air like a hot knife hanging thick with resonance upon the oppressive air, dank pungent vapor skulked off towards the moonlit land a venomous carpet of ghostly serpents in hunt for fresh prey to quench an ever growing thirst for warm blood.

The nocturnal obelisk Alluan commandeered the horizon as it loomed ominous and isolated against the majesty of Alluans silvern light, Rancid water seeped from its amethyst heart like a festering wound as it bled into the gloomy stagnant depths of the surrounding swamp, Slimy repugnant black waters bubbled and hissed as the swamp boiled and simmered expelling forth her noxious venomous gasses into the atmosphere like some immense Wytchs cauldron casting a malevolent enchantment across the realm.

Alluans reflection shone down into the void trapped within the mirrored surfaces of the glacier like a single ray of hope in the dead of night, his hoary silvern disc sat captured upon the dark swamps surface And so was named the Black Mirror of Alluan,

Uthers inner voice drew to a halt, leaving a tense atmosphere in its wake.

Suddenly uther was bought back to reality by a large looming silhouette within the door frame, the boy turned round to see the smyth commandeering the entrance his coppery locks blazing like fire against the sunlight beaming in the windows, beads of sweat caressed his brow, his leather apron scorched and soot ridden, "come lad let us begin" he stated and so it commenced, the teachings of Flamesword and ember enchantment, how to fashion armournents of sorcery, but there is too much to tell here for that would be another tale.

Twenty five Moons later when the Fyre Almanacs flamesword pages all but appeared blank to the apprentices eye, the Flamesword apprenticeship completed with the smyth, the rituals and incantations recited absorbed into his psyche. Uther the warlock rode off towards the setting anwen on the flame flyer minstrel, a glinting golden blade slung across his back catching the sun's rays with its fiery orange steel, he turned round to take one last look at the sweltering forge before his steed burst into a gallop igniting into flames, as the pair soared upwards towards the clouds, a shimmering haze of valour for the next stage of their adventure.

THE TALE OF FREYJA (THIRTY MOON CYCLES EARLIER)

The picturesque little village of Drewsville was situated upon the banks of the river Sabrina, the pace of life was idly serene apart from the lively fishing quarter held at mermaids quay this bustling little port of trade was a hive of activity on market days being visited by many encampments stretching out across the realm, the main feature was its ornate temple spire the only remains left standing of the now ruined temple, it held an obscure curiosity to its visage having been crafted into the impression of a pepper pot, villagers came from far and wide to observe this peculiar sight, A Verdigris crown sat regally upon the spires brow whispering faint echoes of how it had once been a flaming copper beacon but now appeared weather-beaten and dull from age.

The pepper pot as it was called locally was home to a striking stained glass window depicting a mythical being with the body of a woman beheld beneath a pair of innocently majestic swans wings the shade of snowdrops which extended out from her back with an angelic reverence.

In the gardens of the ruined temple crumbling tombstones of the towns ancestors lay strewn about close by as if they were whispering to every visitor that passed by of the ages past and the precedent splendour and once hallowed eminence that still oozed from the ruins every stone block and aperture, a tiny winding footpath lead down from the spire as it wound through the gardens lush emerald grass, snaking past a bed of dazzling flowers splashed in a multitude of colours as if a rainbow had ended their tainting the ground with its multihued blooms, ranging from small round petals of pure crimson laced with cobalt right through the spectrum to abundant cherry pink daisies and violet trumpets.

The path had been created from headstones that had long ago collapsed upon the land under the burden of the ages, smooth and weather beaten in appearance, the epitaphs chiselled upon them were barely visible washed away by many rains, as if they wished to hold their secrets until the end of all time.

The little girl danced down the path skipping and humming to herself as she wound her way downwards from the pepper pot towards the cobbled street below, her hair was long and flowing and glowed in hues of ginger like a crackling flame against streaked golden wisps the colour of summer hay, She had steely grey coloured eyes, flecked with shards of cobalt sapphire, which peered out from beneath freckled features.

Freyja was wearing her favourite yellow dress which her mother had lovingly made for her, a simple tunic dress embroidered with white daisies, The little girls knees told of where she had been previously that day grazed and muddy from climbing trees with her friend.

Freyja loved trees with their immense wizened branches reaching ever upwards towards the heavens like a magical entity, seeming to touch the very clouds themselves, she wondered if that's how rain was made, did the trees squeeze the clouds like a sponge wringing out the water until it began to descend down onto their roots because they were thirsty, She would have to ask her mother her nan or her sisters they would know.

Freyja stepped down on to the cobbles reaching the path beneath the pepper pot, she glanced rightward to gaze at the turbulent river which was swelling to the brim as if threatening to burst its banks at any given moment, like an overflowing washtub.

There were ships, long boats and galleons moored at the edge of the mermaids Quay, they reminded Freyja of tethered up hounds pulling against their leash as they bobbed to and fro, Each vessel floating precariously close to the next with each wave and cross current that lapped at their bow.

A lone galleon rode across the Sabrina river casting an immense shadowy reflection upon the water's surface, the ripples cutting through the like reflections of two setting Suns Alwyn and Anwen, Enormous torn sails flapped powerfully against the breeze whipping and snapping against the tempestuous air, the fearsome sails hung like rags from the great splintered masts of oak, but none matched the prow sail which depicted a vast green Gorgon set upon an ebony background, the serpents danced with a surreal animation as the wind bellowed as if the gorgon were trying to speak, Three jagged masts jutted out of the long ships deck, protruding like horns each had been topped with jagged bronze tips like huge javelins aimed at the sky, Commanding iron guns protruded out from the ship's hull like the fearsome iron tentacles of some great cracken reaching out for whatever prey it could stealthily catch unawares and devour.

An vacuous timber figurehead charted the water with its statuesque expression, the harpies oblivious wooden eyes held a menacing aura about them, her full wooden lips grimaced a sinister sneer as her lifeless features surveyed the village.

Freyja suddenly became uncomfortably aware of being observed, she briskly turned around her gaze was met by pure violet eyes staring back at her, cold soul less and piercing set back within a sallow gaunt face, haggard and almost skeletal in appearance, the lips were thin and pursed, black in colour, menacingly curled down at the edges beholding a sneering venomous expression, two silver fang tips protruded down on to the bottom lip, glinting as the failing light reflected upon them like a vipers kiss.

The ship's captain Raul glared at the girl, long wisps of ebony hair writhed about in the wind like a pit of adders, revealing a woven silver band upon his brow adorned with an amethyst crescent, the necrotic stranger wore a dishevelled sapphire travelling cloak which swept the floor languorously as he paced up and down the deck with an imperial gait.

Silvern moonlight flashed upon the metal scabbard hanging at his side, it was an unusual in the fact it was shaped like a serpentine scythe an with an emerald stone for the eye, freyja was almost certain she saw it blink, it must be a trick of the light she thought to herself.

Raul seemed to beckon to Freyja within her mind with an alluring sense of dangerous enchantment she could not resist but beheld his gaze, half of her wanted to flee in absolute terror and the other half wanted to explore the dangers of the galleon before her ....

A cool night breeze whipped across freyja sending her hair licking across her face and breaking the spell, now she saw a cloaked cadaver upon a pirate ship watching her like a cat watches prey! She broke her gaze as Raul scowled in hatred.

Turning around she saw the setting Anwen reminding her it was getting late, she had best return home to her mother and sisters before they began to worry, she hurriedly turned away to flee as Raul disappeared beneath deck with a swoosh of his cloak, Freyja snapped to her senses and began to run hastily through mermaids quay passing the smaller boats as she darted alongside the river heading back towards the home where her family lived.

The small cottage glowed like an autumn sunset upon the horizon as dusk began to settle upon the realm, the roof thatched with musty old hay was home to many small rodents and birds, it had long since needed replacing, welcoming smoke danced from the chimney giving a seasoned perfume to the air.

The cottages interior had a homely and lived in quality, its centre piece was a vast red bricked hearth which was much used by Freyja and her family in the winter months to roast horse chestnuts, many a finger had been burned by placing them over the embers all too eagerly awaiting them to hiss and crack open revealing the warm sweet fleshy heart that dwelt beneath the hard casing emanating a beautiful sweet aroma as they were shelled, yule was her favourite time of the year with the dark nights, roaring flames and sumptuous treats.

Thick furs and cushions lay strewn around the still glowing embers of the hearth creating a comfortable welcome from the cold red quarry tiles, A picturesque view of pure beauty greeted you from the front windows overlooking a vast lush emerald green meadow set beneath a majestic backdrop of age old immense hills which rested peacefully against the sky line like the silhouette of some great slumbering giant.

Thickets meadow was ornamented with various trees of all descriptions ranging broadly from copper barked pines adorned with cones, right through to smooth trunked hazel trees dripping their catkins from every bough a multitude of squirrels and birds of all species happily dwelt within the branches through the cycle of the seasons, each morrow when the Anwen arose and again when she settled at dusk a beautiful chorus of bird song could be heard resonating from the treetops like a magical enchantment bewitching all that heard its rapturous embrace, upon the sweet pasture dwelt a herd of stocky oxen they dolefully gazed at the meadow through huge docile eyes, occasionally reaching out a mighty pink tongue in greeting to the air as they bayed at each other and trundled back and forth.

Two pastures away slept an ancient mound, surrounded by cairns and barrows it was rumoured to be inhabited by the fay, on a midsummers eve melodious symphonies could be heard carrying on the breeze from the burial ground that was known locally as "Morganas tump", Its summit was commandeered by a magnificent white oak it was fable that the oak had been resurrected from the scorched acorn of Myrddin.

The mighty oak named Duir dominated the Morganas tump, her branches were set like some majestic crown against the murky autumn horizon, the oaks leaves gently danced and rustled in the breeze with an austere magical quality, like the goddess she appeared gnarled and wizened, like a seer of time standing alone against the raging elements of the a eons, as they cut their testimony into her bark to remain ever visible for future generations to decipher, bewitching runic formations adorned the bark as if duir was recounting her parables .

The fluttering leaves formed a dappled shadowy pattern upon the tumps summit, Freyja loved nothing more than to sit beneath the branches and rest against the trees trunk where it was cool and shady taking in the smell of damp earth and watching a multitude of insects furtively crawl and burrow around, Occasionally if she was very still and quiet a handsome crow might come and rest upon the branches crawking quietly to his cohort in the murder as they spied out for unlucky bugs, who in turn would quickly scurry off beneath the half buried roots to hide out beneath the sanctuary of the earth until the threat had passed.

Crows were Freyjas favourite birds, cheeky and intelligent with handsome lustrous feathers as black as coal, they seemed to observe you with an inquisitive secrecy and a mischievous sense of persona.

Freyja had to pass Morganas tump in order to get home, but tonight was a night she was not looking forward to the prospect, having already been spooked by her strange encounter at Mermaids Quay, the young girl emerged from the sheltered confines of the cobbled passage which led down to the immeasurable expanse of Hams common, the wind bit through her clothing as she stepped down onto the grass, hefty gusts of chilly air whipped through her hair as she ventured along the harsh open land.

Freyja began to wish that she had set back earlier now, as she advanced upon the gnarled black silhouettes of trees and cairns, for the moon Alluan was high in the sky, casting down his eerie luminescence to bathe the landscape in nocturnal silvern hues, this gave a different and foreboding alure to the landscape under the silvern illusion.

The Sabrina river ran alongside the common like a deep vein, it seemed to pulse with a darkness she had not witnessed before, as if it wished to draw her in to its deadly frigid waters, Freyja heard it lapp icily against the banks like a cold mocking laughter, she fled down the common heading towards the tree line as fast as her legs would carry her, freyjas lungs were burning and her legs felt like lead as blood coursed through her veins making her feel heady and nauseous, the child entered the lane at speed scattering birds from their roost with her sudden alarming presence, she halted dead in her tracks to recover from her dash with rasping breath, now safely in the village before venturing the rest of the way.

Once freyja, could breathe freely once more and her unknown fear had passed she relaxed taking in her surroundings, her eyes grew accustomed to the inky night. journeying forwards, she strained her eyes against the gloom trying to discern any visible pathway hidden beneath the encroaching darkness, strange noises and the snapping of twigs surrounded her, just badgers and foxes Freyja told herself nervously as an eerie hoot rang out into the night, she glanced upwards towards the silhouette of the chestnut tree above her where a ghostly white owl blinked back at her and hooted in a seemingly cross manner that she had disturbed his hunt, She smiled to herself for being silly and courageously headed off towards the mounds of morganas tump, its silhouette came in to view as she entered the grove but somehow but it did not look quite right?

Freyja ducked down beneath the cover of the thicket hiding from sight as she stealthily crept along the approach to the tump, listening out intently for any peculiar noises, she thought it would be hard to hear anything above her own pounding heart and heaving breath. “Fyngar araghh auth et angarth?” cut through the still night breeze, Freyja froze to the spot not daring to move an inch as she listened to the strange dialect “Fynrirth alsth gilths rirr terreths!” she heard again, What did that foreign tongue mean, and who could be at the tump at this hour bandits, smugglers and worse still whoever they were there were two of them!

Her mother had warned her of Trolls that had been sighted abroad in the next valley of Thygorshire, Freyja slithered down amongst the long damp grass surrounding the brow of the tump like an emerald carpet, she inched silently along on her belly like a serpent towards the crest of the mound, Its pinnacle was bathed in the silvery luminescence of Alluan's light casting it under a ghostly light as if it were caught in time.

To freyjas horror there stood a very odd looking group of silhouettes surrounding the oak Duir, as they lurked menacingly beneath its shadowy form, how could she pass them without being discovered she must get home? Who or what were this group of creatures skulking in the shadows they had an unmistakable atmosphere of mischief and wickedness about them.

Mortally afraid that they were trolls, freyja skulked low down in the long grass until her chin rested upon the earth, as she stared at the peculiar beings in dread, At that moment the hoary moon ventured out from behind the billowy clouds from whence it had been hiding to illuminate the abnormal scene with a stark reverence, she drew in a shocked breath, at the most grotesque appearance, what in Anwens name were they?

Fearfully she edged closer, her every sense heightened to her immediate surroundings nervously the girl licked her lips as her mouth became parched in fear, the drumming of her heart pounding loudly against her temples, The creatures had a vile countenance, with green oily encrusted skin, which oozed with a foul liquid, the beast's eyes were an opaque milky white in colour, like a dead thing with green slits the colour of rotting meat down their centres, their noses were hooked and tapered like beaks scarlet lips curled down revealing tusk like teeth with jutted out over their hooked snout.

Freyja felt sick with fear, her every instinct told her to flee, but she dare not make a run for it and alert them to her presence, she was too afraid, what if they caught her, yet somehow she felt compelled to watch them out of some morbid curiosity.

The beasts were short in stature no higher than a barrel, without any visible hair on their body except for greasy mud coloured tresses which hung lankly from their brows spreading down their backs in a knotted mass, Peculiar looking armour adorned their fetid hides fashioned from scaled pelts and bronze chains, it had been as ornamented with animal teeth, probably for defence Freyja thought and was unlike any armour that she had ever seen before, She watched them transfixed and curious, yet too afraid to move as if she were rooted to the spot.

They had lit a fire on the summit of the tump and were burning the branches of the mighty oak as if to sneer at and ridicule the mighty oak Duir, Freyja could not allow this, but what would she do? She had to act fast! Her mind raced and her blood boiled she felt an insufferable rage!

It was then that something strange occurred, Alluan emerged from behind a wisp of cloud, casting his silver rays down to hit the silver star pendant hanging around Freyjas neck, it was her most prized and coveted possession having been given to her upon her seventh birthday by the resident pendragon daerdrith, Freyja buckled down upon her knees screaming cries of agony, as she felt her bones stretch and contort as if they would snap at any minute, feeling as if her skin was on fire, coarse silver hair sprouted through every pore of her skin as it reached up towards the moonlight, freyja felt her jaw dislocate with a loud snap, stretching out into a muzzle as her bones distorted and deformed, her canine form began to sprout innumerable sharp teeth, every sense was heightened and intensified to the pitch of torment as she heard an insect crawl through the grass beside her.

Her arms and legs extended into paws which grew sharp talons, and the hair on her back prickled, Freyja looked down in fear at her changed form in terror she let out a piercing 'AHWHOOOLL!'she let out an unearthly howl in protest at the pain, which alarmed the leader of the creatures, fearfully he span round just as Freyja emerged from the thicket slavering and snarling in anger, rivulets of saliva dripped from her fangs like blood trickling down a blade.

She bounded leaping off her paws towards the chief troll sending him gambolling through the thicket as she caught him with a surly bite, her fangs pierced through his leathery hide the warm smell of blood hit the air as she released the foul creature in repulsion at the fetid ooze covering his skin.

The vile beast realizing his release scuttled away to clutch at his leg trembling with fright as he submerged himself amongst the refuge of the long grass like a cowering dog, His motley companions began to vanish like beetles in to woodwork, screaming "Ysgarth etallr Lycanthrope silthas!", Freyja span around leaving her quarry behind as she leapt off to give chase to them, growling and snarling as they disappeared from view, she stood hunched scanning the horizon amidst the summit of Morganas Tump sniffing the air for their foul stench, the coast was clear they were not returning, at least not for now, She felt sickened and repulsed by the taste of warm blood upon her tongue, what had become of her and what on earth had just happened? as Freyja padded over to her beloved oak, she Dag into the damp earth spraying soil onto the flames to extinguish them, as the last hiss and smoulder was snuffed out, she patrolled around Duirs base sniffing at the acrid smell of scorched earth that greeted her nose, Dejectedly she circled round a few more times before laying down at the base of the oak afraid and shaking upon her haunches in the cool night breeze.

The lycanthrope gazed up at the mighty Alluan shining down with an unearthly clemency amidst the night-time sky he seemed to dominate the night sky with an unearthly persona even the night air felt as still and soundless as a sepulchre

Freyja the Lycan gazed down at her furry paws in disbelief and fear feeling incredibly scared and alone beneath the glowing stars, now she could never return home, a sad lonely tear rolled down her furry muzzle and dripped upon the dark grass, She thought back to the strange ship in the harbour and its mysterious captain, the trolls upon the tump and lastly herself, what had happened was she cursed? Was it all a dream and she would awake safe in her bed at home?

Freyja lay her soft furry head upon her outstretched paws and curled up into a ball not knowing what else to do she dare not return home even though her mother and sisters would be beside themselves with worry, oh how she missed them all already, Gradually the wolves eyelids closed as the creature fell into a fitful whimpering sleep beneath the branches of Duir.

Freyja the lycanthrope dreamt of a regal lion stood upon a burning hilltop, he held a burning almanac depicting a bronze tree upon its cover, flames swayed mockingly around his majestic form flickering with an encaptivating resonance as they cast his golden fur into realms of ingoted shadow, the beasts eyes smouldered like embers as the fire-light danced within their core, his bulky silhouette personified statuesque and commanding amidst the flaming scene, a dark bejewelled night sky twinkled celestially as a large comet journeyed across the vista illuminating the shadows with its trail of fire, the revered beast raised his mighty muzzle skyward and let out a beastly roar at this prophetical declaration, Fire rained down from the heavens in smouldering cinders which gently burned out to ashes as they fell softly upon the earthen ground, Amadejis the Monarch threw back his shimmering mane bellowing out a commandeering roar which reverberated across the hilltop before cascading down into the valley below echoing out over the realm like a call to arms….

Uther

DUIR AND THE DRYAD

The morning Anwen rose sleepily above the horizon casting a warm blanket over the small girl, a gentle breeze whipped through her coppery hair like a windy caress, Freyja stirred gently from her dreams and visions beneath the oak, to find herself asleep upon Morganas tump, For a fleeting moment she was unaware of her whereabouts feeling alarmed to discover that she had not awoken in her familiar cozy bed back at the cottage with Yllas and her two sisters.

The young girl yawned as she stretched out her sleepy limbs, leaves nestled awkwardly amongst the tousles in her hair refusing to budge as she tried to tease them loose, What had happened and why was she asleep beneath the oak Duir on Morganas tump freyja wondered to herself fearfully, looking down upon her muddy form she noticed briar grazes across her legs and a multitude of colourful bruises which began to throb, but most peculiar of all was the dried blood stain! it could not be her blood she held no visible wounds she thought checking herself over and as for the foul stench it emanated well that definitely could not be her blood!

Freyja had not even a distant recollection of the previous night's abhorations her mind remained chaste and innocent as if it had never happened, nevertheless this did not answer her questions about her strange awakening upon the tump, She lay in the dewy grass a while picking at blades nonchalantly as she tried to decipher the puzzle in her mind and how to explain this to her distraught mother who would probably be out looking for her right at this very moment, Freyjas mind drifted into the realms of semi consciousness whilst she delved into the labyrinth of her memories, she spoke to the Oak Duir, "what tales do you have to tell, do you know why I am here?" she asked not expecting any reply.

At that moment a faint breeze whipped up and a low murmuring like the snapping of twigs whispered upon the breeze, a faint voice could be heard like the crumpling of dried leaves. 'My name is Wynterleaf" said the whisper "I am the spirit that dwells within this mighty oak, thank you kind Freyja" it whispered in spoken splinters upon the wind, "I am the spirit of the oak and you assisted me last nightfall, I have a gift for you" Wynterleaf finished.

Freyja thought she must of imagined this, it had been a strange night with strange dreams and she had awoken not in her bed, she gazed at the oak shaking her head staring at the bark to bring herself back to reality, as she did so something peculiar happened, the Deep set furrows upon Duirs trunk began to pulse and radiate with an unseen life force glowing a verdant emerald green, as if the very heart of the oak was alive and beating within its mighty trunk.

Freyja watched transfixed as the gnarled patterns emerged in to some type of alphabet made up of lines and sticks, as once again the distant splintering voice caressed the wind "Freyja I have entrusted you above all others to receive a mighty gift, You shall become an Ovate to heal and protect the forests and trees from this dreadful curse that has befallen the realm, I bequeath you with this almanac." croaked Wynterleaf, and with this the glowing alphabet began to extinguish leaving the Ogham inscriptions in its wake patterned across the trunk like a myriad of carvings.

A loud creaking and rumbling started beneath her feet, as earth spewed forth into the air, bugs rained down in multitudes unearthed from their hidey holes as Duirs mighty roots began to rise up from the ground, a mighty cracking and groaning sound split the air asunder as the extended root stretched out, writhing in freedom stiff from ages rooted within the soil, it emanated a cloud of dust and moisture in to the air as the thick it reached out towards the warm golden rays of the Anwen, the dank smell of musty damp earth hit freyjas nostrils as the enormous root ball was revealed to the light, a myriad of insects scurried off to find other dark damp refuge further beneath the earth, revealing the treasure which lay tangled amidst Duir son of Myriddins roots, freyja cast her eyes upon the emerald coloured volume, which had lain hidden for centuries awaiting the arrival of the green novice, crawling down between the roots she reached down amongst the woody sinews to claim her reward, grimacing in disgust as a large centipede scuttled along her hand disturbed by the foraging, Freyja tightly closed her eyes after noticing a nest of rather large earwigs and reached deeper into the recesses of the trees root system, as her Small hands triumphantly grasped the Gwersu, Freyja delightedly clutched her prize to her chest and smiled broadly a book bound in green leathery leaves.

At this the mighty root descended back toward its earthen grave with the motion of a wriggling earthworm no longer free of its confines now its task had been fulfilled, it settled back into place with a mighty grumbling creak, the gwersu had a fresh green appearance to it like a spring shoot just emerged from beneath the earths caverns, it smelled of sweet dawn dew, As the small girl examined the gwersu Wynterleaf spoke again.. 'Child go to that clump of mauve blooms beneath the hemlock and pluck the pink heart which dwells within the petals, for it is Luna blossom. Devour this upon the discs full circle and you shall keep your true form child.' spoke the Dryad, She wearily trotted over and harvested the bloom, sniffing the flower tenaciously she raised the magenta petals to her lips as if it were poison, the perfume held pungent tones of sickly sweet decay, she creased up her features in revulsion, closing her eyes she unwillingly placed the bloom into her mouth and held her breath in anguish to bite down upon the peculiar plant.

Freyja was pleasantly surprised as the juices met her tongue, the taste was delicate, the juices started trickling down her throat, unexpectedly another sensation began to embrace her throat as if the plant had mockingly lulled her into a false sense of security, the girls mouth started to become increasingly hot as if she had bitten down into a cinder, causing her eyes to water profusely blurring her vision and adding to the confusion, she started to choak for air swallowing hard, the torment increased as red hot saliva coursed down her throat with each hefty gulp of air that she drew in, sending scalding rivulets into her belly transforming it to a fiery cauldron, her tummy gurgled loudly in protest at the poisonous flora.

The child buckled onto her knees as searing pain swept over her in agonizing swathes, her limbs began to convulse violently and her eyes rolled back into her skull, Waves of nausea pulsed through her body more intensely than her previous night's transformation, freyjas head throbbed as it battled with consciousness and her body protested defiantly, Freyja could not tolerate anymore and so passed out into the realm of dreams at the base of Wynterleaf as the mighty Anwen shone down upon the realm.

The child awoke dreamily in her bed that afternoon with no memory of the strange events save for a stroll in the moonlight, getting home late, and a dream about a majestic celestial lion, She sleepily looked up and saw that her mother Llyas was in the room 'Mother' she asked yawning 'where did I go last night, I have had the strangest dream? 'Nowhere child, you were a little late home that is all." came Ilyas's reply. "you must have been dreaming" she added in a strange tone, Too tired to argue Freyja decided to accept this for now she would try and somehow unearth the previous happenings from her subconscious tomorrow, perhaps she would go down to Druid village and rest her mind by the quiet waters of the lake, freyja gave a large yawn and fell into a deep peaceful sleep filled with dreams of lions, flaming oaks and purple flowers, meanwhile the Gwersu lay beneath her pillow.

The next morning's walk in to the village was crisp and pleasant, dew hung thickly upon the lush bladed grass in droplets which seeped into Freyjas woollen boots with a damp greeting, and the birds sang a sweet songful chorus from their treetop dwellings as the rabbits scattered two and fro on the path ahead, their white bob tails flashing as they darted in and out of their warrens, overhead the Anwen climbed the dusky horizon.

The smell of fish hung in the air as Freyja approached the bridge crossing, Clouds of sea birds circled the harbour as heaving nets were hauled in by burly fishermen, the mariner Octavian stood observing his men delivering the salty bounty, the tides had been most unusual last night, what was Alluan up to he wondered, still it had passed in their favour he considered as he gleefully watched the bountiful catch, the small girl gazed down from the bridge above as she passed watching the fishermen draw in their nets, and listening to the distant chant of their sea shanty dance upon the air.

"Cod, Halibut, Eel, and skate, Which one today will we be our plate? Praise to Alluan our Hoary moon, Honor to his quarry, let us dine with a silver spoon." The Jolly tones faded into the distance as freyja alighted from the footbridge crossing the Sabrina river to advance upon the village, she walked the well-trodden cobbles that wound down towards the village Dachaigh, crossing the boundary her dreamy state was bought back to life by the usual bustling as folk went about their daily business.

Dachaigh had a beautiful Granary in the square, a thatched black and white affair which was always teeming with cheeky crows on the lookout for a free meal of grains, Freyja loved to watch the Miller chase them off, they would Crawk at him in annoyance before hopping off mischievously, soon to return when their beady black eyes had noticed his absence.

The smell of freshly baked bread wafted temptingly upon the air drifting in Freyja's direction, enticing her with a beckoning smell.

She felt a sharp pang of hunger in the pit of her belly like a primordial twist of a blade, feeling like a starving animal she couldn't remember the last time she had felt this famished, her senses followed the warm aroma, eagerly she entered the bake house to discover the welcoming Mrs. Philpotts happily surveying the trestle table which lay before her, it was spread thick with a carpet of baked delights that would put any banquet to shame, cakes, loaves and all manner of biscuits adorned the well-scrubbed wooden surface.

"Now what takes your fancy me dear?" Asked The Rosy cheeked Mrs. Philpotts looking up from her baking, she Smiled broadly at Freyja, as she wiped her floury hands down the front of her apron, and pulled her handkerchief from her pocket, "I would love all of them Mrs. Philpotts, but alas I've only a Hae penny upon me" said Freyja despondently, "Worry not little one you look half starved, why you're nearly drooling come over here, I have some spare cakes that have come out a bit too risen for me to sell" said the kind Mrs. Philpotts, as she began pilling rock cakes in to a cloth.

"Here take these home for you, your mother and sisters they are a gift" said the kindly old lady as she handed over the parcel, "tell Llyas it's a small token for all the good healing she does for us village folk" Freyja delightedly crammed another steaming bun into her salivating mouth" Thank you so much Mrs Philpott's "I shall" came the muffled reply as the girl answered with a mouthful of cake, as she happily hurried out of the bakery down towards the cobbled lane which led towards the lake, heavenly sunshine now broke through the clouds illuminating the day with its golden embrace.

Freyja daydreamed idly of wolves and trees as she approached the lake of tears, what a strange sad name it had she thought, as she reached the bank of the lake she decided to rest a while beneath a Weeping Willow, parting the curtain of branches she sat down upon the damp dewy grass beneath the shade of the dripping leaves.

The late morning sun dappled through the willows canopy to cast a magical mottled pattern across the shady grass, Freyja gazed out across the lakes surface to the opposite bank, no one would discover her here safely concealed in her hiding place, Across the other side of the lake three young lads were playing, she recognized them from Anwens farm in Thygor, Uther, Daermund and Daerdrid, Uther was about her age she remembered whereas his brothers were older and not half as much fun to play with being into more rough and tumble pursuits,

Normally she would have gone over to greet them and perhaps play, but today she felt the need for solace and sanctuary.

Freyjas mind wandered off as she gazed at the dappled patterns of sunlight cast by the willows tendril like leaves, they cast unusual images drawing her attentions to their intricate designs, flashes of recollection darted furtively across the screen deep within the labyrinth of her mind, memories flashed back across her memory, a portrait of bright mauve blooms clustered beneath a gnarled and wizened oak came into focus then panned out to reveal the landscape of a vast hill resting like a slumbering giant against the dusky horizon, A lone wolf prowled the perimeter skulking stealthily in the long grass defending the scared place from unseen attackers, how peculiar this scene seemed to freyja as it played out in her mind with its almost familiar imagery. It felt like DeJa'Vu?

SNAP! the spell was broken, freyja looked up and saw Uther sprinting around the lake to greet her he had travelled to the market with his father earlier that morning, she waved and smiled broadly at him, glad to have been woken from the mysterious daydream.

The young girl emerged from the curtain of the willow and ran to greet her play mate, "Uther i glad to see you, i have had the most peculiar daydream!" exclaimed freyja to the young boy, "Hello Freyja" he replied cheerily, "i saw you skulking beneath that Willow, it is too fine a day to hide in the shadows" he replied, then added. "Tell me of this dream?"

Freyja and Uther engaged deeply in conversation as they headed down to the water's edge, the girl explained her almost vision like dream and how familiar it had felt along with her nagging sense that something was brewing, and Uther listened intently occasionally nodding and adding a “Most peculiar” here and there for good measure.

“I do not know Freyja, it is peculiar but hopefully it is just a vivid daydream” Uther said once the tale had been told, “I hope that you are right Friend” replied Freyja in a slightly worried tone for even the young were superstitious in that part of the woods due to the all the enchantment and sorcery which was rife what with their parents warning them of rough folks abroad and the overlord Saul and his band of regulators.

THE SWAN AQUARIA

The young companions slipped off their felt boots as they reached the lakes bank to tread upon the lush emerald grass, it lightly waved its welcome beneath the breezes gentle caress, Freyja sat down upon the bank and tenaciously dipped her toe into the chilly crystal waters humming contentedly to herself whilst Uther, paddled about in the shallows hunting around for unusual pebbles, He reached down to retrieve a large chunk of rose quartz, it caught his eye as it sparkled beneath the waters like a dazzling enticement, it would make a nice gift for his friend, freyja meanwhile was idly pulling at blades of grass.

Suddenly the pairs tranquillity was disturbed by a loud “Sploosh!” reverberating from the lakes centre as it spread out across the placid waters like a thundering kiss of the lakes surface, Each looked upwards to marvel upon the sight of the elegant Snow kissed swan as it settled down upon the mirrored water sending a multitude ripples outwards across the lake like the spreading of a hushed whisper to announce her arrival, freyja visually followed a ripple created by a wing beat until it ultimately lapped at her ankles upon reaching the bank she stared on in awe at the unusually large swan, looking closer she noticed also that the swans plumage held an unusual silvery blue tinge to it which sparkled magically in the sunlight's rays like the delicate dust upon a butterflies wings.

"She's a marvel isn't she?" remarked Uther in awed tones, "Shush you'll scare her off with your ramblings" Freyja replied shooting him an annoyed glance, the afternoon sun made Freyja suddenly take note of how Uthers silver hair shone like moonlight, she gazed momentarily held transfixed by the illusion, she cast her eyes behind him as the dappled light cast an eerie glow upon the lake reflecting the clouds upon its surface, "Look isn't she magnificent i swear I've seen her on the lake at our farm" Uther added.

For a few moments the children gazed speechless upon the beautiful sight, Uther broke the spell by tapping his playmate on the arm and shouting" Your up" before sprinting away, "Right you've had it!" She squealed and went after him as fast as she could but in her haste Freyja did not account for the slippery mud at the water's edge, "Arrgghhh!.. SPLASH!", Uthers friend plunged into the icy depths, "HELP" Freyja spluttered as she gasped for breath as the frigid waters closed over her, Uther stopped in his tracks twisting around on the spot just in time to see Freyja descend beneath the crystal lake.

Freyja held her breath as she descended like a stone, she was sure that this was just a lake; so why was she still sinking rapidly, it was extremely deep? Running as fast as he could, Uther dived into the icy water without any fear for his own safety, his eyes Stang as he franticly searched under-water for any sign of Freyja, suddenly he noticed a tendril of scarlet hair floating beneath the shadowy depths.

Uthers heart skipped a beat in anguish as he dove further down, desperately he grabbed towards the hair in a last ditch attempt before he would have to resurface, Triumph claimed the moment as he seized a fistful of Freyjas hair, with all his might he began to pull her upwards with him battling against the sucking waters towards the safety of the bank, but alas the under current and extra encumbrance weighted them down, sending them both sinking to the bottom like stones, A dread sense of panic filled Uther turning his limbs to jellied lead as he frantically kicked off the lakes bed and began to swim forcefully upwards whilst tightly grabbing hold of Freyjas arm, air was running desperately low in their lungs, causing the boy to choke as he took in yet another mouthful of burning ice water.

Uther stared desperately around on his defeated descent downwards for any last chance of hope, it was then that he noticed it shinning out in the depths like a glimmering beacon, a single ray of hope lit from within, AN UNDER GROUND CAVERN! If they could just reach it before unconsciousness claimed them, then just maybe it would lead to the cave behind the waterfall?, Summoning every last ounce of strength he could muster, Uther swam upwards towing Freyja towards the opening, his lungs felt as though they would burst, and his head swam with the wooziness of suffocation, unconsciousness lingered within the shadows of his mind waiting for failure, the lake would not take them without a fight! thought uther defiantly.

He battled against the current, forcing life into his tormented limbs, every essence of his being screamed out for air, his lungs and limbs aflame with fiery agony as he towed the unconscious

Freyja behind him, reaching the entrance in the nick of time he clawed at the ledge lifting his head and cradling freyjas porcelain features above the water line, moments before the watery depths claimed the two companions within her drenching blanket of oblivion, he sputtered and choked gasping for air as beautiful life rushed back into his lungs causing him to swoon and feel nauseous, with a renewed sense of vigour, Uther began to haul them both on to the outcropping.

Amazingly there was a pocket of air inside the outcropping "The Anwen be praised!" the boy thought as dragged his friends lifeless form face down on the ground and began pounding on her back with a sense of desperation, "please do not let this saviour be too late!" he added despondently as he regarded her lifeless form, after the third pummelling Freyja coughed and spluttered as she bought up what seemed like gallon after gallon of water, the exhausted boy laughed in triumph as she gasped for air, he cradled her in his lap as they both collapsed into a shivering weary heap upon the wet sandy ground on which they lay, Mercifully Freyja began to cough and started to cry, Uther succumbed to a sense of overwhelming relief and pride, she was all right, he had saved them both!

He hoped that the cavern would be an air fissure to the above world as he rasped exhaustedly for air cradling his friend, "Uther where are we?" she sobbed he had no idea, they were totally lost in a strange watery realm, but he did not want Freyja to know this just yet, he had to work out a plan, and so answered "worry not we are safe for now Freyja" as she slipped back into unconsciousness.

Uther gazed around the dimly lit chasm in confusion, what was this doing here beneath the lake and how was it not submerged, it really was most peculiar, The rocky walls glistened magically as water trickled down in rivulets forming a dazzling transparent curtain which lightly licked at the salty walls, a delicate wind whispered through the stalagmites like a sirens murmur.

Uther shivered profusely as he pondered their next move, it was absolutely freezing down here and there was no chance whatsoever of starting a fire for warmth, he had to locate a passage to the surface or they would surely perish, that breeze must be coming from somewhere he thought as he shivered once more, Uther carefully laid Freyja down upon the silty carpet and began to carefully get up, the fissured ceiling was very low and he couldn't afford an injury at this point, he was only just starting to recover from the severe lack of air moments earlier, The boy began to creep deeper into the caverns recesses half crawling half stooping along, surprisingly it seemed to increase in size and height the further along in that he ventured until before long Uther was able to fully stand up, he blinked hard as he accustomed his eyes to the dim pearly glow which luminesced from within the cavern, slowly his eyes swam into a blurry focus of sorts the boy gazed on awestruck as tucked deep within the caves heart rested a vast nest of swans feathers!

A pair of piercing green eyes blinked back at Uther from within the nest, Uther returned the gaze with alarm for there sat a weird and wonderful entity, It had the appearance of a small human child and yet the creature was covered in an iridescent white down, the Cygnet child appeared to be small at about two hands high, its opaque skin glimmered like an iridescent pearl, Emerald green eyes observed Uther inquisitively from beneath a crop of silvery blue hair which shone radiantly like the stars.

Uther stood rooted to the spot and enthralled by what he had discovered, what had he happened upon, Suddenly there was a loud "HISSSS" behind him! Alarmed the over world child Uther span sharply round and met the very same majestic swan, he had watched earlier that afternoon gliding upon the mirrored lake, only now it did not look too happy! The cob advanced, its huge white wings were outstretched in a threatening display of protection, she totally obscured the entrance to the back of the cavern with her sheer enormity! "OH NO" stated Uther in horror, "I think we have disturbed her nest," added Freyja as she stumbled clumsily into view, she had been silently watching the events from the floor of the caves precipice as she recovered from her watery submersion, "Quick I may know what to do, my mother Llyas has taught me a verse that will befriend beasts and show we mean no harm, it's worth a try" she stated. "*Majestic bird white and pure, By chance we have found your front door, No harm we do intend, Meet with us and comprehend, We only wish to be your friend*" she recited.

The incantation emerged into the air like a flurry of shining poetry, each syllable shimmered in a dazzling light to descend around the swan like a rainbow hued shield between her and the two children, it began to settle in the air. she ceased rearing up her wings and gently lowered them to bow down her supine neck in a peaceful greeting.

Freyja and Uther both heaved a huge sigh of relief, Uther decided to address the cob in gentle dulcet tones, "We are sorry to have disturbed your nest my lady, but we are wretchedly lost and nearly met a perilous end, had we not stumbled upon the shelter of your cave, my companion here slipped into the treacherous waters whilst we were playing, so i dived into rescue her, we were both drowning in watery despair and entered your domain only in the vain hopeful chance of saving ourselves it was sheer luck that we happened upon it", he added, "I am Uther of Anwens Farm in Thygorshire, and this is Freyja of the Druid village, we mean only to find safe passage to the overworld, would you be so kind as to help us and lead the way?" He asked, standing timidly in the presence of the swan, Uther hoped with all his heart that she had understood him and would not engage her anger towards them any longer, The swan appeared to stand momentarily in a sense of stasis, as if she were pondering upon his words blinking her vast ebony eyes in thought.

Something odd then began to happen, the water which lay in the entrance behind the regal bird began to swirl and swoosh like plug hole, gaining in momentum, it made a gurgling sound as it rose to the top of the cavern licking at the stalagmites, as it transcending into a huge mirrored curtain of water which threatened to crash down and engulf them all, with the enormity of tidal force growing as it swirled and danced, to advance upon them.

Freyja watched fearfully as she envisaged the torrent dragging them all out from the cavern and sucking them back in to the icy lake as if it callously wished to reclaim its victims, the wall of water engulfed and swallowed the swan totally obscuring her from view, Uther and Freyja cowered down covering their faces in terror as they awaited their watery fate, believing that they were done for, Suddenly as soon as it had begun the water ceased its command and retreated, the gurgling ceased and it rippled shimmering magically like an underground rainbow.

A glowing silhouette of a human like form stood out against the radiant heart of the mirage as the crystalline waters began to taper and drain off across the sandy floor in rivulets to reveal the presence of the Torrent Aquaria in their wake. "I am Aquaria from The lake of Suns" she said, "I met thee before young master Uther in knightshade forest amid the boggarts grasp, and yet now I find you in the lake of tears, have you a wish to be a Merman?" questioned the torrent, "No Aquaria, I do not wish to keep bothering you" replied Uther slightly fearfully "But my friend Freyja fell in to the lake and I dived in to save her, it is by sheer chance that we cross ways again, but if I may be so bold as to ask how come is it that we meet again?" he asked.

"Child this is the lake of tears, I shall tell you now that all our underwater realms are joined together by a myriad of tunnel systems, certain caverns harbour dead ends just as a labyrinth does to protect us torrents from those who would hunt us, just as the colossal Laganus Water Serpent guards the gates , so take heed, would you confine us Torrents to just one lake young master? she added and then continued, "I shall guide you and your companion Freyja back to the over world, but make not a habit of it young master as not all torrents are as gracious as I" she warned,.

"But Firstly before we go any further, Freyja I have a gift for you" said Aquaria reaching amongst her downy cloak, she produced a pure crystalline feather as chaste as snow, "This is to be yours child, if ever you feel that you or Uther are in mortal peril cast this crystal feather down into nearby waters and we shall come to your aid, but beware tell no other of its existence" she added in a commanding tone.

Freyja was awestruck and apprehensive of this most generous gift, what power must it wield she thought as she turned it through her fingers, the Torrent feather radiated with an alluring luminosity, shimmering like a silken diamond.

Freyja was awestruck what to say and so replied gratefully "Thank you Aquaria, I am forever in your service should ever you need me, it is beautiful just like you I shall keep it safe always." at this remark Aquaria smiled serenely and beckoned the two children towards her, "Now children come quickly we must make haste if you are to return to the overworld you must ride upon my back and be escorted back to the surface before you are discovered, the enemy has many spies!"

Aquaria was once again engulfed by the gigantic wave as she transfigured back to her supine swan like form, The two children climbed cautiously on to her back and nestled down snugly amongst her soft down, how comforting and safe it felt to rest behind the Torrents gracious wings after their fearful adventure, Aquaria swam up to the approach of the caverns dripping entrance which with its raining roaring cascading curtain of water ferociously pummelling down past the sandy outcropping, the children felt terribly afraid and shuddered uncontrollably as they recalled their narrow escape, Aquaria came to a stop and reared up her curved neck and then recited.

"Water so icy cold, No terror from the deep behold, Grant them some air, As we climb up a stair, From the underworld Up to the light, With the overworld in sight."

With this incantation the waters slowly began to part, to allow aquaria through, a bubble of air began to form around the children like an effervescent shield, as they approached "Hold on tight little ones!" said the torrent as she flew upwards to break through the mirrored curtain, the trio began to swim aloft with an immense speed, creating a trailing pattern of froth behind them like the train of a sweeping gown, the bubbles danced merrily upwards towards the water's surface to burst like kisses upon the placid surface of the lake of tears.

Uther and Freyja held their breath intrepidly, fearing they would burst as they clamped their eyes tight shut, before realizing they could breathe, as the air bubbles swished around them, they had no wish to witness the inner lake once more after their narrow escape, they knew that they were travelling fast as the water whistled past their faces, and the air purred past their ears in a bubbling chorus, Aquaria broke the surface of the lake shattering its glassy surface like a frozen mirror between worlds, as the trio broke free into the overworld, the icy water broke with an intense pressure, enveloping the children pressing painfully down upon their heads causing their ears to pop then just as quickly it trickled away in frozen tears down their necks, The sodden trio emerged like newborns into the overworld released from the realm of shadows.

Uther and Freyja felt that they had come to a gentle speed and slightly loosened their grip upon the swan, cool marvellous air embraced their damp cheeks like the welcoming caress of a mothers hand, Freyja dared to open her eyes just a slit and joy rushed into her heart as she saw the green banks of the lake adorned with the sentinels of trees, they were once again in the overworld! she excitedly nudged Uther but he too was already smiling broadly after bravely taking a peep, the pair of friends broke into enchanting childlike laughter at their merciful and triumphant release, the lake had not claimed them, they were free.

Late afternoon had now arrived to cast her shadowy mantle upon the water's surface, the glimmering Anwen reflected like a mystical orb upon the bright water's surface, Freyja gazed down upon her and Uthers reflection riding abreast the regal white swan, was this an illusion or a dream, dare she wake, Aquaria slowly glided level with the banks edge, "Right little ones here is where you alight, i must hurry back to my nest and Cygnet, and remember the feather child" added the torrent.

The children alighted carefully on to the blustery grass, then turned to thank Aquaria but she had already vanished with a splash, freyja and Uther stared wistfully at the ripple which had been left behind as it spread out across the water a poignant reminder of their adventure, they turned away and set off home over the solid earthy ground, how welcome it felt beneath their feet, their bodies felt strange and heavy to them after the weightless feel of the water, as if somehow they had returned back from some shadowy nightmare to their physical form in the overworld, they did not speak a single word to each other as they both raced hastily home from their garish adventure, each was eager to be back within the folds of their families and feel safe once more, What a peculiar day it had turned out to be and what a lucky escape, thank the Anwen for the Torrent Aquaria!

Freyja and Uther arrived at Ilyas's home later that day, feeling some-what tired and excitable from their days adventure, Uther had naturally wanted to see his friend Freyja safely home and would not take no for an answer, "Where have you been little ones?" questioned Llyas Freyjas mother "Your soaked through to the bone, why Uther fetch me a pail of water from the well and I'll boil both of you up a nice hot draught"

Uther wearily grabbed the pail from beside the Fireside and disappeared from the room leaving Freyja with an awkward silence as she thought of a reasonable excuse for their condition, after a moment she decided that there wasn't one and she had better just as well tell the truth, she took in a deep breath and looked up at Llyas expecting a scolding before she had even begun, oh well here goes she thought to herself mother always said I had a vivid imagination, and began speaking…

"Uther and I were playing mother, down by the lake of tears then I foolishly fell in and Uther dived into save me" she added pleadingly before taking a deep breath and relaunching her attack "Uther and i went to this most beautiful underwater world and had a ride on the back of a swan!" exclaimed Freyja excitedly to her mother.

Llyas rolled her eyes at this and tutted "Now don't you be silly child, my what a vivid imagination you have Freyja" she replied, Freyja looked exasperatingly at her mother and whined "But its true mother really it is!" Llyas looked at the child with pity and relief, at least Freyja was home now she had been worried sick about her whereabouts even if she did tell tall tales!

Freyjas mother wrapped a blanket from beside the hearth around her damp daughter and drawing her into her arms added in a comforting tone, "And haven't I also warned you before about the dangers of running by the lakes edge, it was lucky that Uther was there to pull you out." Just that moment Uther returned with the slopping pail full to the brim spilling a trail of puddles behind him like a damp announcement upon the quarry tiles as he entered the room, "Mother doesn't believe me about our adventure Uther," stated Freyja to Uther and then added "Tell her I'm speaking the truth" she pleaded with a desolate look.

Uther wasn't so sure that this was a good idea given the circumstances, but what could he do his mother had always taught him to be honest, and Freyja was his best friend? After a moments silent consideration and a pained look from his friend

Uther went in to great depths and detail describing the day's magical events to Llyas, stopping here and there to receive acknowledgement and agreement from Freyja that it had happened and they were not spinning a yarn!

Llyas listened intently wearing a strange expression upon her face as if she half believed them but really didn't want to, the children looked forlornly at each other sure that they would shortly receive a scolding, Freyjas mother began dropping some strange looking orange leaves from an earthen pot upon the lintel into the hot draught she was boiling up, there not dandelions thought Freyja suspiciously.

Uthers tale drew to a close and the room fell silent as the two children timorously awaited Llyas's reply, the fire crackled and spat in its usual manner but felt deafeningly loud in the silent tense atmosphere, After what seemed like an eon she eventually answered with a most peculiar reply.. "Calm down little ones and worry not" she said handing over two steaming beakers of strange smelling liquid.

And then added "Here drink this down it will warm you both through", The two children looked at each other flabbergasted! had they just heard right? Freyja and Uther gratefully accepted their drinks as they were very thirsty, "come and rest here upon these furs and warm yourselves by the fire little ones" gestured Llyas with a strange undertone to her voice, They both did as they did as they were told stretching themselves out comfortably, Uther took a sip of his draught and stared into the dancing flames within the fire, he yawned heartily and rubbed his eyes suddenly feeling very sleepy and cosy upon the furs.

He blinked hard as his gaze was once more drawn into the entrancing flames.

“She was all white and feathery, ” he murmured, but little did both Uther and Freyja know that they just been given a potent infusion of ‘Black Knight cap’ by Llyas, this potion would erase their memory and act as a sleeping draught, for neither of them could yet know of the task that lay ahead of them, they were far too young and should remain in blissful innocence for a while longer yet.

The troubled woman furrowed her brow as she gazed down upon the sleeping children what a heavy weight rested upon their tiny shoulders, thank the Anwen that they were still to remain oblivious for a little longer, but today’s events had shown that fate was catching up with them, She hastily arose from her fireside chair, she must pen a scroll to Uthers family and send out her owl tonight to deliver the errand, Llyas skirts gently swished upon the tiles as she silently latched the door behind her and headed to the aviary.

And so was woven the beginning of a magical and lasting friend ship between the two children more deep than they could ever imagine, and although the memory became muddled up somehow like a dream, the children knew that they were special, and destined to be with each other, well at least for now for they felt it in their hearts, the friendship continued to blossom until Uther left home to embark upon his smithing apprenticeship, and so we pick up where we left off….

THRITY MOON CYCLES LATER

Since uther had left for his apprenticeship, Freyja felt lost without him, she often found herself daydreaming as if searching the innermost depths of her soul, it was one of these very times, she was sat beside the lake of tears idly watching the swans, when something flashed across her mind, unable to tell if it was a distant memory or a vague dream it centred around, dryads and ovates and the mighty oak Duir upon morganas tump, What could this mean, maybe that Was that to be her passion and strength to join the order of Druids at Knightshade forest, now that uther had gone what else was she to do? she needed a distraction, freyja thought to herself, and although long and laborious in manner Freyja felt that she had to fill the empty void that the friendship had left behind, so with this in her mind she told her mother Llyas and her siblings Breccea and Elspeth of her intentions and headed off on upon the desolate trek towards Knightshade forest.

Freyja felt light and full of anticipation as she stepped upon the well-trodden track, there were many more miles yet ahead she thought as she ambled along the beaten track wondering how many days on foot it would take to reach the valley?

A moment later her thoughts were snapped from wondering by the familiar clattering of a hay cart as it drew level with her. "FREYJA!" sounded the exclamation, She looked up in alarm, from her thoughts, why it was Uthers brothers, Daermund and Daerdrid! "Anwens blessings" she replied joyfully, feeling glad for a couple of familiar faces, "Would you like a ride lass?" asked Daermund, "Were heading home" Freyja smiled broadly this was just the bit of luck she needed and was surely a good omen for the task ahead. "Yes please, I am heading to Knightshade forest in Thygorshire in the vale" she shouted, " Hop on then lass but thygors no place for a girl Freyja" added Daermund " May i ask what takes you there?" he asked. "I'm looking for the druids and the grove is situated upon the forest borders" she explained, Freyja ran up behind and reached out to clasp the hefty hand of Daerdrid who grasped her arm and pulled her sharply aboard, she tumbled forwards towards the back of the cart with the force, which caused the Oxen Yamak to bellow grumpily in protest, "Sorry boy" she said and settled down to make herself comfortable amongst the stack of ricks.

The day long trip was spent reminiscing with Daermund and Daerdrid about the antics that she and Uther used to get up to when they were children, it gladdened Freyja to know he was doing well in his apprenticeship, the two lads were on their way back from visiting him in the local tavern, the highwayman. "Here that reminds me lass he sent this for you" said Daerdrid reaching into his jerkin to hand her a package, "Thank you Daerdrid" she said with a beaming smile, another good omen, he is surely with me still she thought to herself as she eagerly unwrapped the cloth bundle, inside was a small hazel box with a circular spiral pattern carved upon its lid, Freyja carefully opened the trinket to reveal the treasure that lay within, she sharply drew her breath inwards, for within the box there lay a tri-banded ring, Freyja noted that the band had been forged from three different metals, as she freed the ring from the shadowy box to bask in the light of the Anwens rays, Each of the three metal bands glowed in a perfect synchronicity with the next, the ring had been crafted from fragments of copper, bronze and gold, freyja turned the charm over in her fingers, letting the light play across its surface, the Anwens rays caught the underside rim and lit up a hidden inscription in runic Flamesword that she could not decipher, the top of the bands held an ogham inscription reading, ,'Ghilt, vole, ecape' strange she thought the words don't mean anything.

Freyja felt overwhelmed by the beautiful gift which had been bestowed upon her, and although she did not yet understand any of the inscriptions she pushed the ring firmly onto her finger like a begotten treasure, gazing adoringly to admire the way the metals burned against one another in flaming harmony, "Thank you brothers of Uther for delivering me this precious gift, I am most grateful to you both." She said showing off her ring to Daermund and Daerdrid. "My that's a pretty trinket lass" stated Daermund with a whistle, whilst Daerdrid just scowled he had always been a little sweet on Freyja himself but had tried not to let it show.

After a good few hours journey they pulled up at the village gates, "Here we are then lass your journey begins, now off you go and good fortune" Daermund said, "Thank you both greatly and give my regards to your mother" replied Freyja hugging them both tightly, she took a deep breath smiled broadly and jumped down from the cart, freyja brushed the straw down from her tunic, and nervously approached the path leading down towards Knight shade forest, she felt as if her tummy was turning summersaults as she bravely ventured forward into the unknown, freyja turned behind herself to catch one last glimpse of the familiar, watching the back of the hay cart disappear round the bend.

The track ahead looked barely trodden thought Freyja to herself as felt the lush shady grass crumple beneath her boots, delivering a fresh spring odour as its juices were released.

Clouds of delicate butterflies settled in abundance upon the iris coloured bluebells carpeting the shadowy glade, insects gently pulsed their wings like an ornate fans as the sun warmed their tiny bodies, Freyja wound ever further downward to meet the beckoning shadow of the woods, she watched a family of rabbits dart for the cover of the trees their white tails flashing like a surrender to an unseen enemy as they disappeared from view.

Freyjas apprehension was coupled with excitement regarding the new beginnings which lay before her, with a pang of sadness for the life she was leaving behind, The young woman was on the lookout for a grove of trees to signal that she was treading the correct path, looking ahead to the distance she thought that she could spot a ring of treetops up ahead, altering her direction slightly she headed further northwards in line with the distant grove.

Underfoot the mossy path became less trodden as it wound further downwards, the terrain underfoot was becoming more challenging, , lichen and moss covered the shady track beneath its green and silver embrace, Freyja stumbled clumsily upon some loose rocks as she looked overhead at the suns position, it was roughly an hour past noon, dappled light cut through the thick canopy in radiant shafts of brilliance to illuminate the dense covering of foliage littering the glen, An eerie shriek ran out overhead as a buzzard announced an attack upon its quarry, sending it scurrying for cover but alas it was already too late for the rodent as the majestic hunter locked on target and swooped to claim her spoils, freyja saw a dart and a flash before the bird took off victorious, momentarily distracted she had not noticed turning the corner and halted in her tracks when she witnessed the ring of grey sentinels stationed commandingly against the horizon.

The atmospheric majesty of what lay before her was an immense sight to behold, freyja stood and savoured the moment, this was the threshold into her future, she felt humbled as if she could stand and observe the stones forever, a stony portal to the next world, she felt miniscule before this ring of ancients, as if she had been called to trial, dare she enter, or should she flee?

An immense circle of rowan trees enclosed the gatekeepers, to obscure them from prying eyes, protecting the sanctity of the sacred place, they seemed to join heaven and earth together with their roots anchored firmly in the earth and their branches reaching ever upwards as if to touch the very stars themselves, Freyja wondered at her immediate surroundings, taking a moment to rest, bees buzzed furtively to and fro from blossom to bloom gathering pollen, whilst up in the tree tops a murder of crows lurked protectively around their rookery glaring out at Freyja and craawwking in warning, she looked around dwelling on the doorway of time, would her apprenticeship live up to her expectations, well there was only one way to find out.

Freyja tenaciously crept up to the perimeter of the grove to maybe take a just a little peek inside, whilst she gathered up her nerves, holding her breath close in her chest and drawing level with the ancient sentinels, the woody smell of damp bark and rustic stones danced around her nostrils, as she took in the subtle aroma emanating from the grove feeling that all her senses must be awoken, uncertainly she reached out to touch the cracked peeling bark, running her fingers carefully down the wood, if felt rough along the splintered edges, but the intact bark was as smooth as veneer.

Freyja leant against the tree and felt the warmth of its bark radiate against her chilled features, she pressed her ear up and against the trunk and listened to the slow gentle pulsing of its essence, closing her eyes in sheer comfort she drifted off in her mind to an earlier memories of the day, the chance meeting with the two brothers and the beautiful trinket they relayed to her, Minutes drifted by and she slowly began to blend with the environment, feeling at one with her surroundings she gently opened her eyes and peered through the gap between the trees to notice that a strange silhouette lurking deep amongst the shadows of the grove, Intrigued and a little mystified freyja cautiously entered the grove silently placing one footstep at a time as she approached the groves inner sanctum the shimmering silhouette gradually began to come in to focus.

"How extremely peculiar!" Freyja exclaimed as before her sat three enormous toads! each wore a colouring like the autumn's leaves, all three sat there motionless blinking their huge bulging yellow eyes at Freyja with a sense of amusement, Their amphibious hides were slimy and knobbly looking and oozed some type of thick gooey substance, "yuck!" Freyja thought to herself with a sense of disgust, but more importantly the question what on earth were they doing all sat here in a row, was it an unforeseen trap, She was just about to back away when a small croaking voice spoke to her.

"*We are made of leaves but it is not a plant, What lies within does enchant, Though it is bound by roots, Its roots can shoot stalks, Listen hard and the roots shoots talk, The treasure like a seed of knowledge does grow, The answer only you can know!*"

A puzzled look crossed her face as she turned around trying to locate the speaker, after circling completely around and finding no soul present she shook her head in disbelief, surely it could not be? "Did one of you toads just speak to me?" asked Freyja in an unbelieving tone? " Why all three of us did speak to thee, solve our riddle to unfold your destiny so mote it be." Spoke the three toads in unison, Freyja shook her head and gazed closer at the motionless blinking trio before her. “Why toads cannot talk, i ask you to show yourself whoever you are!” she stated, After waiting awhile no one appeared, Freyja grew impatient after a hard mornings travelling and this weird situation, she sat down upon the damp grass and huffed impatiently, “why must I solve this riddle? ” she asked the toads.

“ To venture further upon your route, you will need a magic shoot!” they replied in unison once more, She shook her head again, “so you really did speak after all” she said in disbelief before adding “well i have never heard of talking toads before.

Freyja lingered upon the grass awhile deep in thought, after a while she announced, “well it seems i have no option but to answer this riddle, let me think awhile, We are made of leaves but not a plant!” she spoke aloud thinking hard. “Well You all appear to be made up of leaves,” exclaimed Freyja wearily.“ That is not the answer you need to say, two more chances have you this day!” said the first toad, and with a puff he transformed into a swirling myriad of leaves which settled gently upon the mossy ground leaving behind two remaining toads who blinked at Freyja expectantly, “Oh bother!” the girl proclaimed in annoyance, this would not be an easy task after all she thought to herself.

“What lies within does enchant?” Freyja repeated to herself, with an added sense of urgency, “How do I know that you are not trying to trick me?” asked Freyja observing the remaining pair with a puzzled expression? “ One of us tells truth, one of us tells lies, the other just sat all day eating flies!” proclaimed the two toads mockingly, “I had best be more careful about my answers then” she replied and again repeated the riddle to herself, Freyja sat glaring at the two toads whilst she mulled it over in her mind, “I wonder if that may be the answer you amphibious tricksters, a spell does enchant!" she announced confidently, " An answer wrong again you say, one more chance have you this day." Said the second toad before swirling into a motionless pile of leaves, Oh Blast now I really am under pressure she thought to herself i have only one more chance to pass this test!

Freyja sat thinking hard beneath a mask of worry her head resting heavily upon her hands, she only had one more chance to unfold this riddle, and most probably her destiny depended upon it she just had to get it right!

"What has leaves, is bound and contains talking knowledge?" said Freyja aloud, as she paced back and forth wringing her hands, the remaining solitary toad sat observing her with a smiling expression as his tongue licked the air in search of flies, After a good deal of pacing Freija's expression changed as she burst into delighted peals of laughter, "Aha! at last I have you mr toad" she squealed and proclaimed triumphantly, " A BOOK! A book has leaves, it is bound and contains spoken or written knowledge." She glaring at the toad with a look of defiant victory, "At this the toad smiled broadly, blinked and announced, " Answer right at last you say, now unfold the treasure you may this day."

The final toad swirled upwards in to a vortex of leaves like his two predecessors before him, when the swooshing leaves had settled A beautiful almanac lay beneath the litter, it was not just any old book but the very one and very same magical Gwersu from Freyja's childhood, which she had uncovered at the base of Wynterleaf all those years before!

"My I had forgotten all about this" Freyja exclaimed excitedly as she knelt down to retrieve the almanac, her fingers eagerly reached out to grasp the verdant cover, but as she did so a long writhing creeper shot out from the book like a green sinewy tentacle, it wrapped itself tightly round Freyja wrist, as the shoot sent out runners which began to coil up her arm constricting it tightly like a writhing mass of snakes, "Oouwww" squealed Freyja struggling to pull her arm free from its bonds tearing wildly at the green invader, this only caused it to tighten like a poisonous creeper, the shoots glowed with a verdant light as the thorns penetrated her skin, injecting verdant sorcery into her veins, Freyja felt her head would burst from pain, as the enchantment throbbed heavily through her arm, her head began to swoon sending her toppling onto the mossy earthen floor, stones grazed her skin as the damp smell of earth met her nostrils, she swallowed hard, blinking her swimming vision back into focus, and lay there a second too nauseous to resist, then peculiarly just as rapidly as it had occurred the shoots began to retreat back within the confines of the Gwersu, the last shoot disappeared from view, making a sound like the swooshing of leaves as the cover shut tight with a loud "Snap!" the relic once again appeared normal, leaving Freyja with the painful reminder, as if she had been stung by a trail of nettles, not really wanting to look she cautiously rolled up her sleeve to examine the inside of her arm, noticing a multitude of long green markings left behind by the thorny shoots as a permanent reminder, the markings merged together on the back of her hand to form a single mark shaped like a compass, she examined the peculiar brand aghast, hoping that it was not the venomous tracks of some peculiar poison, she rubbed it carefully before covering her arm once more.

Freyja desperately felt that she needed to retrieve the book but was far too afraid to touch it given the recent event, "why had it left such a mark upon her and would it do so again if touched a second time, she looked at the gwersu timidly, the coppery emblem of DUIR glistened upon its cover with a majestic reverence, She needed the book that was clear to her mind or else why would she have come up against the riddling toads, it was surely protected and coveted for a reason, and had already been bequeathed to her in her youth yet somehow it was a hazy distant memory like a foggy dream, how had she lost it, what was it about, why was it here now, she just had to know? "Oh well here goes nothing" she said, Freyja held her breath in anticipation as she tenaciously snatched up the volume with both hands, she would not give it opportunity to snare her again, no way was she giving it a chance to open again! "Aha now I have you within my grasp you beastly book!" she proposed as she tightly wrapped it in a linen, stashing it away inside her knapsack, "I'm hungry after all that commotion" thought Freyja to herself delving amongst the contents of her bag to retrieve an apple, "I shall sit here and rest a while" she said aloud to herself munching into the apple, my, how lovely and juicy it is she thought, a veritable oasis to the parched savannah of her mouth like a fruity ambrosia.

Freyja curiously surveyed her surroundings, why how beautiful and peaceful it is here she noted, I wonder if I shall train in this grove she pondered nonchalantly to herself, whilst observing all the different species of trees creating the grove, there was the tall majestic oak laden with its bounty of acorns, and next to him sat a lime coloured hazel the two colours contrasted off each other like a perfect symphony, leaves rustled peacefully in the breeze as if they were wordlessly whispering to one other of secrets untold, and a rich variety of blooms carpeted the lush emerald ground, ranging right through from lofty frail yellow honey plants, heavily laden for their furtive insect visitors, their immense petals full of precious pollen they danced around on the breeze like ballerinas, right through to tiny mauve lavender scented kisses of Alluan, their small spiky petals hiding right down amongst the shady shadows of the other plants, the spectacle surely was a sensory banquet to the tired traveller, Freyja glanced back towards the trunk of the large oak, she could not figure out why but she had felt strangely drawn to it ever since she had entered the grove, Tossing aside her apple core now that her snack was finished she decided that she would gain a closer inspection and headed off across the grove towards the mysterious oak tree.

Triad of Alluan

FREYJA AND THE GROVE

The faint breeze kicked up into a small whisper to tease Freyja's face, it gently caressed her cheek like a silken cobweb playfully whipped dancing strands of auburn hair in front of her eyes like flickering flames, she nervously approached the curious oak, her footfalls fell muffled upon the moss carpeted ground, she gazed up in veneration at the tree, taking in every aspect of its vast effigy as it cut out a personified stature against the horizon, the young woman perceived it with fascination, it emanated to her a unearthly malady sung in hushed tones upon the whispering breeze, Freyja and the oak exchanged an atmosphere that was both charged and timeless, from the trees youth as a sapling at the dawn of time to the majestic wizened sentinel of the grove that it was now, her heart pounded heavy against her breast like a sinister drum beat of anticipation against the eerie silent seconds of time experienced within the grove, she could literally feel every second that ticked by as it resonated through her entire being, oblivious to all but the thunderous rustling of oak leaves existent in her mind, The deafening rustling began to travel downwards escaping the canopy overhead, guttural vibrations pulsated through the branches like a sticky sap of sorcery enveloping the bark and any insects that lay in its path within its enchanted ancient sound, it wound ever downwards to reach the oaks trunk like a Childs sticky fingers reaching out for more delights beneath the earth infecting the gnarled roots sunk into the earth like a woody labyrinth of veins tapping in to an unseen life force that lay concealed within the planets soil.

The oak gradually appeared as if it was coming to life, an entity in its own right pulsing and glowing inwardly with a deep emerald blaze radiating out from the crevices and fissures lying within the barks surface, as if touched by a supernatural forest deity, the guttural vibrations penetrated between the ruptures of the pulsating bark joining together in a potent unification with the phosphoresce luminescence, to create a cataclysm of awe striking energy raw in essence as if it were the very spirit of nature herself, multitudes of insects were spewn forth from the bark scuttling and writhing out from the breaches, scurrying back to the safety of the warm moist earthen refuge of soil and leaves that lay fallen beneath Freyja's feet, a littered spectrum of colours and hues like an incapacitating rug of greens, russets and buttercup yellows.

The energy began to pulsate like a vivid emerald heartbeat, sounding out a call to all who would listen, birds stopped singing, rabbits stood up on watch pricking up their lofty ears and every beast was silent, the heart beat resonated in time with the universe and the mighty oaks gnarled bark did something magical, its fissures began to mutate and writhe like busy ants all over the trees surface, as they started to rearrange themselves in to some type of strange alphabet which manifested upon the oaks thick trunk.

Freyja could not read this magical inscription but she recognized it as the Ogham alphabet of the Druids, now she knew why she had felt so drawn to this mysterious oak, it was the portal to the sacred school of Avalire! at last her quest had bourne fruit, the pulsating resonance hushed down to just a mere promise of whispering leaves which murmured upon the delicate spring breeze, the ethereal emerald hue slowly faded out to flickering glow like a trick of the light at the kiss of dusk.

Freyja stumbled toppling clumsily over as the mighty roots beneath her feet began to wrench themselves free from their earthen shackles, the woody sinews sang their creaking protest like a vast sleep drenched yawn of discontent as the tree awakened from its timeless slumber, who had dared to wake this mighty sentinel from where he had nestled in a deep fretless dream wrapped safely in his dusty bed, Albans branches stretched outwards reaching hungrily towards the light of the Anwen like a newborn ushered into the realm of life from the depths of the cauldron, his mighty wooden arms longing to feel form again stiff from all the pleasant ages of dreaming and oblivion to the quarrels of man.

Alban unfolded his barken limbs and gave out one last shuddering tremor as he finally awoke beneath the Anwens stark rays, CRATHULL FINRAELL TISGARTHARL!! Boomed the echo of words commanded by a voice that sounded like splintering wood coupled with the might of thunder, Freyja gazed upwards drawing in a mighty breath of wonderment as the grove around her started to transfigure, she watched in amazement as the trees shimmered and turned a stony opaque white, glistening radiantly as the sun enveloped their frozen bark, Freyja felt humbled as she stood beneath the carved statuesque entrance hall of marble trees.

The potent megaliths had been hewn and crafted from minerals embedded deep within the terra, vast guardians of the inner grove, each wall was a mirrored facet of glinting stone shining like glass as if it were a crystal glacier, every detailed aspect was intensely intricate and glorious, this great hall must have been conjured forth by some marvellous enchantment, Freyja thought excitedly to herself as she took in the breath taking sight, The hall was rotund in shape creating a sphere of inner sanctum to harbour powerful atmospherics of the grove from whence it had sprang, Each meticulously etched marble guardian loomed ominous and glinting in the half-light, their semiprecious trunks bejewelled with quartz moths, butterflies and amber insects, casting the impression that they had been snatched from a moment in time and frozen, the ancient stone council of seers and watchers held their silent deliberation debating unknown secrets yet to pass….

Freyja's attentions were snatched from observation by the spitting and crackling of a smouldering fire which hissed angrily protesting against its stony confines imprisoned within a pit at the floors Centre it blazed venomously like an unruly entity held against its will, The pits circumference was a wall of raised volcanic stone ornately inlaid with mysterious metallic runes set between each stone, the inscription read,

□(7+□/(,9□6:$5'□□+,71□%(7:,;7□
6,7+□□'52:/□1$'□+(7□;(17□

Freyja considered it strange but somehow these runes appeared strangely familiar to her, but where had she seen them before, She thought hard, nonchalantly she brushed a hair back from her face, at that moment a golden glint momentarily caught her eye and suddenly with a blinding flash it occurred to her THE RING!, Freyja squealed with an excited realization, elatedly she closely inspected her ring, the markings around the pit were definitely the same as those upon the ring that Uther had bequeathed her, eagerly she crouched down beside the pit to compare the inscriptions, but for some reason she found it hard to concentrate upon the task, her gaze was repeatedly drawn towards the hypnotic flames within the pit as they danced and frolicked licking at the pits edge like a ravenous fiery tongue, entranced her eyes followed each mesmerizing sway as the flickering blaze merged itself into illusionary contortions assuming a plethora of transmutations weaving Freyja ever deeper beneath its heady spell.

The young woman's mind began drifting back to another time and place back when she had met Uther as a child it all seemed so long ago now, and yet somehow it didn't.

Freyja's consciousness had been cast deep into the fathoms of bewitchment, her glazed eyes sleepily watched the inner confines of the pit as the main body of flames morphed into a blazing hand which seemed to gesture to her, She stared wistfully into the pit of flames and without even battering an eyelid as the disembodied hand beckoned towards her enticingly, some remaining part of her consciousness screamed out in rebellion against the red hot engulfing flames, to walk into them would mean sheer oblivion!

The spark of identity fought valiantly against the spell and with one last thrash she tried to wrench her eyes away from the fires magic but alas her eyelids had grown heavy indeed, the remaining shred struggled once more to resist their closure and with one last almighty effort Freyja wrenched her eyes open as hard as she could, but alas it was to no avail, she sank beneath the intoxicating illusions, her vision became blurred, when she blinked the image that lay before her reappeared she was truly claimed, Amongst the flames writhed an entity created entirely from fire, it glared at Freyja with an impish glint, the mischievous character smiled a smug smile with its sharp features, its ever shifting presence within the flames made Freyja feel very uneasy indeed. "Freyja" it hissed with a voice that spat like a roasting spit" my name is Feanyx, and i have a quest for you, come dance with me to unfold your destiny, revel within the great mysteries of the inner tomb follow me into the depths of the earth child if you dare and see what fate befalls you there?"

The air hung still and silent around Freyja like a thick blanket of suffocating fog, the atmosphere hung like a tense oppressive cloud, but yet somehow it held a strange sense of attraction and a mysterious quality like a beckoning adventure, At what cost and peril do I undertake venturing on this journey asked Freyja? Why only with your life should you fail child! retorted Feanyx mockingly, Well it is already set then, Freyja replied; I have come this far i shall not turn back now.

At this there befell a gruelling laborious groan of age old stone grating its bearing against the earth as it moaned out in protest out from the hall behind them, Freyja turned around to witness two prodigious carved stone oaks creaking inwards to reveal their true identity as a hidden pair of colossal granite doors, undetectable to the crude novice.

The Stone Oak entrance swung open in a steady momentum, slowly swaying inwards with monumental force to revealing the cavernous bowels of the earth which lay behind, Every inch seemed a battle as if the dark resisted the fall of light upon its shadowy confines waging a war of the dark versus the light, the underworld revealing her reluctance to display the timeless secrets that lay within her chasm.

Freyja arose to her trembling feet feeling both apprehensive and curious and stood cowering before the great majesty and hidden terrors lurking in wait behind the enchanted passageway before her, tenaciously she began to tread a carefully placed foot at a time as slowly progressing towards the looming entrance, the acrid smell of centuries and warm damp earth hit her nostrils embraced her senses like a damp shroud, the encroaching darkness invited Freyja's morbid curiosity to venture into the great entrance, like a spider to a fly, "do not be afraid Freyja you cannot go alone" spattered Feanyx, "grab that nearby torch from the wall, hold it at the pits edge close to me and i shall transfer myself to the burning fagot, i shall be your guide in the shadow realm a ray of light, warmth and my wisdom to you my child" Freyja was not going to argue with any offer of guidance whether she trusted Feanyx or not! she hastily grabbed the torch from its bracket upon the wall and went over to the fire pit, carefully she knelt down upon the earthen ground and placed the torch close to the flames.

The entity Feanyx hungrily leapt upon the fresh tinder his face illuminated with a hidden element of benevolence and greed as he let out a raptured hiss, As Feanyx transferred himself so too did the fire within the pit extinguishing itself as the torch ignited with an abundance, EMBLAZEN said Feanyx, I am a Crackle Ember the essence of all flame and keeper of heat, where I leave flame dies, where I appear flame exists remember well the spell of Emblazon that I have given to you Freyja, when you are in need of fire it will summon a crackle Ember to your aid, we are all the same encapsulation of essence we can give heat and light, but we can also take life and destroy so beware this entrusted spell.

THE TALE OF LONG AGO

"Now let us passage in to the dark and unearth the other mysteries that dwell within the hidden realms", he added, and with this Freyja held Feanyx aloft to guide the path ahead of them the strange companions together began the descent down the mighty root formed stairs, Freyja surmised that she would have to be careful of her footing, as she trod on the fourth step, she gazed downwards at her footing and noted that the stairs were constructed of loose earth entwined throughout by gnarled sinewy tree roots, the enchanted briars appeared to take their form step by step, like a writhing carpet of thorny snakes, enticing her down into the very bowels of the earth itself.

The abysses walls began to emerge into vision as Freyja's eyes slowly became accustomed to the damp gloom, she gazed around holding Feanyx aloft to take in her surroundings, the glinting cavern shone back at her like muddy obsidian, secret undiscovered whispering waters trickled down the walls like sweat from the torrid atmosphere, the chasm contained gargantuan stalagmites and stalactites glistening and dripping with water like ravenous salivating fangs of some great underground creature threatening to devour all who ventured in to their domain.

Glittering trickles of water eerily reflected the illumination cast off from the Crackle Ember Feanyx creating a spectral tincture resplendent to the fires of hell, it was humid and sweaty down here, Freyja wiped the back of her hand across her face but only smudged dirt across it making it worse, my it was warm and damp down here she complained to herself as insects dropped down in their multitudes pattering down like raindrops into her tousled mane as they cascaded from the earthen ceiling above.

The monumental stone entrance shuddered ominously as it sealed behind her, casting Freyja into dark realms of muffled silence, She felt very uneasy now that the doors had locked on her only passage of escape to trap her within an earthen tomb, "You are very trusting my lady, spat the crackle Feanyx, how do you know I am not leading you to certain doom?" he questioned menacingly, "I have no option but to trust you, I must venture forth "she replied nervously.

"Well then now we shall uncover some real delights and wonders" Announced the crackle with an evil glint in his fiery eye, but first i shall tell you a tale of long ago about when the world was new and unbroken, before time had passed and things were as they once be-longed, Many aeons ago there were a race of beings called the Alwen they were a peaceful race who ruled over the land of Ashard when it was still called The Vale Of Three Suns, all was at peace, the planet herself was governed by a great god named Zenith, and the very heavens themselves were woven amongst his lofty silken beard of stars, each star was a child of zeniths that had nestled down protectively within the confines of their fathers utopian beard, the children radiated down their heavenly light upon the glittering realm beneath like a promise of hope for the future, Zeniths eyes blazed like phosphorus comets, around his shoulders nestled a velveteen darkness to cloak the world in shadowy swathes of midnight, and Tempestuous echoes of booming thunder heralded the celestial deities voice, Zenith placed his all-seeing third eye amongst the heavens to protectively watch over man and so the mighty moon Alluan cast down his hoary silvern glow amidst the inky night sky.

The three consorts Anwen, Allwyn and Allumayen danced through the cosmos in an utopian synchronicity creating a celestial unity as they wove their vortex in a blissful sonata orbiting the universe, the suns represented light, love and peace within the cosmos their task was to govern the realm when zenith slept throughout the daylight hours, Each majestic stellar, radiated their influence of either light, love or peace upon the realm beneath to form a perfect spectrum of vibes, All men and beasts dwell together in a harmonious union for all the ages of the earth, But then one Aeon long ago a boy child was born to a mighty seventh king named Saul upon a waning blue moon the Child was named malesius but alas as he grew his spirit became evermore restless hungering for power until he burgeoned into a man.

The anger within malesius awakened like a tempest spewing forth venom and spite as it boiled over into a vast greed for possessions, the young squire rampaged and pillaged the land allowing no man to heed his wake of destruction as he clawed his way to power, Malesius cast aside all righteousness in his pursuit for wealth, waging war against all who refused to submit to his rule, a bloody battle waged on for decades which grew into centuries, he sent his sorcerer RAUL the necromancer to cut forth into the bands of time, to disrupt the heavens, angry at the gods themselves with his greed, he set ablaze the mighty tree of life myriddin with the cataclysm of Volava sent by the tumultuous sorcery and necrotic enchantment, as dust dervishes swept across the realms wreaking destruction like a malevolent army of the undead.

The balance of light peace and love was corrupted and thrown into chaos thus emanating a malevolent sickness back to its source which made the goddess Alumayen sick, diseased and full of the despairs of war, So intense was the goddesses grief that her mirrored star Alumayen crashed down from the heavens shattering in to five piercing shards to penetrate the earth, this so angered Zenith that there became a great conflict between the sky and the earth.

The vigorous baneful combat of raged out in legendary fury, the earth spewed forth fire and Volava and the sky rained down vast icy boulders of poisonous hail, the consequences borne were great to man, beast and gods alike.

Raging affliction spewed forth vast billows of dust and hot ash out from the volcanoes as the planets terra ruptured demolishing all in its path like a ravenous blanket of fury spitting out smothering blankets of ash across the land like a rampant infection to cloak and smother all that lay in its wake with a scalding malevolence poisoning the air as it journeyed across the land to devour all who had survived the sorcerers first onslaught.

The spirits of the ruinous sacrifices were consumed and wedded to the fury of the cloud of dust dervishes, creating an incandescent army of the dead, surging and twisting with furious malevolence, ever growing and gaining momentum as the twisted form writhed and contorted, born from the realm of shadows an unleashed unrelenting unstoppable army of malignance travelling in swirling hurricanes of dust bearing the symbol of the tempest upon their brow and so were named the Dust dervishes, Their magic was stagnant putrid and as old as time, it had spread like a disease into the hearts of men like a foul curse to those who would heed its evil bidding, stilling any righteous heart that heard its murmur as it tolled out like a pealing bell of death, creating a foul stench upon the air, And so became the venomous tongue of Shadow speak which bore enchantments that when spoken in malice from this parlance made Shadows peak in to any corrupt form the enchanter Raul wished to conjure for his rancid command.

Zenith could not tolerate such a smothering fury and so he reflected a defence bore of the planets flesh and essence, tremendous earthen dragons were crafted from the ether that remained beneath the soil, hidden stealthily within the roots of plants which had long since been rendered to ash and dust., Burning leaves assembled their scales, soil and roots to contrive their frame, flint and rocks granted them talons and fangs; the soil serpents were created to be protectors of the realm.

A prophecy had long been spoken about an ancient legend concerning a sleeping golden shard rumoured to be buried deep beneath the realm of Ashard vale as it was then called, this golden shard was cloaked in centuries of rumour, some say it held the power to restore the balance and harmony of the land and heavens within its metal, whilst other fables told how one glint of Anwens rays upon its gold would render the dust dervishes back to the shadow realms, The prophecy stated that a peaceful ruler will forge a Matrice sword from the shard and a healer will provide the Ether, this union will restore balance and heal the land, for when Alumayen was shattered all the elements were torn in to five divisions and a state of cacophony and all five elements Ether, Air, Water, Earth and Fire still remain in their state of singular discord to this day, Mighty Alluan rules the Lycanthropes, the sun Anwen governs over the Felinethropes whilst the second sun Allwyn controls the Gryffins, and thus for today ends our tale as we are nearly upon our destination, added Feanyx.

“How does this include me?” enquired Freyja, “you are to learn part of the healing element to bind the union, your destiny was mapped by the heavens before you were born to flesh, but hush now for we are nearly at our destination” declared Feanyx, “Surely, this cannot be! I am a simple girl from Thygorshire.” Exclaimed Freyja in disbelief,

“You have upon your finger a ring with an inscription stating “ghilt vole ecape”, did you not recognize the runes around the fire?”, replied feanyx.

THE WELL OF PORTAL

Freyjas head felt as though it would burst with the cascade of questions, the sheer enormity of her future loomed above her like a vast ominous cloud of uncertainty, insecurities questioned her every thought as she silently journeyed forth, blindly placing one foot in front of the other lingering thoughtfully amongst the shadows cast down by the crackling elemental Feanyx, her consciousness wandering off into the fables and prophecy she had been entrusted with.

enlightenment had released endless questions, bubbling in Freyjas mind, what if she were to fail, what of her parents and her family, were they in danger, what must she do? the questions kept coming at her like a barrage, searing through her intellect like red hot pokers burned mercilessly through her every cogitation, and overwhelming each introspection until she was utterly consumed by one isolated contentious thought, Why has this been bequeathed to me and what is the nature of my quest, how does Uther fall into this as he has forged me the ring?.

"We have nearly reached our destination!" announced Feanyx snapping freyja back from her oblivious state.

Gentle whispering greeted them from the near distance, freyja tentatively tilted her head, straining her ears as she tried to decipher the melodic murmurs., A knowing smile flashed across the embers features as he observed freyjas curious expression, he flickered atmospherically in the underground chasm, watching gleefully as she sniffed the damp dank, notes of Sulphur caressed her nostrils as they drew level with the source, what a curious aroma she thought to herself, unable to see clearly within the gloomy mire.

“SLICK” commanded the Ember elemental Feanyx, a damp sputtering sound spat upon the air, emerald hues lit up the cavernous under realm, illuminating a graceful well hewn in stone, Celtic knot work ornamented its sides, in its heart sat a tear shaped Citrine crystal seated within in the wells centre, The mossy liquid simmered and bubbled as flickering tongues of emerald fire licked and danced across the waters steaming surface, Fire and water were wedded together in an entrancing mirage.

Freyja wore a puzzled expression as she contemplated the under-ground well, how bizarre she pondered who on earth would need to draw water down here, she stooped down to take a closer look at the well, the emerald light cast an ethereal scene as it glinted against an unseen metallic alphabet around the wells edge, a thick crusty layer of dirt covered its perimeter concealing any clues hidden beneath, gently Freyja cleared away the grime to reveal a luminous band of symbols, around the wells edge were cast the same runes as the fire pit above! but this time they had been forged in silver and not copper.

□(7+□/(,9□6:$5'□□+,71□%(7:,;7□
6,7+□□'52:/□1$'□+(7□;(17□

“Decipher the meaning to these runes child and you shall hold the key!” stated Feanyx matter of factly, Freyja was held encaptivated as she dwelt upon the rapturous spluttering of the flames, she watched their writhing forms lick like tendrils across the water’s surface as they reached out as if to escape the wells pit, freyjas eyes were continually drawn to the Citrine gem, it held her fixation as it cast its emerald shadows across the damp walls of the pitch black cavern like some mystical beacon.

The hissing rapturous voice of the Ember snapped her back to reality with a jolt, breaking through the muffled silence as Feanyx sputtered with a loud hiss "And now we arrive at the next stage of your inauguration." And with that, he cruelly extinguished his presence from the caverns below and reignited himself back within the fire pit in the grove hall above.

Freyjas' heart began to race as the damp velveteen blackness engulfed her senses like a cloud of dank despair, cloaking her every breath within its clammy hopelessness, Despondently she crouched down upon her knees, groping wildly at the earth surrounding her like a blind mole trying burrowing its way to the surface, alas she felt desolation and hopelessness she was trapped in this earthen tomb!

Whatever had possessed her to follow that devious Ember Feanyx in the first place?, she hadn't trusted him right from the start, Hot angry tears of desperation began to well up in freyjas eyes anguish engulfing her mind, what of her family and dear Uther, who would find her enclosed within this coffin of clay?

Desolation filled over to the brim blurring freyjas confined perception as tears cascaded down her cheeks creating watery rivulets against her muddy cheeks, Drearily she watched the dark green flames of the well lick to and fro around the pits edge as if somehow they were held captive by the enchanted runes carved around the rim.

This must be an essence of healing, thought Freyja to herself, the fire burns green the colour of the Ovate and Nature, she wondered again at the runes, what in Anwens name did this mean?

Intrigued she began to examine the runes set within her ring, she deftly traced her finger around the bands edge, as if looking for an answer, this was given to me as a token of love and friendship, pondered Freyja to herself, that may be the connection, , but whatever does the rest of the encryption symbolize? she wondered to herself, Freyjas wandering thoughts were suddenly startled by an unseen earthy voice . "Up Worlder' it spluttered "you have been abandoned by the crackle Ember Feanyx left here to perish in the dwarfish realms"

Nearly jumping out of her skin with shock, Freyja questioned whether, a unknown being incarnate or just the crackle cruelly taunting her; perhaps it was even her own mind playing tricks upon her, but whatever it was Freyja knew that she was far too afraid to look behind her, Stealthily she tried to slink unseen in to the hidden shadows, but dread and horror crept upon her like a chill as she tried to move, her boots had become encased in the muddy earth like quick sand rooting her where she stood!, drawing her breath tightly she closed her eyes as a soft unforeseen something brushed against her leg, once more the spluttering sound of muffled dirt again embraced the claustrophobic confines of the dwarven caverns, *"Do not fear little one your time is not yet to pass, you must quench the fire and behold the glass, every flame casts a shadow, and every shadow is born from light, you must overcome your fear and fright*", "My name is Mulch and I am a Morrow" it added, "We are earth elementals, answer my riddle and I shall return you to the up world, but fail this puzzle and these Dwarven realms will be your tomb!"

Freyja swallowed hard, fear parched her throat claiming her voice, shaking, and flustered she tried to concentrate on the task before her," Quench the fire?" Freyja questioned herself, well the only fire that i see is the emerald one burning before me, she pondered watching the green flames dance and lick across the wells surface, "Behold the glass?" freyja mused to herself, this can only symbolize the wells Citrine tear, as it is not the slick surface sustaining the verdant flames, she surmised, before continuing on, "Every flame casts a shadow", and "every shadow is born from light?" This must represent the dusky placid aquas of the well which issue forth and sustain the shadowy potent emerald flames, as all answers revolve around this uncanny spa, now for the last line in the riddle…freyja puzzled "Overcome your fear and fright?"

That has to be my abandonment in this domain, Freyja perplexed to herself, and somehow tied into this emerald font, but what did it all mean?, Her tired mind reasoned hard for she had encountered enough riddles and enigmas already for today and was beginning to tire of them, But fear drove her onwards to plough through the weary shackles of her consciousness.

Freyja and Wynterleaf the dryad

Freyja paced back and forth, trying to mould together a conclusion hewn from all the correlations presented before her, "What terrifies me?" she asked herself, "well right now it is this cavernous realm, black as pitch, gloomy and suffocating with droves of abhorrent Specters inhabiting these desolate confines, "AHA!! my muddy friend" Freyja proclaimed excitedly, "It is a fear of the unknown! she declared as the pieces fell into place inside the labyrinth of her mind, a blinding revelation awakening the true resolution to mulch's conundrum, Freyja began to recite blindly with enchanted reverence as the answer conjured forth from the secluded reaches of her lucidity.

"*I hold the answer to your riddle, and narrate to you i shall, I must immerse myself within the waters of the well, To conquer my fear and fright, I must embrace the darkness and step forth into the light!, Now that i have solved your riddle, release me please from my muddy shackles if you may, and I shall venture forth into the unknown this day.*"

Muffled chuckling resounded around the hidden chamber as the Morrow laughed heartily to himself, waiting for a moment or two Mulch replied in spattering bursts, "*Well done my lady you have solved my riddle of rhyme, so now onwards and upwards we shall climb!*"

Freyja felt the earth around her encased ankles begin to loosen as the clay shackles crumbled around her sullied felt boots, Courageously she journeyed forwards toward the well which babbled voraciously the green hue lit up the cavern as the emerald tear burned with voracity, as if it were awakening to feast upon her form, Freyja took one last look at her gloomy surroundings as she reached the wells edge, this may be the last thing that i ever see she thought to herself apprehensively, Worms wriggled blindly across the soil and insects scurried out of crevices like a network of tiny catacombs, not much of a last memory freyja thought watching them, the only beacon of hope are the runes inscribed around this wells edge, somehow they match those upon my ring which Uther bequeathed me perhaps this shall protect me from any evils that lurk beneath the surface, Freyja took in one last immense gulp of dank fusty air, holding her breath tightly she stepped over the wells runic perimeter to plunge unseen beneath the dark tepid waters.

The supernatural aquas swallowed freyja down with a hungry gulp enclosing her beneath the sodden realms her submersion sent out an emerald ripple across the wells facet, meanwhile beneath the surface Freyja felt strangely charged and invigorated as if a curative surge was flowing unseen around her, she wrenched open her stinging eyes to glean a better perspective on her watery surroundings, she stared hard as she struggled to peer into the gloom as the uncustomary dark waters enclosed her vision like a blindfold.

Freyja fought back blinking hard, a strange golden phosphorescence radiated upwards from the depths below, shimmering radiance, which filtered upwards to cut through the murky gloom, like the outward rays of some underwater sun, Atmospherically the mysterious object luminesced rhythmically beckoning from the wells heart the celestial glow embraced Freyja within the kiss of its golden rays, Where lay the origins of this unusual radiance shining out from the wells innermost reaches, freyja wondered as she descended downwards, its source was a mystery that she herself must uncover, even if it courts peril, It is imperative to my quest that i uncover this light source thought Freyja to herself, i have come this far forward and i dare not venture back it may be the light from the fire pit above me guiding me onwards, or it may be some unforeseen danger; whichever it is, i must overcome my fears to procure my victory.

Descending down through the dank gloomy depths, like a plummeting stone Freyja struggled to ascertain her whereabouts as she bathed as the incandescent flaxen lustre radiated out with a voracious intensity the deeper down she sank, she began to propel herself downwards towards the light source with increasingly ferocity, i must have air she cried out in thought, bubbles of sparkling air flirtatiously kissed her face on their ascension to the wells surface like an effervescent taunting game of chase, her tormented movements began to seem ever more laborious, Freyjas limbs screamed out in agony with their craving for air, her muscles cramped and convulsed like confining shackles of suffering as her head swam with the threat of unconscious oblivion and a watery shroud…..

The bottom of the well begun to emerge into view, casting upon the senses like a shimmering mirage the gleaming water created its illusion in perception flickering in and out of freyjas waning consciousness like a dream, An object had begun to materialize appearing ghostly beneath the rippling waters, could this be the lights source Freyja thought to herself she could not be certain until she was virtually on top of its source as the gleaming waters acted like a cloak of concealment obscuring the bed of the well, blindly she reached down towards the crescent shaped object turning her head away, her eyes tightly closed as she became oppressed by the rays brilliance, Freyjas fingers warily scrabbled around in the wells silty base, she wondered if the glowing crescent would scorch her fingers should she be able to grasp it before she passed into obscurity and the realm of shadows that cruelly awaited her?

Freyjas fingers came into contact with cold hard metal as the object embraced her touch, 'how strange it is not at all hot' she thought as she grasped it within her palm, her grip began to enclose around the crescent, it started to tremble and vibrate with an immense intensity as it cast out a mighty roar 'YNYS AFFALON' rang out like a booming echo shuddering through the waters like a bore, Freyja and the golden sickle vanished as they shimmered through the portal with little more than a ripple.

Freyja materialized with a loud swoosh of water as she reappeared within the Runic firepit in the great hall above, Flames flickered before her eyes engulfing her form, fizzling steam arose from her sodden clothes, bewildered by her sudden surroundings freyja stopped holding her breath and gasped an astonished deep breath of air, at the flames merrily frolicking around the hem of her tunic and licking at her boots like a playful hound.

Then it hit her....SHE COULD BREATHE!! the astonished freyja hungrily drew down huge mouthfuls of hot but welcoming air making her dizzy, she swooned and collapsed wearily upon her knees tumbling forwards into an unceremonious heap, then the world went black.....

After an hour or more Freyja drearily awoke...her head still banging in protest as her limbs toiled beneath their ache, ow what was that? She felt something cutting amongst her palm, painfully she glanced down at the gold coloured crescent within the palm of her hand, the flames from the pit cast a seductive flickering light across its reflective surface illuminating the hidden Ogham runes covering its surface, 'What a curious artefact?' she wondered ' as the day's events flashed back in hurried recognition....I journey through a portals entrance in the well after grabbing this sickle only to exit amongst the firepit and yet i do not drown or burn?' she thought in alarm, her day dream was sharply awoken by the vehement grinding of the oaken stone entrance she had passed through earlier that day, as the doors swung open to produce the form of a wizened Druid in their wake.

The ancient stood wearing a smile across his antiquated face, and his once white robe was now sullied with mud and dust giving the visual impression of a dirty shroud cloaking its master whom had stepped forth from the realms of death himself into the sunlight and kingdom of man."*Heed me now Freyja' he commanded 'My name is Lychan, and you have passed the first test of the cauldron of rebirth whilst you were left alone with your darkest fears in the dwarf mines of Asgaryl discovering the elements of both fire and water, What did you learn there?"*, he enquired in an authoritative tone.

Taken aback but by no means surprised given the strange days events, she replied, "I have learned of fire water earth and air, seeing both vibrant orange flames blazing in the upper realms" said freyja, then pondering a moment she thoughtfully added, "i have witnessed their opposite of emerald flames burning hidden beneath the ground, they can only represent the watery aspect of the cauldron, air feeds all flame and ether dwells in the cauldron, enlightening me to the fact that all forces contain both light and shadows and the five elements." Well done Freyja, lychan replied, you have nothing more to learn here today, come out from the pit and let us address your future', Freyja stepped out from the flames unscathed as the mighty doors closed shut behind

Lychan with one last final rumble. The wizened mysterious stranger walked towards Freyja leaving a trail of dust and mud in his wake, the stranger beckoned towards a spot where an ornate wooden pew had begun growing from roots and shoots, arising forth from the ground like a writhing wooded carpet to plait a myriad of woven knotted seats, creating a breath taking decor, Freyja silently wondered whether it had been a gift from the Elves? She wearily ventured over to the knotted pew to sit before the Mighty Lychan Pendragon of all Druids with a slow and timorous gait beneath his prophetic stance, "Fear not child" laughed Lychan tugging at his beard, noticing her apprehension "all has been foretold in the prophecy of the heavens to be your destiny, Now Freyja I must present you with your outfit and apparatus for the passage of learning that awaits you, You are to wear a moss green cloak of wool as ovate status decrees for you have already Quested to obtained your golden sickle of the first grade, but remember and beware that it is only to be used wisely for it is a powerful tool, Secondly we arrive at your shield, added Lychan producing an armament steeped in regalia.

The heraldrous depictions glinted in unison as flickering light danced across their ornate divisions seeming to speak in whispered tongues reliving tales of battles of old.

A scene of two halves spoke to freyja, the left section bore a deep leaf green as fresh as spring which set a stark contrast against its aged gold counterpart which seemed to burn like the Anwen beneath the silhouetted countenance of an ebony crawbie reaching to pluck a scarlet heart from the boughs of a vast branched oak.

The oak smouldered in deep tones of ochre its entire form displayed in a stark reverence from the gnarled root system buried deep within the terra at the shields base right up to abundant green leaves which reached upwards to adorn the armournents heavenly crown epitomizing the eternal link between the earthen kingdoms and celestial utopia .

Freyja cast Lychan a dumbfounded and awestruck expression, somehow managing to find her voice ' I cannot accept these great treasures Pendragon, it is far too generous i have already been bequeathed the golden sickle' she said meekly, "Child you must accept these tools We almost reach the season where i must instruct you of your future charge" he replied softly, 'Now hand me your cloak freyja" he asked standing before her.

Freyja handed over the sodden dirty cloak over to Lychan who taking receipt of the garment, muttered something inaudible under his breath, as he did so the cloak transfigured into a glistening lush verdant green, he draped the replenished garment over her shoulders ceremoniously, "And now the golden Sickle named 'Luned' " he added…..

She carefully held out the magickal artefact, taking a second to admire it before placing it upon Lychans large calloused palm where it seemed to sparkle and radiate with an unseen intensity, 'Thankyou", he stated as he drew the folds of her collar together placing the sickle against the cloth. "ARMOUR!" he bellowed making freyja jump, With this command the sickle clasped shut with a click sending a magickal golden ripple throughout the cloth, Lychan the Pendragon took a step back and cast her an admiring glance, he smiled to himself and stated, "Beware and remember that this is no ordinary brooch upon your breast Freyja, that conjuration is just a mere charm timorous and meek compared to the true might this clasp bears, the simple incantation should protect you from shadow Magicks by casting your cloak as a shield, should you wish to undo your trinket at any time you have only to recite, WIDDERSHINS", he stated, "So Freyja, are you now ready to step over the threshold?" he asked her encouragingly.

The young woman looked up at the pendragon and smiled a broad smile of acceptance, triumph filled her being as she had accomplished all she had set out to attain, "I would truly consider it an honour to be of service and conclude my fate Pendragon" she replied humbly, "All is well then", he replied and continued, "I have already taken the liberty of packing you a travelling sack, and your chosen assignment should you wish to take it is to govern the Village of Thygorshire where you shall learn to heal the sick using the skills that you have learned from your mother Yllas, Your first step along the trail to scholarship starts with the villagers that you have been entrusted to care for, you must learn patience, healing, and some governorship." He said handing her a glass phial of swirling liquid, the blue tear shaped vessel was adorned with an ornate silver crescent stopper which hung upon a silver chain, "This capsule contains a potent essence of Saints Wort take care that it is only to be employed for deep lacerations and battle wounds, and furthermore freyja you must keep it upon your person at all times." he warned her, 'You are to leave just after dawn then child" ordered the Pendragon in a conclusive tone, "But just one more thing Freyja before you retire to your lodgings for this evening i have one more task set ahead of you for this evening, albeit a pleasant one at that" he stated with a smile, "I have requested that you be appointed a messenger allowing us the liberty to confer speedily in moments of need, the swift flight of feathers is much hastier than human feet" he added blithely, "Journey to the rookery just before dusk settles for you are to select yourself an envoy Crow, at my individual bequest"

The wizened druid laughed heartily at freyjas delighted countenance, for her face had lit up like a beacon upon hearing this, "wow…really?…i mean thankyou Lychan!" she stuttered in grateful reply for it was considered a great honour as under strict custom only druids were ordained such privileges, and corvids were her favourite beasts by far, "Now I'm afraid our paths must unravel as I depart to more pressing matters, you must tread through the crystal gateway to reach the rookeries, love light and peace to you child may the Anwen shine down upon your erudition, until our paths weave together once again" declared Lychan as he stepped forth into the burning pit of flames, the pendragon grew immense in stature within the shimmering heat as he harnessed the blazes potent energy, then casting aloft his arms he disappeared in a wisp of smoke to the unseen realms.

SOLOMONS ENTRANCE

The Quartz gateway, Freyja puzzled arising from her seat, Freyja watched the Elven pew elegantly unravel its weaves as it steadily retreated back in to the earth from whence it had sprang, burying its appendages beneath the soil like a mantle of wriggling earthworms, with a final shudder, once more the ground lay still and calm leaving behind no trace of the preceding enchantments.

"Right where now freyja thought as she surveyed the inner circumference of the entrance hall, looking for any indication or suggestion of what Pendragon Lychan had meant by the 'Crystal Gateway', It must be yet another riddle she thought to herself for the only crystal feature in this chamber is that quartz tree upon the wall, but surely it cannot be an entrance" Freyja wondered as she watched its facets glimmering and blazing as the firelight capered across them like a manifold of entrancing bewitchments," Ah well i shall lose nothing by venturing over to explore" she said to herself?

Freyja watched her distorted reflection grow ever closer upon the trees mirrored aspects, as she approached, her image eerily seemed to appear as if it were somehow imprisoned within the celestial pink hue of the rose Quartz. "Perhaps "she wondered deftly tracing her fingers across the cool glassy edges of the trees skilfully engraved branches, She closed her eyes with anticipation leaning up against the tree to press her face against the cool Quartz, fumbling at the clasp around her neck, her fingers located their prize of the golden sickle whereupon she tightly enclosed the mystifying tassel within her grasp, the word 'Shimmer' rang from her lips from nowhere.

The sparkling threshold enveloped Freyja as she glimmered through the portal, Freyja felt queasy and giddy as she span like a feather upon the breeze, a thousand feathery fingers brushed her skin as she travelled through time and space, wind rushed past her like a Zephyr surging and crackling with a mystical resonance, channelling the whirling vortex into the next aspect, 'THUD!' as suddenly as it had begun it was over, she was ejected from the portals exit onto solid ground with an unexpected clumsiness, for a moment she sat there feeling startled and disorientated, after a moment she announced to herself. "I am a novice at this enchanted voyaging it is unfamiliar and does not yet bear well with me, the last time i was spewn into a pit of fire!"

Freyja cautiously surveyed her surroundings, her head still swimming from the rush of sorcery, gingerly she placed a hand upon the hilt of her dagger as a precautionary measure for self-defence should she need it, for times were indeed dangerous within these realms and uprisings were common place, marauders ran rife under the imperious reign of the monarch Kalthor, Looking around freyja relaxed her grip upon the hilt of the dagger and gave a small smile, this time she was greeted only by an ancient woodland of gnarled sinister looking trees and youthful verdant saplings, the wood teemed with an abundance of flora and fauna as if Freyja had somehow awakened the sleeping birds and beasts with her stark arrival.

The dusky rays of the Anwen shone dappled rays of half-light upon the woods autumnal carpet filtering through the overhead canopy of trees to craft strange and weird shapes born from the shadows, the shadowy forms seemed to magically dance in time with the rustling overhanging boughs, and swaying leaves holding her in an entranced state, she watched the dark emulations writhe and contort upon the fiery coloured leaf litter as they fed off the residual magic expelled by the portal weaving a visual banquet for the soul.

The atmosphere around the passageway felt intoxicating and bewitching, vibrating and crackling as the raw energy of sorcery coursed through its veins seeming to create a separate entity incarnate or perhaps it was the very spirit of the woods herself, Freyja gasped in awe as she turned around and witnessed the majesty that was towering behind her it was a formidable sight indeed met her eyes, the outlet to the Quartz portal stood below the woven jaws of a cavernous tunnel of yew trees, The towering passage dwarfed her blocking out the Anwens rays with its sheer enormity, to immerse her beneath its dense shadow, the contorted wizened Yews emanated a somewhat eerie quality in the dusky half-light, their branches resembling gnarled interlocked hands which menacingly threatened to reach down and capture any unwelcome travellers that may wish to venture into their domain, yet still it was a sacred place and the sanctity stilled the mind and soul from all fear.

Freyja gazed intensely into the blackened reaches of the passageway as she began to descend down the woody corridor, observing the innermost reaches before her trying to unearth any ominous forms lurking within its dense shadowy heart, she gripped her dagger tightly as she advanced but the tunnel was unyielding and impenetrable remaining an enigma cloaked within its shroud of darkness.

Freyja concluded that this could be the entrance to the hidden aviaries of the Druids, for how else could it have remained a secret to the Goblins and Dwarves for all the centuries passed?, "I shall need light to guide the way" she announced stooping over the ground to hunt for a dry bough or some twigs that she could fashion into a fagot. Aha this one will do nicely" she proclaimed snatching up a dry withered branch of Hazel, "EMBLAZEN" she commanded, and the wood ignited with Vigor as it conjured up the Crackle named Feanyx blazing upon its end." Anwens eve Freyja, as you command" he replied with a somewhat mischievous glint, "Anwens eve Feanyx, i am in need of your radiance if you please?" replied Freyja. Request granted, let us journey forth into the unknown" replied Feanyx, Freyja swallowed hard mustering up courage for she did not trust him as they embarked upon their adventure.

Freyja began to feel a little uneasy they further forward they went, they wound deeper into the encroaching darkness, she felt the sensation of a thousand beady eyes tracking their every move, every now she swore she heard a whispered fluttering overhead, Skittishly she spun around holding the crackle aloft as she peered into the shadows which enveloped them, “Do you hear anything Feanyx?” Freyja questioned in hushed tones as fear began to seep into her bones.” No mistress, but let us illuminate our trail ahead” he replied with a crackling voice, “FLARE” commanded the Crackle as he blazed into a torrent of flame casting out his brilliance upon the walls of the forest like cavern.

Freyja looked up at the woven ceiling of Yews and gasped in awe.. there perched the most gratified sight that she had seen this day, excitement began to well up in the pit of her stomach like a thousand tiny butterflies hurriedly fluttering to be released, “CROWS!” she cried aloud barely able to enclose her delight at the multitude of fluffy ebony bundles that stared back at her with inquisition, the burliest creature announced the distress call, rendering the air thick with a thousand “CRAWKKS” curtailed with manic flapping and fluttering as each bird warned the murder of the approaching stranger.

Freyja stared at her surroundings in pure bewitchment oblivious to the descending creepers writhing silently towards her as they sprouted down from the overhead rooftop, she felt a strange slithering run across her ankle as a stealthy runner bound her like a shackle, she screamed aloud in horror as the vine started to tug at her footing binding her fast within its snake like coils, it slithered tightly around her waist, wrists and throat suspending her in midair as it claimed its victim, Feanyx plummeted to the floor as Freyja relinquished her grip upon the torch to claw at the leafy tourniquet threatening to suffocate her, How could she have been so stupid she should have realized that the coops would have enchanted traps! she panicked as her vision started to blur, Without warning a loud yell of "DISPERSE!" rang out echoing loudly around the cavern like booming thunder as the Druid Myllas roared his incantation charging down the darkened tunnel as fast as his legs would carry him.

The creepers released their grip as commanded and began retreating back into the woven canopy above, they relinquished Freyja to the ground with a hard THUD! One more she had been left to lie upon the damp ground gasping for air she thought as the figure came running towards her, "Are you alright?" said the unfamiliar figure "I am so sorry i was warned of your arrival by Pendragon but i must have dozed off somehow, perhaps it was that homemade mead that i have been brewing?"

Freyja looked up through blurry vision as the stranger slowly began to emerge into focus, "You nearly killed me!" she retorted with fury rubbing her bruised backside, The stranger appeared a funny little man, rotund in appearance with a blushed face, his eyes were magnified out of proportion as he gazed out at Freyja from beneath his half-moon bespectacled features, nervously he stroked his tangled white beard.

"My name is Myllas Freyja" he said in a bumbling voice, "You won't tell Lychan will you please, he'll be very angry? "Freyja looked at him considering this prospect, she was angry but felt some pity towards this confused little man, he was almost comical with his wiry white hair, dirty grey robes and his general unkempt forgetful persona, "No Myllas i shall not this time, but i am here to choose myself a flighted companion not be attacked!" she said with an air of amusement, "Thankyou it is not normally how i choose to receive guests" he added jokingly with a flushed expression.

"I have one fellow that I would particularly like to show you, if you would care to follow me" added myllas beckoning towards Freyja before scuttling off down the one of passages of the labyrinth, Freyja arose stiffly to her feet and hurried off after him snatching up Feanyx as she went, dutifully she followed Myllas as they ventured into the labyrinths heart, Eventually after what had seemed like an eternity they reached the innermost reaches of the passages to find a small cramped doorway held together with a few rusty studs and a leather strap; upon it hung a small notice "*Myllas, guardian and defender of flight, Do not disturb before noon, knock thrice before entering*". "Ah here we are , now mind your head won't you?" said the queer little fellow as he laboriously unstrapped the door and placed a triangular key into its lock, Myllas fumbled with the key tutting loudly as the door fought back mumbling and spitting in protest before ejecting the key out onto the ground!

"I've told you before Myllas, NO ENTRANCE without a riddle!" grumbled the door in a haughty tone, "I am in a hurry today, no time for tricks" argued the peculiar little druid, "Now give way if you please Woodrow?" ordered Myllas defiantly shoving the key back into the lock amongst a lot of mumbling and grumbling from Woodrow; "you're not supposed to enter without a riddle, blasted Druids!" came the muffled indignation, Freyja heard the lock click as it was sharply pushed inwards, objectionably it creaked loudly upon its hinges and threatened to collapse into a pile of woodworm and dust.

“Tricky wood that Verdant Damson!” stated Myllas with embarrassment, “Now come inside, come inside” he gestured impatiently, Freyja stooped down and stepped into the messiest place that she had ever seen! a threadbare chair languished dolefully in the corner beneath a Verdigris torch bracket that must have once been dwarfish copper, “Very handy in battle that one” bumbled Myllas noticing freyja observe the bracket, “Dwarf copper illuminates when dark elves are approaching you know” but freyja didn’t think it would do too much illuminating these days, now that it had been filled with a multitude of fat luminescent spark worms who radiated out a dim light giving off a foul stench like cabbages, as they drooled slime down the bracket.

In the centre of the room hid a small table buried beneath a mountain of unrolled parchments and used tea cups, it looked as though its legs were about to collapse beneath the commitment, hordes of books were strewn across the floor, and hardly an inch of carpet was visible in the dim light, On the upper hand though a small fire blazed within the sooty black hearth, hissing and spitting out a shower of sparks to singe a grimy pattern into the hearth rug, over the flames hung a kettle whistling noisily, its lid rattling in seeming salutation to the weary traveller, as it released steam into the air mingling with the soot and smoke from the blocked floo to create a thick blanket of enveloping smog, Freyja coughed at the noxious environment and stepping over a pile of books, “Aha here is the fellow” he announced walking over to the hat stand “What do you think Freyja?” he asked her cheerily as the sooty bundle of feathers fluttered clumsily onto his wrist.

Freyja stood encaptivated by the beautiful ebony fledgling as he perched against the woolly hats, scarves and walking staves, “I have just finished hand rearing him myself, he is a beauty and very tame” added Myllas, but Freyja was not listening for she was much too taken by the baby crow staring up at her inquisitively through shiny bright eyes that burned like smouldering coal, ”KWRAWK” announced the bird puffing out his fluffy ebony feathers in protest as yet another cloud of soot and steam descended upon them, “Oh Myllas he is gorgeous, can i really take him?” asked Freyja in wonderment.

“Why child of course you may he has been reared with you in mind” he replied, “What name has he been given?” Freyja inquired joyfully, “My name is Solomon mistress” said the bird taking flight from his hat stand to alight, he gently alighted upon Freyjas wrist, causing her to giggle with delight, ‘right it is high time i made that pot of tea” mumbled Myllas tottering through the Bric a Brac to silence the whistling kettles tune.

The miniature man cluttered about amongst the debris hunting for teacups. Eventually he unearthed two grimy looking receptacles, he held them aloft and squinted at their state. ”oh dear.” he said rubbing the dust off with his robe, Myllas cleared a space upon the table and placed down the tea cups, and toddled off towards to retrieve the kettle. “now what do you fancy to drink?” he asked freyja encouragingly, “Oh I don’t really mind” she replied. ”but as you’re asking I’d love a hot chocolate please Myllas”she added.

“One hot chocolate it is then if you please spout” he instructed the kettle, she sang happily as she poured a dark frothy chocolate into one of the cups, freyja looked on in amusement as she had never seen a warbling kettle before!

“Go ahead, drink it it’s quite safe” he told her, freyja smiled gratefully and reached for the cup, she was parched after the long days occurrences, this caused Solomon to take flight back to the hat stand! “sorry little fellow” she said, the bird just looked at her with a displeased expression and went back to preening his sooty feathers causing freyja to laugh, The chocolate smelt delicious, a warm sweet aroma met her senses as carefully she took a sip of the steaming liquid, it tasted better than it smelt, delicious, rich and chocolaty she concluded in approval.

“my how thoughtless of me!” exclaimed myllas, “take a seat, by the fire” he told her apologetically, She stepped over a pile of books and sank wearily into the tatty fire-side chair causing its near collapse as the springs groaned in protest at their consignment.

“Tut tut” …myllas grumbled as spout poured him a cup of tea. “let’s see what we can do about that” he said, “BALDERDASH.” ” oh no blast, hang on that’s not it!”. ”HABBERDASH” he declared at the chair, The chairs cushions sprang back into shape plumping themselves up, its feet straightened and the frame once more became sturdy, causing freyja to nearly spill her chocolate, “that’s much better” declared myllas sitting down in the chair opposite freyja, “now how about some cake?” he asked gleefully, freyjas mouth salivated at the thought of cake and her hungry tummy rumbled in approval, “that would be delightful” she replied enthusiastically.

“Thats what I like to hear, now then what was that spell? “he said, “ah I know, SLICE”..he proclaimed, to which a piece of bread appeared out of thin air with a ‘pop’, “oh fiddlesticks that’s not it” he grumbled rubbing his head, after a series of confused mumblings, he hopefully muttered “BUNS” causing a shower of iced buns to rain down upon them, "these will do nicely thankyou myllas" said freyja warily" as she hungrily tucked into a bun.

Solomon swooped over and claimed the bread for himself, merlining his quarry before myllas could reclaim it from him, "ah you best have it then fellow" said myllas in defeat, Freyja delicately sipped her cocoa and watched the spitting hearth as an ember tumbled through the grate to lie amongst the smouldering ash.

Myllas thoughtfully regarded her for a moment then began to speak, "when I was a lad I had a rook named Socrates you know, raised him from a hatchling I did just like Solomon but he is all yours now I shall miss him too, make sure you guard and protect him well as he shall you" he instructed, then continued advisingly, "Now you teeter on the very brink of your destiny freyja you and Solomon must voyage through the portals entrance which lies among the grate of flames, but for now let us talk and rest awhile for it has been a long day" said the wizened little man, Freyja stared at the blazing fire sleepily and listened to myllas recount tales of his youth, the little man's mumbling tones sang like a chorus of lullaby's to the tired girl, the tea cup clattered onto the floor as freyja drifted off to the arms of Morpheus, "Ah I must be becoming a bore" chuckled Myllas to himself as he wearily creaked up on his knees, the miniature sorcerer shuffled over to the hearth and traced a pattern into the ashes with his stave.

Freyja dreamt that the runic bands etched upon the well of portal and around the Fire pit were somehow written into the ashes of Myllas's fire, in her dream she stood to face the little man, somehow he looked sad?

Solomon took flight from his hat stand to perch upon her outstretched arm flapping as if he were in suspended in slow motion, "Very well, I take my leave and I thank you kindly Myllas may the Anwen bless you" said Freyja as she slowly glided towards the blaze, each movement in her dream felt as if she were stuck in treacle until she was mere inches from the flames, she felt the heat sear against her features, Once again she grasped her golden sickle and she and Solomon shimmered through the portal to Thygorshire with little more than a crackle, leaving the humorous little druid and his covert behind them.

Freyja awoke the next morning, what a peculiar dream she thought to herself as it unfolded in her mind, looking around she was not in myllas little hovel, but the healers cottage llette, yawning and sitting up she saw her trusty familiar Solomon observing her from his perch upon the bed stead, the previous day's events came flooding back to her, so this was to be the first day of their assignment together her and Solomon freyja reflected, And so for many years freyja undertook her apprenticeship governing the town of Thygor with Solomon circling ever watchfully above her, they lived a meagre existence from the land and generosity of the villagers.

Freyja became adept at healing the sick, communing with mortals and beasts and as each season came to pass she experienced both the harsh and beautiful elements of mother nature herself becoming wild at heart.

THIRTY TWO MOON CYCLES LATER... THE TALE BEGINS...

It was a misty September morning in the land of Thygor, Freyja was sat idly beneath the great branches of myrddin, watching the swirling mist roll densely into the valley below , meanwhile Solomon was happily nestled within its mighty branches taking roost, the ovate wondered how she was to solve the problem of King Kalthor and his Regulator Saul?

It was a constant dispute Kalthor charged unfair taxes to the villagers, whilst his regulator Raul and his motley troop of Kin trolls rode across the region wreaking havoc in their midst pillaging and torching anyone, that did not pay the kings Tythe when there was barely enough grain to feed the villagers, Only earlier that very day there had been an almighty skirmish between the trolls and the villagers, pitchforks, axes had been locked in battle yet again, Freyja had spent the whole day healing the wounded and was thoroughly exhausted, Saul had sighted her helping those who had disobeyed Kalthor as he rode past into the woods with his vile troop of Kin, surely this would make Kalthor even more angered and ruthless, he would design fresh torments to reign down upon the villagers in revenge for this, Freyja could not bear to think of the consequences that would befall her if she was captured, Solomon broke her concentration calling out a loud 'craw' as he circled overhead hunting for insects or if he was really lucky maybe a carcass left by the foxes from their meal the night before.

Freyja felt that the village of Thygor's only hope lay with the legendary "Warlock" her childhood friend Uther, but what if his skills were just rumour? she thought apprehensively, well there was only one sure way to find out, tomorrow she must go to the Anwen Temple and request leave to hunt for him, or her healing skills would not keep up with the battles, Kalthor was descended from the bloodline of Saeb, and ruled like a pestilence over the land.

The thought of the hunt for the warlock uther was daunting to freyja but someone had to intervene, she may have to ramble far and wide as he had not been seen in these parts for nigh on a cycle or two, but the thought of seeing her old friend again pleased her, she looked down at her ring as the engraved runes burned in the setting half-light, the villagers said he had gone to Khymer upon the Marsh under the wretched regulator Saul's threatened instruction.

Freyja had been to visit Emergaid only the day before about her throng of maladies, she had been subjected to listen to the whole villages gossip whilst treating her ailments, not that freyja minded she loved the old ladies affable nature, the old lady had mentioned that talk had been heard in the oxen and plough of Uther being sanctioned to forge a weapon for king Kalthor, under threat that his father's farm would be razed to the ground should he choose not to obey his monarchs command, as usual Kalthor had sent his appointed cohort Saul to deliver the requisition in person.

There had been muttered discussions between the two, and the warlock not wishing to provoke Kalthor for fear of reprisals had ridden off into the horizon without a word, Freyja had heard tell of his battle weapons they were legendary, but would he come to her aid She would send Solomon firstly to ask him this courtesy, She would ask her order tomorrow if they would send the Warlock a Gryffin as part payment upfront she knew of a fine beast called Pygar who would serve him well, having reached a decision she headed back down towards her little cottage llette in the valley, it wasn't much to look at just a simple cottage built into the side of a hill, set amongst the forest, there was a small winding stream emanating from the forest, which coursed gently down the garden, it was home.

After a pleasant ramble back home through the valleys winding paths, Freyja eventually arrived at the threshold of her home, entering quickly, she barred the door shut behind her, as Solomon swooped back upon his perch, it was a habit she had grown all to accustomed to in these treacherous times, and especially now after yesterday's events.

Freyja crept over to the window and silently drew down the ox skin across, she secured it firmly with a leather thong, sneaking stealthily around the hut she checked that she had extinguished the smouldering embers of the cooking pit and snuffed out the dimly glowing clump of candle wax earlier that morning, ah yes all was safe thank goodness, She strained her ears, listening out for any telltale sign that she had been followed, such as snapping twigs or rustlings for what seemed like an eternity, before decreeing to herself that all was well and it was at last safe to rest, sinking her aching bones amongst the hefty pile of furs she settled down to sleep.

Freyja awoke suddenly shivering and trembling, a cold sweat beaded across her forehead like dew upon grass, it ran down her face in salty traces, awaking fitfully, she licked her fear parched lips, what was meant by the evil portents which had invaded her dreams, she hoped that it was not a vision of things yet to pass, but just an interpretation of her fears ignited by the previous day's events.

The dreams portrayal had been vivid, Freyja stood imprisoned inside a blazing cage of orange fire, it raged like a ferocious inferno, around her feet serpents writhed and coiled like a venomous carpet of malignance, they threatened to extinguish her life's essence with one quick kiss of poison summoned forth from their needle like fangs.

The menacing dreams images the goal's confines haunted her waking consciousness, as images of Kalthor and his cohort Saul flashed across her memory, ready to unleash their regiment of Kin Trolls upon the land of Thygor, she had been powerless to help as the foul loathsome beasts plundered the village, dispatching its inhabitants with an evil rapture, they spared the children to last, ready to be consumed and absorbed by the ravaging army of Dust Dervishes who rolled across the scorched smouldering land like a thick blanket of repugnant fog blocking out the Anwens rays, advancing ever closer to cast the realm into darkness as they devoured their victims with a ravenous fury, and then nothing but silence befell the land as Kalthors depraved cackle roared upon the howling winds of apocalypse echoing out like the victorious battle chant of a legion of fiends.

It was at this point that she had awoken drenched in sweat and feverish as if her soul had been enslaved within the fiery prison of the trance, it had seemed all too real, Freyja could not delay any longer, She slipped from beneath her mountainous pile of damp furs and into her riding gear, she quickly collected her healing bag and a few provisions and whistling for Solomon, she ventured out into the cold night air.

The night air hung still and crisp, Alluan cut his eerie glow through the scattered clouds like a silvern dagger, Freyja scanned the formations carefully in the hope of seeing a prophetic omen or sign for the journey ahead, a shooting star would be good she thought to herself, but alas only the silhouette of Solomon was visible as he swooped down from his hazel branch and landed upon Freyjas outstretched arm with a mischievous peck, She lifted Solomon up to eye level and began to whisper to him, after a moment or two he replied with an affable "craawwk" and freyja released him into the soundless night air, then within a wings beat he was little more than a speck against the brilliance of mighty Alluan.

Freyja quickly headed off towards the pasture where her trusty mare was stabled, At nightfall the meadow held a certain mysterious quality about it, tall grasses danced in the moonlight waving to and fro like rustling warnings, and the all too busy furtive buzzing of the local insects had fallen silent, she almost felt as if she were trespassing as she reached the stable doors.

Upon entering Freyja immediately felt comforted by the familiar aroma of hay and horse dung as Equuleus whinnied her greeting coupled with an affectionate nuzzle for freyja, "hello my lady" she said to the filly, and then continued "I'm afraid that I must disturb your rest, for we are to set out tonight on our journey to roam the kingdom and track down Uther for he is greatly needed here in Thygor", Equuleus, snorted in annoyance throwing her head back as freyja quickly set about saddling her up, after fastening up the last strap freyja breathed an inaudible whisper into the filly's ear, to which she replied with a gentle hoof stamp, In a flash Freyja was mounted upon her charge as they were galloping abroad into the silvery moonlit realm beyond..

Meanwhile the previous moons cycle, The Warlock had ridden off that morrow in a blinding fury relentlessly driving his charge minstrel towards the Khymerian mountains, Uther and the Regulator Saul's meeting the preceding nightfall in the Oxen and Plough had not fared too well…

THE SUMMONS

Uther had been mindlessly working in his forge that morning in the vale of Engor which lay west to Thygor, he had just fed his bellows dragon Vesta a handful of flint chippings in readiment to light the forge when a loud screeching noise had stilled him, He had gone to investigate only to discover in horror that it was one of the regulator Saul's flying snarls, viscous little beasts they were a vivid azure blue in colour with jagged scales covering their thick hides, The Snarls were not much bigger than a small bird who soared around on bat like wings, their features resembled that of a dragons somewhat, but with a slighter snout and projecting barbed fangs, many animals would flee if one was in the air as they feasted upon any small beast they could catch with their poisonous bite and razor like talons.

Uther gazed down upon the ugly little creature it let out a hideous screech and raised a talon which clasped a roll of tattered parchment, The warlock reached down and accepted the proffering, to which the snarl eyed his fingers with a hungry expression as if contemplating its next meal before taking off and swooping menacingly in circles around the warlocks head a few times as if it were trying to torment him before ascending out of sight back home to its masters keep.

What can this be uther thought to himself venturing back inside the forge, his grimy brow bled beads of sweat which trickled down to sting his eyes for added annoyance, he secured the parchment down upon the sooty wooden bench with a couple on nails, and held his breath as he unravelled it to reveal its contents, Uther sighed a heavy sigh as he had read the summons. "*King Kalthor Ruler and Monarch Supreme, summons thee ,Warlock Uther his subject to dutifully attend a gathering this eves night fall at the Oxen and Plough tavern with the Regulator known as Saul, to undertake a commission for the king*"

He had been summoned to a meeting with Saul by the order of king Kalthor, What terrible bequest could this corrupt and tyrannous monarch and his villainous cohort want from me, Ah well I shall certainly find out this eves fall no doubt he thought to himself, i had best go prepared then he reasoned, eyeing the array of armaments that decorated the forges interior.

"We had best prepare ourselves well for this eve" Uther said to Vesta as he chucked her the summons to ignite, she eyed him curiously from her viewpoint atop the chimney breast, she was a miniscule little beast and stood no higher than a tankard, yet she was a perfect little dragon in every proportion even down to her delicate red wings, Vesta blinked sleepily, took one look at the summons and rendered it to a smouldering pile of ash, fragments of parchment floated down to the floor making uther roar with laughter as his days work began in earnest.

The shadow upon the sun dial cast three and half past the hour as Uther hammered out the last smelt, he stood back and wiped the sweat from his brow, his chest heaving against the red hot fury of the forge.

The warlock went over to the pail and immersed his ladle, raising the metal to parched lips he quenched his raging thirst then dipped his hands in to splash his sweltering face, the cool water felt like a sweet maidens kiss to him, Uther glanced up at the sun dial and panicked, he had best make haste he would need to venture out soon if he was to reach the Ox and Plough by this eves fall, hurriedly he began his vital defences and preparations....

THE OXEN AND PLOUGH

Uther the warlock saddled up his charge and raced against the diminishing rays of Autumnal light as if he were chasing the very Anwen herself, as she threatened to descend behind the horizon, Minstrel gasped for breath as he galloped hard, the vapors of his exhausted rasps displayed upon the cool air as he charged towards the inn, luckily their ride through the vale of had been uneventful and had not encumbered their flight.

The warlock gradually slowed minstrels magic down to a trot as they drew level with the Oxen and Plough, he dismounted and led his charger towards the stables "well done boy" Uther gratefully told the fatigued beast as he patted him affectionately, minstrel gave a tired snort of approval in return and headed off towards the overflowing stone water trough, Dusky rays of light shrouded the inn beneath a shadowy veil, candle light gently flickered against the windows illuminating the host of masked silhouettes that lingered within, Uther checked his armaments were well concealed as he made to venture into the inn "who knows what trickery and traps may lie in wait for me?" he thought to himself subjectively.

The sign hanging above the inns threshold, swung to and fro in the breeze its Oxen skull and rusty plough creaked ominously in the wind as if it were a premonitory portent of doom about to crash down upon his shoulders, loud booming echoes of thunder resounded across the heavens in atmospheric resonance, forked lightning streaked across the sky as it cut its path towards the terra like a mighty three pronged sword illuminating the inky sky as it opened its torrential onslaught of rain to pelt down with ferocity, "This is all i need!" stated Uther as the cold hard rain penetrated through his cloak and travelling britches, the chilly water bit into his flesh with an icy numbness like a bite from a frosty serpent.

Uther dashed toward the sturdy oaken door with its rusty brass rivets and grasped the cold metal latch between his numb fingers, he drew in a deep breath and opened the door with a hefty thrust stepping forth into conflict as he closed the stormy night out behind him..

The inn fell silent as its residents stopped their gossip to turn and scrutinize the traveller the warlock threw back the hood of his travelling cloak and strode over towards the bar, folk turned away and began conferring in hushed tones amongst themselves, "Merry eves fall Theo" he said to the inn-keeper, "Merry eve to you an all squire what'll it be?" asked Theo.

"A flagon of your finest Gryffins fire if you please" ordered Uther placing a bronze coin upon the bar, Theo uncorked the dusty barrel behind him and tapped off a pitcher of ale which he placed in front of the warlock, "So what brings you to these parts this eve?" questioned Theo nervously with a glimmer of fear in his chestnut eyes, "I have been dutifully summoned by snarls on request of our most noble and tyrannous monarch Kalthor to discuss a privy commission with his deceitful Regulator Saul" he replied, "May the Anwen be with you then" replied Theo as he gave the warlock a pitying look laced with dread..

The warlock nodded his thanks to Theo and made off toward the crackling hearth supping his ale, he took off his dripping travelling cloak and draped it over the fireside chair, Uther watched it steam as the heat began to penetrate the sodden wool, he stood beside the hearth deep in thought about the evenings assignation, Drawing up a stool he sat beside the crackling amber blaze with outstretched palms, his hands Stang fiercely as the warmth pierced through the numbness of his frigid fingers, the warlock watched the dancing scarlet and orange flames writhe and contort as they hungrily consumed a fagot of wood, giving off the occasional hiss and crackle, the wood smoke had an intensely sweet aroma which filled the inn like an smoky blanket of enchanting perfume, "It must be a fagot of Cherry tree" he thought to himself whilst he waited for Saul to announce his loathsome arrival.

The warlock stared hard in to the flames he could have sworn that that flame had just resembled an mischievous looking fire entity, he blinked hard and rubbed his eyes "must be the Gryffins Fyre!" he wondered to himself, taking a deep draught of his ale, he looked round to observe the inns inhabitants, the chieftain Bynar looked up and nodded in acknowledgement, Bynar was now grey in mane but he still emanated a chiefly persona.

Uther was Abruptly awoken from his complacent state of mind as the bulky oaken door to the Oxen and Plough swung open with an hefty Crash, the fierce wind and lashing rain howled in over the threshold like a banshees cry as it blasted around the inn casting an icy chill upon its inhabitants that no blazing hearth could melt, "GET THE DOOR!" shouted Theo, Bynar arose from his seat and strode over to the threshold, at that very moment a crack of lightning slashed through the heavens illuminating the entrance and announcing the presence of the three ominous silhouettes looming there, A ricochet of pure violet brilliance shot out from the figures, it invaded the room penetrating into its every shadow and crevice, a dense pungent odour of dark sorcery hung thick upon the air to asphyxiate the inns patrons, The central figure stepped forward and withdrew a bony hand from within its cerements, the appendage appeared withered and ashen looking like a that of a cadaver, Saul the regulator pointed into the air with his ring finger and incanted in Shadow speak, "*None shall Tarry, heed nor pass, Before the spilling of an hourglass, lest death consumes them at serpent speed, visible to vision and voice are we three, If beheld we shall destroy thee*" Acrid purple smoke rose up from the bowels of hell, billowing and winding to exhibit the spectral form of a salivating infernal hound as black as pitch with eyes of blazing violet, The smoke began its descent toward the ground as the vestige writhed and contorted in an opaque cloud of torment, weaving its sorcerous malignance as it mutated into solid form, the wispy entrails of vapour slowly departed relinquishing the hideous beast snarling upon the inns floor, The regulator let out a hideous cackle cold and blood curdling as the trio stepped forward into the Oxen and Plough.

The blaze within the hearth spat and crackled, the whole inn fell as silent and motionless as the grave, all eyes were fixed upon the regulator Saul and his two concealed cohorts as they advanced into the tavern.

The threshold of the Oxen and Plough shuddered as its huge oaken door was flung shut by the unseen hands of the cadavers conjurations, it felt like the sealing of a crypt to Uther as he shuddered in repulsion at Kalthor's triad of cohorts, the inn keeper Theo advanced out from behind the bar saying' "We don't serve your sort in ere be gone with you i say", Saul maliciously discerned this impertinence through his putrid countenance, snarling balefully he revealed the tips of his two silver fangs, before Gliding aberrantly fast above the floor, the regulator pointed with maleficence at Theo as he muttered his abhorrent conjuration.

A forked bolt of pure violet lashed at Theo like a scourge, clutching at his chest the publican let out a blood curdling cry as he collapsed into a crumpled heap rendered motionless by Sauls evil sorcery The regulator cackled in malicious ridicule as he descended back down onto the floor.

The inn was deathly quiet all eyes were fixed upon the regulator and his phalanxes, villagers and liege alike were too scared to even breathe, Saul then turned his attentions toward the inns inhabitants and hissed aloud in his decaying voice "Where be the Smythe known as uther?"

No one spoke a word in reply for they were all too afraid to answer, once again the gurgling sound of putrefaction rang out through the tavern, "I command to know the whereabouts of the Warlock uther, answer me now villagers or you shall all be corvid provender upon the gallows!" ordered the regulator scanning their terror stained faces, Not wishing any more confrontations the warlock drew his breath and regretfully announced " I am over here Regulator let us discuss Kalthors assignment", The fiendish hound flanking Saul skulked off across the inn to guard the Oxen and Ploughs threshold it growled threateningly revealing a muzzle of slavering fangs should Uther think of making his retreat, Uthers blood ran cold as Raul drew up the stool opposite him with a sweeping gesture of his corpse like hand.

The warlock observed the regulator with disgust and fear for he cut a truly loathsome and intimidating form, his cerements reeked with the stench of decay and his face lay hidden in the shadow of his cowl, save for two smouldering violet eyes and the glinting fangs, the appearance of his hands made uther shudder for they were pure opaque white tinged blue like those of a fresh corpse, The warlock could not help but notice Rauls ring finger as upon it sat a silver crescent ring set with a jet stone, the stone had a seam of violet straight through its centre which appeared to blink in the firelight as if somehow he was being observed by the artefact, Saul quickly noticed this observation on Uthers part and stealthily withdrew his hand back within the hidden confines of his reeking shroud.

The regulators two cohorts stood guard overshadowing the blazing hearth like stone effigies from a tomb, their heads bowed in total silence their bodies motionless in demeanour, wearing black hooded gowns to obscure their expressionless visages, they seemed to draw upon the silence making the air feel thick and soundless as a tomb, inanimate in time.

It was clearly evident to the warlock that they were pawns of Rauls and Kalthors evil sorcery and corrupt reign of terror….

The warlock returned his gaze to the regulator Raul as he began to speak, "So warlock, here we are ordained to cross our paths upon the orders of my monarch Kalthor." hissed the regulator as his lifeless hands reached into the depths of his fusty wrappings, he extracted a reeking scroll of parchment bound with a black ribbon which he placed in front of Uther.

The warlock reached across to receive the parchment from Raul shuddering save his hand should brush that dead thing,

Turning the stale parchment over in his hands Uther silently mumbled the incantation "screen unfold any masked terrors to behold" noiselessly under his breath, stealthily sliding his other hand beneath the table to rest upon the hilt of his dagger, as his flamesword chant probed for any concealed sorcery that may lie in wait for him upon its opening, but alas somewhat disappointingly none were revealed, "Satisfied master Smythe?" hissed Raul mockingly in his poisonous voice knowing all too well what the warlock had just concluded, his violet eyes observing mockingly from within the hooded shroud.

Uther glared defiantly at the regulator, or at least that which was visible "Ay all seems in order" he replied breaking the wax seal of Kalthor to unravel the scroll, Kalthors seal was easily distinguishable, a violet serpentine eye cast within the symbol of the crescent moon,

Uther carefully opened the parchment with his sleeve should it be dusted with nightshade or fox fever dust, and heard Rauls gurgling sneer in doing so, well he had been wise to take that precaution it seemed, The warlock secured the contract firmly upon the table with his tankard and watched in disgust as the contorted violet wisps of shadow speak came into view, slowly contorting their formation to read.

"Warlock, you are hereby summoned For the commission of one ceremonial dagger and scabbard, upon the order of your supreme ruler and monarch Kalthor, inlaid with these governing runes, Conjure forth, elements of shadows and flame, Hereby bind and entwine, release ye the potency, which courses sublime, To be completed by next moons cycle, Delivered to thine Kings regulator Saul, Failure to obey his majesties bidding shall consequence, The release of his Dervishes upon the citizens of

Thygorshire"

The warlocks blood boiled as he read the tempestuous order, seething in anger he arose furiously from his seat and slammed the scroll down in front of Raul, "What is meant with this threatening insult Regulator?" he fired angrily at Raul, "No man threatens the Warlock with sorcery" he raged bringing his fist down hard upon the table spilling the half full tankard of Gryffins fire.

The regulator just sat there in mocking stony silence glowering at uther through his concealed cowl, answer me you vile fiend shouted uther, by now the inns inhabitants were aghast at the display unfolding before them and looked truly petrified, how am i to know that should i undertake this commission that the dervishes will not be released anyhow, boomed uther angrily.

The utterance of the word dervishes bought gasps and wails from the inns patrons as they fearfully wondered at the subject of the said commission, still the regulator remained statuesque upon his seat in an abhorrent cloud of malignant enjoyment at the warlocks anger, you shall not be so derogatory again bellowed the warlock grabbing hold of Raul's frigid hand, the oleaginous feel of it repulsing him to the bone, Now regulator i shall take my assurance on Kalthors behalf he smirked ripping the ring from rauls cadaver like finger.

Screams hit the air as the regulators pair of motley cohorts lifted their heads in synchronicity shrieking foully ready to advance upon the taverns patrons, meanwhile uther had his own problems, the regulator snatched hold of his wrist with his free hand, the bony fingers bit into Uthers flesh like a serpentine shackle as Raul arose from his pew with eyes of blazing fury, "you dare to grab me warlock" replied Raul with a venomous hiss, “behold thine nightmare” he cried mercilessly throwing back his cowl to reveal a visage of sheer terror, Rauls once handsome features had been sullied to rot by the evil shadow speak, his ashen flesh clung in fetid lumps to his skeletal countenance, the sunken dead eyes ringed with black flickered with an unnatural animation like corpse candles, wispy entrails of once lustrous ebony hair clung to rauls slimy green skull like leeches clinging to flesh, the regulator drew back what remained of his lips over his death like smile, his two silver fangs glowering like daggers.

Uther relinquished his grip upon the fiend aghast in horror at his putrid features and stumbled backwards as Saul let out a vile cackle seeing the look of sheer terror dart across Uthers face, he clawed at Uthers hand to claim back his ring, but the warlock closed his hand fast for even in his shocked state Raul was no match for uther physically, failing to pluck back his trinket Raul was enraged “And so warlock it begins” he spat venomously hurling a bolt of violet light towards Uthers chest.

Throwing up his arm in deflection uther curtailed the blow for he wielded the ring of enchanted shadow speak, Raul let out a vicious cry of anger at this defeat and turned to face his pair of cohorts as they reeked towards the inns inhabitants and screeched “release your horror on these peasants” shadow winders!

Patrons screamed as they tried to scatter into corners, beneath tables or anywhere they could find to escape the approaching terrors, the winders floated above the floor, thick billows of violet smoke swirled beneath their fusty cerements like the writhing coils of a snake slithering onwards to devour its prey.

The warlock had to act fast! “ACCELERATE” he bellowed summoning forth the power of the blazing flames within the hearth, a roaring curtain of flame shot up the chimney burning with an unseen fury as it exited the grate and entered the tavern to engulf the warlock within its ravenous flames, defiant in his rage Uther erupted into an ominous and foreboding stature within the infernos heart, throwing out his arms as he incanted in Flamesword, "*Reveal to me hidden intent, unmask the cohorts that have been sent!*"

The blaze engulfing the warlock raged like a blistering inferno upon this command issuing forth an intense crimson radiance which penetrated the cloaks of the regulators shadow winders, hungrily it advanced toward the mildewed monsters rendering them to charred dust upon the ground, for they were naught but enchanted cloaks summoned for fear.

At this the regulator span round in fury, "how dare you warlock upon this tavern i shall unleash my wrath" he spat back vindictively, Rauls hell hound arose and advanced towards Uther growling savagely, noxious salivations dripped from its rank fangs, "ANIMATE" hissed the regulator in shadow speak.

The dusty remains of the shadow winders began to shift, swirling and winding up into the air like a zephyr, the swirling vortex wove its spinning torrent of sorcery to forge life from ashes, The regulator laughed sickeningly as he ascended into the air, the tavern and its occupants fell still and silent seeing that the spell had been cast, Uthers blood ran cold as he beheld what stood before him.

Two creatures created entirely of volava glared mockingly at Uther through their pure yellow eyes, barbed antlers as black as pitch protruded out from their foreheads like oversized thorns, whilst their volcanic forms smouldered with vehemence, the penetrable heat made Uthers eyes sting and his skin burn beneath their presence, the warlock shuddered, he felt compelled to stare but at the same time he wanted to break his gaze, he felt as though he had been bound by some bewitchment, that the creatures had commanded for he should behold their glorious form and succumb to their ordainment.

These creatures did not have feet like men but stood upon hairy paws like the beasts of the field, razor sharp ebony claws jutted out through their long finger tips like wicked implements of torture, smoke circled their forms half concealing their smouldering skin, but uther noted that it was engraved an intricate pattern of swirls and circles representing the earthly pit of fire and force from whence they had been conjured, Rauls depraved laugh resounded around the walls of the inn as he alighted beside his snarling beast, all eyes in the Oxen and Plough turned in pure terror to behold a spectacle not seen for a thousand moons, the Valanthians….

The warlock stood frozen to the spot as the Valanthians approached, as though he were viewing this event through another person's eyes as he struggled to move in a vain hope to free himself, but alas it was hopeless his legs failed him turning to mush as his heart pounded hard within his chest, the warlock felt his blood coarse throughout his veins in the painful reminder that he was well and truly alive and awake and that he was not trapped in the throes of some terrible nightmare, a scorched odour befouled the tavern coupled with an oppressive heat as the Valanthians drew up level with Uther, Saul stood watching this spectacle with glee as he stroked his malicious hound Zoltar with a diabolic reverence.

The creatures reached out their talon clad hands and grasped the warlock roughly by the arms branding his flesh as they transported him to another time and place and inn fell silent behind them leaving the patrons at the merciless intent of the regulator and his minion.

THE MINES OF ANGOR

The warlock blinked hard adjusting his eyes to the smouldering gloom, where in Anwens name was he? Stumbling upon the loose volcanic rocks he grappled for a foot hold, jets of dust and singing ashes spewed forth into the air riding upon bursts of noxious gases, choking clouds of sweltering torment invaded Uthers eyes and lungs like red hot pollen blinding his vision and making him wretch as he gagged for breath amid the overpowering stench, the warlock gloomily surveyed his surroundings in sheer bewilderment he stood atop an immense valley of burning volava, the valanthians had spirited him into the centre of the terra, to be encased in a fiery earthen prison where Anwen did not radiate down from the heavens, only the silvery glimmer of rock formations glinted back in the intense fire light, cautiously Uther backed away from the mouth of the precipice into the cavern behind him, there was no sign of the valanthians, he must gather his thoughts a moment, how was he to escape this quandary.

The warlock crouched down upon the hot stony ground, wringing his hands together in wretchedness, how could he fall into such a trap? As he did so he felt a band upon his finger, looking down in puzzlement he noticed that rauls ring was still upon his hand, how could this be, surely the fiend would of had his cohorts claim it back, or was this a further part kalthors diabolical plans.

Uther reached down into the pocket of his britches and pulled out a wand carved out of thick briar, it had been a present from his friend freyja when they were just children, he had carried it upon him ever since as a reminder of those childhood days, It was a beautiful trinket to behold small resplendent diamonds jutted out from the wands body in the place of thorns, he gazed upon their shiny facets in adoration, Suddenly a thought occurred to him, i wonder, he mused to himself turning the wand between his fingers, dare he risk it he would be mortified if it broke the briar. "Well Uther it is a vain hope, but your only one at this time" he said quietly to himself.

The warlock held up the wand and incanted "RADIANCE" he waited for a moment as the burning letters issued forth from his lips flickered upon the air, but nothing seemed to be happening, apprehensively he examined the briar holding his breath lest the briar should shatter, patience he told himself as he diligently observed the thorny trinket, After a moment or two a slow and steady dim glow emerged within the tiny facets like a miniature lantern, Uthers heart skipped a beat, dare he hope, A cautious smile began to spread across the warlocks features gradually growing brighter in unison with the glimmering thorns until ultimately both the crystals and Uthers face glowed with a brilliant radiance, "Boy am i glad about that", he laughed, i knew there must be a reason i always carry that with me" laughed Uther with a great sense of relief, At least now i can explore my whereabouts and map a possible escape, he thought to himself as he arose to sand from his crouched position, The warlock stretched out his weary limbs in fatigue, it had been a long hot day at the forge followed by the skirmish at the Oxen and Plough, and now this, well it's just about rounded it off, thought uther cynically.

After gathering his bearings for a moment or so, the warlock decided he had best make haste, and stepped from the earthen cavern on to a large stone which crumbled beneath his boot with a dull crunch.

I had better get a look at the continuity of my footings he thought to himself as he stumbled clumsily like a tottering elder, stooping down Uther introduced the radiant Citrine light upon the cavernous floor, peering down the warlock shuddered, what it had revealed was not a welcoming sight, his hair stood up on end as a chill crept over his spine to freeze his only ray of hope like the frosts of winter within its reapers embrace, the warlock swallowed hard as his gut threatened to expel the contents of that eves supper, he gasped in angst at what lay before him, for the floor of the cavern was thickly littered with bones and human skeletons like a sepulchres carpet of death, he must have been sighted in a catacomb or necropolis uther reasoned to himself against the horror of his surroundings as yet another ancient skull crunched beneath his boot.

The warlock decided to head towards the dark hidden confines of the chasm which lay out of sight, for behind flowed a monumentus river of lava, it was far too sweltering for him to even entertain the thought of looking for an escape route that way, he would be rendered to ashes within moments, not even flames word would save him from that there were special charms and preparations to be made before you could even begin to try and harness the tempestuous fury of molten volova.

Wading calf deep through the bones Uther journeyed forward through his macabre surroundings, after what seemed like an eternity of stumbling over rocks and crunching bones the warlock attentions were suddenly distracted by a golden glint upon the floor which caught the corner of his eye, what was that, he wondered to himself turning back on himself to scan the floor a glint caught his eye, Uther squatted over the pile of glowering bones and lowered down his wand for a better view, "AHA, i see it!" he proclaimed reaching down amongst the skeletal remains.

A golden torque bangle glistened upon the bony wrist of one of the chasms deceased inhabitants, Uther eyed it quizzically "Perhaps i shouldn't remove it it's desecration" he reasoned to himself, "Well this poor soul no longer needs it" his inner voice argued, "I better discover if it holds any bewitchments first" he said aloud to himself as he battled with his conscience, " Enchantments reveal what you may conceal" Uther incanted in Flamesword, The warlock waited a while eyeing the treasure nervously before deciding it must just be a trinket, "well it appears safe, let's have a better look!" he announced calmly.

"SUMMON" he chanted not wishing to touch his bony victim to retrieve the treasure, The metal glinted beautifully as the bangle transfigured into his palm, Uther inspected the prize closely it sure was alluring to the eye an ornate plaited bangle of rare gold inscribed with Dwarven runes which even he could not decipher.

The warlock polished the torque up on his grimy britches before turning it over in his hands, he gazed admirably upon its shining metal fa-cade as the fires below glistened upon its golden surface, he then placed it upon his wrist triumphantly, "well it won't hurt, its owner no longer needs it" he exclaimed in defence, but little did the warlock know that someone hidden had been listening in, “I THINK NOT THIEF” came the rasping challenge.

Duir the oak Solomon pendle and Wilbur

Uther looked up startled by this unexpected reply, only to be met with a cruel blow to the temple from the hilt of a broad sword, “AARGHH” he exclaimed in protest, having been taken totally unawares by his challenger, The warlock had been oblivious to his surroundings bewitched by the beauty of the torque bracelet as he coveted it, he had not detected his enemies arrival until he had plundered the curio, Uther reeled upon the floor the sweet taste of his own blood graced his lips as the thick scarlet liquid trickled down his cheek intruding his vision as it painted it’s blood red water colour, he had been rendered handicapped and vulnerable to attack by an un-seen assailant, SMACK! Uther rolled away just in time as the flat of a broad sword caught him hard on the back knocking the wind out of him, Another blow like that and he would be dispatched, he thought to himself in panic.

The warlock summoned up what little breath resided within his lungs and bellowed “DISARM” in Flamesword, HE MUST GET UP! The warlock battled with the agony of his flesh as he desperately clawed at the ashen ground to heave himself up onto his knees, faltering he stumbled as he arose unsteadily to his feet, The gushing head wound that he had procured throbbed painfully as he fought to master consciousness, woozily he wiped the blood from his eyes with the back of his soiled hand, the warlock swooned stum-bling once more upon the unsteady footings as he regarded his counterpart through bloody hues, “What trickery has befallen me?” he stated in sheer disbelief seeing the opponent that stood before him.

The warrior appeared a formidable force indeed, how could the warlock kill a thing that was already dead?, The bangle was his and he would not relinquish it now, A warrior of bone observed the warlock through hollow orbits, wearing a vacant skeletal mask of death, it seemed to emanate anger at being snatched back from the blissful peace of the grave to guard a mere trinket, it's bony form appeared like a grim reminder to the warlock of his plight stripped of its mortality like an onus of what lies in wait for us all, Uther reached down for his dagger "little use this will be" he thought pessimistically as he tried to square up to his opponent, the skeletal warrior let out an intimidating scream of conflict before charging headlong at the warlock, Uther gripped the hilt of his dagger for grim death sending his knuckles white as he waited for the opportune moment.

The fiend was nearly upon him now, he could hear the sickening grind of bone as they drew up level, Uther ducked quickly beneath his opponent and thrust his dagger upwards into the skeletons ribcage severing the vertebrae of his gruesome challenger with a foul crunching noise, hastily the warlock flung the bony carcass asunder into the river of volava that flowed behind him, he watched victoriously as it disintegrated into all but a mere fizzle of a flame atop the scorching currents surface, "That was close indeed!" he announced to himself in relief and sheer exhaustion as he collapsed unconscious in a heap upon the dusty floor of the cavern, this evenings events so far had taken their toll upon the warlock rendering him completely oblivious to the silent intrusion of dwarves that had entered the void, Uther slowly began to institute the first stirring's of consciousness as his eyelids flickered open into harsh reality.

"How peculiar, i feel as though i am elevated!" he thought to himself to himself, he attempted to move his foot but it would not budge, looking down towards his feet he discovered that he was shackled in chains and being carried aloft on a wooden stretcher,

“He stirs Morath” said one of the entourage of dwarves in gruff guttural tones like the grinding of rocks, Uther heard Morath reply, “Alright Gorlan I’ll see to it, place him down”

The warlock hit the floor with a thud awakening the throbbing of his wounded head, Uther squinted in the half light at the approaching dwarf, a stout little fellow sturdy as a boulder with skin the colour of earth, he was barely visible beneath his vast auburn tresses and beard, Morath regarded his catch for a moment through his dark hazel eyes, then addressed Uther, “Warlock, my name is Morath, and i am king of the inner mountain realms, my troops and i intend you no harm.”, Uther was very pleased to hear this, but puzzled, “Why then is it that i am shackled my friend?” he questioned Morath.

The dwarf rubbed his beard thoughtfully for a moment or two then added, “For your own protection and ours, we thought you may struggle” laughed Morath as he began unfastening Uthers shackles, Morath was now in full view allowing the Warlock to catch a better view of his would be captor, the dwarf stood no higher than Uthers waist, broad and stout in stature, his thick dun coloured hide tautly encased his prominent muscles, Moraths features lay buried beneath his copious moustache and beard which he wore fashioned in braids, interwoven with small intricate golden beads, his hazel eyes observed Uther back, for he sure was a sorry sight to behold, Morath’s thick bushy tresses flowed down to the dwarves waist gleaming in hues of red to mirror the crackling flames of the abyss, Morath secured it in a thick braid which reached right down to his belt, his garb was a thick leather jerkin tailored from oxen hide and ornately fashioned with golden studs, worn over a pair of patchwork leather britches elaborately embroidered with golden thread.

The king of the mountain realms donned a wide knot work belt forged from three hues of gold strapped about his ample middle to announce his status, as such lavish metalwork could only have been forged for a king, the magnificent belt retained a majestic iron axe which hung from a thick metal ring, dwarven runes were embellished upon its two blades, the weapon named Aks flashed in the half-light like lightning.

Uther was impressed by the legality emanated by Moraths raiment's, he delicately rubbed at the sore rope burns upon his wrists, curiously Uther questioned Morath about their destination, "To where am i being taken?" he asked inquisitively, "We are taking you to the hall of our ancestors, it lies east through the pass of the mines of Angor, for you wear a great treasure of our race upon your wrist, and for centuries we had feared that it was lost to us" Morath replied earnestly, 'What this simple gold torque, here take it then" said Uther as he tried removing the cuff, but alas to his astonishment it would not budge!

Morath laughed heartily in reply to Uther generous gesture, "as you see it is not that simple Warlock" he stated, "you did not choose it, it chose you my friend, upon your arm rests the trinket of Velah, we have searched far and wide across many perilous domains to recover it" he finished, "Now that is a tale worth telling" added the dwarf named Gorlan, "And tell it i shall Gorlan fear not for it is a tale once told that is never forgotten." said Morath sincerely.

"We shall rest a while Gorlan, and let our friend here recover his strength and take some sustenance " stated Morath as he released a waterskin from his belt.

“Here warlock let us drink of hidden discoveries and new found alliances” said the king of the mountain realms handing the skin over to Uther, “To hidden discoveries and new found alliances” toasted Uther wearily holding the bursting water skin to his arid lips, the sweet liquor trickled down the back of his parched throat like a welcoming kiss of ambrosia to his desolate mouth, The warlock drank his fill before handing the bulging skin over to Gorlan who repeated the pledge, “Thank you both, the drink flavours like the sap of the gods and yet the skin does not deplete.” Uther declared in thankful surprise, “It is an enchanted Elven skin, i won it in an axe contest with the elves” said Morath, “Aye that you did, i can still remember the look upon their faces even now” laughed Gorlan heartily, “It contains rejuvenating Honeyblossom wine warlock” he added passing the skin back over to his ruler.

The king of the mountain realms took a long draught of liquor, when he had taken his fill he wiped the back of his hand across his mouth and let out a gratified sigh signalling to all that his thirst had been quenched, “And Now for that tale” he proclaimed…..

‘THE GOLDEN CUFF OF VELAH

Gorlan set about unpacking provisions from his back pack whilst morath eyed the warlock with a sense of anticipation, would he make good his escape once the secrets of the cuff had been revealed, to him or would he stay and help them? considered the dwarf, well they would have to risk it, thought Morath, the warlock would soon become lost in this underground realm should he try to escape.

He began to speak, 'many centuries ago, in these mines dwelt a mighty serpent named velah he was fierce and ruthless in manner devouring all who dared to enter his kingdom the domains of Angor, where we are seated now, our ruler Gordhan hungered after the rich seams of magical coppers that run through this place, so he sent scores of his champions down here, but one after another they were all devoured by Velah, hence the carpet of bones which litters the earth beneath our boots, each one of these grisly remnants was once a dwarvian champion, Uther listened intently his attention now fixed upon the dwarf and his tale of old, he had seen draco as a child with the experience in knightshade forest with aquaria the torrent, and the shard of flint, many images flashed through the warlocks head of anguished dwarves battling a mighty serpent of fire.

Morath continued, finally after many cycles of defeat Gordran commissioned his high enchanter to fashion a shackle to control the dragon cast in gold, it was rumoured to be fashioned from the golden scales of the fallen Draco, god of all dragons, he sent his finest knight Mathryl down into these very mines to cast the shackle upon the beast rendering him docile, but alas Mathryl never returned and the bracelet was lost to our race,

He wanted to shackle velah to mine the magical copper that dwells here, once fashioned into a blade it will slay all evils unto mankind, one kiss of its glinting edge is all that is needed to restore harmony to the earth and wipe out this befoul sickness which enslaves the land, The warlocks heart skipped a beat at this new revelation before unheard to him, could it be?..no surely not!

The tale continued…"it is rumoured that he who holds the bracelet is the one who shall forge the blade of power to sully the malevolent overlord and his army of dervishes, and his counterpart shall wield the staff of knowledge that heals all man and beast the two combined shall send draco back to his heavenly abode creating a utopian constellation once more, as told in the tablets of Angor.' finished Morath dramatically.

Uther mind raced with apprehension, had the gods chosen him for this task, and who was his counterpart to be?, one thing was for certain he must conquer the serpent velah and procure the magickal copper Mithralite! for it was the only sure way to turn Raul and Kalthors evil regime upon its tail, how fortunate it would be to cast this evil blade of shadows in the virtuous mineral, A wide smile spread across Uthers face as he considered the possibilities that lay before him, an optimistic twist in the tail of terror that he had been commissioned to unravel, he would forge Kalthors volova weapon but with a twist, it would be enchanted with flamesword runes beneath the shadow speak, and he Uther would assist the dwarves to find this mithril copper and forge an armournents from flamesword, he would have to make haste to complete the forging before beginning Kalthors commission.

Morath regarded Uthers expression with puzzlement, why it looked as though he was smiling at their plight, "what brings jest to you my friend' he questioned the warlock in a gruff tone, "Why i think i may have just the answer to both of our problems, let us talk of my latest commission" Uther propositioned Morath.

And so together the trio drew up their strategy of alliance to overthrow and conquer the evil invasion that had for so long spread its infected campaign of hate, kalthor and Raul would reign no more, uther had forgotten the ring upon his finger it was there by no accident, the red stone pupil blinked as raul observed their conversation through his obsidian scrying stone.

THE TRIUMPH OVER VELAH

The task of winning over the dragon and travelling the mines of Angor would not been an easy one that was for sure worried Uther as he lay awake that night, that mighty serpent of fire would surely be tempestuous to say the least.

Dawn arose outside the mines, Morath, Gorlan and the warlock journeyed toward the hall of the ancestors, unaware of all time they trod the gloomy passage deep within the caverns, endlessly they travelled the dark tunnels over bone crunching scores of gordrans ill-fated champions, their only light set by the flickering torches of the dwarves and Uthers glowing briar, water trickled down the walls casting a glistening facade as it highlighted rich seams of Mithralite, jagged stalagmite teeth threatened to close in around the three travellers as they ventured ever deeper into the mouth of the serpents lair.

The warlock felt that he would go mad as he forever travelled blindly in the darkness like some worm wriggling through the earth.

Upon the seventh day of wandering uther became restless and frenzied stating that he had heard a voice in his head rasping and whispered, the dwarves Morath and gorlan wondered if this was further trickery at rauls hand as Uther still held his ring?

The further that they wound on down into the abyss the louder that the voice became, it chanted, "*Metal ore, copper and gold, these bones do your tale unfold, the closer that you draw to me, you'll manifest your reverie*"

Uther repeated this aphorism over and over again as if he had been bewitched, the dwarves tried to divert his attention but alas it was to no avail for still he continued to recite the sinister rhyme, "what shall we do with him sire" gorlan had asked Morath "leave him be there may yet be a reason for this madness" replied the under realm king in a concerned tone.

Dwarves and trolls were hard to bewitch for it was rumoured that all they could hear were the clashing of boulders inside their dense skulls, oblivious to the rasping voice controlling uther they journeyed on, as they rounded a curve in the passage a fork in the tunnel came into view, "which way shall we take?" questioned gorlan, Morath was just about to answer when the warlock announced, "*To the left lies the labyrinth, dare you to venture there, to the right lies the crypt, your mortality to snare*"

The recital caused an icy shudder to creep up the spine of the two dwarves, "well that decides it then" stated morath, "I've no desire to go right, let us take our chance in the labyrinth" he added, Gorlan gave a dread expression and fingered his axe nervously, "aye let us venture on the left path then".

They followed the warlock as he stumbled off up the left fork tripping over his feet as he chanted under his breath, the underground gloom grew a little brighter as they reached the entrance of the left branch, the torches flickered and water dripped from the stalagmites onto the faggots, "better watch that" commanded Morath as he heard gorlan hiss in annoyance at the damp conditions, a stark change from the arid over chambers running through the volcano.

The underground chasm was as still and silent as the tomb and the air hung oppressive and menacing, as if something were waiting to happen, the trio stepped forward into the labyrinth, where a vile stench of Sulphur greeted their nostrils, The dwarf king held aloft his torch to get a better look at their surroundings, "What on earth" he questioned himself for the labyrinth was made of thick stone walls, who or what had hauled all that stone down here in the damp dark earth, the walls were carved with swirling patterns and geometric designs this puzzled morath even further, gorlan just looked bewildered and as for uther he was in a world of his own.

It was then that they felt it, a gust of hot sulphureous air collided at speed down the passage towards them, it hit them like an onslaught knocking them off their feet and extinguishing their torches, casting them into total darkness.

"Everyone ok?" asked morath fearfully, "aye sire, not sure about him though" replied Gorlan, "*She whistles and she blows, but where she hides no one knows*" laughed Uther manically, "this just gets better" said gorlan cynically.

Picking themselves up off the stone floor the dwarves felt around in the dark like a couple of morrows as they ran their calloused hands across the stony walls attempting to get their bearings, uther on the other hand had no problem he seemed to be being led on by some unknown force, "i vote we follow the warlock sire, we can't lose him that easily you can hear his insane ramblings half a mile off" gorlan offered, "good idea, and it does seem to be our only plan, even if it does lead us to disaster there is a reason for his strange behaviour somewhere, for after all let us not forget that he is the warlock my friend" agreed Morath.

"*Come follow me my merry fellows, let us meet the queen of bellows, For in the labyrinth she hides, Draco's comely flaming bride.*" sang uther in a jestful tone, 'I'm beginning to grow a little weary of these mirthless sonnets" protested gorlan as he ambled blindly along behind the troubadour, they trudged aimlessly on for a suns turn tripping and falling as they met each bend and fork in the maze, throwing their senses off guard and disorientating them even more as if they had been spun round in endless circles.

"I wish he would stop for a while i need a rest" protested gorlan, "aye he can't carry on for much longer that's for sure" agreed Morath, at this Uther suddenly fell silent, You've gone and done it now laughed gorlan, but his leader didn't laugh back in return, for up ahead a fiery surge came into view. "*At the labyrinths heart, dwells the queen of flames, bow down in reverence and announce your names, lest she roast you like a flank of game*"

"I don't like the sound of that one Morath" shuddered Gorlan in trepidation, Morath remained silent as the serpent queen left her lair.

Velahs fiery silhouette came into view, her shadow blazed across the cavern walls like an infernal beacon of terror as she steadily advanced, the air grew arid and scorched with the blistering heat of her form as the mighty dragon closed in upon the travellers, the foul scraping of her claws upon the flagged stones befouled the air striking fear into the dwarves hearts.

Uther stood stark still staring ahead in awe, what manner of beast was this he questioned, his senses had returned all too suddenly as velah released her mental grip upon him now that he had aided her in delivering her quarry straight to her den, Uther beheld the consuming brute blocking their path and swallowed hard, "RUN" shouted Gorlan turning tail and fleeing back down the trail, but Morath and Uther stood their ground, they needed that Mithralite and Velah must be conquered even if it meant their demise, retreat would be futile and their long arduous journey would have all been in vain, Billows of hot sulphureous flames jettied down the passage as Velah snorted her discontent at the intruders, even if she had led them here after all.

Velah had sought to control the warlocks thoughts when she had been alerted to his presence two suns ago, entry into his mind had been easy what with her being the princess of flames and him having flamesword scorched into the very recesses of his consciousness, she had not however been conscious of the dwarves presence, still it was of little matter they would join their ancestors soon enough.

The dragon had learned of the warlocks quest for the mithralite and what need he had for it, she could easily weigh this to her advantage and obtain that dreaded shackle, or so called cuff of velah, an allegiance with the warlock could be a wise move if he were to defeat the tyrannous monarch she thought to herself, and still if not she would render him to ashes and claim the cuff by force, what did she care about the lives of men, for once upon a time she had been passionate about life and men, a certain man by the name of Maleusius, and little good that had done her, for he had betrayed her and turned her into this form.

Uther awaited their demise as the powerful queen approached, holding his breath uther rested his hand upon the hilt of his sword, little good it would do him though, he thought to himself, Morath held his axe in readiment for the onslaught to begin, but much to their Suprise the dragon did not attack but instead she spoke aloud to them.

"Greetings Morath, king of the under realms and mighty Warlock Uther, i do not wish to engage in combat this day, for i have forged a link with uthers mind and your intentions are pure of heart, you wish only to obtain the mithralite to conquer the evil overlord and his regulator, this too would please me greatly indeed, i have your Mithralite in exchange for the Ring of Shadow speak and The cuff for which i have my own reasons, i offer you an allegiance, let me firstly tell you my tale"

The armed duo relinquished the hold upon their weapons and Uther replied, "nor do we wish a fight either for it has been a long and arduous journey, we would greatly welcome a truce, but firstly pray do tell us your tale and then we shall discuss terms of our fealty." to which Morath nodded his agreement and laid down his weapon in front of him, uther followed in fashion laying down his sword beside it, Velah smiled if it can be said that dragons smile, and began her tale of love and treachery to her encaptivated audience of two.

Once upon a time she had been queen Velah a handsome red haired woman and spouse to Maleusius the monarch of the kingdom, but he had become corrupt in his need for power studying ancient Magick and the dreaded shadow speak, she had begged him to see reason and change his ways, be grateful for all that he had which was mighty, but the viporous words burrowed down into his ether corrupting him into a foul beast in manner and appearance, for as his greed and hunger grew so did his contorted features with each act of malice that he performed against his fellow men.

Maleusius grew insane wishing to control the very heavens themselves, he gathered his council of seven enchanters, seers and sages commanding them to recite and cast the ritual of the shattering which would tear draco asunder from his celestial shackles and summon him before the king, the chamber grew heated in this debate, the prophets warned Maleusius that this act could only bring destruction and maleficence, only the kings chief enchanter Raul sought to obey his masters bidding, Six council members held a secret conclave with the queen Velah in hope to poison their monarch at her hand and save the kingdoms celestial and earthly.

To this she agreed and a plan was hatched she was to place night shade essence upon his silver crescent ring of shadow speak, for when this poison was absorbed through the skin it was swift and merciful, at the correct point in the ceremony of the shattering Velah would place the ring upon Maleusius finger, for who would he trust more than any other.

But little did they know that walls had ears, and Raul had screed the plot of his masters demise at Velahs hand, Raul hurried the news of this ill awaited fate to the king, and between the two of them Maleusius and his cohort hatched a diabolical plan or revenge for this intended treason, upon the night of the ritual all were called into the chamber of shadows within the mirrored tower of asgards observatory, Raul led the ceremony, the hearts of the other council members beat hard in fear for the act they were about to commit, little did they know that their best laid plans had been laid bare and contorted to the kings advantage.

As the summoning progressed wispy writhing tendrils of violet shadow-speak whispered malevolently inside the chamber, reflected in the mirrored facets of the chamber to amplify their potency, Queen Velah swallowed hard her heart in her mouth for the time was nigh for her part in the play, she was to place the ring of command upon Maleusius hand shattering asunder the heavens, and capturing Draco within Rauls circle of violet fire.

This must not come to pass she thought to herself in justification as her conscience battled with betraying her beloved spouse, timorously she stepped forward onto the glyph of draco and recited her part. "*Here in fire and shadows we stand, to cast down the celestial land, imprisoning Draco within this fiery band, we place the ring upon the masters hand*"

Maleusius removed his wedded band and placing it upon the black velvet cushion and offered Velah his ring finger, her heart thudded in fear for what she was about to perform and pain, how could he do such a thing, the final act set her heart in stone aiding her in her treacherous task, Velah held her breath as she slid the ring upon Maleusius finger, and the transfixed council held their breath in anticipation as they watched on in hope..

One, two, three, four, five, counted Velah under her breath with each thudding beat of their heart as she waited for the poison to act, "six, …why had nothing happened?

³6,;75$,7256´EHOORZHG0DOHXVLXVWULXPSKDQW O\WKH council looked on aghast with fear, for they had all failed and the monarch knew of their plot so it seemed, how was this so, it could only be one reason and one alone, Raul, 'My dear" the king gestured to his queen in a sardonic tone, "it seems that you wish to betray me, dispatch me even, in favour of your celestial god Draco, well ….SO BE IT!" he raged in anger, "Why i even have a gift for you Velah to bless your union, take my wedded band and pledge your troth." and with this Maleusius gripped Velahs wrist tightly and forcing his wedded band on to her trembling finger, he smiled spitefully as the ring constricted and bit down into Velahs finger drawing a circlet of blood, Maleusius dragged the whimpering queen over to the circle of violet fire, he forcibly held up her wounded hand allowing four drops of blood to splash upon the circle, pushing her hard into the circle he laughed as the sphere closed in.

Velah tried to flee from her fiery jail, but alas the flames spread out into a blazing violet sphere, The council of the watch trembled in fear for they knew what was coming, Raul began the incantation in the foul tongue of shadow speak.

"*Draco we summon thee from the sky, through indigo flames you shall fly, A fiery bride awaits your lionize, to rest forever at your side*"

The violet wisps and tendrils of contorted words snaked upon the air weaving their portent they cast a maelstrom to greet the violet flames of the sphere, a blistering indigo inferno consumed Velah ravaging her mortal form with merciful speed, amid much shrieking and wailing from the council, "SILENCE" ordered Maleusius venomously, Raul observed laughing manically as the raging flames grew down to all but a flicker revealing the transfigured Queen in their wake, for trapped within the sphere loomed a vast and horrific sight, The once beautiful queen Velah had been transformed into a huge serpent of flames, all that remained of her once striking features was the colour of her form, red and copper flames licked and blazed like a distant echo of her lustrous tresses, A huge tear welled up in the beasts eye threatening to spill over into steam as she observed the world anew.

"My dear you certainly look ravishing today" taunted Maleusius pitilessly, then continued, "Now what have we here?, the six traitors of the council of the watch, what to do with you, let me see, spat the king venomously, "Well you had certainly been loyal in my service until now, i should hate to lose your services, it seems that we may have new 'openings' for you all" laughed Maleusius sardonically, With this Raul aimed a violet jet of light at the council, it raced through the air and bound them tightly within its noose like embrace, the sorcerer tugged at the line with his finger, laughing in glee as the helpless companions were tugged off their feet in unison, Maleusius cohort beckoned to them, his finger pulled the binding line of sorcery closer towards him with each tug, When the trembling prophets were inches from his cruel grasp he shrieked, gestured a throw towards the sphere casting the line of six elders to their fate amongst the consuming flames, "*Six traitors do we cast in stone, bequest draco from his celestial throne, i cast them to the shadow realm, to govern our armies at the helm*" The six seers were rendered to ash as the flames engulfing them created the first dust dervishes over the shadow realms to command and oversee Maleusius and Raul's abhorrent legions that would follow them there, celestially Draco roared a fiery blaze of anger as he shimmered onto his golden glyph, and the heavens shattered asunder as he plummeted to his cavern beneath the terrain OF knightshade forest.

But that was now aeons ago, And Velah though fearsome in form was not the beast she often portrayed, a human heart still beat within her mighty breast, she would strike a bargain with the King of the Under realms and the warlock named Uther, Draco must be released from his shackles and returned to the heavens, and the repugnant overlord that was her husband Maleusius must be dethroned from his campaign of terror, too long had he dwelled within that earthly form, shadow Magicks had taken their toll upon his appearance, creating the foul beast that lingered between the two worlds, why even Raul had perished and ruled in the realm of shadows a between worlds cadaver, commanding the six elders of the council and the ever growing legions of darkness.

She would offer the mithralite in exchange for the cuff and Maleusius ring which Uther had taken from Raul, for when the king had cast her into the sphere the ring had withered his hand with the potency of the Magick he had summoned, the ring had then passed to the sorcerer Raul, who Maleusius had appointed to govern his campaign for the ring controlled and harnessed the dead realms releasing the foul tongue of shadow speak into this world, to claim diabolical inheritance over all who used it.

The overlord had all but forgotten about his draconian queen festering down here in the bowels of the earth, as he controlled the realms towards his twisted ends, but the pure and true mithralite would banish his diabolical deeds sure and true, Mithralite was rumoured to be the very blood of the planet herself its healing properties were legendary.

One blow struck home at the hand of a true champion would dispatch the evil duo and return Velah to her true form once the cuff was placed upon Maleusius withered wrist, And so was struck the Guild of Virtue.

KALTHORS CONSIGNMENT

Three seasons had passed since Uther had received his commission from the regulator Raul, and rumours were rife that the warlock was dead, for as yet no weapon had been delivered to Kalthor, Raul however had kept quiet about the warlocks encounter with the valanthians at his hand,

Kalthor had granted the warlock a lunar cycle to deliver his consignment and many cycles had since passed, uther had not heard tell of any conflict yet against thygorshire from the tyrannous monarch, luckily they had been idle threats, but why had Raul sought to render him to valanthia was the regulator working under his own counsel to overthrow kalthor, for without the blade of shadows his campaign could not continue, greed must be driving him towards treachery, still uther didn't care it played in his favour that he had delivered to Velah to forge the mithralite blade to dispatch his ruler malesius and overthrow Kalthor and his troops, Uther would soon put a stop to them both, he could not wait to see Rauls face when he arrived to deliver the sword to kalthor, the moment would indeed be his!

The king Kalthor had surely been unaware of Morath and the cuff of velah, but it had worked to Uther and the dwarves advantage for they had gained a fierce and mighty ally in the dragon of Angor, and he still held Raul's crescent ring upon his finger should he need it.

Velah had helped him to forge the blade of shadows in shadow speak from the volova, she had bound vengeance and hidden incantations to corrupt its power that only she knew, for she was there in the beginning when draco had crashed asunder, she incanted the tongue of shadow speak as she breathed her fiery flames upon the volova, entwining the sorcery within the metals form, it was well hidden incantations, the dwarf king Morath had assisted with his forge in the mines of Angor, the commission for Kalthor was completed, and now Uther had set about the task of the mithralite blade of virtue.

The warlock stood amidst the ruin he had created, the Mithralite ore bubbled and smouldered amidst the volcano, the blades mould was cast and the molten ore was smelted and ready for pouring, Uther grabbed the crucible with his tongs and began to forge the sword of virtue that would ensnare Kalthor and his motley band of cohorts, Driving home the hammer upon the red hot blade he incanted, "*Armor piercing, Blade of blue, Strike home only, Those untrue*"

Pendle and freyjas farm cat gobblers

The so named blade of virtue would not strike a killing blow to anyone save for the unjust, happy with the blades shape the warlock plunged the glowing metal in to a vat of blessed water, it boiled furiously throwing tumultuous billows of steam as the Mithralite cooled, the air fizzed with the potent charge of raw magic, when this was done he would set to work on kalthors blade for the consignment from volova a double pronged task.

The heat and fumes were making Uther feel sleepy, strange visions crept up on him in his dream like state, all around the barren land had been lain to waste, once pure spring water festered in stagnant pools spreading disease and pestilence, the villagers were crying, and the beasts of the field lay still, farmers crops failed, and death hang imminent on a massive scale due to starvation or plague, suddenly a colourful flash burs across the horizon as the scenery changed into another picture.

A tall red haired woman stood amongst a grove of oaks wielding an oaken stave its knotted sinews were woven as all the colours of the rainbow entwined together as one, She stepped forward from her wooded enclosure into the picture of despair, as she did so her footfalls sprang forth new growth as the land became healed beneath her shadow.

The warlock himself stood atop the Temple Of The Anwen, holding a shard that he recognized from the caves beneath his Fathers farm, then just as quickly the vision faded away blending back into the sweltering reality of the volcanoes inner realms, Uther wondered if the magical fumes had gone to his head or, perhaps it was the herbs he had used, or maybe it was just the heat down here, but what he did know was that he sure needed a good rest, He felt an overwhelming sense of accomplishment as he admired his handiwork, the blade of virtue glinted mercilessly against the fire light as the Mithralite burned in copper hues like a spirit of fury that it would unleash itself upon malesius, kalthor and his evil regulator.

The flamesword runes smouldered like whispering tongues of fire across the blades edge as they burrowed unseen down into the mithralite inlaying their hidden mantra of righteousness, he Wrapped the sword of virtue inside a woollen cloth concealing it beneath his britches the warlock made good his leave with the two blades.

THE DELIVERANCE

The keep at Khymer was the best part of a day's ride away on horse-back it would be a dawn start for Uther, he endeavoured to retire early to get a good night's rest once he had retired back to the halls of Morath, after eating his supper of bread, cheese and ale, he, entered the bath house and took an icy plunge into the pool of Elgard, the chilly waters washed away the heat and strains of Uthers laborious day as it embraced his skin within icy rawness, the warlock washed down with a dark orange foaming flower which grew by the water's edge, grimy bubbles floated across the water's surface as he submerged to rinse off the day's toil, Uther shivered as he arose from the pool, he dressed quickly into his clean garments and wandered off to find Morath.

Winding through the labyrinth of passages he eventually Arrived at the outer hall, the dwarven king was sure to be here awaiting his arrival he thought as he knocked upon the golden doors, the sound reverberated into the vast cavern beyond as the warlock waited to be granted his entrance.

Footsteps rang out across the flagstones as Morath's counsel Dwergan headed towards the entrance, a teeth gritting grinding announced the drawing back of the bolts behind the door followed by a loud clunk as a key unlocked the huge mechanism unravelling the patterned locks guarding the chambers that lay within, Slowly and steadily the door swung inwards as the guards hauled their brute force against the might of the vast golden doors, Dwergan once more returned the key to his belt and bowed to the warlock, “Greetings Uther, Morath grants you entrance to our halls and invites you to dine with him this eve, he wishes to know what news have ye of the commission?” asked the elderly dwarf hopefully.

“The commission is sealed my friend” replied Uther triumphantly, “This is wonderful news, sire will be greatly pleased” added Dwergan merrily, “IT IS DONE, IT IS DONE!” called out the counsel as he hurried off to deliver the glad tidings, Uther gave a happy smile at the elderly dwarves sudden Vigor at the news, when the warlock reached the inner chamber it seemed the spirit of things was infectious, loud raucous cheers rang out echoing through the cavernous stone passages like an acoustic anthem of praise, it seemed that celebrations were already underway as the clan raised their flagon’s in toast to Uthers entrance.

Morath arose from his throne almost tripping upon his great trailing beard as he hurried to welcome Uther, the king of the under realms raced towards the warlock knocking him heftily to his knees as he slapped him heartily in the small of the back, “Dwergan has delivered the glad tidings that you have completed the commission, what say ye warlock?” boomed Morath in jubilation, “Aye it is true, the Sword of shadows is forged and the mithralite holds her secret true and steady, for the fealty of virtue stands tall beneath the shadows.” replied Uther gaily, “A banquet, a banquet!” proclaimed Morath in exaltation.

That eve a hearty banquet was held for the honour of triumph bestowed upon the warlock, laughter and merriment flowed like an infectious zeal to all that heard her, The Guild Of Virtue had been sealed and celebrated with much ale and back slapping, joy flowed through dwarf and warlock alike and for just a moment the world seemed a lighter place, and so this Positive energy seeped out into the misery drenched ethos which drank its fill like a parched animal, and within the wizened trunk of Myriddins ancestor Gwenhefayr the magical flower of arcadia started to bud as the heart of hope began to beat once more.

Moraths banquet of virtue danced merrily into the early hours like a band of drunken minstrels, Uther had drawn a skinful of ale and belly full of hog until till he felt his seams would burst! As the Anwen rose to kiss the horizon the birds serenaded her with their jubilant chorus of welcome, and the warlock headed off to the bed chambers.

Uthers plans of an early night had been in vain in return he had been granted an exuberant banquet of mirth, triumph, mead coursed through his being as he troubled over the long trek that lay ahead of him, and what skirmishes he would meet on his path to perdition as he delivered his quarry to The regulator Saul and his evil Overlord Kalthor, a warm and fretful night lacking in slumber plagued Uther like a pestilence as visions of a Firebird invaded his dreams, The feanyx smouldered and burned with the pure essence of red-hot flames crafting its own form and being, the beast spewed out searing hot jets of yellow and green flames to scorch and charr all that surrounded it, leaving in its wake a pile of ash and dust billowing beneath the shadow of its wings.

Devastation was wrought as the fearsome beast beat its infernal wings on its trail of annihilation, the churlish brute soared off overhead as it headed towards the jagged tower in the distance that jutted out to pierce the inky cloudless heavens like a rapier of torment, As the wing beats died away the swirling dust settled to sear its mark into the earth, Uthers dream self-watched the spectacle in horror as the cinders cast their token into the scorched terra, the symbol of a crescent moon.

Uther awoke that morning in a cold feverish sweat, he was drenched right down to the straw beneath him and back up through to the furs above, battling tiredness Uther protestingly roused into consciousness, his head still swam with the ale and mead he had consumed that morrow, His mind raced with troubled thoughts of the flaming feanyx, what did it signify and how would its interpretation play against his fate and the battle that lay ahead?, and there was still the problem of removing Velahs cuff from around his wrist he thought as it glinted against the flickering candle light, it must be released before i can place it upon the evil overlord.

The warlock vacantly washed the sleep from his eyes splashing the cool clear water against his furrowed brow he stared aimlessly in to space, Uther dressed more out of sheer habit and routine than the result of conscious thought then gathered a light meal of apples, bread and cheese, he filled his waterskins with honey blossom wine from Moraths elven skin, in preparation for the long journey ahead, he collected minstrels magic and rode out into the rising Anwen, the mist lay across the land with promise of a pleasant days ride ahead..

It was a season later that the warlock arrived at the Keep, the looming twin towers greeted him with their evil countenance, cutting against the sky like a knives edge, the pair of black foreboding towers jutted in to the sky like a knives edge as if to pierce the blood red sky, the keep was surrounded by a pitch forked fence impaled with ghastly troll and human heads upon its spikes like a constrictment of agonizing torment, Uther shuddered at the grisly spectacle and drew his snood up over his face to cover the fetid smell and the scores of swarming flies.

Khymers gatehouse was always posted by a pair of Great Troll sentry's armed with charged obsidian Polearms, its port cullis gave off the appearance of prison bars as if to say that once inside there was no escape, A foul moat surrounded the keeps circumference oozing slime bubbled in its depths like a pit of venomous snakes festering beneath its waters.

Upon approach Uther was greeted by the intense stench of insipid decay, his mount reeled back stamping his hooves in protest, rearing up almost unseating his faithful master, "Easy boy, it is just new to you, we will be fine, I will not let any harm befall upon you." said the warlock as they set out to Cross the moats rickety bridge.

Uther felt every clopping step resound in his ears like a fearful beat of his heart, as the wood protested splintering beneath them, he could overhear the jesting of the trolls as he advanced across the bridge, "Here comes our breakfast Faedale!" "An' our dinner all dressed in finery, some rich spoils that's a bonus 'ay Grafton?", Crossing their Pole-arms, the sentry Grafton raised his hand in a halting gesture and questioned "Hold, what business have you here? State quickly or be gone, or stay and face our wrath!"

"I am the Warlock Uther, I have a consignment for Kalthor and bring arms for your master! Is this not the keep of Khymer upon the Marsh?" said Uther, producing the rich purple felt bundle, carefully he unwrapped a corner to reveal the glimmer of volova beneath.

The greedy trolls eyes lit up in reverence, as they hungrily coveted the bundle "The Sword of Shadows" stated Faolan and held the mighty blade aloft, to catch the mornings gloom, it gleamed dark and menacing revealing the inner black-hearted fire enchantments that it wielded, Grafton was taken a back in awe. "That it be, we will let you through! Rise the Cullis" he ordered.

The rattle and clank of heavy chains, grated against the turning cog wheels as the cullis gate lifted, Uther nodded and rewrapped his offering as he rode through as the cullis to meet his confrontation, the cullis crashed down behind him with an imprisoning clunk, as Uther entered the keep goblins spewed out from every orifice, like maggots upon rotting meat, surrounding uther like a pestilence, "A Guide to the Keep do you need one silver piece is the price?" bargained a creature glaring at the warlock through its shifty yellow eyes, "Show me the way to Sauls Chambers." commanded Uther.

The loathsome beast went to grab the mounts reins causing the others to beat him away, none were willing to share the prize of this rich looking visitor, causing a brawl to break out in the forecourt, a flash of violet smoke announced Sauls arrival for he had seen the warlocks entrance in his obsidian glass, the cowering goblins scattered from their master and scuttled off back into the battlements as fast as they dared.

Where is my ring warlock? snarled the regulator as he slowly approached uther aided by an amethyst staff, his face lay shrouded beneath the pitch-black cerement that hid his ghastly visage, wisps of ebony hair escaped his hood to lick like venomous tendrils in the wind, Saul lifted his head toward the warlock and his eyes burned through uther like violet fire boring into his very soul depositing dread in their wake as he awaited the reply, “All in good time regulator” snapped The warlock, “I have been somewhat disposed what with my little sojourn to Valanthia” retorted Uther.

The regulator cackled in fiendish malice at this reply then added, “My overlord has long awaited your return, you are well overdue delivery of your consignment warlock, his anger is great at your failure, show me the blade of shadows for my own eyes”

The warlock unwrapped once more the violet wool to reveal but a flash of the hilt for the regulators satisfaction, Satisfied that Uther had concluded his task Raul continued, “fortunate for you that you carry the blade for i have been ordered to consign you to the dungeons, and a word of warning warlock it would not pay you to speak of valanthia for if you do so i shall render you to the oubliette, try no tricks warlock now follow me.” hissed Saul through his silver fangs as he hobbled slowly toward the overlords tower, whilst overhead an unseen messenger circled watching the events below intently.

The warlock seethed with repulsion longing to render the foul beast upon the blade of mithralite, but he must bide his time and effect the attack as planned, summoning all his self-control to rein in his anger, he nodded curtly at the regulator and took up the rein, as in the distance Solomon took to the wing.

THE WARLOCK AND THE OVATE

Freyja hoped with a heavy heart that she would be able to enlist the help of the Mighty warlock Uther, for if he chose to aid her and the villagers in their plight, he would be well repaid in ranking and honour by the order of the Anwen Druids for it was Unbeknown to Freyja that the Warlock was already plotting to take down the evil overlord and his motley band of cohorts, like a trojan horse with his Mithralite blade of shadows.

Equuleus hooves thundered underfoot as they approached the forest that surrounded the borders of Thygorshire into the county of Thygor itself, Freyja would try here first in Uthers home town perhaps folk had heard tell of his whereabouts what with him being local and all, Freyja slowed the mare down to a gentle trot as they met the forests edge, she ducked down to avoid the branches as they entered the tree line, the snapping of twigs and rustling of leaves alerted the forests inhabitants to their entrance, birds took flight and a den of rabbits scattered thumping their paws upon the ground in alert, their white tails bobbing off into the distance like little flags of surrender, Leaves whipped about on the gentle breeze as they tumbled down from the canopy overhead to meet their fate upon the littered foliage below.

The trees watched on, freyja yawned in her sleepy state, her sleep had been troubled that previous night and the ride had been long and hard to cover the distance of the counties, mindlessly she noted the rich fiery tones of the autumnal leaves as they frolicked before her, feeling more tired than ever she decided it was wise to make camp for an hour or two, poor equueleus deserved it at the very least she had galloped tirelessly since before dawn!

The ovate scanned around for a suitable spot to set up bivouac for an hour or two, noting two hazels closely aligned she steadied the mare to a gentle halt and dismounted, wearily she tethered the horse to the trunk of one of the trees and offered her a sweet juicy apple from her saddle bag, Equeleus crunched it up in no time then affectionately nuzzled her appreciation, “Right, i had best set about making good my camp” freyja said to herself in an orderly tone as if instructing herself upon on a task that must be done.

Freyja strode over to her saddle bag and withdrew a length of sash which she tied between the two hazel trunks when the knot had been secured she threw a blanket over the taught cord to fashion a temporary shelter, removing her golden sickle brooch with a click and fastened it upon the tent with a sound click, she stood back for a moment to admire her handiwork then incanted, "CONCEAL", to which the clasp reverberated shimmering the tent from vision, The ovate gave a smile of satisfaction as she unfastened her saddle bag, then climbed unseen beneath the shelter.

Freyja dropped her bags with a thud upon the forest litter, then rubbing her saddle sore behind she stretched out her weary limbs and un-fastened her sleeping roll and cast it over the ground, she sat down upon the blanket and drew a green bag from her travelling sack, "I must discover if i follow the right track", she said aloud to herself as she drew a circle in the dirt with a stick.

Freyja carefully withdrew her gift from Myllas, the 'Oracle of Myriddin' from within the green bag and steadily placed the golden apple in the circles centre, it had been a gift the previous solstice, and had come with a curious note, "*when all hope seems lost, and the world is affray, spin this apple, to guide you on your way*" then standing back she incanted the charm. "*Golden apple that upon myriddin grew, Point the way to lead us safe and true, to the way our warlock flew, seeds of knowledge do tell us true.*"

The air fell deathly silent around the encampment as freyja and Equueleus held their breath in anticipation, a gentle breeze stirred across the forest floor whipping up the leaf litter as they eagerly watched the golden fruit.

Slowly the apple tilted upon its axis ever so slightly as it started to rock from side to side gradually gaining in momentum until the rocking grew into a steady spinning, The oracle of Myriddin span the circumference of the circle for a few turns then shot off widdershins breaking through the circle and out of the tent, quickly freyja quickly followed its course as it rolled off down the leafy path.

Myriddins eye was literally rolling downhill now and freyja had to break into a run to keep up with it as it coursed through the bracken momentarily once or twice it became obscured by the ground foliage and she thought she had lost sight of it, only to be relieved when a golden glint appeared once more amongst the leaves, rasping for breath the ovate wondered how much further the apple would lead her before it stopped she couldn't run like this for miles! Then just as suddenly as it had set off the apple fell still nestling beneath the corridor of two overhanging willow trees, their catkins dancing merrily in the breeze as if joyfully announcing her arrival, "Well i see no warlock my golden friend, what is it you wish to tell me?" she questioned the apple in breathless gasps.

But the eye of Myriddin remained as motionless and still as the tomb giving away no clue to its recent behaviour, "Oh bother!" exclaimed Freyja in annoyance, trust Myllas to give me a useless trinket she thought dejectedly as she collapsed upon the floor with a defeated thump, Catching her breath she looked around for any visible token of the apples behaviour, was it perhaps another portal she wondered, or am i just to wait here and see what happens awhile? she puzzled, well the latter of the two seemed the most alluring at the moment for she was in need of a good rest now at least after her sprint, she would investigate the possibility of the portal after gaining forty winks she reasoned to herself, snatching up the apple and noting its location she headed back to the tent, disappearing beneath the bewitched camp she lay down to close her eyes, the soft mouldy litter embraced her form like a autumnal blanket as she relaxed her limbs and lay her head upon the earthy floor beneath as sleep invited her to play in its entrancing waltz as her eyelids started to fall, a distant thundering met her ears as it coursed through the ground like a planetary heartbeat, da dom, da dom, DA DOM, DA DOM..hang on that's getting louder freyja noted in her half-conscious state, she listened again only harder this time pressing her ear against the ground as she battled slumbers embrace to rouse her senses into action, DA DOM, DA DOM, DA DOM.... "Aha!..you clever apple, that is not the heartbeat of the forest, but the thundering of hooves!" she exclaimed triumphantly.

Overhead an unseen enemy scout settled in the branches of sycamore tree, the beatings of its leathery wings were drowned out by the rhythmic beating of the approaching hooves, Could it be the warlock and his mount, dare she hope, or perhaps it was a messenger or travelling troubadour who had seen sight of Uther recently? Freyja quickly arose to her feet, i cannot be too complacent she thought as she went to grasp her sickle brooch, "Blast!" she thought it is back at the encampment how careless of me, i was in such haste to follow myriddins eye that i did not arm myself accordingly she stressed in hindsight, well there was no time to loose thought freyja as the thundering grew ever louder resounding through the earth she could almost hear it now!

With swift dexterity she climbed in to the branches of a nearby chestnut tree, despite her tiredness, she would lie against the branches unseen until the friend or foe had revealed their identity.

The thundering hooves clapped through the pendulous air like a forges hammer as the king entered the clearing, Announced only by his vast crop of antlers which grew like a majestic crown from his furry brow, The stag tossed his back head dramatically as he came to a halt as if he wished to make an impression of regal grandeur to an unseen audience for he was Hearne the king of nature, he who let all creatures revel in his glory, Freyja held her breath aghast, she could not believe that the eye of myriddin had led her to the Mighty Hearne the king of the forest, it was not such a useless trinket after all and nor was Myllas..

Hearne Strutted right into the middle of the path beneath the chestnut tree, he turned upwards and cast his hazel eyes straight toward freyja, who hardly dared to breathe they locked gaze for a brief moment as one considered the other before them, It was freyja who ultimately broke the silence, "forgive me my lord, it was i who not certain who approached upon the trail, i only wished to be certain that they meant me no ill", Hearne replied in a soft and gentle voice "That was a wise and safe move my child for there is much unrest and peril in these parts these days not like the days of old, now please do come down from those branches and let us talk awhile.", The ovate beamed a smile of gratitude at the stags pleasant demeanour for he was indeed the king of the forest as she deftly swung down from the trees cover.

Freyja's felt boots met the ground with a soft thud as she landed before Hearne, hastily she dropped down onto one knee to kneel and pay homage to the ancient monarch of nature who commanded such reverence in all who met him.

NATURES KING OF THE FOREST REALMS

The stag king seemed mighty pleased with the ovates display of respect, and so bowed his head in return to gently touch freyjas shoulders with the tip of each of his antlers, "May the blessings of the forest rest upon you freyja" he bequeathed and then added, "now please lady arise for you read the wrong path we must talk of matters most pressing", Freyja stood up dusting down the forest debris from her tunic and smiled gaily at hearne who shook his antlers in reply, "Now let us return to equuleus and discuss the problem of kalthors reign of terror upon your village. "said the stag in a hasty tone, "we cannot dwell here too long, the enemy has many spies" Nodding agreement freyja stealthily headed off to lead the way back to her camp, a loud jittering rang out from the overhead branches as a snarl ruffled its leathery wings in a bid for take-off, moving fast freyja swung down and scooped a rock from the forest floor, she hurled with all her might as the horrid creature left the branch in a wings beat, the stone hit home catching the snarls body, it let out a vile screech of anger as it tumbled from its flight into a spinning descent, the beast flapped and fluttered manically as it descended like a stone, then by sheer luck it caught an updraft and regained its balance, freyja watched in horror as the cretin now hell bent on vengeance procured her in its sights, then locking in on its target, it swooped down like an arrow its fetid talons extended like scythes, She ducked down drawing her scabbard from its hilt as the snarl narrowly missed her, a stinging on her face told her that it hadn't quite missed as she slashed the air with a swish.

Hearne reared up in anger as he tried to butt the beast with his antlers as it once again circled round for the second attack, his hooves hit the floor with a thud as he lunged at the air, The ovate stood with blade extended ready to skewer the snarl like a rabbit on a spit, if only she could get close enough, why oh why had she been so careless as to leave her golden sickle brooch at the bivouac she cussed herself, the overlords emissary must be captured, she could not let it escape!, Wicked green eyes bored into freyja as the snarl launched itself like a blue thunderbolt of fury at her face, luckily she tumbled over as she slashed at the snarl narrowly missing the snap of its barbed fangs as it aimed at her nose, cursing under her breath she leapt back up in defence, but was knocked straight back down onto the floor by the swoosh of ebony wings in mid spin.

A loud CRAAWW rang out as the ebony dart sang out his battle cry, the flurry of swirling black wings collided head on with the azure snarl, as each was pinioned to the other locked in combat as they nosedived towards the forest floor, the snarl let out a hideous screech as Solomons talons pierced through the already wounded reptilian wings, in a last ditch attempt to secure a footing it sank its barbed fangs in to the corvids wing, Solomon flapped hard as he tried to loosen his assailants grip, but the beast sank his jaws ever tighter like a poisonous vice, Solomon glared at the foul snarl through his intelligent eyes, it would take more than that to deflight him he thought, he must defend his mistress to the last.

The crow heaved with all his might as he pulled at the beasts wing through his own pain, his sharp talons tore through the paper like wing as he shredded it to tatters, Piercing fangs released their grip as the monstrous snarl thrashed around in agony trying to free itself from the astute bird, Solomon released his quarry which sank to the floor with a vile thud, the snarl screeched and thrashed around as it tried to take off back to its master.

The crow half fluttered half fell at Freyja's boots for he was mightily injured by the snarls poisonous fangs, Freyja leant down and carefully recovered up her precious champion, nestling Solomon in the crook of her arm she gently stroked her companions ebony feathers and cooed to him, "Thank you my mighty warrior you saved me from the hideous beast, you are truly valiant. "She said softly through a veil of tears.

Solomon stared back at her through pain filed eyes knowing that he may not recover from his festering wound, she was his mistress and he had served her well an honourable death would be his, "Place him before me" instructed Hearne in a hasty tone, freyja looked up at the king of nature torn between obedience and love, "but if i place him upon the ground he will surely perish alone" she pleaded, "Do as i say child for all is not yet lost" he ordered, The ovate knelt upon the ground and gently lowered the wounded animal before his master, solomon lay there in a bewildered crumpled heap, blood oozed in rivulets from his wing to drip soundlessly upon the fallen carpet of leaves beneath him.

Solomons eyes threatened to close as the tide of eternal sleep gently began to sweep tenderly over him in drowsy swathes, Hearne looked down pityingly at the fallen champion, concern courted his hazel eyes as he spoke to the valiant little bird.

"Friend you have saved us both from the teeth of the poisonous snarl and you cared not for your own plight, you are a valiant little fellow, night invites you to dance with her in the halls of eternal peace, but not this day shall she claim you.", And with this the mighty stag threw back his regal antlers shaking them from side to side in a slow steady rhythm, trails of green light began to dart to and fro between the protruding tips of hearnes crown until a ball of verdant emerald light glowed within his antlers, Steadying his swaying head hearne bowed over the injured crow as he wavered between the worlds and chanted. "*Light of nature, light of power, bestow your healing, now this hour, rain down fettle, with this shower*"

Hearne then tipped his antlers down over the nearly sleeping solomon, verdant light engulfed the mortally wounded soldier buzzing and snaking it weaved its magic upon solomon restoring his life and Vigor as it girded his black form, slowly and steadily the weary crusader began to stir, firstly his jet coloured eyes peeped out at the green hue which embraced him, With this development the shimmering aura began to vibrate at a high-er resonance until it seemed to sing, solomon cautiously began to ruffle his feathers steadily extending his wing as if waking from a long and heavy slumber, Freyja held her breath as tears of joy sprang into her eyes, clasping her hands together she bought them up to her lips in feared excitement, dare she hope her beloved companion was to be cured, snatched back from the jaws of death, it certainly looked that way!

She watched hearne steadily raise his antlers from the ground carefully holding the awakening solomon within his antlers embrace until he once more gained his regal stance, The verdant brilliance gradually diminished to all but a glow, "*Natures breath has healed thee, now once more you shall fly free.*"

commanded the stag, Solomon flapped and fluttered with a vigorous new animation as natures breath vanished into the air for it had healed the valiant champion and restored him back to vitality, the enlivened crow flew on to one of hearnes antlers and began to preen himself as if nothing untoward had happened, Freyja and hearne laughed together in jubilant relief, "How can i ever repay this debt to you my liege" freyja asked hearne.

"Thanks are not needed my lady" replied the stag "our little friend saved us from the poisonous bite of this treacherous little blighter, now what are we to do with him" he added observing the squirming reptilian upon the ground, "I shall heal him enough to return to his master but place a memory shroud charm upon him, lest he disclose our whereabouts. "he added to himself, solomon let out a disgruntled craw from atop his crowned perch, causing the king and maiden to fall about in peals of laughter, once the matter had been dealt with the stag and the ovate sat beneath the veil of the enchanted camp, Freyja and hearne discussed the plight of thygor for most of the afternoon until the anwen sank level with the horizon, they had reached the decision that the warlocks help must be employed no matter the cost as the eternal balance of male and female must be honoured as spoken by the prophecy.

The ovate was relieved that she did not have to go it alone, but there was still the problem of joining uther, Solomon had located the warlock that was for sure and he could easily lead the way back to the keep, but it still left the problem of entering the fortress and overcoming the defending hordes of trolls and goblins hanging in the balance, perhaps the apple of myriddin could help them, it was worth a try.

That night fall after releasing the snarl, Hearne, equueleus and freyja journeyed forth to Morganas Tump, with Solomon nested on the antlers of Herne like a branch, natures king raced at a gallop towards the oak upon the summit of the hill with the ovate close at his heels and the rejuvenated Solomon circling overhead, their task was to place the oracle of myriddin amongst the earth beneath the shadow of the oak Duirs mighty branches to see if it could foretell if they were to be victorious or doomed in failure, thundering hooves once more pummelled the ground as hearne led the band of companions, damp breath exhaled in tired snorts leaving a swirling vapour trail in their wake as Morganas tump drew level on the horizon like a welcome sentinel, the band of travellers gratefully slowed their pace somewhat, Freyja steadied equeeleus down to a gentle trot as they approached the tumps incline, the ride through the forest had been swift as her steed had flown as quick as the wind, causing freyja to duck and swerve to avoid the fast approaching boughs and branches that hung like nooses between the trees, she had narrowly avoided being unceremoniously unseated on more than one occasion, she thought as they laboriously plodded up the hill, Freyja was suddenly distracted from her thoughts by hearnes commanding but gentle voice, “we have arrived at our destination my lady, let us begin the divination if you will”

The mighty branches of Duir cut a regal silhouette against the dusky sky, the anwen had retired to the heavens and Alluan now cast his unwavering eye upon the world beneath, the silvery glow lit up the writhing formations of clouds with a surreal luminescence adding to the occasions ethereal atmosphere.

Gnarled branches cast their shadows black as pitch across the silvery grass engulfing the smaller regal crown of antlers projected from Natures king as he observed the clement scene with a hopeful reverence, Overhead Solomon swooped down to rest upon a wizened branch, fluttering and flapping he quietly crawed as he settled down to roost awhile.

Freyja swiftly swung down from her saddle to alight upon the moonlit panorama, purposefully she strode over to the mighty oak and knelt down amongst its network of gnarled roots, she glanced skyward to check the threat of any circling spies, with none visible the ovate withdrew the golden oracle of myriddin from her saddle bag, Bowing her head in reverence to the wizened sentinel she incanted. "*wise old oak standing steadfast and true, please share with us your secrets, on this day do.*"

The oaks leaves seemed to rustle a little louder than normal in the breeze as Freyja ceremoniously placed the golden apple of Myriddin at its base, she retreated back to equueleus giving both the oracle and Duir some distance for who knew what could happen thought freyja to herself? "Now patience is our task" instructed Hearne as he pawed the ground with his hooves, "Yes i agree we may as well settle down awhile" replied Freyja wearily as she grabbed a blanket from her bed roll for she had still not managed to catch any sleep from earlier, chucking the blanket down on the floor she collapsed onto her back with a heavy thud, and lay gazing at the celestial vista above.

Natures king himself drew weary also and so settled down upon his haunches to rest his velvety antlers upon the stygian sod leaving Equueleus to graze contentedly whilst Solomon kept watch from the oaks branches, As blissful slumber engulfed the pilgrims Duir made his move with Stealth and silence he gradually released a tuber from its earthen encasement, steadily it began creeping towards the golden oracle until the gnarled tendril constricted its accolade.

THE ORACLE OF MYRIDDIN

The mighty oak had waited centuries stretched out into long aeons for the return of its blessed oracle, when the world had been new and innocent before the shattering came the oak had held all its knowledge and wisdom a secret to pass down to its seedlings in this one golden fruit which hung from her branches, but alas when the shattering came to render the planet to dust and ash she had been mercilessly destroyed her regal silhouette transforming it to cinders and loam, but the oak she had been clever and held a great life force within her roots the Dryad Wynterleaf, and with his help she had cast forth the gwersu of Root-stalk and rejuvenated from the ashes to be Duir born of Myriddin, Long had she waited for the missing piece of the puzzle to be returned to her, this single golden apple contained the very essence of knowledge, love and virtue itself.

Furtively and soundlessly Duir drew the oracle of myriddin towards his wizened trunk, where a knot gradually started to open until it was an apple sized aperture, with covert haste he swallowed the golden oracle with little more than the rustling of a leaf.

Solomon awoke suddenly from his dreamy sleep to let out a loud craw of alarm, Duir looked to all the world as if he were on fire!, Both Hearne and freyja quickly awoke in a state of alarm at the distress call, defiantly shaking the sleep from their heads they were just in time to see her gnarled form begin to pulse with an eerie green light as the oracles knowledge once more began to seep its essence into myriddins son, strange symbols began appearing within his cracked bark like a distant memory of unwhispered secrets, The knowledge tasted like a honeyed ambrosia to the parched oak who had long awaited the oracles return, the apples power was immense it held the all forces of virtuous knowledge within its golden lustre, Beneath the cloaked veil of night The mighty oak Duir began to weave his formula of allure.

The merry band of companions witnessed as a multitude of shoots began springing forth from the earth around them, leady appendages writhed and danced in the air to some unheard Sonnett as they entwined their tendrils together in an intricate rhythm creating an ornate weave which then grew straight and true flourishing into a Plaited Oaken Stave!

The staff crackled Magically as myriddins essence transferred through Duirs wooded flesh, ripening buds appeared upon its sections ostensibly threatening to burst into bloom at any given moment, Freyja unfastened her sickled clasp and mumbling she rubbed it lightly causing it to burgeon in readiment to harvest the sceptre of myriddin, and bowing down in humbled reverence to the mighty oak she addressed the heavens, "mighty Anwen giver of light, blessed be on this day for Duir marks our path with this oaken sceptre"

The ovate then arose and strode over to the stave in readiment to hue it free from the sinewy tendrils from which it had germinated, holding the golden sickle, she reached out to grasp it, but to her surprise it effortlessly came free, as if it wished to be in her hand, Freyja deftly span it around to try out the balance, the weight felt perfect, as it twisted effortlessly through her hands, it was a truly beautiful object to behold, what magical powers did the staff possess? she wondered as she cast her eye over the woven intricacies which made up its formation, green ogham runes burned with a jade reverence up its seams as the moon Alluan glinted upon its surfaces.

A peaceful rustling embraced Freyjas ears as the oak Duir retreated his tendrils and shoots back into the silvery earth, the soil rippled as it swallowed back the myriad of enchanted vines, Son of Myriddins leaves whispered softly upon the gentle breeze as the emerald hue pulsed through the oak like a reverberating heartbeat, drawing down to all but a distant glow an echo of its former brilliance, Freyja bowed to the oak and turned around, she headed back towards Equeeleus carrying her prize, the sceptre of gwenhefayr, smiling she scanned around for Hearne, where was he? she thought to herself as Solomon swooped down to settle upon the front of her saddle.

Hearne was nowhere in sight and she had not heard his hooves departing nor had he made his leave she noted, Well he was the king of the forest, his work here must be finished she thought as he had already surrendered a great portion of his time to her this day had he not, meanwhile in the distance a shadowy pair of antlers silhouetted against the moonlit realm diminished as hearne vanished into the tree line.

"Ah well my girl we had best bed down here for the night "announced Freyja, Solomon crawed appreciably at this and tucked his tufty black head beneath his wing, giving out a final little ruffle before settling down to roost for the night, "that just leaves us then" said freyja to equeeleus, loosening off her travelling pack, she began unfastening the leather straps of the pony's encumberments.

When camp had been set up and a blanket tossed over her mount Freyja settled down to sleep, it was too risky to make a fire up here it would be seen for miles around she thought to herself, wrapping her fur blankets around tightly as she shivered profusely, “Oh blast!” she exclaimed noticing that the sceptre of gwenhefayr lay on the ground, “i had best put that treasure safe and unseen” she said to herself arising into the cold dark night air from her equally cold damp bed roll, Snatching up the stave she retreated back beneath her make shift tent and disappeared beneath the conceal charm covering the fabric.

“Right where to put you” she thought aloud, “well this should be safe enough” she announced sinking the sceptres base into the earth behind her pillow, A loud crack tore through the air like a clap of thunder as the sceptre of gwenhefayr ejected a bolt of brilliant light which illuminated the shelters interior with a blinding flash, Reacting swiftly freyja shielded her eyes against the foray closing them as tight as she could until the brilliance subsided, when she felt it was safe she cautiously opened her eyes peering into the eerie glow cautiously surveying the camps concealed interior.

Gwenhefayrs sceptre projected a beam of light across the shadowy floor, but it was like none other she had seen before for it played out a vision of time, Freyja could see the warlock Uther riding out on horseback as he entered the keep at khymer, she saw the fracas with the trolls and goblin kind, even Solomon circling overhead, suddenly Raul appeared in the picture in a violet flash and then the picture changed, the warlock was being led off to the mirrored chamber of Asgard where the overlord awaited his arrival a Siberian prowl lay curled upon his lap, a roost of snarls began hissing venomously from their stone turreted windowsill as Uther entered the room.

The warlocks reflection cast across the many fractured countenances as he stepped forth into the mirrored glare of the serpents lair, trapped like a bug in a jar, a heated conversation was taking place but freyja could not make out the dialogue for it sounded muffled and far away as if she were listening underwater, suddenly the overlord raised his deformed hand towards Uther, the purple smoke of shadow speak fouled the air as the evil sorcerer bestowed his curse upon the warlock reflected upon the mirrored walls like a plague of pestilence.

Uther drew the sword of shadows which he had been consigned to forge, but alas it was already too late, the overlords foul cackling poisoned the air as the trapped warlock was little more than a sword wielding reflection cast within his mirrored prison, the warlock smashed the blade of shadows against his glass gaol, but alas to his avail nothing happened, or at least nothing he knew about, for deep within Knightshade forest a crack appeared across the Knight Gondrils stone encasement, as each blow of the blade threatened to release him from his centuries old shackles, deep within the hills of Asgard the soil serpent let out a hideous cry as he too felt the blow of the virtuous blade, ejecting a blast of dirt from his earthen snout the mirage faded to dust upon the breeze.

The light from Gwenhefayrs sceptre died down and the air ceased to vibrate as the vision ended trickling off to little more than a shadowy remnant, etched into the ovates mind, Dread filled her heart, what was she to do, however could she defeat such an evil sorcerer, the warlock had been her last hope to defeat the over lord and his tyrannous regulator raul and their motley band of cohorts, and now her plan of attack had been lain to waste for the warlock lay trapped within the mirrored chamber of Asgard, and now Hearne had left her side, whatever was she to do, but still a ray of hope flickered in the dark for the knight from legend had been seen to crack, what could this mean, a forked path lay ahead, travel to the keep and rush head long into conflict, or journey to the innermost depths of Knightshade forest and seek out the stone family risking the attack of Mist wraiths and soil serpents, Freyja sighed as her plight rested heavy upon her shoulders, which way should she choose? well at the very least she would sleep on it for nothing could be done right now she must devise a plan of attack, with a heavy heart freyja crawled under her blankets shivering and succumbed to a troubled sleep plagued with portents of doom.

The ovates dreams, saw Solomon rise skyward into the velvety black night, he circled a black tower, ornamented with a coat of arms on the highest turret illustrating a violet background set beneath a heraldic wolf and Gryffin, Locked in the tower was the young freyja but now a red headed ovate healer in green robes, the girl was crying and in despair at being incarcerated, a golden knight on Gryffin back was flying through the night sky to her aid, Freyja still held the stave of Gwenhefayr in her dream it spoke unto her and declared "I am bound to your Staff and my name is Wynterleaf, I am a Dryad the spirit of the oak that you saved from the trolls in your youth, I am to guide the way for the stone warrior has awoken and the time has almost drawn nigh" announced the woody voice, as freyjas thoughts drifted into another scenario from her childhood within her dream.

KNIGHTSHADE FOREST

The next morning freyja arose somewhat fretful and tired, she must begin the journey back into the forest, and decipher the meaning behind the vision displayed by Gwenhefayrs sceptre, she was sure it had shown the stone knight crack asunder, and after last night's prophetic reverie she was sure of it, the trio of companions Solomon, Equueleus and Freyja travelled most of the day to reach the threshold of knightshade forest, as the evening began to fall the trio began to grow uneasy, they had travelled all day and were dusty and tired.

The trio broke through the treeline and entered the forest, gnarled shadowy trees loomed overhead like a dark and ominous predators, the ovate scanned her eyes across the canopy overhead, feeling the glare of unseen eyes bore into her neck, Shuddering she pressed on, Saying "Come Solomon, Equueleus let us hurry about our task for i cannot wait to be free of this place, it fills my heart with dread fear and eeriness seeps from its every appendage."

Knightshade forest was as black as pitch with only the light from an occasional glimmer of the setting Anwen through the trees canopy, each footfall forward felt like an intrusion into danger, Unable to bear it any longer freyja declared to her animals "This darkness is unsettling allow me to illuminate the area, steadily focusing upon Gwenhefayrs sceptre she incanted, "*Anwens Light within my grasp, Fire bright until nights past!*"

The tip of the stave welcomingly against the gloom like a flickering candle amongst the shadows, Freyja felt sure that she could hear strange whisperings upon the air and knew all too well that the forest was rumoured to be swarming with mist wraiths, for had they not enchanted Gondril in the legend of Knightshade forest, the very Knight she sought to find.

Equeeleus lead the way as the ovate kept watch for wraiths and soil serpents, Freyja felt as if they were in a labyrinth, the trees appeared to move around them like a game of hide and seek, the ovates heart skipped as the horse nervously stamped her hooves, whinnying in protest at the strange and unearthly shadows, “SSshhh girl” whispered freyja comfortingly as she leant down to give the horse a consoling stroke, Nervously she glanced through the approaching trees, what was the horse skittish about? Freyja was sure that she could make out a strange glow in the distance, but when she had her vision fixed on it, it seemed to blink out like a snuffed candle, it was most peculiar, fear crept into her heart like a seeping infection attacking her confidence, What if it was a trick by the wraiths to lure them into the forests heart? freyja thought to herself, but no matter how afraid she was that was where the stone knight was rumoured to sleep, they must press forward to find Gondril, no matter how perilous it seemed, and anyway besides her curiosity had now gained the better of her, “let us follow close girl” whispered Freyja into the mares ear as she signalled to Solomon to scout ahead with a sweep of her arm, the corvid quickly read the instruction then stealthily swooped off ahead to scout for danger.

UTHERS DISMAY AND THE PLOT OF PESTILENCE.

Uther dismally surveyed the aspects of his confinement, the dank amethyst dungeons, construct of vaulted mirrors portrayed all the sombre imaginings of a sepulchre, the fetid stench of decay invaded his nostrils like a poison, Rotting meat and decaying cabbage leaves were strewn about the stone flagged cell.

The warlock could hear the squeaking protests of a family of vermin that had set up residence in the fusty heap of straw in the corner, they noisily bickered over the spoils of the last unfortunate inmate.

Uther anguished at his desolate fate, he the warlock could not meet his demise in this rank dungeon, the safety of the realm lay upon his shoulders, destiny had dealt him a cruel hand this day he thought dismally to himself, idly he pushed the straw along the flagged stones with his boot, he must think hard and do it fast, for time was of the essence if he was to defeat the evil overlord and his rotting cohort Raul, still he held the trump card they would not dispatch him just yet he thought as he turned the crescent ring around his finger thoughtfully, why had raul not reclaimed his ring and why did he still have the sword of shadows with him, the very item he had been consigned to forge and deliver?

Surely there must be some trickery or sleight of hand at play here, the diabolical union must have other plans for him yet else he would not still be drawing breath, he had best uncover the plot before it thickened further, closing his eyes the warlock gave Rauls ring a half turn widdershins and closed his eyes, he hated to do this, to unleash the vile corrupt language of shadows peak but his circumstances provided little option he must divine their ulterior motives.

He was to discover too late that this too was in their plan for him, for raul had thought ahead that the mighty warlock would use his ring to unleash visions of the future, for many moons and seasons it had now slept upon Uthers finger, seeping its corruption into his flesh little by little barely noticeable to the unseeing eye, The warlock had played straight into their hands, or so he had led them to believe, he had used flamesword to create a mental shield against its sorcery, and hide certain things from its all prying eye, he must get word to the Guild of virtue that attack loomed imminently in the offing they had best prepare to besiege the keep and mirrored fortress before the moons cycle was out.

The soupy night air circled the mirrored chamber of Asgard like a poisonous vine, it snaked and writhed around the amethyst facets, Mighty Alluan emerged from behind the clouds, illuminating an eerie vista with his silvery Hoare, a thick bank of fog swept along the chamber, its image reflected upon the crystalline formation, ghastly reflections stared out trapped across the countenances, wailing phantoms terrifying to behold screamed in torment, their human like features twisted out of all recognition bound within the fractured aspects.

They had once been mortal beings who had dared to defy the overlords pawn King Kalthor, they had paid the ultimate price of being cast into dust dervishes, the other side of the mirrored walls, purple shadows twirled across the chambers, as Raul observed Uther through the glass and sneered as he sat hatching out further plans for his reign of terror, Maleusius meanwhile, reclined upon his throne an intricately woven myriad of stone serpents made up its construction, each arm bore the head of a python upon its end the mouth agape to reveal the fangs biting an amethyst between their teeth.

Snara sat nestled upon the overlords lap, her snowy Siberian fur set a stark contrast against the archaic black velvet and tattered silver brocade fashioning Maleusius tunic, she dag her claws into a Rats carcass, looking up to regard the regulator with a glare of disdain, Raul stood hunched before his master, his reeking cerements invaded the chamber like a pollution of decay, his cadaverous visage defiled the many mirrored walls like a necromancers army.

Slowly he bowed his head and stepped forward onto the silver glyph of Draco, and addressed Maleusius, "My lord we had best to strike while the iron is hot" debated Saul in a hissing ravenous voice for he was all too eager to see the warlock's demise.

"Saul you charge forward with haste, when patience is the key" floated Maleusius reply emerged from his lips like acrid purple smoke upon the air, So many foul curses and abhorations had the overlord cast that shadow speak had now become a part of him, his voice no longer flowed from his lips only the foul tongue which had invaded and soaked into his very soul, Saul and Maleusius discussed their diabolical conspiracy of rule governing their marionette Kalthor and the sword of shadows, and how they would dispatch the warlock, the diabolical pair discussed plans for his future enslavement and despatch as the kingdom glowed beneath Alluans silvery Hoare.

Meanwhile Uther considered his fate as it swung in the balance, , for the moment at least he was safe for malesius still required uthers services to wield the sword of shadows, uther needed to show Malesius the art to master its secrets to conquer the land and all manner of man and beast that dwelt upon it, he considered how Raul had allowed Uther to claim his ring in the Oxen and Plough so that the corrupt energies of the ring could seep into uthers flesh corrupting him to forge dark Magicks into the blade for the pair had already surmised back then that he would forge the sword, but uther had noble properties he knew they would sully and twist this to their advantage, playing on Uthers noble qualities like an inner conflict.

Maleusius thoughtfully stroked snara's silken fur with his withered hand as he considered their next move, the warlock still carried the blade upon his person due to the overlords error, he had been too hasty to imprison Uther before retrieving the blade and now that he had confined him to the mirrored chamber he would no doubt be most unwilling to part with his consignment, they could not risk a conflict inside the chamber for to crack the mirror would be folly as it would lessen their sorcery, for the shadow speak flowed and ebbed through the amethyst crystal, morphing and amplifying its power seven fold, Crushing his tankard with the power of his silver gauntlet Maleusius arose from his throne, Snara leapt to safety as the overlord tossed the goblet sending it clattering across the marble floor, "AHA" he cried triumphantly in dense shadowy dialect, the purple fog pouring from his lips like the kiss of death, "Raul we must strike a bargain with this warlock, we shall offer him parley and armistice out of this place in exchange for the blade and its secrets, then when he is most vulnerable we strike, claiming the blade for ourselves and deliver the fatal blow, we shall christen the blade with its creators blood!" thunderous silence reigned as the treacherous scheme hovered in the air like a creeping poison, for even the mighty moon Alluan had retreated behind the clouds to cast the chamber into inky isolation, A thunderous crack rang throughout the chamber as the evil Regulator Raul banged his cane triumphantly upon the marbled glyph of Draco to the symphony of Maleusius's venomous laughter resounding off the mirrored walls.

DESOLATE GLIM

Solomon flew as silently as a whisper hardly daring to beat his wings as he approached the mysterious glow up ahead, one minute it shone crystal clear like a beacon only to blink out in a second into an echo of a shadow, Misty air gnawed at the crow sending penetrating fingers of cold through his downy plumage, moist drops of air beaded off Solomons feathers in dewy rivulets as he glided towards his quarry weighing him down like a moist blanket of hinderance, almost soundless drips descended from the sky and pattered with a hushed resonance upon the mouldy leaf litter below like the falling of a silent tear, unheard by all but Glim the desolate, as he tracked his path towards the forests heart.

A host of squirming insects spread out before him like a writhing carpet squelching and scuttling as they squirmed across the forest floor to further advance their territory alongside the guardians every footfall, Glim held aloft his lantern, it flickered gently as the myriad of moths fluttered around the lamplight momentarily shadowing out its brilliance like a dim blinking eye of solitude, The hermit knew they were following; he had done well in luring the ovate to her destiny guided her by his lamp he had hoped to cast a dim ray of hope against the bleak wilderness of Knightshade forest, She had been wise in sending the corvid ahead to scout for danger, for Glim had heard the mist drip from the birds feathers, it had been such a very long time since he had heard anything but the sounds of the forest centuries even, he had long since forgotten the noise of the outside world and why he had retreated here.

Slowly and steadily he crept towards the barrow at the forests heart, he felt sure that it would be guarded by an army of myst wraiths but they were no match for glim the desolate for he was the man with no name, humanity had left him as he had spent many a long century in the forests heart drawing ever further into his minds labyrinth growing stony and gnarled like the forest that surrounded him.

The hermit had blended into the forests background so much that now even the insects swarmed to him in their legions and strangely what was left of the man welcomed their company, Glims silent footfall began the approach towards the gateway of the neolithic sepulchre, soundlessly he entered the passage of archaic yews which marked the barrows mouth, solemnly and respectfully he trod towards the house of the ancients, Overhead solomon discreetly settled amongst the branches of a yew trying to conceal his presence as he mapped out the entrance, tucked away in his bower the crow lay hidden to all but glim, the corvid watched the hermit suspiciously as he shuffled along with his lantern.

Glim smiled secretly to himself as he felt the crows gaze bore into the back of his neck, but that was not the only pair of eyes which had spotted him, the horde of myst wraiths circling the barrows' top had also felt his approaching presence, they swiftly evaporated into all but a whispering of mist as they tried to conceal their presence from the man with no name, they loitered above the ground tenaciously billowing and swirling like a foggy trap waiting for the opportune moment to ensnare their victim catching him unawares, Glim the desolate rounded the bend with unwavering audaciousness, for he knew what would lie in wait for him, the myst wraiths.

The bank of foggy predators drew upon the hermit's scent as it drifted upon the breeze, sucking through their skeletal teeth they pinpointed his location as he trod the barrows entrance, a thick writhing carpet of insects scuttled from the concealed shade of glims robes spilling forth like an infestation as they hurriedly burrowed and crawled into the sanctuary of the barrow, The hermit stood his ground as the myst wraiths unravelled their treachery to reveal three phantom like countenances each as hideous as the next, but glim did not falter as they closed in around him, a distant flap told the hermit that Solomon had flighted back to Freyja to relay his findings, Glim turned his cowled head upwards to observe his captors through ancient eyes of pitying solace, as he traced three lines in the dirt with the stick of his lantern and intoned, "*CALLOR KERIDWEN, I am the earth, I am the sea, i am the wind, i am the fire, Anwen emblazon these three, so mote it be*"

With this a mighty ray of light burst forth from the barrows entrance to illuminate the vicinity beneath swathes of fiery brilliance, rendering the myst wraiths to naught but ashes and cinders laying strewn across the ground, And so the man with no name turned to face the forest, he stood alone like an aged sentinel against the barrows looming silhouette as he awaited Freyjas imminent arrival

The beech tree rustled gently signalling to freyja that Solomon had safely returned to a nearby branch, Freyja took hold of Equuleus's reins and steered the mare slightly westward drawing up alongside her feathered scout, "how looks the path ahead friend?" she questioned the corvid, Solomon gave a hearty reply by avidly flapping his wings and letting out a deep bellied craw, the ovate laughed earnestly at her little charge then added, "as good as that eh my little fellow, let us venture forth then" to which

Solomon took to the wing once more to guide the way back along the secluded trail that he had followed.

Foliage and tree cover began thinning out as their trek gained ground, the Anwens light beamed down through the overhead canopy like the welcome embrace of a long lost friend, up ahead on the horizon freyja spotted the approaching outline of an earthen mound, blinking hard against the stark sunlight she squinted to gain a better look but failed to do so just as the terrain underfoot became more challenging causing her mount to stumble upon the stony incline, giving up she figured that they she would find out soon enough, As they wound higher up the hill the lay of the land changed offering freyja a better view of Knightshade forest, she could clearly see the stream as it snaked its course through the forest like a vein of life running through the eerie place to the valley yonder, mist snaked and swirled around in odd soupy patches across the autumnal verdure, probably Myst phantoms she thought to herself with a shudder.

The ground under foot began to level off somewhat as they started to round the bend, Solomon swooped down to perched upon the front of freyjas saddle ruffling his feathers comically, signalling to the ovate that they had reached their destination, Freyja drew in breath as the barrow appeared before her, the majestic temple of the ancients stood looming before her, the vast entrance pillars seemed to draw upon the atmosphere commanding dignity and respect from all who stood before them, the guardians of the ancients.

Lifting his cowled head Glim became visible as he observed the red headed ovate through dim and weary eyes, it had been a long trek for the primordial sentry of the forest, for so many centuries the hermit had resided with the solitude of nature that he was barely visible to mortals with his gnarled overgrown appearance and cloak of mossy foliage.

Freyja remained seated observing the wizened warrior as he ambled towards her, dried leaves were strewn the forest floor as his silver beard swept along like a besom, Multitudes of moths fluttered around him like a cloud of defence obscuring his geriatric features, beneath their flickering mantle as they danced around the dim light emitted by his lantern, As Glim drew nearer the squelching carpet of bugs became clearly visible to freyja, Equuleus whinnied and began backing up as restlessly stamping her hooves at the carpet of writhing invaders, the furtive spilling and screeching of the insects became deafening as the Hermit drew almost level, freyja was having a hard time controlling the spooked mare from bolting, whilst Solomon just eyed the writhing mass with a veritable delight that a feast had indeed been bequeathed to him.

Freyja felt both uneasy and intrigued sat before the commanding backdrop of the barrow and now this strange looking old man constructed from insects, had he lured her here to meet her demise, who was he and why had he not perished at the hand of the foul phantoms that dwelt within the forest, “I AM THE MAN WITH NO NAME” announced the wizard, desolate glim, as if somehow he had read freyjas thoughts, I am the essence of solitude and I offer you sanctuary against the perils that lie in wait for you within this place, he paused allowing freyja to contemplate, she nodded in agreement, glim continued, But first you must overcome your horror and embrace the lessons that age and decay offer to teach us, to enter the hall of your ancestors, for does not all that is verdant in the spring perish to lie dormant beneath the soil in winter only to flourish again akin to the fate of all mortals child?

The wizards words created a poignant atmosphere as freyja considered Glims thesis, eventually after a few seconds that ticked by like an eternity of time the woman smiled a welcoming smile and hung her head, "forgive me, i am sorry it has been an arduous journey through this perilous place and i have grown weary and afraid." at this she dismounted from Equuleus and bowed in humble apology.

Glim laughed gently like the babbling of a stream at the sudden display of regard and replied, "it is the folly of the young to fear the old, but remember as the years grow heavy on your shoulders age will be your counsel, and now I have something to show you." he announced fumbling awkwardly at the lanterns catch as he squinted beneath the Anwens rays, a small click sounded the release of the glass mechanism as the lantern's door swung outwards, the radiance of the Anwen faded behind a cloud as Glim the desolate reached inside the lantern with a gnarled hand, the dim glowed suddenly extinguished beneath his grip casting the scene beneath a shadowy milieu, Slowly and steadily the wizened old creature withdrew his hand from the lantern and stooping before freyja he whispered into her ear in a friable voice, "hold out your hand", Freyja was dreadfully unsure as to whether or not she wished to do so, but she could not insult this aged guardian a second time, trembling slightly she extended a sweaty palm toward the elder who clasping her palm between his soft wrinkled hands and transferred a delicate something onto the skin of her palm, holding her breath freyja hardly dared to look as she timorously opened her fingers one by one and let out a startled little gasp of delighted astonishment for nestled within the crook of her palm was the most beautiful bloom she had ever seen.

Each delicate petal began sedately unfurling one by one, firstly a crimson petal the hue of rubies unravelled to reveal the dim gleam of its resonance, shortly followed by an ochre sepal coloured as the essence of desserts, continuing with, flaxen yellow like the Anwens kiss, viridescent emerald, deep cobalt, intense orchid hued indigo, completed with a rich violet petal like a viola in the shade, Until ultimately each refraction had fully opened to reveal the Corolla of rainbows, a knowing smiled danced unseen across Glim the desolate's face as he observed freyjas obvious wonderment at the mystical blossom, "It is better known in legend as the "Flower of Arcadia" plucked from the pastoral paradise of Pans meadow itself, and i myself have spent many a long century waiting for the bulb to blossom and unravel its beauty, for whence it opens is a signal to me that the time is nigh for me to guide the temperant one through the gateway, for it will only open in her hand"

Glim informed the entranced ovate, who was wistfully reminiscing back to childhood tales of how the bloom was rumoured to hold enough magic to vegetate all the kingdoms of heaven and earth beneath a swarthy carpet of botanical lustre and in so doing the door to pans haven would unlock allowing the liege of the sidhe and all his subjects to tread once more upon the mortal realms, Freyja could not believe what she held in her palm, she could not fathom the fact that it even existed for it was the stuff of bedtime fairy tales told to her by her mother when she was just a tot, an article of pure myth, legend and fable was sitting in her hand, her freyja from Drewsville!

The tale of long ago went something like this.... once upon a time eons ago when the world was still new the sidhe and the mortals dwelt side by side amidst the luscious haven of arcadia, then came the great shattering and the tearing the worlds asunder by the expulsion of the dust dervishes and shadow speak.

The sidhe felt pity for mortal men cast out from arcadia and so sent a gift, one precious bulb from a flower plucked from the garden of Fay by the very lord of the dance, Pan himself, it who bequeathed into the charge of Hearne the Stag ruler and guardian of the mortal forests, Hearne concealed the mighty treasure deep within the trunk of myriddin hidden away from harm and consigned its care to the Dryad Wynterleaf, when the time of reckoning was nigh the flower would sing to opened and claim the forests back to the elegant folk, Wynter leaf had tended the bulb attentively for the long span of centuries until the constellation of Lyra governed the celestial heavens, the bulb began to sing like the gentle tone of a harp wishing to be awoken from its everlasting slumber, Seers and sages noted the portent of the meteor shower Geminids streaking across the desolate heavens signifying that soon two children would be born to liberate Nimrod from its fractured stellar.

The dryad had witnessed this also and so summoned Glim the desolate guardian of Knightshade forest to retrieve the shooting bloom and tend its welfare, taking it deep into the forests heart where no one dared to venture save for the hermit and the foolish, there it would be safe from mortal hands until the time of flourishing was nigh, and so the promise of Arcadia had budded and flourished just as Freyja and Uther had grown and thrived from seeds in their mothers bellies until the heavens aligned into sequence whereupon it would omit a heavenly rainbow.

Freyja was snapped back to her present surroundings by the hermits intoning reverberating around the glade, looking up from her palm she saw that Glim had shuffled to stand before the megalithic sentinels his arms cast aloft as he raised his blue lantern before the dark chasm of the ancients gateway, "Caer Sidis" he cried over and over each chant resonating off the stones until they in sang their applause and started to vibrate in chorus at first it was like the hushed whisper of gentle breeze fluttering through the apple blossom until it steadily arose to the deafening cacophony of mighty thunder resounding through the milieu, Freyja's hackles stood on end as the atmospheric acoustics penetrated her very ether.

All fell silent as Glim the desolate ceased chanting, he stood motionless and frail against the mighty backdrop suddenly appearing very small against the threshold displaying the wizened old creature that he was and not the powerful conjurer he had been just moments earlier, the air inside the barrow whipped up and began to stir spinning leaves in a merry dance as it travelled out into the glade, sucking up soil it span ever faster gaining momentum with every second as it cut a deep pattern into the terra, Freyja watched on astounded, what could this be, would they be sucked up, the whirl wind was spinning dangerously close?

Then within a trice the elemental Zephyr ceased revolving, and the tumult of leaves gently cascaded to the floor to settle upon the indentation left in the zephyrs wake, the glowing mark of the Triskele, Slowly the hermit lowered his arms and turned around to face freyja and asked, "Behold the mark of the threshold where the world of light meets the world of darkness, do you dare to tread in the wake of my footsteps?", "Yes i dare to tread the hidden path" replied Freyja boldly, to which Glim nodded his head in receipt of her answer and instructed, "leave your mount tethered to this tree for she will be quite safe in this glade alas Solomon must also wait behind." to which the crow let out a disgruntled crawk, causing freyja much amusement as he ruffled his feathers and glided off with a most dejected expression.

Freyja carefully Wrapped the flower of Arcadia amongst her skirts and Lead equeeleus over to a sycamore, lashing her reins around its trunk she gave the mare a gentle pat as if saying her goodbyes, for who knew what lay in wait for her in the barrow she thought as she stroked the horses mane, Gathering courage she ventured to stand beside Glim the desolate and nodded her readiment to enter the under realm, together The hermit and the ovate stepped onto the Trilithon and vanished from the glade in a swirling cloud of dirt.

Inside the tomb a wizened old man and a young red headed woman spiralled back into existence as the token safely conveyed them between worlds to land with an unsightly thump upon the damp floor, Freyja instinctively she threw out her hands to steady herself, she would never grow used to this method of travelling she noted to herself, Somewhat woozily the ovate tottered to her feet with her head still spinning she clambered up onto unsteady feet and viewed her dingy surroundings.

The reeking centuries of decay violated her nostrils like a fusty cerement cloaking her senses, damp mildewed air encroached upon her lungs as she coughed in protest, reaching around her neck she drew her snood up across her mouth for alas who could tell what myriad of entombed plagues lay down here awaiting release. for she could not even make out the form of her boots amongst the pitch black gloom of the barrow, as it ransacked her senses like a stale assault of putrefying horror, Feeling the presence of Glim draw up beside her freyja felt a little more steady in her confinement "The flower if you please child?" instructed the hermit.

Why she had forgotten that she had not yet returned the bloom to its keeper, her heart leapt a beat until she remembered that she had stashed it safely amongst the apron of her skirts, letting out her held breath she retrieved the radiant flower and offered it out to glim.

But the hand that reached to recover it was not the frail hand of the hermit as she had expected, freyja watched in horrified dread as a skeletal appendage appeared in its place, Her heart thudded in her chest in absolute petrification rooting her to the spot unable to move or breathe, with just one thought branded in her mind had the evil overlord and his foul regulator Saul sent Charion to reap her for the crypt, "Fear not my shrivelled form" came the rasped instruction, "For i am the Draugr keeper of the necropolis." As he finished speaking the flower of Arcadia burst into glorious reverence like a whispering hope of light to illuminate the cavernous underground chasm that imprisoned Freyja.

Myriads of light invaded the dust reeked orifices and recesses of the subterranean catacombs to reveal the grimacing horde of long dead ancients as they smiled their endless greeting of mortality, Gaping mouths of tunnels loomed to her in the distance each snaking off to perpetual darkness, who knew what lay in wait for her down those dark alleys she worried as she surveyed the endless passageways of the labyrinth that constituted the enormity of the necropolis carefully concealed within the barrow.

A deep shudder travelled down the girls spine as she realised with dread that there was still one more horror yet to come, for she had not yet gazed upon the visage of her guide Draugr, With her heart pounding like the beat of some sacrificial drum freyja slowly turned to face the ruler of the necropolis…steadily and fearfully she raised her head from its cowered position to gaze upon the countenance materialized before her.

Archaic grime encrusted wrappings adorned the Specter standing before her as the mummified Dragur stood swathed in the decay of ages shrouding the now withered body that lay beneath, Even in living death he cut a commanding silhouette towering in stature above the girl, An animated glow radiated out from where his eyes would have once been seated and yet Somehow he seemed to ponder the girl before him with a sense of serene benevolence as if he were patiently awaiting her reply.

The strange sensation put freyja a little more at ease as she observed her otherworldly preceptor against the imposing backdrop of grimacing skulls, stacked row upon row and piled as high as the earthen roof covering the necropolises inlet with a stark reminder of mortality, As terrifying as he seemed freyja observed that the king of the necropolis Dragur tentatively cradled the flower of arcadia amidst his dusty palm as if it were some rare jewel.

He shows a rare solicitude she thought earnestly to herself and anyway besides what choice do i have but to venture forward, for i am incarcerated down here like some rabbit trapped in an unfamiliar warren, with no seeming means of escape, And if somehow by the luck of the gods i were to make it back to knightshade forest in one piece i would surely perish at the hands of the Myst phantoms, so no i must venture forward in my quest however frightening it may seem on my journey to find The warlock for if i go to his aid i will surely gain his enlistment in the battle against the overlord and his foul regulator, the villagers are relying on me and me alone to release them from kalthors corrupt clutches.

A distant memory of home flashed across freyjas mind as she thought of the villagers, suddenly stabbing her unawares with a pang of homesickness, for she had not thought much of home since the quest had begun, The ovate recalled the ploughed fields, lowing cattle, lush meadows and rambling countryside of home, the starkness of the land amongst natures bountiful harvest true beauty manifest in all its seasons, The Warbling bird song of spring visitors returning from their winter travels played across her memories as she remembered walking the well-trodden paths of home.

Freyja thought back to the villagers with their trivial ailments and petty squabbles, the chubby little tots paddling in the stream with their elder siblings a broadening smile crept across her face as she remembered her village and its inhabitants, and images of her two beloved cats tatters and tangles nestled by a roaring log fire amidst the winters snow, solomon on the wing and Equeeleus prancing playfully in the glebe, Fear and dread crept into freyjas heart like an icy spear as the realization hit home, what would happen to all this if she were to fail!

Maleusius, Raul and kalthor would surely raid and pillage her beloved little village to the ground and what of the villagers and the animals when he wielded the rumoured weapon of destruction, unleashing command after command of foul abhorrent legions from the shadow lands, NO!! i must be strong too much is at stake, i am just a pawn in this game and i must advance now casting my fears aside whilst i still have the chance, Courage and valour welled up in her heart as she thought of her adversaries, they would not conquer all with an expression of steel determination and the boldness of a warrior the girl swallowed hard and addressed Dragur in a bold voice “I am ready keeper of the Necropolis, let us venture forward.”

CREEPING VENOM

Alluan once more unveiled his presence from behind the wispy clouds concealment, his radiance shone down to be forever ensnared beneath the bubbling surface of the fetid black mirror, Hoary silvern moonlight illuminated the despicable scene unfolding within the mirrored chamber of Asgard, Snarl retreated into the shadows with a leap and a growl as her master painfully arose from his silver throne, the withered deformed hand grabbed hold of the sovereign arm in anguish as the corrupt overlord agonizingly dragged himself to standing.

‘Let us make the preparations” instructed Maleusius to Raul as he laboriously hobbled over to the Altar of ‘shadows and remnants’ his velvet cloak dragged across the floor like a furrow of restriction wishing to hinder his progress against its weight, the dark magics had paid toll to the overlords unnaturally long existence, draining every last drop of strength and virtue that may have once made the man leaving only a shrivelled blackened heart to course poison through his veins, Raul took up his place behind the silver crucible and its billowing pit of violet flames awaiting his masters behest.

The overlord bowed his head in reverence before the altar as he gathered up his ceremonies, firstly picking up a sceptre of pure jet blacker than the blackest heart, Maleusius ran his eyes over it admiringly as he recalled how he had plucked it from the dervishes wake, ashes baked hard by their tempestuous fury, the ching of a silver chalice rang through the air as the overlord removed it from its plinth, it was a gory sight to behold for it had been fashioned from a skull, a leering smile crept into the corners of Maleusius lips as he reflected upon the fate of the champion slain on a harvest moon, the equinox of approaching shadows, then most carefully of all he retrieved a small amethyst phial with a silver stopper, the liquid inside swirled and contorted with menacing portent forever waiting to be unleashed, this insignificant little bottle would be their greatest triumph of all a consortium of shadow and flesh, Maleusius let out a rasping cackle as he grasped the dripping tears of the goddess Ophidia, "We begin!" commanded The overlord as he moved with eerie animation towards the crucible as if somehow he were drawing strength from the foul deed that they were about to cast, Raul raised his arms aloft and began the mantra of summoning opening the gateway between the shadow lands and the mortal realm "*The steady fire of violet flames, forever burns and never wanes, for every flame casts a shadow, darker than the deepest barrow, engulf the fire with tears of ice, they tread within the tunnels of thrice*" The atmosphere in the chamber hung heavy and pendulous as the mist swirled tempestuously awaiting its liberation.

Maleusius uncorked the dusty stopper and unleashed the writhing liquid into the atmosphere, it morphed and writhed in exaltation at its new found freedom taking on the form of a vast serpent as it slid into the silver chalice, tumbling over itself with a bewitching gait as it rolled into the goblet like a soupy violet mist slithering in adder like tendrils around the chalices brim awaiting the alchemy that would procure its release.

The overlords withered hand viciously plunged the jet sceptre into the goblet piercing the snaking mass like a dagger of pitch, the misty tears of Ophidia cried out in a tortured wail and clung to the athame like a pleading victim as the sceptre thrice stirred widdershins, Each turn saw the tears swell to fill the chalice like a venomous potion until they spilled over the goblets sides like the shedding of tears, Letting out a rasping cackle the overlord steadily withdrew his athame from the serpentine elixir and stood with malicious imposition upon the glyph of Ophiuchus, Holding aloft the billowing skull Maleusius and Saul intoned their summoning of the enchantress Ophidia. "*Tears of Ophidia you no longer shall weep, We awaken you from your eternal sleep, to cast you onto the flames of violet, to release you the celestial harlett.*"

Raul and Maleusius arose into the air gliding with surreal animation towards the fiery crucible like a pair of villainous harpies, their cerements and cloaks flapped like the wings of death as the corrupt winds of shadow speak pulsed throughout the mirrored chamber of Asgard like an infection coursing through a vein, At the first charge violet lightning danced across the crucibles flames, Malesius cast the grizzly chalice and its venomous potion onto the red hot coals, a loud hiss embraced the air as the tears extinguished the magickal flames like a damp mischief, Asgards mirrored surfaces were cast into blackest pitch as Alluan refused audience to the diabolical scene and took retreat behind a billowing cloud as the foul act took play.

Beneath the veil of darkness Ophidia's tears smothered the extinguished coals beneath their constricting embrace wrapping ever tighter around each simmering ember as they squeezed and extracted the last of the heat to fuel the transmutation.

The reptilian enchantress had slept beneath the curtain of centuries corked up by that vile stopper, but now, she had been granted freedom the dying cinders fed her cold blood like a fountain of youth as the heat penetrated her very essence transmogrifying her tears into violet steam allowing her ethereal form to transmutate into existence, Maleusius and Raul watched in awed bewitchment as the crucible began to glow with a dim violet hue, wisps of vapour were emanating from the extinguished fire like a beast drawing its first breath into the world, sulphur invaded the air like a choking miasma as the wisps became more solid in form, licking at the air like a multitude of serpents tongues hunting for victims.

Ophidia could feel her strength growing as the heat fed her cold hunger, why she could almost taste the world around her for it would soon be time for her to step through the veil into the realm of mortals once more, the Lashing tongues of violet vapour retreated back amongst the now dead coals as the mass of steam gathered itself up writhing and thickening into a dense body of acrid smoke which lingered within the silver crucible to create a charged atmosphere as Maleusius and Raul watched on in agonizing expectation, magickal smog seemed to grow in brilliance as if alight from within, slowly and steadily the tears of Ophidia began swirling like the gentle dance of leaves upon an autumns breeze spinning and dancing like a charmed serpent to some unheard cacophony playing on throughout the universe, the swaying smoke halted its swirling motion as the distant sonata ended, the once wispy tendrils of vapour had now become a thick bank of sulphureous violet smog, Unexpectedly the crucible burst into life as a vast wall of purple flames sprang from the dead coals, Maleusius and Saul fell suddenly to the floor their bewitchment broken by the unexpected turn of events.

The motley cohorts cowered in awe as the violet Serpent Ophidia slithered down cutting through the bank of flames like a serpentine dagger, her black tongue licked the air voraciously as she tasted long awaited freedom, Smooth scales as black as shrouded night glinted like ebony diamonds against the crucibles flickering blaze, Ophidia's cold dead eyes fixed upon the grovelling duo, the hiss of her flicking tongue vibrated through the air like a sacrificial chant as she approached her quarry, awakening from the sleep of ages had thrown the serpent into a ravenous hunger and here quaked a feast before her, what cared she if they had granted her freedom, they had outlived their usefulness, and why was it not a great honour to be sacrificed to the goddess and sleep eternally in her belly?...but what she did not know is that Raul had already foreseen this turn of treacherous events and armed himself to the fore against the harletts treachery, His bony hand scrabbled frantically amongst his reeking cerements as he hurriedly extracted the frozen breath of Ofrir the god and keeper of the serpents, the milky crystal glinted ostensibly beneath the moonlights luna hue as Alluan once more reappeared to illuminate the profane ritual.

The regulator swiftly threw the glittering gem into the silver crucible with his cadaver like hand and with a quavering voice recited, MELTA, a loud crack rang out through the air as the Nordic summoning wove its magic, the once solid crystalline formation melted into a frozen puddle of ice, chilly drafts of air arose up into the chamber like a freezing gale of the gods, the mirrored facets of the chamber froze instantly cracking beneath the icy blanket of winters frigid kiss, the icy vapours spread through Maleusius court covering every surface beneath its hoary embrace.

Ophidia the serpent advanced ever nearer to her quarry, flicking out her ebony tongue she could taste their fear as it escaped into the frozen environment like an equilibrium of dread, she clicked her jaws in anticipation for their dislocation stretching out the stiffness of centuries, what a joy it would be to devour once more!

Raul looked up in horror as the serpentine harlett slithered towards him and his master she was nearly on top of them now, there was no time to waste! shivering amongst the arctic atmosphere he traced a single line across the frosty glyph of Ophiuchus the rune of IS.

A crack like thunder rang out through the chamber as Thor smote his hammer, The face of Ofrir appeared in the chamber hovering in midair like a wavering visage, The mighty Odin was greatly angered et this abrupt and crude summoning, he eyed the chambers inhabitants with vexed fury until he spotted Ophidia his onetime concubine, furious rage invaded his celestial being, who had dared to release the harlett that he had locked in a lagoon of tears, Ofrir exhaled his gelid breath like a blast of rimy demise stilling the serpent as she loomed over the overlord Maleusius and his regulator Raul, her jaws outstretched in a ravenous gape of engorgement.

The mirrored facets of the mirrored chamber of Asgard cracked under the gods frozen breath, as the enchantress Ophidia became trapped within odin's icy shackles her blood chilled to ice and her voracious animation stilled instantly enslaved by Ofrirs kiss, the trembling regulator observed the frozen ice sculpture that was Ophidia towering above them her glinting serpentine jaws of ice agape in a famished kiss of oblivion as she hovered in stasis between the worlds not dead but not alive either her body slowed down to just a quiver of a heartbeat.

Meanwhile Maleusius was more concerned with the icy visage of Ofrir still hovering in midair amidst the chamber, he looked anything but benign at his summoning, the overlords poison heart beat faster in his breast as he awaited Odin's wrath as he watched his icy breath rasp upon the air in strangled exhalations, But strangely it did not come, the god of Norse observed the motley cohorts through his glacial eye smouldering with arctic vehemence, A commanding boom echoed throughout the chamber shattering the mirrored walls to a thousand twinkling shards of frost as the god Spake his malediction upon the diabolical duo in a voice like the ravenous blizzard of yuletide ,*"By the dominion of the serpents coil, i sentence you to Blood and toil, saved are you for a year and a day, then the ultimate price you shall pay"* Icicles crashed down around the overlord and his regulator as a whirling squall of snow signalled Odins departure back to Asgard in a blinding torrent of snowy rage.

The air fell still and silent as the remaining snowflakes fell softly upon the marbled floor leaving only the devastation of ofrirs wake in its midst, Alluan radiated his silvern touch upon the shattered fragments of glass and ice cast around the chamber like a thousand twinkling diamonds of portent, Maleusius's fearful expression turned to one of urgency as he observed the dripping formation of Ophidia, the icy shackles of IS would not hold her for long, the chamber of ruin would soon return to a temperate climate unleashing the now much angered harlett, Staggering and sliding over to his throne the overlord Maleusius collapsed with a weary trembling, closing his scarred eyelids he steadied his composure, what did ofrir mean, 'blood and toil and the ultimate price'…he was the overlord centuries old, blacker than the blackest night, he alone commanded the foul army of dust dervishes and wielded the tongue of shadow speak, none so ever could defeat him and his regulator Raul, but there was still the pressing matter of the serpent Ophidia, opening his dead eyes Maleusius turned to face his regulator addressing him in an urgent tone. "Raul time is against us, each second heralds the dripping of the ice if we do not gain control over Ophidia it will be our blood spilling upon the ground…Fetch the prisoner…..we must make her an offering!"

The regulators silver fangs flashed maliciously as his cadaverous visage displayed a sickening smile of hatred, he would relish watching the fate of the warlock uther his nemesis and adversary "It is done Master" he replied in a rasping cackle…and with a swish of his cerements he had gone leaving Maleusius to watch the watery gleam of the thawing serpent…..

Freyja at the temple

THE LABYRINTHS OF MORT

Dragur nodded a gesture of readiment to signal the beginning of their dark and mysterious journey as he led Freyja toward the trio of dusty tunnels gaping before them, like the ravenous mouths of some three headed worm of the deep dark earth, “Each passageway is an instant in time, the past, the present and the future, what you must decide freyja is which path you wish to take to aid you on your journey” stated her chaperone, a puzzled expression spread across the girls face as she pondered the conundrum, “each tunnel is an instant in time?”…she questioned Dragur, “well how is it that this may aid me, it surely only seeks to delay me or throw me asunder from my path, For if i journey into the past i am treading away from finding the warlock, and if i seek to change my actions i may not arrive here at all, now if i continue to journey into the present then i am merely stepping forward with no real danger from time, yet i may wander aimlessly amongst the dead while the hour of reckoning draws nigh, which just leaves the path of the future, this also holds danger for i may witness our defeat or triumph over Maleusius, Raul and kalthor and become complacent or abashed, but yet it may hold the key to unlocking Uthers whereabouts by means of destiny that i may await his arrival in time.

…Meanwhile inside the chamber of Ruin the corrupt overlord Maleusius sat perched amidst his dominion like some black corbie of spite, gazing into the obsidian scrying glass of malefaction his withered claw tenderly caressed the pallid fur of his Siberian snarl Losanne..”aha, they have reached the jaws of the creeper”. Rasped his necrotic breath…as he hissed in miscreant delight as he placed the glass back upon its plinth.

Freyja suddenly felt very uneasy as if a thousand eyes were boring into the back of her neck, she shuddered violently as she span around half expecting to see eyes watching her, but only the pitch black gloom reached out his stifling embrace, with her mind half made up already freyja questioned Dragur, "If i step into either of these tunnels, how shall it be that i am not trapped in time for surely one cannot return back here? "Alas that is the paradox that you must decipher for this is your next task, there are those who spy who would wish to see you fail, but you must defeat them and their beasts of many "stated her mummified retinue, these were not the type of words she needed to hear as she was just about to venture in to the mouth of the future she thought to herself with another shudder, but she must not delay for the weight of the future hung heavy in the balance, quite literally.

"Thankyou Dragur" freyja replied timorously, what manner of beast could he mean, and how many of them were there, he could only be referring to one person alone, the evil over lord Maleusius, how could it be that he could spy on her down here in the blackest pitch, were those his dead eyes she felt upon her but a moment ago, drawing her cloak around her to stave off the damp chill like a child's comfort blanket, she declared her intended direction, "I have reached my decision on which path to tread, the past and present have already been cast, but the future may still hold the element of surprise, be it bad or good for it is the only uncertain factor left before me"

Dragurs glowing eyes seemed to ignite with a discarnate ferocity as he held out the flower of Arcadia to Freyja once more, "Then take this you must for its future lies with you" The ovate delicately received the bloom from him, gratefully thinking that at least there would be a glimmer of hope and light to guide her on her way, as the soft velveteen petals touched the soiled skin of her palm, the bandaged remains of Dragur stood like a watcher at her departure, ”Heed my words well, for the enemy comes in many guises” he added as final warning.

A ferocious wind whistled down the tunnels like an advancing army of Zephyrs, screeching its hunger toward the sacrifice about to enter its jaws, Freyja’s legs began to tremble slightly as she trod upon the threshold of time, poised upon the equilibrium of that which is, and that yet to pass, she cast back one final look at her guide only to see his encrusted form as the archaic cerements began to unravel falling upon the floor like the gentle shedding of leaves in autumn, as his disanimate glowing eyes erupted into a fulvous blaze, consuming his shrivelled form like a dried up faggot on the hearth, rendering the once mighty warrior Dragur, king of the Necropolis to dust and ashes once more, Tears welled up in her eyes as Freyja watched oblivion once more grasp Dragur within her lamented seas, well there is no going back now she thought to herself and swallowing hard the ovate stepped into the gaping mouth of the creeper.

THE COILED MANACLE

Utha sat forlornly in his cell as he pondered means of escape, he could try to smash his way out of the amethyst walls with the hilt of the blade of shadows, but to what purpose would that serve, it would use up the last of his strength and alert his captors to his impending freedom, alternatively he could use the fire Magick of flamesword, but alas that may only cause deeper peril given the potent inscriptions of shadow speak engraved all over the crystal walls like an unexecuted stony death warrant.

As much as he hated to admit defeat, his magic was useless in here, his only seeming option was to await the return of Raul, this was a thought he did not relish after their previous skirmish had cast him deep into the bowels of valanthia, still it had put pay to his advantage in the end, for he and Morath had won the Allegiance of Maleusius darkest enemy Velah, he thought rubbing the cuff around his wrist, luckily Raul had not yet noticed the ornate trinket disguised beneath his leather smyths cuff, The warlock idly Pushed the straw around the flagstones with his foot as he listened to the distant approach of the Jailer and his clattering armour, he would have made a last ditch attempt at freedom if he had only known what the regulator had planned for him!

Uther listened to the impending footfall of the armoured enemy as he approached the stone cell, his metal boots grated like knives upon the flag stoned floor like an executioner sharpening his axe, there was no point feigning sleep to launch an attack even he thought to himself for any escape would be futile, he must deliver the blade of shadows in order for the guild of virtues plan to work, outside the cell the guard drew level with the threshold, raising his gauntlet the guard traced a razor sharp finger across the doors elegy, *"lock them tight without a key, never again shall they roam free, nor flee o'er the boundary"* almost wordlessly the guard muttered the incantation that would unlock the crystal cage that held fast the mighty warlock Uther, *"unfasten the bolted tongue of shadows, relinquish the quarry for the gallows"*

As the jailers finger traced across the chilling epitaph the crystal barrier ground across the floor opening with a gritty utterance like a thousand nails scratched down a blackboard, uther winced painfully at the unsettling clamour as it cut through his consciousness like a scathing torment, the warlocks attentions were momentarily distracted from the here and now as he clasped his soiled hands over his face and ears in a vain attempt to block out the grinding wail of the entrances admission, uthers brow furrowed into a myriad of deep lines as he scrunched up his features in vexation, closing his eyes he bore the agony until finally the assault upon his senses ceased as the slab of amethyst once more slid shut to seal his escape route, A more fitting noise could not have been found than the scratching grinding torment of stone against stone like the sharpening of some vast whetstone, as the final screech announced the entrance of Maleusius gaoler adorned in its razor sharp armour black as pitch, hardly daring to move his hands lest the racket should continue, uther steadily uncovered his ears, wincing in anticipation for an assault which did not arrive, relaxing a little he lowered his shoulders and opened his eyes only to witness the barbarous horror towering over him, WHACK, a knife edged gauntlet cut deep into the warlocks cheek as the guard Tulon dealt a cruel blow of subservience, sending uther crashing to the flag stones beneath a visual curtain of sticky crimson.

The flag stones rose up to meet Uther with a painful thud as his muscles absorbed the stony blow, a searing pain cut through his cheek as the deep laceration opened up like a grimace of pain, Resistance would be futile against such an opponent even with sorcery, the warlock could not stand to take another hit such as this, so silently he bore his malice beneath a masquerade of subordination as his captor dragged him to his feet by his hair, gritting his teeth in anger the warlock turned upwards to observe his counterpart... "Alright...alright...Parley...i submit...i request an audience with Raul, shouted Uther defiantly.

The ebony helmet leant down to meet uther face to face casting its shadow of domination over Uthers bloody features like a gloaming omen of dread to blot out the last ray of hope, Drawing upon his last ray of strength the kingdom could not forever be enslaved by the evil overlord and his regulator Raul he would play along for now.

Meanwhile the ovate Freyja had a strange feeling wash over her, like a sixth sense telling her she would be in danger if she did not move, a vision of masonry crashing about her, Dust started to descend from the ceiling to the floor spattering onto her cloak and hair, a rumbling resonated like thunder in the distance, freyja dived down to the floor, drawing up her knees to her face and wrapped her arms around her head, protecting her face and neck from any falling building "SORCERESS!" she heard Raul hiss as he began to charge up the tower staircase, oh no in the name of Anwen, opening her eyes to slits Freyja noticed a hole in the wall cracks had appeared in the walls of the labyrinth like fissures into hell, the last thing she saw was a big black cloak billowing towards her at ferocity, like a large black bird blotting out the light, "SMACK!" she reeled over onto her side in pain as the tears welled in her eyes as flying debris hit her in the back, She pulled herself up on her elbows looking upwards she was met with a boot coming at her face, "Ovate Sorceress I have warned you about your trickery, how dare you breach my castle walls with incantations to escape!" Freyja, full of anger felt the taste of blood upon her lips, she faced toward the evil lord, She had not caused this onslaught to the castle walls, little did she know the tunnel that she had chosen was a portal taking her straight beneath the warlocks prison!

The rumbling had created a cracking fissure into time ripping asunder the dimensions as she stepped forward drawn to her warlocks aid as that was her innermost thought, manifestation had played its hand, dealing a hand of aces, the regulator had seen the ovate breaching his spiritual defences in his scrying glass, hissing he had fled down to the labyrinth beneath the crystal prisons, she had escaped the tunnels viper who slithered away in the past and present tunnels like a worm of despair licking the air unable to find her scent, enraged at his plan foiling he had underestimated the ovate and the warlocks bond, still it mattered not he would incarcerate them together.

Grabbing the ovate cruelly by the hair, he dragged her through the crumbled wall up the towered staircase into the mirrored chambers above, Freyja clawed at the dead hand repulsively clawing off necrotic flesh but still the skeletal grip held her fast like a bony manacle, tight and unrelenting a grip of death, each stair reverberated through her body like a sharp blow to her back sending cold pain shooting through her being at each strike, she screamed and cursed at the regulator, release me you fiend, to no avail he returned a blood curdling cackle of delight in retort to her protests, grabbing her hair tighter and moving with deft speed up the staircase.

Freyja panicked where were they going?, what had he planned for her she could not perish, blood ran down her face, she felt as though her hair would be torn from her scalp, with one last almighty summoning of strength she fought against the pain and drew forth her Ogham blade from its hilt beneath her fur lined boot, raising it aloft, she looked Raul straight in his dead eyes with a glare of malice and bore down the hefty blade with an almighty force into the cadavers hand twisting it until he relinquished his grip upon her hair, an angered scream emanated from the evil sorcerers lips, sorceress!! He clutched at his deformed appendage oozing with coagulated blood curling up his lips in venomous anger as the ovate clattered down the turret stairs her blade still in hand…

Up above Tulon the gaoler dragged the warlock forcibly by his manacles before the evil overlord Malesius, like a horse dragging a plough, Uthers feet dragged across the floor as the enchanted suit of armour paid him no heed and followed its enchanted orders, slinging the warlock clattering at the feet of the black throne.

Uther hit the marbled floor hard, the cold stone met him with a sharp welcome stinging his knees and elbows as he was strewn upon the floor like a sack of flour, uther gritted his teeth in anger and tried to control the bubbling anger rising in his blood as the Flamesword scorched through his veins in readiment for battle.

Still not yet he must give the element of surprise, he heard the clatter of Tulons guard descend into the distance as it walked back to the Gaol, Uther arose to his knees. "Warlock you have been summoned here spat the overlord, purple tendrils of venomous sorcery licked the air with each syllable, you had a consignment to carry out which is already two moons late, where is my blade." Stated malesius.

Controlling his anger the warlock replied, "I was somewhat dispatched down in the realms of Valanthia my lord and unable to gain access to the surface had it not been for the dwarves, " for he knew intuitively that the ring had been spying upon him, yet velah had shrouded the rest of the quest with her sorcery, I believe this is your regulators ring scowled uther, tearing it from his finger and throwing it at the thrones base, "very clever warlock" came the reply, as the cadaverous overlord leant forward upon his throne to observe his prisoner, dead eyes bored into him with a milky malevolence, time seemed to stand still as one observed the other, the air charged and heavy each one conscious of the others sorcery, the pendulous atmosphere was interrupted by the entrance of the festering Raul as he pulled the ovate freyja across the marble floor by her hair, Uthers heart skipped a beat, surely it could not be, he had forged the ring of oaths as a gift to bind them , but he had not expected it to be so strong and fast! The hidden words flashed across his mind, "*The veil grows thin betwixt this world and the next*" for it was the ring that had helped freyja parry across the time thresholds into uthers location, from knightshade forest to beneath the fractured mirrored chambers of Malesius kingdom to the captured Uthers aid, The warlock observed the dishevelled countenance of the fellow captor before him, he would recognise those flame coloured locks anywhere, even though it had been many moons, he looked down to Freyjas hand and noted the ring he had forged, he felt his blood boil the Flamesword was upon his tongue before he could stop it. "*Evil deeds here you weave, let her alone you leave!*" with this a bolt of flame licked across the floor like dragons breath scorching the cerements of Raul causing him to release the Ovate, fury flashed in the warlocks eyes as the regulator snarled utter hatred muttering and cursing under his breath his robes extinguished to smouldering rags as he cast counter Magicks, glaring at Uther he announced "I have a gift for you warlock here is your little friend as he pushed the unconscious freyja towards uther with his boot.

Malesius laughter rang out across the chamber like a tolling bell of doom as he observe the clash with glee, "enough for now, for there is plenty of time for that" he added, uther breathed hard calming himself he must think straight and strategically, he pulled the dormant freyja towards him, shielding her from further harm, "Now where were we" he added raising his skeletal fingers up to his chin as he drummed his other fingers upon the thrones arm, "ah yes the sword of shadows if you please", Uther drew the scarlet package from within his leather tunic and slid it across the floor towards malesius with a clattering as it slid across the marble unravelling from its cloth bundle.

Rauls eyes lit up with a greedy animation but Malesius noticing his sorcerers greed incanted "*Blade of shadows to me you come, all sorcery and portent to come undone, when the moon blots out the sun.*" with the blade of shadows rose up into the air in a cloud of violet smoke, and floated towards the black throne to be claimed by the hand of its master. The overlord Malesius grasped his trinket with adoration holding it aloft he observed its snake shaped blade as the shadow speak runes burned with a violet fire, the serpent shaped hilt held a single green stone, smoke seemed to billow within its core as he turned it in the shadowy light, You have done well warlock, he stated, although late it is a potent armournents, Raul looked on through jealous eyes as he plotted his masters downfall and how he would claim the blade for himself, he would be the supreme ruler of the realms, and sit upon the black throne of sorrows.

Freyja meanwhile had begun to stir from her oblivion, pain met her with its stark embrace as the events leading up to her capture raced across her memory like a burning dread, unable to get up she lay there listening feigning sleep lest it be discovered she was alive, where was she? The ovate felt a presence beside her it felt strangely familiar like a dream from her childhood, opening her eyes to slits she glanced to her side, freyjas heart filled with joy for the welcoming form she recognized instantly, although dishevelled and sullied from his encounter with Talon, and age kissed his countenance with furrowed Magicks, the ovate would recognize Uthers silvern locks anywhere, she felt immense relief, she had found the warlock, the counties and kingdoms could be saved! But how were they to get out of this predicament, she gently touched her cloak checking for the sickle, thank the anwen it was still there, but where was her ogham blade? Last she remembered she stabbed Raul with it before the world went black, wiggling her foot she felt for its presence in her boot, the welcome of cold steel met her skin, she felt relief as she found it was back in its place, for she had placed a charm upon It, "*Ogham blade oak and yew, if we part keep your promise true, return across forest land, back to my scabbard, back to my hand.*" that if it ever she and blade became separated it would tarry back to its scabbard.

The warm presence of uther at her side was a blessing indeed, she must signal to him that she was awake for they must escape, looking upwards through her slitted vision she saw the foul overlord Malesius and his regulator Raul defiling the chamber with their reeking authority, they seemed otherwise dispatched momentarily as they poured gleefully over the blade of shadows, now was her chance, timorously she slid her hand across the floor and touched the inside of uthers palm, cutting him a quick glance as he turned to meet her gaze, their eyes locked for a second each welcoming the others presence with a familiar reverence of unspoken words, and childhood memories, each glad at the others welcome presence, Uther was pleased that Freyja was mostly unharmed by her ordeal, he must come up with a plan to get them out of there before the evil pair of cohorts unleashed more trickery upon them.

Malesius and Raul happy with the consignment of the blade of shadows, turned their attentions back to The warlock and the ovate, they observed the pair strewn across the floor like a bundle of rags, now it would be time to christen the blade, but little did they know that concealed in Uthers tunic was the mithril blade of oaths.

Rising up from the black throne of sorrows, malesius swept across the marbled floor like pestilence towards the silver glyph of Ophiuchus hewn into its Centre, beckoning to Raul the sorcerer he pointed towards freyja and Uther, the warlock had been observing this and was ready to wage a battle of enchantments or armoury whatever may unfold, he glanced over to freyja who had been observing the malicious duo with intimidation, Raul floated across to his master to join him upon the glyph ready to do his evil bidding, time hung heavy in the air as they waited for Alluan to cast his silvern rays upon the glyph.

The argent Alluan emerged from behind his cloak of clouds and cut down a silvern beam of light like a sword from the heavens, it hit the glyph with a supernatural glint lighting it up in eerie incandescence, malesius held aloft the blade of shadows it gleamed terrifyingly in the moonlight as if awaiting its christening with hungry poise.

The warlock surmising what was about to happen, whispered to freyja, "when they take us, upon the glyph, turn your ring one turn widdershins, with this he revealed his left hand to freyja for her to see an identical thicker band of oaths he had forged, around the band was the same runic inscription in flames word, "*the veil grows thin betwixt this world and the next*" freyja thought back to the druidic grove, this band was also around both wells of portal, fire and water, That's what it is! It suddenly dawned upon her these runes are an incantation to open portals of movement between time and place! She nodded in agreement and grasping Uthers hand for comfort she gave it a squeeze then let go, a small smile broke across his troubled features, she smiled back.

Fetch the prisoners Regulator, time is of the essence, commanded the overlord, Raul held aloft his lifeless hand to the sky, his shroud dropped back down his arm revealing necrotic skeletal remains where once there was flesh eroded by the pungent shadow speak, and incanted, "*shackles of torment bound to you, fetch us a sacrifice of hearts good and true*" with this vivid violet ropes like thorny vines shot across the floor from beneath Rauls cerements, the overlord looked on in glee, licking his rotted lips hungrily in anticipation for the power he was about to wield, uther looked at freyja to hold her position until his signal, the ethereal shackles snaked across the marbled floor to claim their victims, the vines wrapped tightly around their ankles and wrists, as the thorns cut in drawing painful pricks of blood lest the victim should struggle against the bindings.

Freyja and Uther were dragged unceremoniously across the floor on their backs, sliding at speed until they reached the triangular plinth containing the glyph of Ophiuchus, Raul and malesius loomed like shadows of death over their captives, the repugnant stench of putrefaction met the ovates nostrils, repulsed she held her breath awaiting uthers command.

Malesius held the dagger aloft with both hands, Raul sneered in malice and incanted, "*Shadow of moon, shadow of night, I deliver the pure of heart to their plight.*" At this incantation Uther gave contest and threw flames word to counter the shadow speak,

"Evil blade, dark and cold many secrets you do hold, the smyths hammer bold and true has bound Magicks unto you, enslave your maker you shall not now swiftly untie the knots!" at this the violet shackles loosened and dispersed into smoke, the warlock shouted NOW!

The warlock and the ovate turned their rings of oath one turn widdershins and disappeared into the caverns below the glyph, leaving the regulator and his overlord empty handed.

Malesius let out a cry of rage , Raul scowled hissing utter malice through his metal fangs in disgust, their quarry had escaped, the Blade of shadows had not been consecrated!

Raul fetch Fenrir's breath commanded the overlord, the regulator strode over to the crystal cabinet and drew a symbol upon the glass opening the doors, smoke poured out like a waterfall as Raul withdrew the bottle, gliding over to his master he handed over the phial.

Malesius strode over to the fractured mirror containing Ophidia's trapped reflection, pulling the stopper from the bottle he commanded, *"breath of ice cold and blue, now your petrification undo."* With this the mirror began to mist over obscuring the countenance of the mighty serpentine giant trapped within its facets, the mist ran down the glass in rivulets collecting once more into the phial as its sorcery called it back into containment.

When the last drip had been captured, the overlord replaced the stopper and handed the phial back to Raul, who stashed it amongst his swathes.

Malesius looked upon the glass watching as gradually the glass began to thaw, "hurry we must make haste" the overlord commanded, the motley pair headed back within the sanctuary of the triangular plinth of Ophiuchus, turning to face Ophidia the overlord held his hands aloft sword of shadows in hand and commanded, *"crystal glass sharp and cold, the serpentine prisoner you hold, the mirror will shatter and unfold, release the serpent from its despair, snaking writhing through the air, the portal gate shall now release the serpent queen to find her feast, down unto the lair you go, hunt them down, now you go."*

With the incantation complete, a cracking sound filled the air as the mirror holding the serpent shattered like ice, Malesius held his sword of shadows in her direction as warning not to come near, Ophidia spilled out onto the floor like a gush of water, snaking across the floor towards the plinth of Ophiuchus, Raul pointed a bony appendage at the glyph upon the floor and incanted " UNCHAIN" with this the glyph slid open to reveal a large eye shaped hole which cut through the triangular plinth, the motley pair of cohorts watched as the serpent Ophidia licked the air in readiment sending out her forked tongue like a great barbarous whip, hunting for Freyja and uthers scent, before disappearing like a vast worm into the earth as she encroached upon the tunnels below, with a final slither, once more the eye closed shut upon the plinth and the overlord and his regulator stood looking at the glyph, malesius let out a rasping laugh, and said "And so begins the game of cat and mouse.", and with that the overlord left the chamber his cloak billowing behind him like a thundercloud.

THE TUNNELS OF CHARON

Freyja was overjoyed to have found Uther, but they had been thrown into the thick of it there was no time to catch up, it was black as pitch down here and soundless as the tomb, she withdrew the stave of Gwenhefayr from behind her back and tapped the base on the ground with a dull thud, the ogham runes lit up in a verdant green giving an eerie hue to the tunnels confines, "it seems once more we are reunited, but alas we must hurry " stated the ovate, Uther smiled kindly, "I am glad to be reunited once more, I fear we should leave in case we are dispatched" he replied, off in the distance cold coils dropped from the ceiling down into the tunnels.

The warlock and the ovate made off down the tunnel in the dim green light, "we must get passage to the overworld" stated Uther, "i must get reinforcements I need to deliver a blow to the overlord to stop his reign of pestilence, and then there is the matter of his regulator and their pawn Kalthor, I shall call upon the dwarves Morath and the chieftain Bynar and their armies." The warlock felt relieved that their quest was the same to free the realm of the evil reign of terror, it meant she did not have to explain, "when I travelled these tunnels earlier Uther there are three of them, past, present and future, we must pick one before we reach our destination, "I decree that we should choose the path of the present for it keeps us on our course, the past would only lead us further from or goal whereas, the future may take us again further away", Uther pondered this for a while and considered before replying, "we must use Magick to scry the tunnels, it is too dangerous to use flamesword down here for it will burn up the air, what enchantments have you freyja?"

"I have my stave of Gwenhefayr and my 'rootshootstalk', the Magick of ogham, replied freyja hopefully.

Meanwhile behind them in the not too far distance, Ophidia was hunting her quarry, with a slithering famishment, her tongue licked out at the air tasting for scent, she could sense the heat of blood upon her tongue, and sped up her coils, creating earthen swirls upon the tunnel floors as she disturbed the dust of ages upon the tunnel of the past, and focused her sights upon the path of present where her meal wandered, she had not eaten in eons and felt sluggish from her icy confinement within Fenrir's breath.

We must find a underground clearing to allow the visage freyja said, let us journey on further, uther nodded in agreement and on they ventured, uther told freyja the tale of Valanthia and the dwarves and what plans he had to overthrow malesius, kalthor and restore Draco to the heavens, After what seemed like they had journeyed a mile or two, an echoing sound came up from up ahead as they ventured forward into more open space, freyja banged her stave upon the ground with reverence, the ogham runes lit up in emerald hues as they danced around on the stave as if to tell a story, the runes huathe, straif and ohn came into view floating upon the air, the ovate explained, we have protection, no choice and wise choice before us, I determine this to be the tunnels, let us scry and with this she incanted the charm " *wood of oak, wood of light, show us peril, valour and might, down in the tunnels of night."* With this freyja became entranced a vision of coils flashed across her mind white and cold, moving ever faster towards them, its tongue licked out like a lashing torture encircled by barbarous fangs of poison, she could hear the reptilian in her mind hunting for them in the tunnels, Uther snapped her back to reality, Freyja can you hear that, it sounds like something is moving down the tunnels, as he said this the ovate felt the floor shudder as if someone had stepped upon her grave, the earthen ceiling vibrated loosening soil like a cacophony of dread, as bugs rained down upon their heads, and the acrid smell of upturned earth met their nostrils within the humid atmosphere.

Freyja quickly put the events and the vision into place, “Quickly Uther we must move, we are being pursued by a large serpent,!” she exclaimed, the warlock swallowed hard he was not a fan of snakes, “we must head towards the tunnel of present she stated breathlessly, struggling to draw air in the oxygen starved tunnels as she ran, Ophidia on the other hand could feel the vibrations of the pairs feet thundering upon the floor, this would only aid her in detecting her feast she surmised, she felt the tremors they were not far now she thought to herself as they exited the tunnel of the past, she would catch them unawares.

The warlock and the ovate skidded out of the tunnel into the mouths of the three gateways, taking a moment freyja bent over and rasped for breath as uther surveyed their surroundings, after a moment of contemplation he questioned, which one shall we take, which is correct, freyja looked around, it was peculiar as the appearance was not as it once was before her encounter with Raul, the three tunnels had similar openings, earthen strewn with gnarled roots cascading down from the ceiling, as if cramped trees wished to stretch out their appendages from age old confinement.

However in the centre of the labyrinth stood a square tomb stone encrusted with earth, around the edges was the same runic inscription freyja had encountered before in the well of portal and fire pit where she had met the mischievous feanyx.

□(7+□/(,9□6:$5'□□+,71□%(7:,;7□6,7+□

□'52:/□1$'□+(7□;(17□

Atop the tomb were three stone skulls each one facing a tunnel.

Suddenly the pairs attention was drawn from their riddle, a loud swooshing could be heard travelling up one of the tunnels like a cold icy wind threatening to envelop them, they quickly stood back to back to view the remaining two tunnels, the warlock brandished his mithril blade of oaths at the ready, whilst the ovate stashed her stave back in its place and drew her ogham blade, for darkness would shield their whereabouts a Littlemore.

The warlock and the Ovate stood back to back facing the two opposing tunnels before them with intrepid breath, each heartbeat felt like an ominous ticking of the clock as they awaited their fate, battle in the darkness loomed.

The rumbling grew ever louder like some impending earthquake, Freyja and uther blinked hard in the darkness as their eyes adjusted to the gloom, loud hissing met their ears as Ophidia exited the tunnel, her gaping mouth loomed before them with barbarous fangs of death poised to strike, her long tongue licked out tasting the air to locate her prey, uther dodged as it nearly missed him, freyja sliced at the air narrowly missing Ophidia, for although sluggish the serpent was too fast.

Warlock I see you hissed the serpent, freyja dove behind uther as he slashed at the air with his mithril blade of oaths, the serpent advanced towards freyja her coils expanding and diminishing , hissing menacingly, ovate where are you I smell you?

Uther incanted flamesword, "*Down beneath the earthen lair, to trap us within your snare, this day it will not be, light of feanyx set us free*." With this the crackle ember Feanyx ignited the cavern glowing menacingly within the pile of skulls atop the sarcophagus, casting light upon the abhorrent sight before them.

A pure white snake filled the passage way, her milky pink eyes full of malice and hatred, huge barbarous fangs protruded from her jaws like a vice of death dripping with venom which threatened to burn its victims into paralysis, her coils curled and unfurled as she navigated the small space in hopes to catch her quarry.

Freyjas blood ran colder than the serpent before her what a petrifying sight to behold, she stood stock still unable to move transfixed as Ophidia slid towards her, uther noticing this leapt upon the sarcophagus launching himself onto the serpents head, he Dag his mithril blade into her eye, the serpent let out a bellowing hiss as she writhed and contorted to throw off her attacker, the onslaught snapped freyja out of her bewitched state.

The serpent was partially blinded she had only her taste to rely on, she licked the air looking for warm blood, and made good her attack driving her fangs in the direction of the scent, Ophidia snapped at the air harrowingly missing freyjas neck as the daggers of demise sliced thought the air like venomous cutlasses.

The ovate slid on her footing narrowly catching back her balance, standing on the serpents blind side, freyja signalled to the warlock atop the serpents head, she waved her hand down signalling to uther that he was to drive the serpents head down and she would strike upwards, uther nodded downwards in agreement showing that he understood her instruction, Uther raised himself up onto his haunches Stradling the serpent as if he were riding a horse, he twisted the bade in the serpents eye causing Ophidia to lash her head to and fro with ferocity as she hissed in venomous anger, uther struggled to stop in his seat as the serpent thrashed wildly around, freyja pinned herself against the tunnel walls, until the opportune moment to strike.

The warlock withdrew his dagger and drove it hard into the skull of the snake, she slumped downwards at the sharp pain searing through her skull, the ovate taking her opportune moment skidded across the dirt encrusted floor and drove her ogham blade with force upwards through the mouth of Ophidia, the two blades drove home the fatal blow as the mighty serpent fell still, her coils twitched one last time before her head lay slumped upon the ground.

Upstairs in the mirrored chamber Raul let out cries of disdain and anger that Ophidia had not defeated their emissaries, he covered over the obsidian scrying mirror and retreated to his potions tower, Malesius threw a goblet across the chambers in anger and stormed off to have counsel with his troll army guarding the gates.

THE RIDDLE OF BYGONE, EXTANT AND YET TO COME.

Uther slid off from his mount and ran to hug freyja, they would take a moment to catch their breath and rest before considering their next move, the warlock and ovate took good draught from Uthers skin bequeathed by the dwarves, and ate freyjas dried griddle cakes, they discussed their journeys up until now amidst the gleam of feanyx, under close observation from the pile of skulls, past, present and future.

Once they had rested Finally freyja spoke, regarding the current predicament, I state that we claim these barbarous fangs as a weapon for they would be of aid with the poison so long as we take care, she stood up and went over to the serpents head, uther joined her as they cleaved the fangs from the serpents mouth wrapping them deftly in cloth.

The crackle of feanyx blistered in the background lighting up the sepulchre with an eerie eminence, lighting up the runic inscription around the tombs edge.

We must decide which tunnel it is that is the tunnel of the present for we must find a way out of these caverns, stated uther, considering their next move the pair gazed forlornly at the mausoleum, it was then that it happened, one of the three skulls, spoke. "*three tunnels is it that you see, all are shrouded in mystery, three guardians stand at the gate guarding the answer to your fate,"* at this freyja looked over at Uther who appeared perplexed, the ovate on the other hand was not surprised and was now quite used to tasks, she pondered a moment before answering, "*three of you before me sleep, on a sepulchre cold and deep, what is your task if I may, instruct us both now I say*". The air fell silent and heavy, as if you could slice it with a blade, a gentle flickering blew into a gust as the crackle ember Feanyx extinguished himself with a pop and a cackle, casting the cavern once more into darkness.

A chilling voice cut through the air, " *Bygone is my name I say, I am the past not today, bring forth blossom to light the way, place it where the words do say"*

Freyja considered the riddle in the darkness, whilst Uther added, "it refers to light, but my Magicks have extinguished, and we have used your stave, what say you freyja, she pondered a while longer mulling over the words, light the way? Well that's the darkness, blossom?, thinking hard it occurred to her the flower of arcadia! I have it uther, carefully she placed her hand inside her tunic and deftly pulled out the delicate bloom, it glowed with a soft lilac light as it nestled in her hand, Uther smiled a broad smile gently lit up by the dim light, as he observed the ostentatious flower casting delicate nymph like shadows across the cavern walls, put it where the words do say?, he considered the riddle a moment, ah Freyja you must place it with in the jaws of the skull, where words are said, she nodded in agreement and stepping over the carcass of Ophidia she observed the pile of remains, but which one is it uther, there are three.

That we shall have to try out he replied, freyja stood before the skulls and incanted, "*reveal to me now this day the ancestor for which the flower I lay,*" with this the middle skull opened its jaws, freyja smiled and gently placed the bloom within its jaw, the skull closed tightly with a snap, before casting the cavern into swathes of bright violet light, the orbits of eyes burned like crystal amethysts from the flowers hue, freyja stepped back and with uther they awaited the next riddle, they did not have to wait long.

"*Extant is my name I say I am you here this day, a stag inside this chamber lies, hunt him out claim your prize.*" A stag inside this chamber lies considered freyja, well I see no deer or elk only us two, uther added, agreed let me try something, he strode over to the tomb and faced his three judges, using flamesword he conjured, "*Extant is your name you say, to the riddle an answer if you may, I command it now this day.*" With this the skull laughed a copious laugh and opened wide his bony jaw, the warlock and the ovate waited, watching intensely, nothing happened, freyja went over to join uther, and peered inside the skulls mouth, what appeared to be crusty layers of dirt and foliage were rammed into its orifice, she cleared it out with her fingers, as she did so something scuttled across her hand, drawing it back in disgust she took a step back, and looked at the graves lid, a large green stag beetle with antlers crawled out from the foliage and seemed to observe her back.

Extant instructed. "*Now the stag you have found, on his head he wears the crown, claim him now as your prize, taking care he doesn't fly.*" Uther pulled an empty elk drinking horn from his britches, placing foliage inside it he laid it atop the vault for the beetle to take refuge within its confines, once the insect had scuttled from view the last skull gave its ode.

"*Yet to come is my name I say, journey forwards one more day, journey forth into the tomb, be it escape from this earthen womb, or lead to certain peril and doom.*" Well that can only mean one thing stated the ovate, it is referring to this sepulchre which lies before us, do we journey forth, or remain in these tunnels and try our luck she asked uther, the warlock considered a moment and replied, we have had our fill of darkness and caverns, it is wise we take the risk, for air down here is limited and we have no light or supplies on us, we could wander around for days or end up back in Rauls Gaol.

Freyja considered and replied, then we must move this lid, and see where it is that we may go, carefully she retrieved the bloom of arcadia and stashed it amongst her tunic, The pair leant against the tombs lid, digging their boots into the earth as they pushed the lid with almighty force, it gave off a loud grinding sound as ages old stone ground against stone a grinding of teeth, like the deathly grimace of the three skulls atop its sepulchre, Bygone, Extant and yet to come , dust descended in clouds from the lid as the fusty stench of decay and damp hit their nostrils, the lid was half off as they peered into the gloom of the crypt, but nothing could be seen.

Let us use enchantments for the last part stated freyja, for it is tiring and the lid remains stuck, the inscription around the tomb is similar to other portals I have travelled, let us try this together, uther considered a moment, it may be dangerous to use flamesword and rootshootstalk together, but what choice did they have, agreed let us try he replied to freyja.

The warlock and the ovate stood before the tomb of the three skulls, Bygone, Extant and Yet to come, and incanted together, □(7+□/(,9□6:$5'□□+,71□%(7:,;7□6,7+□ □'52:/□1$'□+(7□;(17□WKHYHLOGUDZVWKLQ betwixt this world and the next, as they did so the rings upon their fingers burned with a fiery eminence, burning vines surrounded the pair, like fiery tendrils as they shimmered through the portal into the enchanted realm of knightshade forest.

The overlord malesius and his regulator raul watched the warlock and the ovate in the obsidian glass as they shimmered through the sepulchre portal into knightshade forest, the location of attack had been determined, malesius summoned his Tulon guard, ordering him to fetch the head of the troll army for war counsel in the crystal chambers, raul withdrew to his dungeon of enchantments to summon his army of dervishes and concoct sorcerous armournents of shadow speak, malesius turned the blade of shadow speak in his hands, maliciously admiring the glint of its cross shaped metal.

HEARNES COURT.

Meanwhile freyja and uther arrived in knightshade forest with a thud, taking a moment to survey their surroundings the pair arose from the leafy forest floor rubbing their knees and backsides, dusting the dirt and dust from their clothing.

Where say you we have landed, uther asked freyja, freyja looked around at the dense covering of trees and dappled light cutting through the canopy, it looks like we are in a forest but as for where yet I cannot say she replied, uther looked around surveying the forest, it felt strangely familiar to him, as if from his childhood somehow.

Still let us rest a while it has been an arduous day he added, the pair walked over to the leafy sanctuary of an overhanging Alder tree, resting against the trunk uther passed his dwarven drinking skin around, whilst freyja summoned forth some apples with her enchantments, drawing a circle in the soil she intoned, *"ground of earth, rich and true, sprout forth apples for us two"* with this two rosy red apples sprouted out of the leaf litter with welcome appreciation, uther strode over to the hazel tree and harvested them some nuts to go with it, whilst the ovate picked some, goose grass and chick weed to add to it.

Finally the warlock and the ovate tucked into their forged meal, and went over the day's events, why that reminds me exclaimed freyja, we must release our little friend into the forest, before he perishes, uther looked at freyja perplexed, why the stag beetle silly! Stated freyja. Ah yes the little fellow, smiled uther tapping out the contents of his elk horn onto the forest floor, freyja slid a piece of mulched apple over to the dazed beetle, he clambered on the offering and started on the juices, resting against the tree trunk the pair dozed off to sleep in the warm afternoon, tired from their adventures beneath the crystal gaol.

It was late that evening when the pair awoke, freyja sleepily rubbed her eyes as she battled with consciousness, her mind had been racing with dreams of large white serpents, tunnels and jeering skulls, she had been crawling through the earth and emerged from a tomb covered in stag beetles, peculiar she thought, then remembered her previous adventures as the chill night air and pitch black hit her she was not in bed in llette, she was in a forest, damp, dark and spooky.

overhead a loud flapping and craaw rang out, as freyja fully awoke solomon swooped down to greet her, cocking his inquisitive head and observing her through beady black eyes, he hopped over to her and jumped on her boot, hello my companion she said, eagerly stroking his black feathers, glad of the welcoming familiar presence of her corvid familiar.

Solomon crawed back in agreement, freyja looked around for Uther but he was nowhere to be seen, oh no she thought, where could he be? Solomon gave a loud craaw and swooped over to a nearby tree, freyja gradually got up to her feet, her eyes accustoming to the light she looked over to where solomon was beckoning, squinting into the darkness she made out the silhouette of uther, she would recognize him anywhere, taking a sigh of relief she walked over to the warlock.

Ah freyja you have awoken he exclaimed, I was just following our little friend, he awoke me rubbing his legs together frantically, so I am following him it seems he wishes to go over to these stones, the ovate looked at the small beetle plodding across the leaf litter, almost invisible beneath the moonlight, miniscule and majestic displaying his pincers he trundled towards the mossy stone megalith jutting out of the earth like a ragged tooth, even solomon did not seem interested in devouring the bug which was a welcome outcome, freyja had not seen the megalith before it was carved with a triskele, worn and dirt encrusted from ages, but still visible.

We shall see where he goes, she added they followed the stag beetle as he progressively reached the monoliths base and began his climb up the stones face, the warlock and the ovate observed somewhat laboriously as the insect gradually reached his destination, not daring to interrupt for they were all too well aware that there must be a motive to their encounter with the beetle.

The stag beetle was now halfway up the dolmen, and ventured on to the bottom rung of the triskele carving, ceremoniously almost he began his promenade around the grooves of each circle like the path of some miniature labyrinth, until eventually he reached the heart of the triskelle were he halted, the gleam of the mighty Alluan cut through the clouds hitting the monolith with stark reverence, as alluans rays hit the triskele harbouring the little explorer illuminating the beetle like a mighty crusader as he opened his antler shaped jaws in three clicks, There was a flash and a bang of bright white light which obscured the stone and its inhabitant for an instant, the light diminished to shadows once more revealing the king of the forest, the mighty Hearne stood before the sarsen in regal atmosphere, his horns glowed with white fire beneath alluans embrace.

Freyja and Uther took breath before bowing their heads in reverence to the king of the forest, Solomon crawed in acknowledgement before fluttering down before Hearne.

The air hung thick and pendulous like soup as the warlock and ovate waited instruction, after an elongated pause Hearne shook his antlers and stamped his hooves as if stretching out his new form, then regally addressed his subjects, freyja and uther I have journeyed with you since the portal of catacombs, I had leave to take a form to deter detection by the overlord and his regulator, and now we are in Knight shade forest for the next duty of your quest.

The fate of the realms hangs in the balance and that of the planet nimrod also, we must quest to the forests shady heart and defeat the soil serpent Terrafurn, to release the dragon rider from the temple mount at theadran from ages past, he is to ride Draco to the heavens, his children love and virtue must be freed of their stony shackles to assume balance in the skies, but it will be treacherous as before we can find draco and complete our quest we must free the realm from our oppressor and his minions, and then there is the matter of kalthor so it is not a slight task, the first step in our journey is to free the knight of the temple, i alone as king of the forest know his resting place, but it is guarded by Terrafurn.

You warlock and ovate shall follow me, and with that he shook his head, tossing his antlers to and fro in regal dominance, after a moment he stopped and raised his head bellowed a defiant war bark that rang out like a woodland trumpet.

Beneath the light of the mighty Alluan, Hearne king of the forest lead the warlock and the ovate and the trusty Solomon on their path into the heart of knight shade forest, the valiant trio began their quest with in trepidation, by the light of the anwen I hope we are victorious stated freyja to Uther, to which he replied, by the Anwens fiery bellows I hope that you are right, the travellers disappeared into the forests shadows as Alluan observed his inhabitants.

THE CHAMBER OF CONFLICT

The overlord malesius sat scornfully at the head of the table observing those who he summoned together with disdain and annoyance, his mood as black as thunder emanated into the room like a black pendulous cloud. The council of motley cohorts sat within the chamber of conflict, awaiting instruction, observing their overlord fearfully, the mirrored walls would guard their planning with enchantments of shadow speak.

At malesius right hand sat the festering cadaverous Raul enchanter of the necrotic, his skin glowed a deathly grey in the candlelight and the stench of putrefaction oozed from his cerements, to his left was seated the head of the guard of trolls Maluck the destroyer, his green skin oozed with slime, thick yellow tusks protruded from his bottom jaw, a large copper ring was set in his nose, contrasting with his bright orange slimy hair, slicked back in braids, he grunted in annoyance as flies buzzed furtively around him.

At the base of the table directly facing the fetid Overlord sat the puppet king Kalthor, he appeared meek and cowardly before the three imposing characters surrounding him, like some diabolic inquisition, his thin brown hair hung down limply sticking to his thin ferret like features, he wore the crest of the realm of Malesius upon his emerald velvet tunic, a coiled black serpent breathing purple fire, he was largely concealed by a huge black cape covering his distorted form and crooked spine, a pair of beady green eyes peered out at The blade of shadows forged by the warlock Uther, as it sat in the obsidian tables Centre coveted by four pairs of eyes.

The overlord banged his walking stave three times upon the glass floor to command attention opening the counsel, "I have summoned you here today on a most pressing matter, he began as the words spilled out of his mouth in purple vapor lingering upon the air, we are to discuss strategy for defeat of the warlock and the ovate, in governing our realms, they seek to unleash the

Knight Gondril and restore draco to the heavens, undoing the sorcery we wielded eons ago to control the land through sorcery, Raul and myself had laid many traps in wait for the pair, even imprisonment to which they have escaped, our serpent Ophidia has been slain, power hangs in the balance should they succeed, our task is to intercept them at the edge of knight shade forest once they have released the knight Gondril from his stone form, for if we take them all at this precise moment, the threat of the rider is eliminated and they shall all three be our captives, upon this table sits the consignment of the blade of shadows forged by the warlock, I shall wield this in attack at the opportune moment to bind and capture all three within its shadow speak sorcery, once they are captured they are to be bought here to my crystal chambers.

You kalthor are to govern the realm under my instruction of tyranny, if the warlock and the ovate persist in this line of attack then we shall release the dust dervishes under sight of Raul, at this remark Raul grinned gleefully at the prospect of causing mayhem and destruction across the land, Maluck you are in charge of gathering your troll army to attack and surrender the warlock and the ovate over to me, upon their exiting knight shade forest covering all aspects of the forests perimeter should they try to escape, we will not attack before as I require the knight Gondril, Draco must not be released.

And with this he banged his sceptre upon the floor three times, the counsel of conflict was closed, the minions departed back to their duties.

Hearne king of the forest led the warlock and the ovate into the forest, he trotted along steadily following a snaking path through dense foliage and uneven footing. The journey was slow and stumbling with many incidents of getting your foot trapped in roots and vines, your clothing and hair snagged in brambles as if the trees wished to hinder you.

Solomon kept the look out from atop Hernes's antlers, the tree canopy was too dense to allow flying and swooping, Herne was only too happy to oblige for they had met before, wood flygths were a source of great amusement and annoyance, as they swooped and swung in from the branches throwing acorns down like missiles at the trio, Solomon narrowly missed snapping one with his beak, giving out a disgruntled craw at narrowly missing his quarry, the wood Flyght swung away in the nick of time giggling and sticking out its tongue, Hearne laughed heartily at his mischievous subjects, whereas freyja and Uther were weary of being pelted with acorns.

The further they wound along the path the darker and stiller the air became, thick and heavy as if it were awaiting something, the bird song was less, and they felt as though they were being watched, no conversation was flowing as freyja and Uther were mindful of their quest to defeat the soil serpent terrafurn, and the pair were intent on listening for any sign of the earthly beast, shadows danced in illusion across the forest floor resembling all manner of shapes and patterns, freyja and Uther were accustomed to such sorcery in their training and paid it no mind, the air felt colder as they reached a fork in the road the path ahead seemed to lead up a brighter trail where dappled sunlight hit the forest floor up ahead like a welcome kiss, the warlock and the ovate hoped this would be their direction but assumed that they would not be so lucky, the trail to their left loomed ominously shady and covered by thickets of brambles, dark and menacing the path appeared narrow and tumultuous.

A breeze whipped up as Herne grew to a halt, his antlers outlined against the setting daylight atmospherically, like barbed branches fighting against knightshade forest, leaves swirled across the floor making faint sounds of foreboding, the king of the forest began, "*Two paths at crossing here do meet, for travelling weary feet, one track lies to peril and gloom, a wrong choice here will seal your doom, the path less trodden may be the way, or does the sunlight guide the day.*" We will take the left path replied the ovate, for the path of sunlight seems too easy, she replied with a shudder, Uther added, it is agreed for as ominous as it looks I think Terrafurn would lie amongst the shadows.

Herne bowed his head down in acknowledgement, and began, "a wise choice they have made this day, leafy portal guide the way." With this incantation a patch of swirling leaves swept across the forest floor like a carpet of enchantment, they swooshed and danced gaining in momentum as they rose up into the air, the wind whipped up making a whistling sound as a circle of leaves surrounded the trio like a cacophony of shrieking foliage, all three companions were encircled by the spherical leafy portal as it transfigured them down the shady path through the thorny brambles and snagging branches, gaining in momentum as it cut through thick low-lying boughs and wizened old trees until it reached the paths end where the leaves began their steady decrease in swirling and the whistling winds grew to all but a murmur as the three plus solomon were placed down upon their destination, the crypt of knightshade forest, in front of their eyes a family mausoleum of three stared back at them through dead lifeless eyes of stone, two twins Love and virtue, their small hands raised up to their faces against the hot rasping breath of Terrafurn that had ultimately encased them like asphalt, with their beloved pet goose Wilbur frozen to stone at their feet, shielding them stood the mighty knight Gondril, sword in hand raised before his face against his earthen attacker, the soil serpent Terrafurn, his garments rendered to marblesque form, the heraldry upon his shield, petrified like the encasings of a tomb, horror aghast on his statuesque features, Freyja and uther looked upon the ghastly view with a feeling of sorrow, at the sad expressions, but still they, the warlock and the ovate were here to release the trio from their timeless sleep, for the fate of the realm and Draco depended upon it.

Solomon swooped down to the forest floor eagerly eyeing a wandering beetle, the ovate swung round to search for the king hearne but his silhouette was gradually disappearing into the vegetation, to attend to kingly matters no doubt, it is just us then brother let us begin our onslaught but be aware for the soil serpent freyja stated.

Uther nodded in agreement, aye I shall stand guard whilst you make preparations for Magick, I shall aid thee when required, he added.

With this the ovate walked before the melancholy trio thinking hard as she considered her next move, maybe I shall try an incantation she thought, "*Thaw out stone to flesh and bone*" she incanted in rootshootstalk, verdant green light bounced off the statues, the ovate waited awhile, yet nothing happened.

Ah that approach has not bourne fruit uther, so I see he replied, I shall try, the warlock approached the stone family and in Flamesword, incanted "Smelt" but again alas to no avail, there must be a way reasoned freyja to herself, what skills do I have?, Magick and healing, perhaps it is that they are to be healed she considered, I can give this a try she reasoned, the ovate drew a triskele in the air, incanted "luibhghort" and pulled out her ogham healing bag from thin air, freyja spent a few minutes rifling through the contents, and pulled out some agrimony and mug wort, rubbing the herbs between her hands, she deftly blew them over the stone family and incanted, "iacháu" the herbs settled gently upon the faces of the trio, resting there like a verdant kiss, freyja and uther watched on expectantly, very gradually it happened the herbs began to dissipate across the stone glowing green as they reassembled in shape and form, to produce ogham alphabet spelling out FIRE FLAME FLICKER, uther and freyja considered this, I think it's telling us we need a joint effort, I shall try flamesword stated uther in response, freyja stepped back as uther stepped forward before the trio of stone, raising up his hand he incanted, "*words of fire, I call upon deaths crone, render stone to flesh and bone*" with this red hit flames licked through the air wrapping themselves around the three statues like a warm breath of spring, stone started to crack and fall onto the ground like a tree shedding leaves, warmth and colour began to radiate from within, glowing across the families faces like sunlight as life was breathed back into stony form, the trio stretched out their limbs towards the Anwen above as dappled sunlight cut through the canopy, to welcome them back beneath her rays.

The newly awoken Wilbur honked and quacked in delight as love and virtue dashed into their fathers arms once more, it was a teary scene, the warlock and the ovate watched on happily at the reunification and Solomon observed the waddling goose carefully.

Gondril turned around to face uther and freyja and remarked, "I cannot thank you enough you have freed us from our stony tomb, last I remember was hunting for the twins when I was met with hot soil raining down from dragons breath.

Uther replied you have been encased here 500 years under the reign of malesius and his regulator Raul, their evil puppet Kalthor reigns the lands as monarch whilst the celestial draco sits in chains beneath the earth, Gondril considered this a while, and then said to uther, come let us make a plan, so the knight of the temple mount and the warlock sat beneath a silver birch making battle plans, whilst the ovate, took love, virtue Wilbur and solomon off to, wash and play in a nearby stream, uther would fill freyja in later on the details of attack, the children laughed playfully splashing about seemingly oblivious of their previous predicament, whilst Wilbur scooped up babbling water with his beak like a scoop, throwing and splashing it about amidst much quacking, freyja looked on laughing at the funny little ale jug.

When the forest sky began to grow dim the ovate and her small companions headed back to uther and Gondril, they had already set up camp and had a rabbit stew and fruit ready, uther had used summoning as the ember feanyx danced mischievously in the fire pit, observing freyja with a mocking glance she had not forgotten their underground adventures before, Uther filled freyja in on the battle plans and mode of attack as the children filled their bellies with stew sat upon gondrils knee, After many after dinner stories and tales between the knight, warlock and ovate, the trio lifted the sleeping twins off to bed and settled down for the night.

Meanwhile down the path less travelled, the leaves rustled as Alluan sat observant in the sky watching the leaves form into a menacing form, as the soil serpent Terrafurn manifested from the forest floor,

The mighty soil serpent was created from dark red leaves overlapping like scales of armour, jagged and barbed around the edges, spiky in touch and appearance, her long thorny tail lashed about like some woody serpent licking to and fro as it sweeped across the dead leaf litter, thorny talons cut into the mulchy wood underfoot as terrrafurn drummed her paws menacingly tasting the air, bright yellow eyes observed the dense gloom of knightshade forest, licking the air with her forked tongue of brambles, like a scourge she tasted for her quarry, as she began her advance down the pitch black trail.

Meanwhile in the camp, uther stirred waking up in a sweat something felt off, his dreams had been troubled clouds of swirling dirt before him unable to see, he gently shook freyja awake not wanting to wake Gondril or the twins from, their slumber, he whispered his feelings of discontent and foreboding to the ovate, the pair hurriedly made fast their position to the edge of the camp, hunkered down behind the thicket, blended in amongst the deep dark shadows they observed the gloomy trail.

The warlock and the ovate placed their hands upon the hilt of their swords in readiment for terrafurn for they could feel her entrance was imminent, poised on a knives edge freyja and uther crouched down behind the thicket staring intently at the dark winding path waiting for any sign to indicate the soil serpent was advancing, Strange winds began to whip up dancing around the clearing, throwing soil up into the air as they gave off whistles like a banshee, what seemed like a dark a pendulous shape began to grow ever larger like some vast entity blocking out alluans rays from the pathway, what seemed like two faint glowing yellow pin pricks came into view in the distance blinking like a distant sparks, as terrafurns eyes glowed menacingly in the gloom, freyja tapped uther to go wake up Gondril to assist, he quickly dispatched to the camp and woke the sleeping knight concerning the impending peril, coming towards them, quickly and stealthily Gondril gathered up his armournents and crept over to the thicket releasing freyja to go defend the twins as they slept, she quickly surrounded them with an enchantment of protection, the ovate touched her sickle and incanted "circle of gold, so strong and wise, protect all who here do lie, sleeping underneath this tree, be us safe so mote it be. "green shoots of glowing ogham runes encircled the encampment creating a verdant circle around freyja, hope and virtue, solomon perched overhead whilst Wilbur had his beak tucked beneath his wing fast asleep, the ovate stood on the threshold of the perimeter sword at the ready.

The warlock and the knight crouched behind the bushes as the glowing yellow slits grew bigger as terrafurn advanced towards her prey, the wind grew to a howl ripping down the path to bluster through the trees snatching the branches to and fro violently, as the air filled with the deafening sound of rustling leaves growing ever louder as the earth dragon advanced, as terrafurn reached the midpoint of the track she let out a cry of fury, the trail lit up beneath the glowing blast of white hot burning soil as she spat earthen asphalt into the air, the scorch of burning earth invaded the night acrid and menacing like a looming threat of her capabilities and their fate should they fail, Gondril would not allow that again he was still stiff from ages beneath her stony kiss and was wary of her ashen breath, uther signalled to Gondril as they crept out from behind the bushes and crouched one either side of the path as the soil serpent drew ever nearer, hot soil rained upon the ground as terrafurn glided into the clearing raining hot breath on all beneath her, the hot ashes and soil bounced off freyjas protective enchantments enraging the earthen dragon, who roared menacingly, uther and Gondril charged out from their hiding places to slice through the leafy assailant, but alas to no avail for as soon as the cold steel of their weaponry cut through her leaven form it reassembled around the blade, Terrafurn turned her mighty thorn clad head in anger behind her and spat a torrent of poisonous barbs like scourges at her attackers, the warlock incanted, “Cinders” causing each poisonous thorn to fall from the air in ashen wisps, the furious terrafurn turned her attentions towards the camp and began to stamp off in the direction of the children love and virtue, Gondril roared out in anger for his family had befallen to her spell once before, he ran charging over to the ovates side as did the warlock the three stood guarding the camp as the soil serpent terrafurn approached like a cascade of burning leaves, I hope the magic holds out stated freyja as the trio stood face on to the onslaught of the soil serpent raining her hot soil upon the verdant dome of protection, after the fourth blast cracks began to appear upon the spherical surface as it glowed green beneath another hot blast, let us execute the plan said Uther to freyja and Gondril, for they had previously come up with their plan of attack the eve before, on his command Gondril exited the sphere waving and flailing his sword wildly as the enraged dragon lashed her tail like a cudgel upon the ground making great earthen dents and mounds as she slashed it around, Gondril took shelter beneath his shield dodging the many rasps of hot soil rained down upon him, as the protection around the warlock, ovate and children began to disarm freyja and uther began their enchantments, weaving together rootshootstalk and flames word in to burning stalks of sorcery, stepping out of the circle freyja threw a handful of herbs into the air, they swirled around inceptively as she commanded the charms, “rootshootstalk, and soapwort swill, soil and leaves we wish to spill, we bend the dragon to our will.” With this a great swirling cloud of soapwort enveloped the dragon from head to claw sticking to her leaves like a blanket of moss as it lathered and foamed with enchantment, swilling and disembodying her very form, swilling away the soil and grime holding her form together, damp leaves began to fall onto the floor as the Soil serpent began to dissipate, at the crucial moment when her angerous cries and lashings had ceased the knight Gondril charged forward from beneath his shield and hurled the fangs of Ophidia through the air, they took home within the exposed woody heart of terrafurn rendering her to a pile of mulch upon the forest floor with the last beat of her woody heart, as the air stood still once more the final crack gave way upon the camps protection shimmering to the ground, Gondril uther and freyja heaved a huge sigh of relief, the twins and animals slept on unscathed or bothered, there is one task left to do stated Uther, in readiment for our next assignment, he stepped over towards the pile of damp leaves and brambles that once begot the terrifying form of gondrils captor terrafurn, and using Flamesword charmed, “fire scorch, leaves and soil, smoulder burn and broil, collect the ash of soil and briar, to defeat dust dervishes, cast under fire.” Snaking flames of fiery tongue licked over the smouldering leaves burning them up into rising ashes, uther held out a leather pouch to which the ashes of the terrifying terrafurn floated towards collecting within the smyths pouch.

Once the last ash had settled in a clump, the warlock uther closed the bag and stashed it safely amongst his tunic, for it would soon be needed he could feel it in his bones, the evil overlord malesius and his regulator Raul would soon attack.

And with that the warlock and ovate along with the temple knight Gondril took leave for the night, it had been arduous but they had been victorious thank the anwen and her bellows, and so they settled down to sleep, as the morrow set a greater task.

Meanwhile in the realm of shadows as Alluan cast his illusions across the mirrored chambers of sorrow, preparations for battle were underway within the gatehouse, Raul observed the companions through his obsidian glass with a sneer of disdain, the dawns light they would unleash their attack.

THE AMBUSH

The dawns light caressed the horizon like the opening of a veil, as the Anwen began her daily reign over the kingdom beneath, whilst Alluan retired to his celestial chambers.

The warlock, ovate and temple knight were fast packing up and making preparations for the battle ahead, it loomed like an overhead thundercloud, they knew it was coming, just how and when, they had planned for most eventualities, lobe and virtue sleepily rubbed their eyes, nuzzled by the comical wilbur as he waddled around the camp, Solomon observed the land from overhead, he circled around scouting for any sign of the enemy.

The trio quietly discussed their last minute plans, if kalthor and his men rushed them at the forests edge they would defend with magick and armournents, if they were lying in wait on the borders of the village that would allow time to get the children to maeves cottage where the wytch and pendle the shapeshifting cat could protect them, they hoped it was the latter, they would head along the hawthorn path to maeves cottage on the woods edge, for gondril although slumbered many a century could remember the way, for to him it seemed like yesterday, and the wytch and her cat were not mere mortals.

With the last of their provisions pulled together they set off on foot down the trail of prickly hawthorn bushes, the warlock leading, the ovate and twins in the middle, and the temple knight taking the rear.

The path wound deftly through knightshade forest narrow and secretive beneath the thick ancient canopy of trees, the anwens rays flickered upon the ground as she rose into the sky, hawthorns on either side protruded their sharp branches as if to scratch a droplet of blood to quench their age old sorcery in the menacing enchanted forests heart, white blooms adorned the hawthorns their scent hung on the air like bewitchment, the travellers wound on ever deeper down the path treading over gnarled roots which protruded like pulsing veins across the trail, as if the hawthorns were a living network, each connected to the next, rooks and jackdaws crawed overhead as if to warn the explorers and menace Solomon, the shady confines of the snaking path were a welcome respite from the anwens rays, the forest felt forgotten by time, magic pulsed through its very heart, as if somehow it was watching and holding its breath.

Steadily the hawthorns began to thin out, freyja felt her hair being snagged less, as the trail widened out and became more even under foot, “it is up ahead” said gondril, we are almost at the forests edge.

The travellers felt as if somehow they were being watched, did the enemy have spies amongst the dryads and Faye, the corvids could not be trusted either, freyja touched her golden sickle and incanted, “Mirror mirror shining bright, conceal us may conceal us might, hide us beneath your golden light” with this a resplendent golden sphere enveloped the band of voyagers, within the chamber of shadows, Raul obsidian scrying glass clouded over with smog as the anwen cast her enchantment, we are here Gondril said joyfully, a black cat darted across the path up ahead of them as if to confirm their arrival, pendle had gone off to inform her mistress maeve of her visitors, Freyja gave a big smile and looked happily at uther as the trees and bushes thinned out to reveal a welcome sight for they had journeyed through the dawn, they were still tired from the previous night’s escapades.

At the forests edge nestled the wytches cottage, sunlight barely caressed the moss strewn floor, the crooked ramshackle hut crouched rather than stood at knightshade forests perimeter, branches cut through the roof like struts holding the very fabric of it together, and bug littered ivy adorned its walls as if holding the structure together with its gnarly tendrils, smoke wound lazily from the crooked chimney to adorn the air with herbs and seasoning bubbling from the cauldron below, birds buzzed furtively around the cottages thatch darting to and fro as they collected midges and bugs, the three guardians approached the winding path of cobbles strewn with moss, a large patch of herbs growing in clumps alongside the paths, weeds covered the terrain like a small forest, a rabbit darted into cover as uther, freyja and gondril stepped onto the path, the twins, followed steadily behind remaining silent in awe of the spectacle, wilbur waddled like a little jug at the rear whilst solomon hopped mischievously at the back, pecking at wilburs feathers.

A dim light glowed through the cottages grimy windows like a firefly at sunset, the children were hushed as Gondril took the lead he had previous dealings with maeve and pendle and was hoping they would assist in the fight against the evil over lord malesius and his regulator Raul, freyja touched her sickle slightly nervously, for maeve was a mighty wytch of legend, uther kept his hand on the hilt of his sword.

The cottage door hung partly off the hinges, strange symbols were carved over the doors surface, strange runes cut jaggedly up the doors frames, as the dying sunlight hit them they glowed with an intense blue ferocity, they formed in the air to create a poetic song whispered upon the still air, "*the way to the cottage from the lady who appears upon the water in caerfyrddin, lies through mist and memory, walk without fear for the old voice calls you, through waves and woods.*" One the echo had whispered its tale onto the dusk night air, the symbolic threshold swung open with a creak, like age old bones stretching out from slumber, the three travellers looked at each other uneasily and stepped over the threshold. The inner confines of the cottage were dark and shadowy, the air hung dense with the aroma of magick, burnt sage and candle wax, with ghostly floral under tones of pungent lunar blooms, dust swirled like spirits in the dim light of firefly's
, crooked shelves adorned the walls like jagged teeth, glass vials full of mystery, dried out herbs and bones were stacked and balanced teetering on the shelves edges, in the rooms centre rested a star shaped table, on brass clawed feet, the table drew back barking and snarling like a wooden hound, flashing teeth along its splintered edges, at the unwelcome visitors to its abode, almost sending the crystal ball crashing, the crystal ball reverberated like an amethyst heartbeat as it filled the room with energetic vibrations resonating like a hum of time through every living thing in its presence.

A croaky voice commanded, "disarm" and the defensive table fell still and silent, the band of travellers looked up to where the voice had emanated from, a huddled form stood shrouded and bent over cast into shadow by the embers of the dying grate which spat and fizzled in discontent at the lack of wood, long wisps of grey hair clung to the wizened form like a silver cloak, she stood by the hearth like a distant shadow a memory of youth, cloaked in midnights shroud the wizened crone, her face hidden to face the fire, slowly and steadily she turned to face the warlock, the ovate and the knight, the twins huddled behind freyjas skirts in fear as maeve let out an unearthly cackle of delight, the firelight licked across her features casting shadows to create the illusion of a skull with hollowed orbits across the aged features sunken and toothless, her eyes glowed the colour of storm lit seas, candles flames licked towards her as if drawing on her power, and smoke curled around her like a shield of protective enchantment, it felt as though time herself had stopped in awe of the triple mother and her presence.

The shapeshifter Pendle, pure black cat of ebony fur snaked around the wytchs feet, observing the visitors with judgement through her emerald green eyes, she flicked her tail almost mockingly as she slinked across the crooked floorboards, weaving amongst the companions, as she brushed against their legs as if marking her prey, pendles fur shimmered obsidian, violet and midnight as if unsure which form to reveal which truth to uncover, she blinked at the twins and purred majestically as they giggled back in delight, At the enchanting feline, then almost tauntingly she disappeared in a puff of violet smoke, like an enchanters trick.

Freyja, gondril and uther observed the formidable witch maeve with revered respect as her countenance settled back to that of a wizened old woman, bent over stoop and fragile.

The air cut a commanding atmosphere as the witch maeve spoke, the triad visits me to discuss the plans for battle concerning, the overlord malesius, his regulator raul, and the puppet king kalthor, the celestial wyrm rests beneath the terra in shackles, you the knight of stone wish to unleash him back to the heavens, restore the equilibrium, but you warlock you fear the dust dervishes born from rage and fury, and you ovate you fear the fate of the village peoples.

The triad of light versus the triad of dark, you request safe haven for the twins love and virtue, and my assistance in protecting the forest, I do not grant favours to mortals, all is born out of the cauldron and all returns to the cauldron, but in this instance per chance as my forest is under threat from zephyrs and dervishes let us reach an alliance of understanding, the witch maeve fell silent once more as the five observed her expectantly, uther went to speak first, but the witch drew her finger to her lips in silence, behind her the fire spat and crackled sending out eerie shadows across the quarry tiles, the brass footed table sat still before them as a quiet wind stirred, the scent of thunder and storm clouds caressed the air, the familiar pendle flashed into brilliance before them, a beautiful raven haired woman, her green eyes glowed with emerald fire, pendle drew a circle in the air and incanted, "*luxor in ventris exspectatum apparetum* " wind swept across the table leaving in its wake, silver platters overflowing like a cornucopia, berries, bread, goblets of mead, cooked meats on the bone, cheese and Welsh cakes adorned the table as if it would burst and buckle under the weight.

The little table waggle wick, jigged up and down delightedly as if threatening to spill its consignment, the twins giggled at its antics, as their bellies rumbled at the sight of the feast, maeve waved her bony hand across the air and seven chairs appeared around waggle wick, she nodded to pendle, maeve sat at the tables head and pendle at its base, she motioned to the others to be seated, wilbur honked dejectedly at being ignored, whilst solomon observed from a rafter beam, for there was a cat down there, be it shapeshifter or not.

Maeve and pendle drew their hands up in to the air and incanted, "*by wind and flame by sky and stone, bring forth the feast from lands unknown, from fruit of earth and beast once fed, let table rise with wine and bread, by stars light and hearths old fire, fulfil the call of hearts desire.*" With the final word, the air hums softly and silvern coils of light rain down on the food invoking the blessing, Pendle purred delightedly as maeve declared, let us dine and discuss our intentions to disarm the triad of malevolence, Uther, gondril and freyja nodded their heads down in thanks, smiling broadly at the warm hospitable host, they had not expected such a warm welcome, but they were glad of the feast and offer to assist them in their monumentus battle task.

The seven confidants planned deep into the midnight hours of the plans of attack and counterassault, sorcery and disguise, until the fire blazed low in the grate, the twins slept a peaceful slumber upon the bursting couch, solomon and wilbur roosted their beaks beneath their wings by the hearths warm glow, the plan was set.

Meanwhile across the plains a foul army of trolls and goblins marched towards the county of thygorshire beneath the silvern luminosity of Alluan.

THE TWO TRIADS.

The triad of companions, the knight, the warlock and the ovate would venture out into the dawn of their battle at first light, their hearts holding anguish and valour both, at the same time, but for now they would rest with the twins, maeve and pendle now preparations had been made and provisions packed.

Many hectares away uthers flint dragon sparks swooped on to the open window ledge of hross hall, quested to deliver a scroll to the viking lord Bynar, the miniature dragon was comical in appearance, bright red in colour with large bat like wings edged with sharp thorn like talons, which gripped onto the windowsill tenaciously, sparks had elongated flappy ears, and a large snout lined with razor sharp teeth which snapped at bugs voraciously, flint dragons were used to start fires and uthers sparks was employed to light the forge and man the bellows by blowing hot air, he was fed with Welsh slate which he chewed up with a grinding daily, much to the warlocks amusement.

Sparks had been dispatched that morning from uthers forge summoned by flamesword under consignment to deliver a scroll, the flint dragon blew hot ash out of his nostrils sending embers floating on the air, like singing fireflies then tapped on to the window frame with his snout to gain attention, tendrils of smoke wisped out of his nostrils as he awaited being noticed, inside hross hall a boar roasted in the firepit sending out the sweet succulent aroma, mixed with the spilt mead on the straw from the previous night.

The chieftain bynar looked up from his wooden throne, rubbing his long beard he tried to discern where the tapping noise had come from, sparks becoming increasingly impatient at being noticed sent out a jet of flame, bynar let out a raucous laugh arising to his feet, why it seems we have a tempestuous little fellow in our midst remarked wandering over to where sparks was perched.

Bynar observed the small red dragon with amusement his comical little features displayed annoyance at being kept waiting, sparks snorted out a jet of hot ash narrowly missing bynars beard bouncing off his red leather breast plate, like a warning not to approach too close, the small dragon extended a claw towards the viking chieftain,

Laughing at the beasts fiery attitude bynar took the scroll extended by sparks claw and bowed graciously in merriment, why thankyou small dragon, you are now released, but first attend my smyths forge to fill up on flint for your troubles, at this sparks appeared to give what was a grin before flapping off in the direction of the village forge, disappearing like a red crow into the distance.

Bynar strode back over to the long table with purpose, what could this be he wondered uneasily, that was the warlocks flint dragon, most flints were brown in colour only uther owned a rare red dragon from Anglesey the isle of the dragons, home of the druid lords.

The chieftain unfastened the leather fetching securing the scroll and unrolled it onto the table, he weighed each corner down with a tankard, and holding aloft a candle to illuminate the words in the dim light, he began to read, it appeared to be blank on sight, what manner of trickery was this he wondered, he would inspect the scroll closer lowering the candle close to the parchment to gain clarity a droplet of wax spilled onto the parchment, catching alight from the wick, as it did so flame spread across the parchment like a glowing ember, burning words appeared in the wake of the ember as it extinguished itself, for the warlock uther had cast the scroll inflames word lest one of Rauls corbies should intercept the call to arms, bynar could not understand the strange runes which burned voraciously, annoyed at the sorcery he threw the parchment into the fire pit, as he did so the scroll ignited like a furnace summoning the crackle ember feanyx, for the scroll was a sorcerous flamesword incantation.

Feanyx cackled and glowed malevolently within the fire pit, chieftain bynar he began, I feanyx have been summoned here to instruct thee by my master uther, bynar observed with awed bewitchment and an element of fear, he stepped back lest he singe his beard or plaits, feanyx continued, firstly I must ascertain I speak with the chieftain for my message is urgent and confidential, you must show me the sword bradweith so I convey instructions to the intended party.

Curiously bynar considered the request, what choice did he have he was however having a conversation with a flame!! That alone spake of uthers presence, precariously Bynar drew the lion headed blade from its scabbard, the golden lion adorning its hilt appeared to roar in the fire light under command of its runes, bynar shook his head, must be the dimly lit room, the flames and last night's mead he told himself! Feanyxs eyes burned with voracious delight at the sight of bradweiths roar, so it is set, viking draw the window coverings and seal the door, summon your chief of arms as well I shall wait, bynar snapped his fingers for the page to call the counsel of the watch and attend to the room, momentarily a stout viking entered the room adorned with copper bangles, and bronze beads throughout his hair and beard, he bowed to bynar his beard sweeping the floor and asked, what say you bynar.

Bynar observed the chief of arms faolan with an aura of concern for what he was about to reveal, we have a visitor faolan and he pointed towards the fire pit where crackle danced to and fro, the chief of arms mouth fell ajar as he set eyes upon the ember.

Feanyx spoke, "*now that we are all gathered and the hall is secured, I have an urgent matter from the warlock uther, he is with the ovate freyja, and the knight gondril, they have freed the stone rider from knightshade forest to unleash draco from his shackles to ride to his celestial home amongst the stars, there is peril at large for there is to be a large skirmish on the outskirts of thygorshire, the overlord malesius and his regulator Raul are making haste with their goblin army to take the village by force and slay the warlock ovate and the knight gondril, for dracos reinstatement will undo their sorcery, the puppet king kalthor awaits command with back up, raul has threatened dust dervishes should we not submit to rule under their command, they hold the blade of shadows, the triad of alluan versus the triad of anwen, good battles evil, the warlock holds a weapon of surprise for he holds the mithril blade of oaths cast by the dwarven king Moraths allegiance under instruction of malesius consort velah, in the mines of angor, uther has called upon your you bynar as a companion to help defend the fate of the realm and its people including your own to tarry with him in combat to defeat this pestilence, should you see fit he requests your help for they are only three warriors, he would have one of your men at arms light the watch towers to summon the dwarven king morath and his kin to aid us, he bade me to instruct you to head to thygor and the edge of knightshade forest for place of the skirmish is not revealed, the fate of us all lies in unity.*" And with that a big wisp of wind cut across the firepit extinguishing feanyx with a pop.

Faolon drew his breath and asked, "what say you sire?" bynar turned to his counsel with a grave look and a heavy heart, he pulled at his beard for a moment and replied, we must have counsel for war, draw together our warriors and shield-maidens in the long hall at sunset instruct them to prepare for battle, we leave at dawn, call upon the witch Arianwen to ride out with haste to light the watch towers, faolan solemnly nodded and stamped his foot, turning on his heel he left the hall, bynar strode back over to his throne and seated he awaited the counsel for war with a concerned expression, his eyes gazing off into the distance solemnly, meanwhile chief of arms Faolan stood in the centre of the village and blew his horn with the command for assembly in hross hall, then made way to the hut of the witch.

Faolan looked at the foreboding hut with dread, arianwen scared him it was plain and simple, the two ravens sat perched atop the roof observing him through beady judging eyes, their craws warning and mocking as they hopped up and down the thatch like a couple of guards, the wind blew the skulls of animals hanging from the threshold and odins runes adorned the rafters around the door, he drew in his breath and took a step to make way to her door taking a step forward he was surprised as the door swung open, out stepped arianwen, seer and sage of the elements and the stars, healer of the sick, caster of sorcery, teller of prophecy, the wind caught hold of her snow coloured hair as it whipped in the wind like silver tendrils of a serpentine goddess, silver beads flashed in the light, a stark contrast against the purple and green gown the colour of sages, a midnight blue cloak adorned her shoulders cowling her striking Nordic features, steel grey eyes like that of a wolf observed faolan inquisitively, he cleared his throat which had suddenly become very dry, but she interjected, “warrior, you have come here to bade me to light the watch towers to summon assistance, have ye naught.”

Faolan looked at arianwen bemused, how did she know that, he looked at her and nodded in agreement, that I have sorceress, bynar requests your help if you may.

She looked back and cut a small smile, nodding curtly she announced it is done, arianwen pulled her cowl to cover her face and stepped out in to the yard, a shrill wind whipped up spinning all around her like a tornado, she out stretched her arms raising them aloft into the air, and began to rise upwards causing dust to spin beneath her in intricate patterns, she span so fast she became almost a blur, arianwen shrieked out her spell with intent, the cry of “LOGI” filled the camp, on her command jets of bright blue flame shot out from the tornado like thunder claps headed in the directions of the four watchtowers of the cardinal points, in the distance four fires ignited with conjorous power as the witch alighted back on the ground.

Faolan nodded in servitude and gratitude and bowed before taking his leave from her audience, the witch observed him depart with an inner knowing, the gift was a blessing and a curse.

At that moment in Angor, Morath was alerted to a reflection in the over mirrors, cast down into the mines viewing mirrors an intricate system of mirrors to reflect the overworld into the mines as a method of surveillance, he peered into the telescopic device enquiringly.

He observed a while before retracting the device, looking at his cohorts, he furrowed his brow and said, "the time discussed is nigh, let us prepare." the dwarven cavern filled out with raucous battle cries as they headed off to chambers.

That eve the chieftain of vikings Bynar, and the king of dwarves Morath held counsel for war as all, prepared to come together to bear arms against the triad of alluan Swearing allegiance to the triad of anwen, led by the warlock, ovate and the knight, in the dawns dewy mist two large armies rode out into the land for valour against the pestilence that was malesius, raul and kalthor.

The morning light cut through the clouds, throwing dappled patterns across the earth like the slain ghosts of battles past from whence they lay, the rays highlighting the frosty dew to decorate a multitude of spider webs hung like silken flags of battle.

MYLLAS THE STRANGE CONJOURS GOLIATHS GORGE.

The morning air was light and lofty like the heavens blowing a kiss, the black feathered crow Solomon soared up ahead on the thermals, his feathers guided him upon the wind as his instinct guided back towards his home roost at myllas grove, he felt carefree with not a care in the world as he soared above the tree tops, Solomon the brave had been charged with the quest of petitioning Myllas the strange with a consignment to aid the triad of Anwen in the battle.

The ground below looked small, the roaming cattle appeared like dots as they grazed upon the pastures below, birds scattered from the tree tops as solomon swooped close by, he was excited to revisit his home roost once again and his first keeper myllas the druid.

Solomon began to lose height as the landscape beneath changed, he descended, downwards into the dense treeline as knightshade forest approached, the line of oaks swallowed him up from view, as he hunted the corvids entrance to Myllas rookery, solomon alighted onto the leafy undergrowth with a gentle thud, tenaciously he hopped over to the silver birch known as termondd, its branches hung down like a welcoming hug from an old friend as its familiarity reminded solomon of his former days.

Solomon observed the cracked wizened bark with his beady black eyes, the white bark was split into fissures, the corvid observed the patterns, looking for a key hole, he tiled his inquisitive head to the side and began tapping on the bark with his beak listening for a hollow sound, working his way around and up and down the trunk, he struck luck, an echo resounded from beneath the bark, solomons eyes lit up with delight, he taped again, yes this was it he was sure, Lifting up his right wing he revealed a silvern blue feather hidden amongst his black wing, the blue feather resembled a key from a lock, gently Solomon slotted it between the barken fissures, and gave his wing a quarter turn, a dull click rang out amongst the wooded environment, Pulling his back his wing the crow hopped backwards, as a small bird sized doorway swung open on Termondds surface, giving off a squeaky wooden sound.

A faint green light emanated from within the barks concealment, Solomon let out a loud crawk and hopped inside, as his tail feathers disappeared from sight the door snapped shut behind him, inside the tree trunk solomon was transported back to myllas roost.

Myllas the druid pottered around the rookery, talking to the small black crows as he filled up the bowls with seeds and grains, water trickled down the trees roots in rivulets offering up a gentle stream for the myriad of fluffy black chicks, the silver birch Termondds bark glowed a glistening silver, as his roots lifted from the rookeries earth like waving tendrils reaching out to stretch their aching limbs, they peeled back to reveal a somewhat disgruntled Solomon.

Myllas face lit up at recognising his old friend, and fond recollections of freyjas visit.

The druid waddled over to Termondd, stooped over his beard swept the floor, as he shuffled along almost tripping over his mucky white robe, muttering to himself in delighted under tones chuckling to himself, "why little fellow what a delight to see you again" he remarked holding out his oversized sleeve for solomon to hop onto, the cheeky crow gave it a cautionary tug with his beak before deciding it was safe and alighted on to myllas out stretched excitedly as he fed him a fat juicy grub, "what brings you my friend" enquired the little druid, Solomon eyed the little druid beadily and then tucked his beak beneath his wing to draw out a small scroll, made from leaves, myllas gently took the rowan leave parchment from solomon and unfurled it, alas there was no visible alphabet on it, he alighted solomon onto an outstretched branch and touched the tip of his birch wand on it, green ogham runes of rootshootstalk lifted from the parchment swirling in the air, a leafy green face appeared in thin air made up from the runes and spoke, "*The circle stands in time and space, the goliaths slumber without a trace, stone and moss, earth stood still, they rest they sleep like time stood still, the tribe of colossus awake once more, three times we come and knock on your door, the triad of Anwen calls your name, giants of stone arise again, the warlock ovate and knight of anwen, request that myllas do hereby summon the slumbering circle of giants to aid in the battle against malesius, raul and kalthor, the triad of Anwen, versus the triad of Alluan."*

My my oh my my replied the little druid, well well, I best be getting ready he paced across the rookery, fidgeting as he rubbed his long beard thoughtfully, what to do, what to do? He remarked, solomon interrupted the panic with a loud CRAWW, ah yes little fellow replied Myllas, Awake the giants, come let us go friend, Myllas out stretched his robe once more as Solomon glided from his perch.

Myllas lifted up his arms and incanted "Apparition, no hang on that's not it, Appear, no oh bother. Hmmmm… Apparate!" he resounded eventually and the crow and druid shimmered through the portal into claddachs cave with a glowing incandescence.

On the portals end the pair of travellers emerged inside the confines of a salt scoured cave, the sea permeated the rock with its salty aroma, the clan of claddach slumbered in silence, time wrapped around them like an ethereal blanket soft as moss, they formed a perfect circle around the rock formation, the triskele inside Merlins cave, crafted from lava rock, anemones crawled over its facets and groves, pebbles lay strewn around and starfish adorned its surface exposed by the low tide, they waved their tentacles expectantly at the salty breeze, the clan surrounding the monolith thirteen gigantic stone giants hunched and reclined in postures of ancient sleep, set in stone their faces blank and expressionless, stared lifelessly at the foamy waves rolling into the caves entrance like the licking tongue of some mythical sea creature, heads tilted devoid of emotion yet tinged with sadness, each giant is unique, one shields his eyes from the sun that rendered him to stone, whilst another's stony fist clutches a tankard, they dream listening to the call of the tides, The cave of clan claddach hums faintly with the seas rhythm, the air is dense with power, thick and heavy, with the promise that the giants will stir once more.

Myllas tread tenaciously to the lava rock triskele, carefully eyeing the giants for any sign of movement, drawing his hand into his leather pouch he withdrew a large handful of soap wort, placing it on the grooves of the symbol he quickly retreated back to the caves mouth, turning around to face the sea he drew his arms aloft and faced the incoming tide, he cleared his throat and in rootshootstalk conjured, " *waves wash clean, soapwort do swill, rid the clan of time stood still, awake with waves to wash them clean no longer shall they slumber and dream.* " With the last word said, he motioned to solomon and incanted "elevate" he uneasily and unsteadily rose up into the air to alight on the hill opposite a safe distance from the clan, and the pair bird and druid observed the awakening.

The crashing of the waves had fallen silent, only the sound of its breath remained, echoing in the distance, in the pool of still water trickling down the caves inside where the fresh water meets the sea water the mirrored pool of crystalline dew shimmered as it arose into a form, then she appeared, Aquaruia the torrent! She stride commandingly to the triskele before the clan, standing atop it she commanded "Awash the clan of claddach"at this she transmuted into a violent gush of water splashing the soapwort into a swirling torrential downpour of freshwater as the mirrored pool arose like a whirlpool, to engulf the sleeping clan, an almighty roar could be heard as the waves rushed into the cave like the thundering hooves of a hundred foamy horses galloping at the water's edge, then suddenly the cave began to drain rapidly, the waves retreated, and aquaria once more had vanished, as the last trickles of water sank once more into the sandy floor the clan lay exposed once more, one of the giants shuddered as dust crumbled from his shoulder, another yawned low and gritty like the grinding of boulders, the awakening was slow and steady the clan, arose like old trees in spring stretching their limbs, dust cascading as it crumbled from their form aeons in sleep, they arose once more surrounding the triskele as it glowed an azure blue, sea creatures scattered as the blue light hit each of the giants awakening them fully from their slumber back to the world of the living, once its task was done the light hued down to a mere glow then extinguished as if nothing had happened, still and calm as the rolling waves.

Once more aquaria took form before them, glowing ethereal and translucent like a humanoid jellyfish of sorts, she spoke, "clan of claddach you have been awoken and granted freedom from your stony shackles, cast by malesius and raul, we have need of your assistance, the fate of the kingdom hangs in the balance the triad of Anwen battles the triad of Alluan, we need your help it is your turn for vengeance, seven hundred years you have slept clan, the water around aquaria rippled as she spoke sending out waves of emotion which lapped at the giants feet, With this the head giant Gideon Titan of the clan claddach vast, colossal and imposing let out a mighty roar shaking the inner confines of the cave, the rocks trembled as stalactites and rubble descended from the ceiling in protest, his face loomed like a weathered rockface furrowed with the passages of time, skin coloured like stone, deep cavernous eyes loomed like stormy skies, his wide noble brow arched above them marked with ridges like the tally of battles long past, Titans nose was broad and flattened as if centuries of waves had washed it away, his crumbed lips were framed by a vast long beard like tangled roots, he spoke in his own tongue a battle cry, *"Ghurm -dok ar va telkun Bragg ul gorr"* aquaria reverberated the cry a she dove into the waves "forward we go strength to the stone as Gideon the titan Raised his massive arm aloft, turned towards the ocean he bought his arm down commanding his vast battalion forwards in battle, the terra rumbled as the colossal warriors ventured out of the gorge for the first time in centuries.

That sunset myllas the druid and solomon the crow stood atop merlin's cave and watched as the clan of claddach take to the cliffs, as the gentle crash of waves serenaded below, the goliaths left their gorge, vast silhouettes disappearing into the horizon.

THE TRIAD OF ANWEN

That morrow the warlock, ovate and knight arose from their slumber at dawn, deftly creeping around maeves ramshackle cottage to gather their belongings together save waking the twins love and virtue, for they were to stay under the care of pendle the witches cat along with wilbur the goose, here they would be safe from the perilous journey and encroaching battle, the twins father Gondril watched them adoringly drawing up the blanket around them tighter as the embers of the fire spat and hissed in the gate as if grumbling at being disturbed at this hour.

Uther wondered out to the well to draw water, standing in the half-light he stripped off his shirt and splashed chilly water on his face and body to awaken, dipping his head in the bucket the cold water ran in rivulets down the silver copper tinged spirals of his hair, crackles of fire licked up and down his skin like sparks protesting at the water from the flamesword etched into his being.

Freyja was out at the front of the cottage drawing herbs for her apothecary healing pouch, cutting st john's wort with her golden sickle and chanting to herself uther watched her adoringly for the years they had known each other, they had aged but she was still the same, flame haired and tempestuous, her green cloak camouflaging her against the long grass, making the ovate visible only by the wispy tendrils of orange hair whipping in the dawn breeze.

Uther wondered how they the triad of Anwen would fare against the evil overlord malesius and his regulator Raul and puppet kalthor, what hell awaited them on the battlefield, goblins and orcs no mind and all manner of sorcery no doubt he wondered, still he had sent his flint dragon to enlist Bynar and his crew and freyja had dispatched solomon to request myllas to awaken goliaths gorge, they had the mithril blade forged by velah he pondered rubbing the cuff still shackled to his wrist, they had released the dragon rider and they had their flamesword and rootshoot stalk, it would be an almighty skirmish that's for sure, they had advantage anyhow, by the anwens bellows he hoped they would be victorious.

As the anwen kissed the horizon a damp drizzle began to fall as the triad of companions set out upon their trail, like the tears of a thousand slain warriors, soaking through their cloaks and muddying their boots, a clap of thunder rang out across the sky and lighting illuminated the scene atmospherically as if thor and odin wished valour and victory on their campaign, bowing their faces against the rain the warlock, ovate and knight began their quest as the triad of anwen, with a final peal of thunder and flash of lightning they disappeared from view, wilbur honked dejectedly as the twins turned in their bed murmuring inchoatively, pendle watched on protectively from the windowsill, and so it was to be written in the stars, the battle of evermore.

THE TRIAD OF ALLUAN

The metallic grinding of wheels cut through the heavy smog of concealment whipped up by the regulators shadow speak sorcery that surrounded the diabolical triad of malesius, Raul and kalthor, the grotesque battalion of goblins whipped the large scaly beasts pulling their war carts, the gurlds had dark skin stretched across muscular hind legs, built like stocky oxen, they grimaced through huge protruding jaws of razor sharp teeth, red slitted eyes blinked ferociously and their heads were adorned with poisonous spikes running down their backs, the goblins would use the shed quills for poison darts in battle.

The war carts were laden with axes, arrows and all manner of armournents a fierce match for the triad of alluan with naught but their personal melee and sorcery thought the overlord laughing gleefully to himself, he would soon dispatch the knight gondril, he would not be releasing draco from his earthly shackles and undoing all his harm and sorcery over the millennia, control and power would be his, little did he know that the warlock and ovate had sent word to bynar and morath to join the fight, and myllas was raising the circle of goliaths gorge.

The wind whipped the foul cadavers black locks around like writhing eels which stuck to his rotting features, the tips of silver fangs flashed in the half-light as raul muttered inaudible spells in shadowspeak, the remnants of purple breath hung in the air like a cloud of decay, he lifted up his hand to point the direction of ambush Deadman's fingers revealed from beneath his cowl, a loathsome and foul sight for the living to behold, the head of the goblin horde commanded his legions in goblin tongue, "Krashul Dragga mak vo'rr Hrak'nul trog urzga GRIMNOK VAGH!!" which in man's tongue translates to forward troops move as one tear the earth with your march, blood for the war god, the cry reverberated out down the line of stinking goblins as they excuded their hatred for anything borne of the light and echoed their masters battle chant, Vultures circled overhead awaiting their battle spoils not yet slain following the party like a pack of hyenas, earth became mud in the sleeting rain and iron wheels trudged on thought drawn by the gurlds, malesius eyes glowed red in malevolent delight as he hovered above the floor using sorcery to travel, and kalthor sat atop his black stallion knightshade, a fearsome beast of jet cobalt black, imposing and regal, battle hounds trotted along dutifully at their masters behest following knightshade, big blue dogs with powerful jaws like an alligator covered in short dappled fur.

Triskele portal

The rain sleeted down on the grim looking entourage like a spectral army cut free from the otherworld as they marched on against the elements, the battle was set fate had been cast.

THE ALLEGIANCE

The battle horn rang out through the Viking village, bynar stood regal and imposing, his face painted black for war, his long hair braided with wolves teeth, like a true ulfhednar, he stood to face his finest warriors and shield maidens alike, their faces etched with sheer determination and defiance was a sight to behold, ready to claim their seats in valhalla should it come to pass, they would go out victorious against the triad of alluan if odin called it, Bynar let out the cry let out "FOR THE ALLFATHER, TILL VALHALLA!! And the lid, beserkirs and ulfhednar began their advance, standards raised high the hrafnsmerki, they hoped the raven fluttered that day, the cry of horns rang out like a shrill cry of the victorious dead once more to be remembered and fight aside their kin in the ensuing battle, they would celebrate a feast in the hross hall or valhalla either way before the dawn arose the next morrow.

Deep in the mines of angor morath was assembling his clan, the watch fires had been lit, it was time velah was to be awoken from the recesses of her cave for her long awaited revenge on malesius, once lover and husband, he had betrayed and tricked her casting her into the form of the dragon all those centuries ago, she would release the cuff and shackle malesius the plan was set out the mithril blade had been forged to cut Draco's shackles.

The dwarven king morath pulled thoughtfully at his long beard as he considered the arduous battle ahead, would the viking clan be joining them he pondered, in the background the fires in the forges raged like the anger of valanthia itself, the air was hot and heavy and humid, within the mines, the dwarves were ready to embark there had been arguments about leaving gold behind unguarded, this had now been resolved Thrainor stonehelm the ingots keeper had vowed to stay behind and guard the horde whilst the party were dispatched at war, the dwarf vaults were held in forge hall, situated beneath the mountain roots where the anwen dare not shine, the realm of shadow and flame, parallel to valanthia, the land carved by dragons flame, hand and hammer, the air is warm and heavy and the heartbeat of forges, columns of grey stone pillars support the rooves etched with dwarven runes telling of battles long ago, and fiery dragons, like ancient underground tree trunks.

Walls are adorned with glittering veins of precious ores and stones running like veins to the pulsing heartbeat, firelight caresses metal and anvils ring like bells, and at the heart of the hall lies an eternal flame, said to be taken from the world's first star, the breath of draco, beneath it sits the vaults of gold accessed only through flames word enchantment allowing passage through the flame, passed onto the ingots keeper thrainor stonehelm.

That dawn the dwarves set out across the mountain halls tunnels and ledges as they journeyed towards the realms surfaces, careful to miss the passage to valanthia, the first task would be the descent down the mountain pass, snowy and perilous, all the while the watch fires burned on like the hearts of all warriors as they set out on their quest.

The allegiance was set to aid the warlock and ovate and the dragon rider, morath and his dwarves, velah the dragon, bynar and his ulfhednar warriors, beserkirs and shield maidens, the clan of claddach from goliaths gorge would aid the triad of anwen against the triad of alluan, the overlord malesius, his regulator Raul and puppet king kalthor, with their goblins, orcs and gurlds, it would be a battle of light versus dark, good versus evil, draco must be restored to the heavens once more, the fate of the kingdoms and realm of the planet nimrod hung in the balance, the sun began to rise on the horizon hot and blistering to scorch the earlier rain into a humid agony like an added tormentor, and so it was set, the battle as foretold in prophecy down the ages.

Maeve the wytch sat beside the fire observing the twins love and virtue as pendle her familiar entertained the children with card tricks ad basic enchantments, much to the twins amusement she had bewitched a dormouse to speak, he was running around furtively panicking about his whereabouts in a small squeaky voice as he tried to escape pendles clutches, although in human form she flicked her long black tail voraciously.

Outside the rain had pelted down like a cascade of tears as if the gods themselves had cried out in vain for the coming onslaught, now however the anwen was high in the sky to illuminate the scene, vapour arose from the damp sodden ground as the sun turned it into steam creating a shimmering mirage across the land, as if to conceal the army breaching the horizon, Bynars troop were first to arrive in Kinman ship to aid the triad of anwen, the thunder of hooves kicked up dust as the stout horses broke the horizons line, concealed amongst the steam and dirt cloud, they shimmered like a welcome mirage across the windswept plain, the ground trembled with the distant drum of hooves, war drums and the shrill of horns a most imposing but welcome call, cresting the line emerged the troops broad shouldered ironclad Vikings, helms adorned with sigils of snarling wolves and fluttering ravens of the allfather, their cloaks flapping in the wind fashioned from the beasts of their slay, at the front rode the chieftan of the ulfhednar, wolven warriors eyes like fire and bare chested painted for war, crying out in howls, the sound hit the ovates ears like a dog whistle reminding her of the incident at the oak duir all those years ago, that would explain she held ulfhednar heritage!, it felt like a familiar pack calling, the troop moved as one, a pack answering an unseen ancient call to arms, dark versus light.

At the foot of the plain awaited the triad, The warlocks sword of oaths pulsed with flamesword, the hidden sorcery awaiting its call uthers silver hair flickered in the sunlight like moonlights kiss, beside him stood gondril the griffin rider in black plate, the symbol, of the griffin on his armour plate, helmets visor raised in welcome, the ovate freyja completed the triad, beside gondril her fiery red hair burned in the light of the anwen like regal fire, robes of green adorned her form signifying her status as a healer, the three forces held a charged silence like the drawing of breath before a thunder storm, the oath of allegiance had been held by bynar and his kin.

From the shadowed crags bordering the plain the terra groaned a rumble that announced stone born kindred, Moraths dwarven army emerged in ranks of four, short in stature hobnailed boots thudding like anvils, upon the earth, bearing arms forged in the mines of angor thick axes with rune etched heads, swinging hammers that sang with dormant fury.

Moraths army wore copper and bronze beads braided into their beards and locks, helmets crowned their brows and round shields slung across their backs, they oozed the scent of forges and the pulse of the mountain, holding aloft the standard of the feline thrope Tharion the lion of rage, fury and courage that burns within all of us forged from mountains fire, the roaming mountain lion tharion the root of bravery shield of the defenceless, the banner flapped noisily like a roar as the wind picked up, the bronze pole capped with a lion's head wrought from dwarven gold, deep crimson fabric displayed the image of a majestic lion in rampant stance, manes swirling outward like solar flames of fury.

Morath sighted the triad of Anwen in the distance, a broad grin broke his stony countenance, memories of the forging of the blade of oaths from the rare mithril and the encounter with velah played across his memory, there was oath and kinship he thought , the armies of the wolves of the north flanked the triad of anwen, morath and his dwarves joined the battle ranks as equal ancient allies long absent but not forgotten, the triad, wolf and steel formed an allegiance ready for the reckoning.

Hand slaps back saps hearty laughs and bearlike hugs reinforced the oaths of kinship, even the vikings took part, old grudges buried beneath the common good for victory over the triad of Alluan.

Once formalities had drawn to a close the militia awaited the air hung heavy with anticipation, birdsong ceased and the forest animals paused mid step pricking their ears to some distant pulse beyond mortal ears, the ground quivered like the breath of a goliath, gradually it grew stronger then through the mirage of steamy vapours and dust they emerged, the clan of claddach, beings of earths oldest bones, capable of thunder and ruin, gargantuan figures wrapped in cloaks of moss and shale, antlers of petrified wood protruded from their brows like antlers, they moved slow and laborious but with marked intent, their eyes glowed like ancient starlight and the power of the waves from whence they came, at the centre was the leader Gideon of the clan of claddach, he bore a stave fashioned from lightning struck root, a toped With pulsing lava rock which bubbled voraciously with sea water trapping the power of the waves in its essence.

The clan of claddach were a mighty sight to behold, all parties held their breath in awe as solomon circled them overhead, myllas had been victorious in their raising, slowly they encroached upon the territory of the plains.

That day gathered beneath the anwen the last of the great allegiances stood in unity, the triad of anwen, flesh and fang, forge and flame, the realm would thunder and swords would clash, it would begin here thought uther, and so it was formed as they stood in rank waiting for the triad of Alluan.

SKIRMISH OF THE FEUD

The allegiance waited the air was tense and pendulous, the mighty anwen retreated behind sudden cloud as the wind whipped up and the air fell cold like the tomb, they were coming cold and darkness announced their ascent upon the realm, the breath of the wolf warriors hung on the air and standards flapped furiously in the wind, the army waited with baited breath watching the horizon holding steady their line of defence and attack, hyping themselves up for the fight, the drums and horns were silent for now lest they give their position away and ruin the element of surprise.

Lightning descended down from the heavens like the forked tongue of some great serpent as thunder boomed across the heavens in outcry, the vikings feared thor was angry, sorcery hung thick and heavy in the air as the foul mist rolled low over the plains horizon, tinged with a purple glow rich in shadowspeak like putrefaction made visible, the triad of Alluan emerged spectral and sickening atop skeletal steeds that decayed the grass beneath their hooves, first came the overlord malesius, gaunt and gnarled his face stretched tight over bone, eyes glowing with a pale pitiless flame, beside him the regulator raul, taller and crueller cowl snatched back to reveal rotting visage, silvern fangs and black eel like tendrils of hair, held the razor like reins of the skeletal beast with twisted limbs and hands like talons, his black cerements snatching in the wind like fetid shrouds, the two silhouettes bled perpetual shadows, cloaking almost rear of the overlord and regulator to conceal the puppet king kalthor portraying his subjugation, his rusted crown perched lopsided atop his weaselly features, his crooked spine and hunched form positioned him unevenly upon his death horse, pain and agony etched upon his features like old royalty gone insane, shadowspeak pulsed in their wake like oil on water, they were not alone the ground shook under the march of goblins like a fury of ants advancing on their quarry, a horde of snarling misshapen creatures in rusty oozing armour, eyes wide with madness lashing on the ghurls, spined backs eyes like black coals and jaws crammed with fangs, the howls split the wind and the booming thunder storm.

For a tense moment the triad of anwen observed the triad of alluan. Then came the call SKAL! Horns rang out in battle cry and drums thundered, The triad of Anwyn stood tall, the knight sword drawn, the warlock wielding the blade of oaths burning with divine fire, and the ovate her stave held high encircled with runes of light, the clan of claddach rumbled forward like rumbling mountains, flanked by ulfhednar snarling with battle lust, dwarves advanced swinging axes and hammers forming a living wall of stone and steel.

The attack began across the plains before flesh met flesh, cold violet shadowspeak flashed across the air meeting with red-hot flamesword, wrapped in verdant green rootshootstalk, the spiritual war waged and underway before the physical battle had begun.

Lightning cracked the sky as the ovate and the regulator locked spells, blasts of raw sorcery licked the tumultuous air, light against dark good against evil, the knight gondril rode advanced into the goblin ranks atop the griffin pygar who had come to aid the event from the temple mount at theadran, he span like a falling star, his blade cleaving through shadow and flesh alike, giants swept their clubs through the ranks of the snarling beasts flattening and stamping on dozens, pressing them into the earth like fossils.

The battle was borne of chaos and legend blood and fire, the triad of alluan fought with fury born of ancient vengeance but the triad of anwen held fast, stone did not bend flame did not extinguish the house of lycanthrope and feline thrope had come together despite age old grudges against a common enemy, the triad of alluan.

The battle raged on pushing the triad of alluan into the village of thygorshire as the triad of anwen gained ground over the plains, villagers fled in terror and barricaded their doors against the foul and loathsome beasts and assailant of sorcery, fyngar and tarog retreated to the gatehouse, this was not their battle, the shutters went down at the oxen and plough, Casualties were littered everywhere like the earth had spewed out her dead for judgement, the remaining survivors battled out on foot in hand to hand combat, the clan of claddach had retreated back to the sea for they were unable to set foot past the plains due to magicks as they were bound to the waves and the oceans, to tread beyond that boundary would render them to dust.

The village had lain quiet prior under the shroud of dusk, muting out the birdsong like a thick blanket as if anticipating the coming onslaught, the atmosphere shattered like ice under hobnailed boot when the triad of alluan had entered the city walls, the church bells rang out in protest one low chime like the coming of doom, from the shadowed cobbled alleys figures emerged, villagers but changed murmuring in shadowspeak tongue, the pestilence had spread from Rauls sorcery, purple mist hung heavy on the air, malesius emerged from the town square well, in a torrent of brackish water a scream rang out as uther hurled flamesword toward the foul apparition, gondril and kalthor clattered onto the hard cobblestones amidst a full on hand to hand melee, meanwhile the regulators necrotic chants were being held back by the ovates rootshootstalk blooming and twisting, the regulator scowled and hacked at the verdant blooms with the blade of shadows rendering them to dust, the air shimmered as Raul ascended to the turret of the keep, freyja charged the tower steps ogham blade extended like justice and celestial wrath, inside the keep the air pulsed with sorcery, uther charged the battlement with malesius dispatched out cold by the well, standing atop the keep he called out in flamesword “DEFEND BY FIRE” a golden sigil erupted underfoot an ancient sigil, he pulled freyja close on to the sigil as raul descended from sight in a cloud of violet smoke, beneath the keep tower battle raged on, dwarven hammers and axes swang and battered like an anvil, and viking warriors hacked and sliced through goblin meat with voracity, the glyph of triskele reverberated in flame casting the enchantment out of the villagers who fell to their knees.

Charging down the turret stairs, the warlock and ovate were met with gondril and kalthor still clattering around the cobbles rolling around in the dust and grime like a pair of fighting dogs, over by the well the rat from the cellar malesius had stirred from his unconscious sleep, and disappeared from allsight, the treacherous slimy snake, cowardly and spineless had retreated, raul stood in his place hovering over the well, uther and freyja joined hands, a loud crack rang out as the sky split and bled rain the warlock raised his sword of oaths, and the ovate her ogham blade, they chanted in tongues of sorcery combining their flames word and rootshootstalk into a multitude of burning vines, freyja ducked down to the earth and began drawing symbols in the soil, together they incanted "*symbol of Wonder, sigil of Light, In the Darkness, Show the Light*"

Summoning forth a vortex of unravelling force holy and absolute, raul charged cloaked in shadowspeak, his filthy cerements glowing purple, the combined magicks of the warlock and the ovate struck like a lightning bolt, a heavy silence where his chants were not heard, a muffled void of light to absorb the dark, he screamed as the spell unmade him wrapping him in burning vines silencing his chants and cries, like the thorns of the Christ, cutting into his flesh, the foul necrotic sorcerer folded into nothingness leaving nought but a piled black stinking shroud lain upon the earth.

Now with raul dead this was his opportunity to retrieve "The Sword of Shadows" that he had made for malesius as it has been misused Daemons and Disease had been called forth from the blade, he strode over to the pile of black rags lying before the well and rooted through until the glint of cold hard steel met his eyes, the amethyst stone blinking out like a vipers eye, reaching down he grabbed it and concealed it within the confines of his jerkin, this would be needed for dracos shackles, This blade not been the promise of what it would be wielded for malesius had told uther it was needed for summoning Harvest Spirits and ruling the land, instead ,the evil overlord had wielded the blade of shadows for Greed, malice and Blackened Heart and his own personal gain, and not for the good of all, the results had been catastrophic with crop failure and plagues across the realm.

The warlocks quest was to obtain "The Sword of Shadows" and right the wrong that he had created, the Ovate and The Warlock would heal the land, and release Draco from his shackles with the help of gondril the golden phoenix rider, uthers life had taken him back to the underwater caves with draco and the shard from his youth, the Ovate freyja and he were connected, from childhood.

Cries rang out all around them as the battle raged on, gondril morath and his kin and bynar and his warriors were still in combat, there was no time to rest, the overlord had fled, there was still the matter of kalthor, At that moment an arrow swished towards the warlock, released by a foul stinking troll, it sped home to its mark burying itself deep in his leg, Uther reeled as first wood then repeated fire seared through him. Sending him crashing to the ground, but the warlock knew that it would only be temporary; he knew he would have to move fast in case it was a ghurl spine, in flamesword he incanted, "Multiple Shafts of Fire Bright, Smite thyne Foe within my Sight "with this a jet of flame coloured arrows sped through the air taking out a troop of goblin archers, The Warlord may been injured but that was a more damning blow to the army of stinking goblins he thought as he pulled out the arrow and singed the wound closed with his finger tip.

Overhead solomon circled, looking for a spot to land, the courtyard looked most likely, the Guards would probably run at the sight of him, goblins were superstitious about crows And if they did not, he would squash them with a barrage of rocks from overhead.

Freyja looked on in disbelief aghast! What had happened there they had cast protection magic how had those arrows gotten through to pierce uther, She looked out through the hole in the tower wall to see the littered bodies of goblins being circled by the massive spectre of a Gryffin, the rider gondril astride his back releasing arrows into the skirmish below in defence against the goblins, the knight had slain kalthor whilst rolling around on the cobbles dispatching him with a single blow of his cudgel to the head.

It appeared as if the temple mount at theadran had seen the lit watchtowers and dispatched a griffin, to aid the triad of Anwen, Freyja watched the Gryffin circle to land in the courtyard, she began the descent down the tower steps Sword in hand and heart in mouth, the warlock uther followed closely behind, she could literally hear the blood coursing through her veins like a drum.

Freyja was stopped short as midway up the stairs by a troll charging the steps, she must have been distracted not to see the beast, as all of a sudden, “THUD” Her world went red, as the blood from her head wound streamed in to her eyes, behind her unseen by the goblin the warlock let out a cry of flamesword, upturn and burn!! Sending the foul creature gambolling down the turret in a ball of flames, uther helped steady freyja back down to the battle in the courtyard beneath.

The griffin pygar was back winging to land when a Bluster thrown by snark the goblin chieftan at arms blew up in his path, What now? Thought gondril as he tumbled from his mount, As the dragon rider fell from the sky his luck changed, a Hay cart broke his fall!

A second Bluster drew ever nearer, without a second thought uther who was watching summoned a Fire Ember, it would take a short while to coalesce into form, until then he would have to fight the Bluster by himself a being of air and fury an elemental!

Freeing the Shield from his back and drawing "The Sword of oaths" the warlock was just in time to parry the first blow from the Bluster, I just need a few moments more, and then your history Bluster, he thought, luckily the fire crackle feanyx apparated into being igniting the bluster like a torrent of flame, as the two elementals span off across the ground bluster igniting ember and ember trying to engulf bluster, At that instant six of the overlords personal guards appeared at the top of the stair turret, "INTRUDER" bellowed taron the suited gaoler, footsteps echoed from all directions. Gondril charged back into the attack, rolling to the left to avoid another strike from the flaming Bluster, at that point more summoned Embers roared into life engulfing their prey in a torrent of flames.

Now was his chance to engage taron in combat thought uther he had not forgotten the events in malesius castle gaols, "May my aim be true, swift and just" he thought, in the background the chants of viking and dwarf met the roaring of embers, ringing out like battle fury as the Embers crackled hungrily devouring Blusters to fan their flames, Rushing forward the warlock swung his Sword of oaths in a sideways arc, crashing into tarons shield, the gaoler glanced the blow and swung his broadsword overhead in return, CLANK! CLASH! SMACK! The battle cries of swords cried out in rage and competition, with the union of cold steel rang out a metallic symphony, Uther and tarons battle raged on, the warlock lost his footing and stumbled to the ground, availing him an opportunity to stab upward disarming tarons defences.

Meanwhile although raul and kalthor were demised, there was the matter of the goblins who would fight on whilst their measly overlord lived, although the serpent had slithered away in retreat.

The ovate and the knight took breath and water considering their next move, they would regroup and rest before hunting out the evil overlord malesius, but first let us escape this castle of terror, They engaged the staircase, where had the warlock gone? Thought Freyja, as they approached the bottom of the stair turret Freyja noticed there was a struggle underway in the courtyard between uther and taron, she lifted up her Ogham wand and recited in rootshootstalk, "*While we tarry, Protect us three, Keep us safe, Me you and Thee, So mote it be*"

Immediately a jet of green light shot out of the wand tip presenting a shield of light like an umbrella, freyja and gondril huddled underneath and advanced towards the scene keeping their wits at a knives edge, Freyja looked with a heavy heart at the number of goblin guards in combat with dwarf and viking alike, "Mighty Anwen what shall we do?" Solomon came to the warlocks aid, flying about the gaolers head obscuring his line of vision desperately trying unseat his helmet uthers luck was in, taron too busy swatting at solomon was distracted enough for the warlock to jab upwards with "The Sword of oaths" impaling taron beneath his ribs, it went straight through and punctured his armoured chest, bright white light emanated from the blade as light battled dark and drew the sorcery from the suit of armour, no longer animated it clattered to the ground noisily, Uther lay on the floor exhausted and triumphant! He had won the battle for the moment, but time was fleeting and they must make good there escape first, the triad of anwen must regroup to find malesius.

Across the courtyard bynar had the head goblin beneath his axe, AARGHH! cried the beast as he reeled his head swimming, gasping for breath like a fish floundering, he smashed on to the cobbled yard with an almighty impact, and cracking cobbles as he landed, The foul creature lay twitching, then silence as his eyes rolled back into his skull.

Freyja was making an easy meal of the trolls with her newfound companion pygar the griffin who was swooping and plucking up goblins, then dropping them from great height like bugs, "EASY PICKINGS!" she cried she loathed the foul ugly beasts, with their vile smile and evil ways, morath was also tallying up casualties and kills alongside bynar, she stood victorious by the pile of troll carcasses, with gondril by her side, pygar with head bowed in exhaustion rasping for breath, he was an almighty but magnificent sight, blood spattered but true and pure of essence.

"QUICK LETS BE GONE BEFORE MORE ARRIVE" the warlock shouted as he gestured towards the Gates. "FOLLOW ME." He instructed, addressing the band of companions, "I'LL SECOND THAT!" shouted Freyja as they all charged toward the portcullis.

As they approached a pair of Great Trolls with Poleaxes barred their way." I thought we had done, but still there's more!
Ah well One each" gasped Freyja, Out of breath and rasping, they were all exhausted as they began the onslaught, The troll on the left saw them approach and roared a chilling sound, the stench of

its breath hung heavy on the air like rotting meat, hearing this the Troll on the right began to charge towards uther, The warlock raised up his right arm digging his Sword with all his might in to the troll's heel, sending him crashing down towards the ground, causing it to roar in pain and confusion as it crashed down to the hard earth!

The second troll was enraged as it lumbered at speed towards Freyja, she waited until he was nearly on top of her, then quickly dived underneath it lying on the floor with her ogham sword pointing upwards, she drove the sword in to the underbelly of the troll both impaling and disembowelling it with one move, foul stinking fluid oozed from the troll as it lay diminished on the floor, She lay there for a few seconds catching her breath, Thank Anwen that's over she thought, There was just the final hurdle to overcome, the gate it would need an incantation.

The triad of Anwen all began to head towards the gate Freyja and uther chanted in unsion, "*While we stand, Sword in hand, Gate asunder, By The Anwens hand, Into Cinders ash on ground!*"

CRASH! A plume of smoke arose as the gate erupted into flame then dust upon the winds, creating an exit to freedom, At last the band of travellers were victorious, it had been a hefty task to escape the triad of alluan, the evil overlord malesius was missing, but for now at least the regulator raul and the puppet king kalthor were out of the picture, they would devise a strategy for draco and malesius after rest.

Uther, freyja and gondril departed in haste to the cover of the wood, towards maeves cottage as the sound of dwarven hobnailed boots and viking warriors departing into the distance victorious rang out like a cacophony of triumph, there would be much feasting in hross hall and the mines of angor, and the triad of anwen, they were all in need of rest and a meal, before planning their next move, the sun set on a graveyard of goblin carcasses raul and kalthor were lain slain to cross the river styx with charon, in the crystal tower malesius observed his obsidian scrying glass with bitter anger, he would unleash the dust dervishes like a pestilence across the kingdom, they would pay for this, meanwhile in ingots hall in angors mines velah eagerly awaited her summoning, the gold glinted in the light of the forges like hope and valour in the hearts of men.

BROODING VEHMENCE

The triad of alluan had been hit hard, malesius had not bargained for the house of Lycan thrope and feline thrope to offer allegiance to the triad of anwen in battle, an easy pickings had turned into a catastrophic blow, the evil overlord had lost his immortal necromancer raul, his puppet king kalthor and the decimation of his goblin hordes, not to mention the loss of his gaoler.

Malesius slumped on his thorny throne gleering and scowling vehemently, he was much injured from the sorcery aimed by the warlock and ovate and had shimmered out of the wells portal just in time save for the looming jaws of eternal death threatening to devour him, but vengeance would be his he thought as beheld the jar of ashes watching the sands swirl violently beneath the stopper.

Malesius laughed with an ageless malevolence not human in tones but pure malice, with a slow deliberate twist he loosened the ancient stopper from the blackened glass jar, a loud screeching sound like a thousand whistling winds escaped as the seal broke, spewing forth from its orifice a torrent of swirling dust dervishes, spectral wraiths of ash and malice, insatiable and hateful they shrieked as they spiralled upwards like a tornado skywards spinning widdershins, beginning their cloaking death across the realm spilling out like poisonous smoke in a choking gale, crops withered to bine dry husks, livestock were rendered to skeletal remains, and men fell coughing blood as the plague ridden pestilence consumed all in its wake, Villagers scattered in terror but alas it was to no avail, the overlord observed from his obsidian scrying glass and cackled in hatred and the anwen hid her face as the sky fell black.

Back in maeves cottage the triad of anwen were slumbering peacefully with the twins love and virtue after an arduous battle, blissfully unaware of the raging massacre, pendle watched observantly from the windowsill as the wytch gathered herbs for potions in knightshade forest, the pestilence would not reach there it was banished and sacred unable to encroach on the boundaries, protected by age old magicks.

Deep in the mines of Moria a red winged serpent stirred, in the stone halls where the dwarves whispered her name in fear and awe, velah stirred, the ancient red dragon bound in darkness for an eternity she felt the call of the villagers cries with a cracking roar that split the mountain asunder she erupted free like molten lava, wings unfurling like flaming banners, eyes ablaze with flame born wrath, the air reverberated like a cry of triumph as she arose a living furnace streaking towards the blighted lands.

The scorned bride Velah came not as destroyer but as purifier, no ordinary dragons fiery breath, but cleansing sacred defiance, a cry for her own vengeance and a cry for draco and now the villagers against malesius mad scorn and delusional grandiose plans of dark sorcery.

Advancing into the swarming cloud of malevolent dervishes she remained untouched for malesius sorcery was still vehement in her form a layer of protection against his unleashed army of cremated dead, with each beat of her wings swatches of red light poured down cutting through the swarming blackness like a red hot knife, the dust dervishes shrieked in defiance unravelling midair scorched from existence in ravels of holy red flame.

Velah cut through the cloud of demise like a red dart heading towards the crystal tower where her estranged husband waited or what was left of him, he felt in his blackened heart her return as she gained distance, the part of him that was once human had a knowing, her shadow engulfed the obsidian tower shadowing the glyph of Ophiuchus malesius arose to greet his doom, he could sense the end was near he had not bargained for the release of his traitorous bride, his, cerements cast a shadow across his features as he stood and waited too weak to wield shadowspeak.

The glass dome shattered sending crystalline daggers through the air like razor sharp portents of anger as velah crashed into the scrying tower and landed with a cracking thud upon the glyph of Ophiuchus,

Her talons scratched the gilt edges as if to erase the memory of aeons ago when draco had been shackled and she had been cast to scales by her insane husband, for a second their gaze met one observed the other tentatively the air like heavy soup waiting for words to be spoken but only hush fell heavy and deathly silent, velah observed the rotting carcass of dark sorcery with human eyes, as a tear spilled down her scaled red cheek, malesius wishing forgiveness, for those eyes sparked memories that he had not felt in many a century, sorcery had devoured him, greed hunger and power had ravaged his form like a principality, and for what he was defeated, his army gone, his kingdom and riches, he had long forgotten about his bride Veah but now it came flooding back to him the love, the moments before the insane greed, he bowed his rotting head his misshapen twisted form a shadow of its former self, he fell to his knees in a crumpled heap before the tear stricken red dragon observing her one last time through milky eyes he felt terror at his fiery demise, with putrid lips he said, "*Maddeua fi, os gwelwch yn dda.*" Velah drewa deep breath filling up her bellowing chest, as she let out a final roar and flapping her almighty wings, the scorned bride incinerated the evil overlord, once her traitorous spouse to a pile of ash smouldering upon the ground like his dust dervishes, the pestilence was ended the realm was scorched but plague free.

As the last embers of the overlords throne guttered to ash velah arose amid the smoke, her massive form outlined in flickering crimson, slowly the fire that wreathed her scales began to draw inward her wings folded into nothingness, talons softening spine collapsing like coiled shale unbound, flame danced and coiled around her like tongues of embers, from the heart of the brightest flame stepped forth a woman, tall flame haired her eyes aflame with the memory of dragon fire, her naked form and bare feet upon scorched ground she stood in silence, the echo of wings still rippling through her mind, her skin aflame with fire and heat her breath like the winds of a forge, she observed her form in the amethyst mirror before her, taking in her hands and arms she examined her feet and touched her face and hair, then blackness as she passed out from exhaustion and heartache on the floor of the ravaged mirrored tower.

Inside maeves cottage unbeknown to the sleeping warlock uther, a golden bracelet unclicked, the cuff of velah fell from his wrist into the bed sheets, the dragon was free the allegiance and oath upheld.

In its place bore a mark not unlike a scar from whence it had sat, the warlock and ovates two rings glowed with a resolute celestial hue in the dim room, it matched the inscription on the rings.

THE GROVE OF THE THREE RAYS

The early hours caressed the thatch of maeves cottage, the soft breeze curled sinews of smoke from the chimney as the dawn bled into the rise of the anwen, inside the cottage crooked cottage the hearth crackled with delight casting shadows upon the stony walls like spectral puppet shows of the underworld, the warlock uther stirred the cauldron mindlessly his eyes off deep in thought for he had found the discarded cuff of velah, so it was done, the ovate freyja sat by the window sifting dried herbs between her fingers humming a tune only the dryads knew and the fae, the knight gondril polished his blade in silence his jaw set as he recalled the previous day's battles, he had a timely reminder in a deep gash from kalthors sword, which had been packed with st john's wort a medicinal plant by the ovate healer freyja.

The wytch maeve observed them like memory ageless and swathed in cloaks of time, on her lap curled pendle the cat with eyes of obsidian a regal but mischievous shapeshifter, half dreaming half listening, the goose wilbur stood sentinel by the fire plump and proud like an ale jug, a small enchanted guard from a distant realm,

The twins love and virtue played near the spinning wheel, but neither touched it feeling it should not be messed with.

Maeve stirred from her silence and announced, "*you are ready the hollow of the three rays calls, this eve under the kiss of alluan we go.*"

The dragon rider questioned "will the veil part?" as he stood by the hearth, to which maeve replied "it requires the three blades and to walk in truth, then yes be wary though for what waits beyond knows your names."

That nightfall the five and the two children accompanied by solomon and wilbur set off, warlock ovate knight witch and cat to perform the rite, into the ancient woods where elder trees leaned into listen, moss muffled their footsteps and silver moonlight lit the way.

In a clearing curtained by hanging ivy and branches three stones arose from the earth to form a ring, the sentries older than forgotten kings, each bore a slot shaped for a blade.

The ovate freyja with her Beltane crown and cloak of forest green drew her ogham blade and placed it in the eastern stone, next the warlock uther unsheathed his blade of oaths whispering in flamesword he set it in the northern stone, and the knight gondril, silent and steady drove his broad sword into the third.

The air shimmered, around the floor leaves span pendle arched her back hissing wildly, wilbur the goose honked alarmingly and stepped back, from the circle burst forth a ring of light gold and green flame with UXQLFLQVFULSWLRQ□(7+□/(,9 □6:$5'□□+,71□%(7:,;7□6,7+□□'52:/□ 1$'□+(7□;(17□WKHWUHHVEOHZEDFNZDUGVDVLIERZ LQJ to some ancient force remembered, the portal ripped asunder, not a door but a wound in time undoing malesius sorcery, the air rippled like water.

The twins love and virtue clutched at each other eyes wide as the ovate took their hands, it is a path she whispered but not all who walk it return the same.

The knight gondril the griffin rider from the temple mount at theadran stepped forth first for this was his quest to release draco to the celestial heavens, second was uther the warlock, unshackler of chains, third freyja the ovate protector of the ancient places, the children followed into the hollow land.

Pendle and the witch maeve waited at the threshold for this was not their battle, wilbur however waddled in defiantly unshaken and brash as maeves voice drifted upon the breeze, *"only the brave may open what was sealed, only the true may carry light into the dark."*

THE HOLLOW WORLD THE UNSHACKLING OF DRACO

The triad of anwen shimmered through the portal, the air thickened oppressive and muffling, scented with star dust, iron and the distant echo of bells that had not rung in millennia, the hollow world was not empty, but vast, a twilight realm caught between breath and memory, trees hung upside down from the sky and stars floated in the air like unmoored lanterns, the atmosphere sparkled like a thousand diamonds at dawn.

In the underground galaxies heart a commanding stone basin chained by flames and bound by runes lay the celestial majesty

Draco the dragon. Scales shimmered like molten silver bathed in starlight although the dust and ash dimmed their hue they still glowed with celestial reverence, dracos wings loomed vast as cathedral arches trembled with each shackled breath, chains glowing with the age old magick that confined the majestic serpent, bound around hid limbs and neck, Draco opened his eyes to observe his visitors, one eye golden one eye violet, he met their gaze with a vista of ages.

Uther the warlock stepped forth no fear for he had met the beast with the shard from his youth and no harm had befallen him then, the scar from the shards cut burned like white hot metal, he held no fear just recognition, The warlock unsheathed the blade of oaths forged in mithril and sealed in truth, its edge glowed a soft cerulean, humming with promises, "*do you remember me oh mighty Draco?*" the warlock asked.

The dragon did not speak with words but the ground shook with transfigured reply, a memory shared a vow once made between a celestial dragon and a small boy that he would come back for him.

The warlock raised the blade an brought it down upon the first shackle, it shattered with a scream that turned the air to glass, one by one he sliced through the iron shackles, wrist, wing, neck, and with each blow of freedom the blade of oaths sang louder freer purer, as the last shackle fell into the basin with a clank the mighty celestial Draco flapped his wings and arose, the ground quaked stars serenaded in the sky realm above the hollow land, the mighty perched on the basins edge stretching out his cramped form majestically stretching his limbs with grateful expression.

Now it was the turn of the knight gondril, he stepped forward amour glistening with griffin glyphs and spake in the old tongue, words of deliverance release and ascension, "*by sky and scale by breath and bone, rise now o flame of the forgotten throne.*" Sorcery rippled from his sword into the air runes spiralling, golden, alive.

Draco lifted his head, outstretched his golden wings and let out a fiery roar that shattered the false sky, light emanated from his chest like a flaming heart starlight unbound.

With one mighty leap, the celestial dragon Draco soared upward, beyond the hollow, beyond the veil, into the tapestry of stars where dragons are written in fire and fate, the ovate freyja wept softly knowing a prophecy had been fulfilled, the twins love and virtue clapped not fully understanding but feeling the sanctity of the sacred event, The warlock blade still glowing turned and whispered , the veil grows thin between this world and the next, and let out a huge grin amidst the tears of victory.

As draco vanished into the heavens the sky itself opened up , deep velvet torn by silver flame, a new light ignited above them brighter than any star that had shone before, The dragon dracos form, majestic, eternal and etched itself in the constellations, wings stretched wide across the firmament, his tail curling around a cluster of stars like a guardian encircling a forgotten realm.

The knight gondril dropped to one knee, sword pressed to the earth, the ovate raised her hands in silent prayer, the twins gasped pointing upwards their faces illuminated in hoary swathes of starlight, and the warlock with the blade of oaths resting on his shoulder, looked skyward and smiled, his heart echoing with old promises kept oaths fulfilled.

The over realm shuddered but not in fear but in remembering sending out a ripple of enchantment across the land, from the tree roots to the mountain tops the planet reverberated with a low harmonic resonance, a sound that was a hushed whisper of pure light breaking through the darkest shadows, rippling through stone and river, penetrating essence and bone, all who stood upon the terra felt it, a pulse a heartbeat, life's breath, a return to the light.

The hollow world shimmered shedding layers of shadow revealing its bare truth beneath the illusion, luna flowers bloomed where ash once lay, runes burned out released by freedom, he would never be forgotten, draco the sentinel the north flame, celestial serpent of the heavens the glyph of Ophiuchus.

THE PLANTING OF ARCADIA.

After the light of draco had embraced the world beneath its healing eminence , and the stars had sang his name, the ovate freyja took leave to complete her task, leaving the shimmers of where once the hollow world stood freyja walked to join maeve the wytch, pendle snaked around her ankles excitedly, wytch and ovate walked hand in hand through the waking woods past trees now glimmering with dew and bird song, knightshade forest leaned into listen no longer did it feel imposing and shady but instead cool and welcoming, swathes of bluebells carpeted the floor.

At the forests heart the navel of rebirth where no shadow dared linger, the great boughs of white leaved oaks and silver birches formed a cathedral canopy like an elven hall, in the centre pulsed the green mound a living alter of moss, fern and root.

Here the ovate freyja knelt and laid down her medicine bag of silverleaf and crystallin the dirt she traced three lines and three dots, the wytch maeve wild haired and barefooted drew a single symbol in the dirt a triskele, then they began to chant inaudible sacred sounds only known to the crone and the goddess.

A spiral of wind whipped up and pollen arose around them , the leaves danced in patterns like waltzing wraiths unseen by mortal eyes, a flute could be heard upon the wind drawing nearer, the air became thick with mischief and magnificence, then atop the navel the living altar he appeared, hobblesnot the faerie king, small in stature and crooked as a gnarled branch cloaked in moss and adorned with a crown of ivy and holly his eyes gleamed with ancient knowing, his voice although impish was music made strange by the light of a magical moon, like laughter echoing in a cave of stars.

“well sisters” he said twirling his stave made of elk antler, “so the world is ready, many a moons turn we have awaited, it is about time, from whence there was dust I shall summon bloom, where the dervishes danced I shall make green.”

The ovate freyja reached into her medicine bag and bought forth the flower of arcadia, a bloom that pulsed with pure life, its petals shifted colour with every blink, and in its heart glowed a soft verdant flame, freyja passed the flower to hobblesnot who planted the flower of arcadia at the centre of the green mound.

The earth shivered once more then exhaled, from the single bloom vines spilled forth like tendrils reaching in radiant arcs weaving through rot and stone, pushing through decay, trees bloomed with blossom and leaves, fruit grew instantly like the garden of Eden not seen since the first dawn, rivers cleared streams ran free singing happily with fresh clear water, the dervish dust long choking the land turned to loam rich and black fragrant with rebirth a fertiliser life from death, and so it was the forests heart was arcadia reborn, creatures stirred in their burrows and nests, dryads sang happily, spirits peeked from their hollows, fauns danced and Herne galloped asunder from the cauldron to spread the news, even the wind smelled of honey and mead, the twins laughed and span dancing in the daisies, freyja looked at hobblesnot eyes brimming, the wytch looked at hobblesnot and asked, "will it hold?" the faerie king grinned as wide as a hunters moon, "aye so long as ye guard it, the flower is eternal but hearts must be too." And with a thunder clap the faerie king vanished in a shimmer of acorn dust and laughter, upon the singing wind could be heard the mischievous chant of the fae, hobblesnot and his court, "call upon us again, but only if you are dancing beneath a beard of stars. "with a swirl of pollen and grass hobblesnot slipped back into his realm of faerie rings, nettle patches and mushroom thrones where the air holds secrets and songs linger like perfume, and the land sang once more, with the flower of arcadia planted and the land renewed the crystal megaliths reverberated a new pitch across the planet, the fetid amethyst glacier where once protruded malesius lair turned a pink hue of rose quartz, pitch perfect with the crystalline formation of the quartz megalith the mirror of anwen, healing all disease and sickness casting out malevolent sorcery that lingered like a sickness, from the baptism of dracos rising and arcadias rebirth,

A GREEN FEAST.

The forests heart was left glowing and alive a verdant pulsing heartbeat, a lush emerald sanctuary reborn from the ashes and bones of pestilence, malesius, raul and kalthor had been defeated, death to the triad of alluan, draco had been restored to the sky, every knee would bow to the true king of light and truth, news of the renewal spread fast and quick as if the trees gad whispered leaf to leaf, root to root, the warlock sensing harmony in the air lowered his hood and let the wind caress his face, the ovate still shining in reverence too his hand in hers and they enjoyed a quiet unspoken moment.

The wytch maeve gave an unusual cackle of laughter, as the twins danced and spun singing happily *"flowers and petals and sun and bloom, we the triad defeated the moon!!"* wilbur the goose honked triumphantly as if he too had cast some enchantment, and the shapeshifter pendle sat upon a tree stump, purring through half lidded eyes of satisfaction, and the knight gondril still bearing the echo of dracos ascent in his soul raised his sword towards the clement constellation above.

That dawn there were vast celebrations, the warlock and ovate, the knight and the forest folk, as well as the halls of moria and the long halls of bynars lodge, fires were lit along the watchtowers in celebration, the oxen and plough and the highwayman were brimming with tankards of dragons rage ale, and Hernes hops, finished off with tatters mead, uncorked with cheer, songs were sung and fables made, bards made poems and tales about the battle, and jesters entertained the small villagers.

The ovate sang songs, the warlock drummed a tune and the knight banged on the table, whilst the children chased maybugs and fireflies, and wilbur well he fell asleep on his back, feet in the air snoring like a goblin, whilst Solomon observed disapprovingly giving the odd peck when no one was looking.

Pendle watched all with knowing eyes, tail swishing to the music, whilst above the constellation of draco shimmered a guardian of light a promise etched in the stars, for that night they did not worry, they did not fear the dust dervishes or whispers of war, battle cries were a distant memory like the echoes of a nightmare now forgotten, they celebrated joyously and the new land blessed them in return.

THE CROWNING OF REALMS

Dawn broke softly, golden mist curled through the trees like a waking yawn from the world itself, dew sparkled on every new leaf and the air sang of rebirth and happiness, the nights fires had burned down to embers giving off a faint warm glow, as the triad of anwen awoke and first light kissed their sleeping features, they awoke not as wanderers and outcasts but as something regal and victorious, their fallen comrades looked down lovingly from valhalla whilst draco rested in the anwens glare.

Beneath the blossoming canopy of knightshade forest uther the warlock and freyja the ovate stood side by side radiant in morning light, the earth itself seemed to bow as the forest crowned them not with golden crowns but with woven circlets of star vine, oak and luna blossom, the dryads whispered king and queen of the realm, and the trees bent in silent witness, their reign would be one of wisdom, light and truth.

Meanwhile gondril and velah the woman with dragons blood in her veins and fire behind her eyes made a fitting bride for a griffin knight, for they had both sworn and proven their allegiance to protect draco, velah lifted the twins love and virtue into her arms now guardians of both flame and innocence, at her side gondril bound not by oath but by heart, together they descended into the cauldron deep caverns of root and stone, into the forgotten places where echoes dwell and the shadows recall, there among the crystalline springs and glowing fungi they were crowned king and queen of the underearth, keepers of the hidden, protectors of the lost, the twins love and virtue would be raised in both worlds as above so below walking in both worlds.

That night the stars sang it was a sound no mortal could hear a weaving of light and music, memory and fate, constellations shimmered in harmony led by the north flame Draco, for a time long or short depending on how you measure peace the realms were one.

No dust stirred, no blade was drawn, all who dwelled in light shadow or twilight lifted their eyes to the sky to observe draco the northern flame keeper of the heavens.

Time passed not in the measurements of mortal man but as dryads do, seasons turned, and the realms blossomed beneath the crown of those who had earned the crown not by blood but by the weight of their heart.

In the overworld king uther and queen freyja, ruled from a throne of stone and sun, beneath branches that never withered, halls of fire and green where druids taught old magicks and smyths taught flamesword, rivers sang with healing light, the villagers spoke their names with reverence and the land was one again, in the underworld, deep in caverns of sapphire fire and silver roots, king gondril and queen velah reigned raising the children amongst forgotten cauldron magicks and truths hidden from the sun, their court was quiet lit by glowing blooms and frequented by laughter of ages past, pendle and wilbur they stayed with maeve, visited occasionally by love and virtue, the flower of arcadia never faded, and draco ruled as the northern star but legends do not end, they sleep wrapped in roots in underground caverns, maybe in the halls of moria, who knows. But time herself.

PREQUEL TO VOLUME TWO THE WHISPERING STAR CHILD

Many millennia later in the constellation of caleus the elemental a child born of both realms, light and dark stood atop the star hill next to the ancient oak duir and looked to the sky, their eyes ancient holding in their hand a shard of something old, a scale gleaming with starlight, and above them Draco flickered, not in warning, not in rage but in awakening.

A whisper rose into the air, like smoke from a forgotten flame, all peace is a momentary breath between battles and stories, and somewhere beyond the far edge of the sky something from dreams stirred, the stars watched and waited.

Long before malesius divided the realms or enslaved draco there came a whisper through the fabric of time, the whisper became light and light became thought and from that thought caleus was born, he was not of flesh but of stardust, language and memory, he governed the weave between worlds, guiding those who wandered too far from truth, gentle ageless and silent he spoke only to those who listened with more than ears, legend says that he does not walk but floats in the hollow world, his eyes hold the reflection of every star born and in his presence time folds like silk, the warlock knew him, the witch saw him in dreams and when draco arose it was caleus who steadied the breath of the sky.

Now he waits in the constellation beyond dracos tail the watcher , until the next tale…..

Author Freyja and son of uther

9 781918 038408

Printed by Libri Plureos GmbH in Hamburg,
Germany